The Dead Don't Dream

Mauro Azzano

Novel Voices Press Inc.
Radnor, Pennsylvania
Ottawa, Ontario

Novel Voices Press Inc.

Copyright © 2012 Mauro Azzano

Azzano, Mauro
The dead don't dream / Mauro Azzano.—1st ed.
2012954121

ISBN 978-0-9854464-6-8

www.novelvoicespress.com

Printed in the United States of America

To Alison, who has always had more faith in me than I had in myself and who still makes me smile every morning.

PROLOGUE

There is a scene at the end of *Sunset Boulevard* where William Holden floats dead, face down in a swimming pool. I wonder how they filmed that scene; I'm trying to figure out how long he held his breath.

I am lying in the gutter of a rainy Toronto street, trying to lift my face out of the water, with my groceries scattered beside me on the sidewalk.

The bullets in my chest make it hard to breathe. A streetcar clatters by, empty at this time of night. I'm glad that I won't be embarrassed by being found this way, but irritated that nobody will likely come to help me.

Reflected in the slow-flowing stream I see someone coming toward me, a gun in his hand. My own revolver is pinned under me, useless.

CHAPTER ONE: THREE WEEKS EARLIER

My bed is soaked in blood. There are deep slashes on my arms and legs and stomach.

I am still bleeding, and there's not enough blood left inside me to breathe. Like a fish out of water, I suffocate, unable to take in enough air. I am too weak to get to the phone, and my voice is too faint to call for help. In the distance I hear a fire bell . . .

I sat up and turned off my alarm clock, the fire bell fading. Six am: time to get up.

I tore the top page off the hall calendar.

"Hello March," I mumbled. I pocketed my rosary beads and left the apartment.

Old shag carpet, covering the plank floor, muffled my footsteps as I walked down the hallway. Hopping quickly down the stairs, I pressed my elbow against the revolver under my jacket to keep it from jiggling. I braced myself for the cold blast and stepped out to the back lane.

The recent snowfall had given way to freezing rain, leaving icy slush on the roads and a chill in the air. Now, at seven thirty in the morning, last night's clear sky had clouded over, and the low sun was just a haze in the southeast.

I shuffled cautiously to the garage. My "summer" car sat covered in a tarp, my unmarked cruiser beside it, dwarfing the little Fiat.

The Fury's blue-green hood blended in with the morning sky. I fired up the V8 and waited for the windshield to clear. A minute later, I was cruising up Silverthorn Avenue, past houses with bare trees, barren stucco without landscaping, and the odd corner store.

I turned north onto Keele Street, then into the driveway of a neat brick bungalow.

Short grass struggled to poke through the stubborn snow in one corner of the front lawn, while a plaster wishing well in the other corner waited patiently for someone to drop coins in. I stomped up the steps two at a time, knocked at the door, and let myself in.

"Morning, Helen," I sang. I wiped my shoes on the front mat.

A small, pretty woman with impossibly black hair and a Jean Simmons face smiled at me. "He'll be right out," she said apologetically. "He had trouble getting to sleep last night."

I sniffed the air, pretending to just notice the coffeepot.

"Would you like coffee and toast?" she asked slowly.

"Gee, I dunno. Well, maybe, sure," I said, rocking my head from shoulder to shoulder.

It was a routine we both knew. I sat down, and Helen popped bread into the toaster.

"Frank ready?" I asked.

She shook her head. "He was mumbling in his sleep. Doesn't remember a thing, he says."

She waited for the toast to pop up, then buttered it and handed it to me along with a large mug of coffee.

I took a bite and a sip, choosing my next words carefully. "We had a tough week," I started. "A fifteen-year-old runaway who'd ended up on Jarvis Street. She picked up a john who went too far. We'd been after him for weeks. He didn't get away with it, but she didn't make it out alive."

Helen stared at me for a few seconds. She was also choosing her words carefully, I thought.

"He didn't tell me," she said softly.

From the back of the house I heard footsteps, and we both put on pleasant smiles. Frank came out in a blue-black suit, clip-on tie in hand, humming softly. He looked every inch the ex-Green Beret he was: "five eight and a hundred sixty pounds of whupass," as he described himself.

He looked at us. "What?" he asked warily.

"Helen says you need more sleep," I said, not a total lie.

Frank looked at Helen. His eyes narrowed in mild irritation, then relaxed. "She's right. I have to stop watching Carson. He's funny, but he keeps me awake."

We all waited patiently as Frank finished breakfast. By eight thirty, the sky was overcast and threatening sleet. Frank swilled the end of his coffee, grabbed a beige trench coat from the hall closet, and threw it over his elbow. He swept his other arm around Helen and pulled her close.

"Will you miss me while I'm gone?" he asked.

She smirked. "I suppose. The mailman and the plumber always ask me the same thing, though."

"Hah! I keel them. I keel them all!" he barked in a mock Greek accent. He grabbed an umbrella and poked at the air, like Errol Flynn battling pirates. "Like so." He planted a passionate kiss on her lips.

She giggled and shoved him playfully away. "Go to work, you nut."

I bit my lip, pouting. "You know, since he married you he doesn't kiss me anymore," I said in a hurt tone.

Helen laughed out loud and moved forward to kiss me, her lips puckered.

Frank took the bait and stepped between us. "Time to go." He rushed me out. "Bye, sweetheart." He pecked her quickly on the mouth and headed for the door.

"Oh, wait." She waved at me, remembering something. "We're having a bake day at the center. Can I get your carrot cake recipe?"

"Sure." I shrugged, then said, "Would you prefer me to bake one instead?"

She smiled. "Would you mind? I'd really appreciate it."

"My pleasure. Wednesday night?" I thanked her for coffee and turned to go.

She waved me back again. "Take care of him," she mouthed silently.

I nodded. I shuffled back to the car, dodging the wet snow and puddles in the driveway.

Frank slid into the passenger seat, tossed his coat and umbrella into the back, and opened a Moleskine notebook to the first page without its corner cut off. "Looks like an easy day. We've got two kids at Northwestern, hit by a train."

"Accidents? That's not our beat," I said. I drove north up Keele Street, the gray skies filling the Plymouth's windshield, on toward Northwestern General Hospital.

Frank looked past me at the traffic streaming downtown. "Kid was crossing the tracks with a buddy. One kid's in a coma, the other got clipped. He told the doctors they were being chased by some creep and didn't see the train." He looked solemnly at notes on his page.

I looked right for a lane change and glanced over at his open book. Frank's shorthand was a marvel: this page had a small Ankh icon and a letter *X* followed by a capital *I*, his way of noting "boy injured crossing railroad track."

Northwestern Hospital was a large cement block, a dozen stories of pigeonholes, operating rooms, and garage space masquerading as a hospital. When I was dating Melissa, I'd visited her there after her rounds. A resident's life was hard, especially for one of the few women in her class.

The hospital was on a hill, looking out over North Toronto. I wheeled into the *Police Vehicles* spot. Frank jumped out before I stopped. I caught up to him by the main entrance and let him in first.

He went to the admissions desk, flourished his badge, and nodded at mine. The nurse, a slightly plump woman in her thirties, gawked at the ID and directed us to the elevators. Frank pushed the button and looked around to make sure we were not being overheard. He stared at the elevator door, willing it to open.

"She's cute," he remarked.

I thought about it for a moment. "By cute, you

mean big boobs?"

That question surprised him. "Yeah. Your point?"

We got in the elevator. As if we'd choreographed it, we faced each other, turned ninety degrees more, and faced the door.

"You have a lovely wife at home," I chided.

He nodded. "I may not buy, but I can window shop."

The elevator door opened; a nursing station in the corner held two swivel chairs, a rack of clipboards, and a forlorn vase of wilting daisies on the counter. A lone nurse typed at a Selectric.

"Wait here," Frank said.

I stood back. He strode to the nurse and displayed his badge. She did a slight double-take. They spoke for a minute. She pointed with her left hand, nodding quickly, then she shook her head and picked up the phone. He nodded me over.

We entered a hall with a sign above it that read "Intensive Care." Through a leaded glass window we saw a child, stretched out under a sheet, connected to IV drips and monitors. Beside him, hunched over in prayer, was a slightly overweight man, his suit jacket crumpled on the floor behind his chair. We left him alone and returned to the elevator, then headed down two floors.

We found a ward whose door was propped open, with six beds in two rows. It smelled of iodine, Pine-Sol, and urine. The bed nearest the window held a small body, a boy around nine years old, with a bandaged right foot and a cast on his right arm.

Frank pulled up a plastic chair and slid up next to him. The boy looked over, a mixture of fear and curiosity in his eyes. Frank sat down and smiled, a warm, inviting, relaxing smile.

"How ya doin'?" he asked softly. "You must be Victor. You've had quite a time, haven't you?"

Victor nodded. Frank pulled out his badge and offered it to the boy, who reached out his good left hand and took the leather wallet greedily. He rubbed it, like a beachcomber rubbing a magic lamp.

"You're a real detective?" he finally asked. He had

a little girl's voice, all singsong and softness.

Frank nodded. "See," he explained, "my warrant card has my name and rank. I'm Detective Sergeant Frank Burghezian, and this is Detective Constable Ian McBriar." He nodded at me.

The boy handed the badge back reluctantly.

"Let me ask you," Frank said, frowning. "Do you want to be a detective when you grow up?"

The boy nodded enthusiastically.

"What's your favorite TV show?"

"I like watching *Rocketship Seven*. And I like *Adam-12*. And *Columbo*."

Frank feigned surprise. "Your parents let you watch *Columbo*? Wow! I like him too." He leaned forward in the chair. "Now, I have to ask you some questions, OK? You're not in trouble or anything. We just need to find out what happened."

The boy nodded warily.

Frank pulled out his notebook. "OK," he started, "you and—" he read his notes, "—Nick Palumbo went over some railroad tracks yesterday. What happened?"

The boy tried to speak without crying. He looked at the notebook as he spoke. "We didn't do nothing wrong. Nick said there was this crazy dog, and he could make it bark and jump and stuff. So we go to this backyard."

"The backyard where this dog lives?"

Victor nodded. "And he was just talking to it, but then the old guy in the house chased us down the street. So we ran, and Nick said, 'Slow down,' but I'm faster so I'm way ahead. We get to the tracks, and I keep going. That's when the train hit us." He stopped for breath.

Frank looked him squarely in the eye. "Good. Some more questions, Victor. That's what we do. If you become a detective, you'll do this too, OK?"

The boy nodded.

"Why were you running toward the tracks? That's going away from where you live."

Victor thought for a moment before answering. "There's a cool lot on St. Clair Avenue, next to this mattress place, and they got old TVs and sofas and stuff there. We were just going to play jungle. My mom says it's dangerous, but it's way more fun than Hughes School field."

Frank nodded. "You go to Hughes School? Who's your teacher?"

"Mrs. Cox is our teacher, me and Nick's."

"You like her? Is she a nice teacher?"

The boy nodded.

"Where is the house with the dog?" Frank asked casually.

"On Gilbert, where you cross the tracks."

"What does it look like? What color is it?" he pressed.

The boy thought for a moment. "It looks kinda like my house. It's got a door on the side, and it's beside the lane, and the dog's house is under the back door." He stopped for a moment. "We wasn't hurting the dog. Nick just wanted to play with it." His eyes teared up. "But then the guy in the house started chasing us, so we took off. That's all. Nick was yelling, 'Run, run.' He was real scared. Then the train came, and we got hit."

Frank scribbled quickly. "What was the man like, the one who chased you?"

The boy looked up. "He was funny-looking. I don't remember."

Frank nodded. "Any questions you want to ask me? Anything I can tell your mom and dad?"

Victor stared out the window, then back at Frank. "I'm sorry 'bout Nick and his dad. They said he got hurt real bad. Is that true?"

Frank nodded.

"He's going to be OK though, right?" Victor asked.

Frank shrugged. "I'm not a doctor. Just worry about getting yourself better, OK?" Frank stood to go. "One last thing," he added sternly.

The boy shrank back.

"You have been very, very good at describing what happened. You will make a good detective one day. So, to get you started, here's a badge for you. Just like mine." He pulled out a vinyl wallet and handed it to the boy.

Inside the wallet were a shiny plastic ID card and a plastic badge. The boy's eyes widened. He held it gently, as if pressing too hard might make it vanish. "Thank you," he said in awe.

Frank backed away from the bed. "You take care now. If you remember anything else, my business card is behind the badge. We'll be back to see you soon, to make sure you're better." He smiled warmly.

We drove toward 52 Division for our weekly briefing. I dismissed Frank's conversation with the nurse and thought about work instead.

Frank was scowling at pedestrians as we drove, checking for suspicious faces. Something was burning him, but it was clearly not up for discussion. I went for a safe topic.

"So, Chief Adamson will be joining us this morning," I said, stating the obvious.

Frank slowly smiled. "Should be fun. Captain Hook can tell us how the Chief's pants smell at ass level."

We drove on in silence until I pulled into the parking lot. Frank jumped out and walked ahead, not looking back. The sky was gray and darker than it should be at nine in the morning. Frank hopped over wet patches in the asphalt, pausing briefly to choose the next step.

A low, flat brick building with anodized aluminum window frames and smoked glass doors, 52 Division was the poster child for bland 1960s architecture. Dark bronze letters on the brick read *Toronto Police Department* and the address. In the entryway, a terrazzo floor carried through to a waiting area behind the counter and further on to the detectives' squad room in back.

Captain Van Hoeke was already talking, pointing to a chalkboard full of notes. As we entered, he stopped and stared at us. "Ah. If it isn't the Burger man and Tonto." A small laugh rose from the gathered detectives.

Frank smiled. "Sorry we're late. I went for doughnuts." He pointed at one detective, a lumpy, fortyish man in a wrinkled brown corduroy suit. "Unfortunately, Parker got there first. Carry on, Captain." Frank saluted quickly, and we sat down on the edge of a desk.

Van Hoeke scowled, went back to his blackboard, and read from a crime sheet: robbery at a corner store, assault on a man outside a bank, car theft, bad check written at a TV repair shop. As he hit on specific cases, he called on individual officers for an update. Van Hoeke was clearly trying to become Eliot Ness, his bright white shirt and suspenders adding to the image. He was rake thin, a tall, lanky Brit who'd come to this side of the pond after shooting down bombers in World War II.

His graying hair, slicked back over a small bald spot, made him look more like the evil butler in a bad movie than a career policeman. His cultivated, pencil-thin Howard Hughes mustache moved before his lips did, giving him an overly emotive face, and he wore heavy wool slacks year-round, which hung on his bony hips like towels on a rack.

He used expansive gestures, swinging his arms across the room and poking the end of his finger into the blackboard to show emphasis.

In the corner, frowning slightly and nursing a Styrofoam cup of coffee, sat City of Toronto Police Chief Harold Adamson. The Chief, looking like a hockey coach, smiled and nodded at the appropriate phrases.

Frank leaned over to me and whispered, "Did you ever notice the Captain can't speak when the Chief is drinking?"

On cue, the Chief took a sip of coffee; Captain Van Hoeke paused and glanced over at him. Frank and I snickered softly. Van Hoeke gave us the look a teacher gives the class troublemakers, and went on.

Twenty minutes into the meeting, Chief Adamson glanced at his watch, and the Captain abruptly wrapped up.

The Captain introduced the Chief and asked him to give us a few words. Chief Adamson spoke for about thirty seconds. He thanked us for our good work and told us to keep it up, then sat back down to polite applause.

Van Hoeke fired off instructions to the junior staff and ordered the detectives out by ones and twos with their assignments. Frank and I were now alone in the room with Van Hoeke and the Chief. Chief Adamson stood, deliberately slowly, and strolled over to us. He stuck out his hand.

"Good to see you again, Frank." He smiled at me. "And you're Ian McBriar? I've heard good things about you. How are you?"

I took his hand. I felt I was in the principal's office, but I wasn't sure why.

The Chief nodded. "Captain Van Hoeke tells me you put in good work on that murder, the last few weeks. Found the man who's been slashing prostitutes. Long hours, lots of shoe leather, solid police work. Well done. You both deserve the time off. Frank, you still fish, right?"

Frank gave a plastic smile. "Not since they closed that aquarium."

The Chief chuckled flatly. He turned to me. "Ian, you haven't seen your father—in Alberta, isn't it? Good chance to visit him." He smiled, a smile that did not go all the way to the eyes. A smile that said "or else."

I smiled back. "Thanks, sir, he's in Saskatchewan. We speak on the phone quite often."

The Chief stopped smiling. "Nice again to meet you. Good day." He nodded at Captain Van Hoeke and left, office staff parting before him like the Red Sea, staring after him as he passed.

The Captain watched him disappear and turned to us. "Do you know why the Chief was talking to you?" he asked, hands on his hips.

"Because he went to university?" Frank deadpanned.

Van Hoeke ignored him. "You two were supposed to take this week off. I told you—I do not want burnouts on my team. He doesn't either. I need you both fresh and thinking clearly. The Chief just told you as much. Go home, both of you." He wagged his finger, his Canadian accent slipping into the Cockney of his youth.

Frank leaned forward and looked up at Van Hoeke. "Look, I still want to chase down the incident from this morning—the boys hit by a train. Then I'll go home. Really."

I looked back and forth between them.

Van Hoeke thought for a moment. He pointed at Frank. "Five o'clock, you two better be watching hockey or drinking or something. Agreed?"

Frank smiled. "Fine. Five o'clock I'll be taking the wife out for dinner, and I'll let the file sit on my desk until next Monday. Promise."

Van Hoeke nodded. "What exactly are you two up to then?"

Frank told him about the boys in hospital and the house with the dog.

The Captain sighed quietly. "Check it out. Know what to do then?"

Frank shrugged. "Capture Tinker Bell?"

Van Hoeke glowered at him. "Piss off."

We walked to the car. Frank smiled, looking at his shoes as he walked.

"What's so funny?" I asked.

He chuckled.

"Went to university."

I shook my head. "Clown."

Gilbert was a short dead-end street with small bungalows on one side of the street and a low wire fence on the other side. Beyond the fence was a berm about five feet high, with railroad tracks on top.

At a gap in the fence, near the dead end, was a pathway over the tracks, worn smooth and rutted by hundreds of pedestrians cutting across.

We parked just down from the pathway. The house Victor had described was a small bungalow. It had a pair of bedroom windows and a larger living-dining room window on one floor, beside a short side lane that led to a longer back lane. It was covered with pale yellow aluminum siding on three walls and soot-stained stucco on the back wall.

As Victor had said, a brown wooden door covered by a metal screen door faced the lane. The screen door had a flock of aluminum mallard ducks flying across the lower half, their teal neck paint faded and chipped. It did not seem to have been opened recently. The backyard also faced the side lane and led to a rickety garage. A rough, low wooden fence separated the lane from the yard.

The back door steps sagged to one side; a cinder block propped them up to roughly level, but it was obvious they wobbled under load. Frank squatted and found the doghouse under the steps.

It was completely out of place. It had a crisp coat of dark blue paint on the side panels, cedar shingles on the roof, and a painted faux window on the side. A fluffy plaid pillow protruded from the arched opening. Mangy gray paws hung out.

Frank whistled; the dog raced out, barking wildly. It was some kind of terrier cross, bouncing up and down on its hind legs as it yelped. He let the dog rant. When it stopped to return to its kennel, Frank made a deep "woof" sound; the mutt ran back and barked madly again.

A moment later, the owner stormed out of the house, waving a broom furiously over his head. He was a short, stout man, early middle-aged, with a crown of thin sandy hair and brass-colored glasses. He looked like Tweedledee, a small pasty ball in cotton shorts, with skinny legs poking into ratty slippers.

"Dixie. Dixie! Go to your home, girl. Go," the man called to the dog, a sad, moaning voice, almost pleading. He turned toward us. "Get out! Get away! Leave her alone!" he screamed. He charged Frank with the broom, waving it in front of him. Frank stood back from the fence, just out of reach.

The man got to the fence, still swinging. Frank stepped forward just before the next swing, caught the handle in his left hand, and pulled it back. The broom slipped harmlessly behind him, popping out of the fat man's hands and clattering to the laneway.

"We're police officers," Frank said with a sneer. He held his badge out. "We want to ask you some questions."

The man stared past us, at nothing in particular. "Go away. I don't want to talk to you. Go away," he said, his voice softer and softer. He shoved Frank in the chest.

Frank's hand came up fast, grabbed the man's

wrist, and rotated out; the man's arm bent unnaturally away from his body, his back curving out to follow it. He stared at Frank but still seemed to be thinking of something else. Frank glared back, sizing him up for a fight. The man melted at the visual assault. Frank slowly let the fat man's arm go.

Something seemed odd. I touched Frank's shoulder, and he stared at me, ready to hit me.

"What's your name?" I asked the man gently.

The fat man rubbed his arm, looking surprised by the question. "Gary," he said.

Frank moved his arms as if playing an accordion. "Gary . . ."

Gary nodded. "Gary Hrojic." He spelled it and Frank wrote it down.

"Gary," I started. "Do you live alone?"

The fat man seemed offended by this. "I can be alone. I'm old enough."

Frank gave him a puzzled look.

"How old are you?" I asked.

Gary thought about this, pinching his thumbs and forefingers in a link in front of him. "Forty-two?"

I nodded, mentally confirming something. "Gary, could we come in and talk?"

CHAPTER TWO

Gary seemed uncomfortable with guests. He still looked like he was somewhere else but trying hard to focus on our presence. We sat at his dining table, a Formica and chrome square, barely big enough for us, with four mismatched chairs.

The house was sparsely furnished, with a small sage-green sofa in one corner of the living room, flanked by a 1930s easy chair and an ancient lamp with a fringed shade. It would have looked at home in *The Maltese Falcon*.

A door opened to a room stacked with TVs, TV parts, radios, and boxes of vacuum tubes. A workbench held a soldering iron and some test equipment. Gary disappeared into the kitchen, frowning.

Frank turned to me and whispered, "What made you think he's retarded?"

I nodded at the kitchen and whispered back, "I think he's autistic, not retarded. I don't think he meant to hurt those kids."

Gary came back with a teapot and three mugs, instant coffee, and a can of condensed milk. He carefully placed mugs in front of us, filled each with a spoonful of coffee and hot water from the teapot. Frank added milk and took a polite swig. I looked between the two men, rolling my mug back and forth in my hands. Frank no longer seemed antagonistic.

"Gary," he started. "We need to talk about the two boys who were here yesterday. What happened?"

Gary looked down at his mug. "People say I'm stupid. I'm not stupid. Kids are mean. They tease Dixie. But I'm not stupid. I got a job—a good job. I work real hard." He nodded, affirming the statement.

"Gary," I said, "we don't think you're stupid, either. I think you have a handicap. That's OK. It just describes someone, like blonde or tall or Armenian." Frank smirked.

Gary looked at me with sad eyes. "I got a good job," he repeated. "Some guys I know don't got a good job. I got a good job."

I smiled. "What do you do?"

He brightened. "I fix TVs and radios." He nodded again.

Frank sighed. "Look, we still have to ask you about those two boys."

Gary looked glumly at Frank. "They were scaring Dixie. They were mean."

"Is that why you chased them across the tracks?" I asked.

He looked puzzled. His dog, staring up at him, seemed to be waiting for his answer. "No," he said. He shook his head. "Didn't chase them there, no."

I hadn't expected that.

"Can you tell us what happened?" Frank asked.

Gary silently walked out the back door, his dog beside him, wagging her tail. We followed. He exited the side fence and shuffled gingerly down the laneway. He stopped suddenly by the aluminum side door and pointed across the road. "They went there," he stated simply.

"We know that," said Frank. "How far did you chase them? To the pathway?"

Gary shook his head firmly. "Don't cross the road. Don't like traffic." He pointed at his garage. "They bring me the TVs and radios. I don't cross the road."

Frank made some notes. "So what happened?"

Gary pointed across the street. "The boy was running so fast, so fast. The other boy was not so fast. The man grabbed him, then the train came and hit them."

Frank's face dropped. "What man?"

The question seemed to puzzle Gary. "The man," he

repeated. "He chased the boys. They were teasing Dixie, so I yelled at them. I said, 'Leave her alone!' They ran away. He chased the boys."

Frank wrote this down. "Can you describe the man? Height, weight, age, skin color, hair color, so on?"

Gary shrugged. "I don't know people. I don't know."

Frank sighed. "Was he taller than me, or as tall as Ian?" He held his pen at eye height, moving it back and forth between me and him.

Gary looked frustrated. "I don't know." He shrugged. "I can't tell people, just TVs and radios and stuff."

Frank scanned the street, desperate for inspiration. He waved at a van parked across from us. "Was that van there when this happened?"

Gary nodded.

"Was he taller than the side mirrors on the van?"

Gary thought for a moment. "Maybe. He was taller than his car." He nodded again.

"Ok, Gary, can you describe the car he was driving?"

Gary furrowed his brow. "Sixty-five Impala. Two door hardtop, dark brown, blackwall tires."

Frank shook his head and wrote it down. "I don't suppose you could tell if he had an FM radio or power steering?" he joked.

"I couldn't see." Gary didn't get Frank's humor.

"Could you see the license plate?"

Gary shook his head.

"Where was it parked?" I asked.

Gary pointed to a spot just ahead of my car.

Frank looked across the street, thinking out loud. "Why didn't he go after the first boy? Didn't he see him?"

Gary thought the question was for him. "He saw the first boy. He ran after the second boy. He chased him on the train tracks and knocked him down." He nodded for emphasis.

Frank imagined the mystery man gaining on the boys. "Victor thought Gary was chasing them. That's why he ran." He scratched his head with his pen. "Why did he wait for the second boy?" He turned to Gary. "Had they been here before, these boys, teasing your dog?"

Gary nodded. "I think so. Lots of kids come after school."

Frank crossed the street and stood by the van. "Was this van parked exactly here yesterday?"

Gary nodded.

Frank stepped back to where the Impala had parked. "Have Gary stand by the side door."

Gary stood obediently by the aluminum ducks. I stood by the curb.

"Is that where you stopped chasing them?"

Gary nodded. Frank couldn't see him. I nodded.

Frank came back, deep in thought. He gestured with his pen again. "I'm in a car down the street. I see two kids running. I'm after the second kid. Why?" He looked toward the tracks. "From my car, I can see them but not Gary. I hear the dog. I think they're running from the barking dog." He stared at the house. "I never see Gary."

Frank went to the van, along the sidewalk, then back to the van, looking toward the railway. He turned to Gary. "After he pushed the kid down, did he see you?"

Gary thought for a moment. "He looked around and came back. He pointed at me and drove away."

Frank wrote that down. "What do you mean, pointed?"

Gary lifted his fist and made a gun.

Frank rested his wrists on his hips and walked in small circles, shaking his head. "Shit," he mumbled. "Gary, do you have someone to stay with, a friend or relative?"

Gary shook his head. "Just my mom. I can't go there. They don't let me."

"Where is she?" I asked.

"Sunnydale nursing home. They don't like me. They don't like Dixie, too."

"Anyone else? A neighbor, someone on the street?"

Gary shook his head. Frank grimaced and blew air out the sides of his mouth.

"OK," I said. "Stay indoors. Don't go out if nobody's

around, and keep your dog in the house, OK? If anyone bothers you, pick up the phone, call the police. We'll have a cruiser come by regularly to check on you. This is important. Understand?"

Gary nodded.

I arranged for a cruiser to drive by randomly. Gary took his dog in and locked the door. We canvassed a dozen or so houses on the block, but nobody had seen an Impala. Frank looked at his watch: twelve thirty.

"Let's grab lunch," he mumbled.

I drove past the lot where Victor said he was going. To one side was a warehouse with a handful of cars parked near the doors. No Impalas. To the other side were tall trees, perfect for young boys to climb, and a pile of old appliances to play with. A scruffy bush lined the path to the tracks.

Two blocks along I knew a decent burger place, with red vinyl booths and paneled walls. An AM radio played behind the cash register. Every time a streetcar passed by, the music was drowned out by the hiss of static.

The Leafs had lost the game last night, but there was another coming up Wednesday. We argued about their chances of winning that one.

Over dessert, Frank flipped though his notes. "We have to talk with the other injured boy's family. I want to find out why he was the target. Was it a whacko, someone he knew, mistaken identity, what?" He sighed. We paid and drove to the boy's house.

A drizzle started, a damp snow blown by a rising wind. It was heavy enough that I had to use my wipers, but not heavy enough to wash away the road grime.

The boy's house was near Victor's school, in a good—definitely not working class—neighborhood, yet this house was larger, almost opulent. A neat hedge sheltered a lawn, struggling to grow through the snow. A white fountain on the lawn sat empty.

The second floor had a curving balcony jutting out from recessed French doors. A wide driveway pointed up to a cream-colored double garage. One door was partly open, exposing the tail end of a Sedan de Ville. The other garage door was closed, blocked by an equally plush Buick station wagon.

I parked behind the Buick. Frank studied the house, the way a mountain climber might study a cliff.

"Let me do most of the talking," he said.

"Why?" I asked.

"Just let me run with this, OK? I know this guy."

I grunted a yes. I wasn't happy, but I went along with it.

Frank sprang up the steps to the front door and rang the bell. From inside, I heard the sound of wooden shoes getting closer. The door opened to reveal a tiny old woman. She had a black kerchief on her head, a dark black and blue polka dot blouse, and an inky blue-black skirt. She craned her neck to look up at me, then down slightly to look at Frank.

"Ya?" she squeaked, her voice a shrill rasp.

Frank nodded politely. "Mr. Palumbo?"

She shook her head, waved her hand at us, and dabbed her eyes with a handkerchief. "No. no. *Va via.*"

She tried to close the door. Frank stuck his foot out to jam it. He took out his warrant card and thrust it at her.

"*Polizia,*" he said. "*Signor Palumbo?*"

She sighed and shuffled off, waving us behind her. We followed, past a spiral staircase wrapped around another, smaller fountain, to the end of a long, dark hall. I heard the clatter of chinaware from her destination, apparently the kitchen.

The kitchen was blinding after the dim hall; its fluorescent lights made my eyes sting. It was the size of my whole apartment, with a huge dining table and gas stove.

A handful of men huddled around one end of the table, talking quietly. The woman nodded to a balding, middle-aged man in a gray suit. He was about Frank's height but with extra weight. I recognized him as the man in the hospital, sitting by the boy in the coma.

She mumbled something in Italian and pointed at us with the palm of her hand, then sat with the men, her head in her hands. A glass of red wine faced her, and she took short sips.

The man stared at me. I'd been focusing on the old woman, but now I saw him glaring at me, eyes filled with rage and sorrow.

"Mr. Palumbo?" Frank asked.

The man nodded. "You're police?" he started, in a perfect prep school accent. We showed him our ID. He squinted, reading the names carefully. "Detective Sergeant Frank Burghezian." He looked up. "I remember you. Russian?"

"Armenian," Frank said, smiling politely.

"And Detective Ian McBriar, then, you're the Canadian."

My turn to smile. "Scottish, French, and Cree."

Palumbo turned back to Frank. "Have you arrested the man who did this?" He was blunt and forceful, but his voice quivered.

"Mr. Palumbo," Frank said, "I just want to say how sorry I am for your son's injuries."

Palumbo glared at him. "Do you know my son?"

Frank shook his head.

"Then you don't know shit." Palumbo turned to me. "They were being chased, Nick and his friend. Do you know by whom?"

"We're doing everything we can to find the person responsible," I said softly.

Palumbo ignored me, turning back mid-sentence to Frank. "What about this moron with a dog? Isn't he the culprit?"

Frank stiffened. "You don't appear to have all the facts, sir. Please let us deal with this."

Palumbo sneered. "What, how you gonna stop me?" The prep school accent had disappeared. He moved toward Frank menacingly.

I moved forward to separate them. Four of the men at the table instantly surrounded us.

Frank's eyes didn't leave Palumbo's, and vice versa. Frank carefully, slowly folded his hands in front of his waist. The men sat down.

Frank spoke, softly and precisely. "Your son and his friend were teasing a dog in a backyard. The dog's owner, a mentally handicapped man, yelled at them, and they ran off. Our information is that someone else chased your son and knocked him down. We are investigating that now."

Palumbo gritted his teeth. "Go on," he said evenly.

Frank reached into his jacket. One man stood up quickly. Palumbo glared at him. He sat back down.

Frank pretended not to notice. He casually pulled out his notebook and flipped to the page after the cut corners. "Do you know anyone who drives a brown Impala, mid-sixties?"

Palumbo looked at the men. They silently shook their heads. "Brown Impala, you solid on that?" His voice was now gruff, a trucker's voice.

"The man with the dog is terrified of traffic," Frank explained. "He can't cross the street. But he saw a man in a brown Impala chase the boys."

Palumbo said something in Italian, and the men left. He smiled softly and the prep school voice returned. "I'm being very rude, excuse me. Would either of you care for espresso?"

Frank's eyebrows went up. "We would love some, thank you." Frank faced me. I nodded silently.

Palumbo whispered to the old lady, and she shuffled quietly to a kitchen cupboard. She produced an ornate coffee maker and placed it on the stove. She pulled out three demitasse cups and saucers and set them in front of us with a plate of biscuits. For Palumbo, she set down a small bottle with a label that read *Grappa*.

The coffeemaker rumbled and spewed steam. The old lady served us, mumbled something to Palumbo, and kissed his cheek.

"*Si, mamma,*" he whispered. He stared at Frank. "My mother thinks you're a good man. Prove her right."

Frank sipped, squinting at the strong coffee. I did the same, wincing as the hot caffeine flowed into me. We had symbolically broken bread, I thought to myself, and we were more than just visiting police officers. We were guests, an extension of family.

Palumbo poured a dash of grappa into his coffee and offered it to us. We declined.

The smell of evaporating alcohol filled the room. He took a sip, pinching the tiny cup handle while cradling the bottom of the cup in the other hand. Frank put down his coffee.

"Mr. Palumbo, what business are you currently in?"

Palumbo thought for a moment. "I import food. I also assist small businesses that want to expand."

Frank nodded. "We last met when I was in Vice. You finance businesses and take them away when owners can't pay you back."

Palumbo shrugged. "You have a mortgage on your home?"

Frank nodded.

Palumbo asked, "Would your bank repossess if you don't pay your mortgage?"

Frank frowned. "Yes, but they wouldn't break my legs."

Palumbo smiled slightly. "You watch too many movies. I am far more successful with completely legal means than by using old Chicago tactics." He looked down at his cup, as if reading tea leaves. "A man in my position often attracts people who are . . . envious of my success. Sometimes it's necessary for me to assert my standing in the community. I would appreciate any information that would allow me to bring this to a swift conclusion." He looked up, his eyes drilling into Frank.

"I understand your desire for peace," Frank said slowly. "Please understand that we will do our job; we will prosecute the guilty, whoever they are." He stressed the "whoever."

Palumbo nodded. "I will leave you to it, then. Please realize, however, that even a place as removed as a Don Jail holding cell holds dangers that are unavoidable."

Frank acknowledged the threat. "I understand. Rest assured we will investigate this to conclusion. I am again sorry for this accident. This must be very difficult for your family."

Palumbo poured more grappa into his cup. He took another sip, longer this time. He stared at Frank again. "Do you have children, Detective?"

Frank shook his head and looked down.

"Then you don't understand how devastating this is, after last year."

Frank stiffened.

Palumbo picked up on the reaction. "What?" he barked.

Frank and I looked at each other. Palumbo's eyes stayed on Frank. "You didn't know? Some cop," he said with a sneer.

I asked the obvious question. "What happened last year?"

Palumbo leaned back. "I have—*had*—two sons. Nick Junior is my younger son." He looked down sadly. "My older son, Peter, was on vacation in Italy last year. He drove off the road . . ." His voice trailed off. The silence was painful. I spoke first.

"You named both sons after great saints: Peter, the fisherman, the Bishop of Rome; and Nicholas, Bishop of Myra, St. Nick, Santa Claus."

Palumbo nodded. "Peter was named for my late wife's father. I am grateful that she did not live to suffer this. Nicholas was named for me. We're very close. Even though he was our youngest, we were always close." His voice trailed off again. Palumbo studied me now, curious. "How do you know about the Bishop of Myra?"

"I studied religion. You will be saying novenas?"

He leaned forward, squinting. "Religion is one thing, but novenas?" He shook his head. "What are you?"

Frank coughed and smiled. "Detective McBriar felt he had a calling in the church, but decided he could help mankind more by catching bad guys." He lifted his pen. "The accident last year. What happened?"

Palumbo leaned back. "Peter was on spring break, third year U of T. Good kid, nice friends, no troubles. He wanted to see the sights, get some culture. He drove too fast." He looked down at his cup. "They said there was a girl waiting somewhere. With Peter, there was always a girl."

Frank stopped writing. "Who would benefit from Peter and Nick being gone?"

Palumbo eyed him, suddenly cold. "You think the events are related. I can't imagine why."

Frank smile sympathetically. "You said you lost your wife, too. I'm very sorry."

Palumbo looked back down at his cup, now just a trace of coffee in the bowl. "We were married twenty-six years. Three years ago, she got sick. We went to doctors, but they couldn't find anything. Within nine weeks, she was bedridden. She made it to our daughter's wedding then went into hospital. She died of cancer. It was a very difficult time for us. The kids were supportive, and my mother was great, but it was still hell."

Frank gripped his pen like a fisherman with a fly rod. "Could we speak to your daughter?"

Palumbo pulled a business card out of a box on the counter and handed it to Frank. "She owns a furniture store on Finch Avenue. I'll tell her it's OK to talk to you."

Frank put the card on the table and made more notes. "Your daughter is . . ." he read the name, "Maureen Zimmerman?" It was a question.

"She was named for her maternal grandmother, Maureen Fitzpatrick." Palumbo turned to me, answering a question he'd answered many times. "Yes, I married an Irish girl. And my son-in-law isn't even Italian. He's Swiss."

Frank looked at his watch. "We should leave you in peace this week. You have medical concerns, and it would be rude to get in your way. I will call on your daughter next week, then, and I may ask you more questions at that time." He placed the business card gently into his notebook. Palumbo stood up.

"Please keep me informed of the progress in your investigation. I will leave this matter in your hands—for now." His mother appeared from another room.

Frank shook Palumbo's hand. "You have my word we will resolve this as quickly as possible. Good afternoon."

I silently shook Palumbo's hand, and the old lady led us to the front door. Frank bent down and clasped her hand.

"*Signora*," he said simply.

Her eyes welled up again. She caressed the side of his face and covered her mouth.

We walked back to the car and got in. I sat still for a moment.

"Frank, why shouldn't I have talked to him?"

He shrugged. "I wanted to take the lead, that's all."

"Yeah, but you brought up my past in there—you threw me under the bus."

"Yeah, kid, you're right. Sorry," he mumbled.

The rain now fell softly, on the verge of wet snow, as the sun moved west from due south. Soon it would be dark, and I would be on vacation, like it or not.

I drove us back to 52 Division. Frank walked ahead to the detectives' room.

The receptionist had a jazz LP for me; she would bring it next Monday. I thanked her and followed Frank. He was telling a joke.

"So the Queen says, 'If Margaret was here, we could have saved the Rolls, too.'"

The detectives guffawed.

We sat facing each other, filled in activity logs, skimmed over the day's events. Frank, expressionless, ticked boxes on a page and wrote three-word sentences. He threw down the pen and sighed.

"Who would benefit from two deaths?" he mumbled. "Were they witnesses to something? Did they know something?"

I nodded. "I thought about that, but why hurt a nine-year-old, unless they're going after the whole family? Mom had cancer. Older son was luck; now bop the other son?"

Frank mulled this over and sighed again. "Nah. Again, who benefits? Too far-fetched." He crumpled the top page on his pad and tossed it at me. I caught it and wind-milled it into the garbage can.

"Good thought, though," I offered.

Van Hoeke walked over and sat on Frank's desk. "How did it go?"

Frank got him up to speed, the Captain nodding intently.

"Now," Van Hoeke started, that principal's office feeling coming back to me, "I expect you to go home. Don't make any waves before next week, or we'll get crapped on like a beach umbrella. Go home." He went back to his office.

Frank looked glumly at his desk. "Hate to say it, but he's right. We can't do shit till next week without looking stupid." He pushed his chair back, stood up, and stretched. "Take your time. I'll hop a banana." Frank spoke to a uniform and begged a ride in his yellow cruiser. He turned back as he left and pointed to me. "Monday!" he yelled.

By five thirty, the sky was dark. The rain stopped, but the forecast was for snow overnight. The sidewalks were slippery in spots, and pedestrians walked carefully, gingerly stepping over puddles and dodging the splashes from passing cars. It was a good night to stay home with my jazz. I stomped up the stairs to my apartment.

It took me five minutes to get into jeans and head back out. I thought I looked cool in jeans, but Frank said that my long hair looked hippie. The push broom mustache didn't help. I hugged the inside of the sidewalk, far from the splashes and the wind. Street lights flicked on reluctantly. I walked to my grocery store, following the smell of warm bread, olive oil, and coffee.

There was a deli on one side of the shop and vegetable bins on the other side. I grabbed some groceries, remembering the promise to make Helen's carrot cake. I would bake it tomorrow. Tonight I would relax. Four dollars and eighty-three cents poorer, I headed home.

I took a nap before dinner. Twenty minutes later, refreshed, I made eggs Benedict. I relaxed, finally, enjoying my eggs while Miles Davis played on the hi-fi.

A knock on the door, familiar but insistent, made me jump. Frank sauntered in, a Bundt pan in hand.

"Here," he said, thrusting it at me while casually

looking around. Whenever he came to my apartment, he always looked around like he was seeing it for the first time. "Helen said you'd need this for a second carrot cake."

"Second cake?" I asked, pretending to be stupid.

"Sure. You're making two, right?"

"Sure. Two." I put the pan on the counter and looked longingly at my meal. "Care for some?" I asked. "I could whip you up an omelet."

He grunted. "Helen's waiting—going to some play or other." He was still looking around, searching. I almost felt I should say, "No dope here, officer." He shook his head. "Why hurt the kid? He waited. He *waited*. He hurt that *specific* kid. Why?"

"I'm on vacation. So are you. Monday—let's talk Monday."

He ignored me. "If he's a skinner, a perv, he could go to a school yard and grab a kid—the short one, the slow one, the blond one, whatever. But no reports of kids being harassed in the area—zip, zero, squat." He looked at my stereo, projecting Miles's trumpet into the room. "Teak?" he commented. "Funny name."

I chuckled. "TEAC. It's pronounced *tea-ACK*. When did you check on Gary?"

Frank didn't seem surprised by the question. "An hour ago—he's fine." He eyed my eggs. "Looks good. Enjoy your evening."

CHAPTER THREE

I am floating in blood, in a swimming pool but with no walls or bottom.

I am tired, and I can't keep my head up much longer. I roll onto my back.

I see a body drifting by. A young woman, still in her teens, her mouth open, lifeless, with slashed arms, throat, and chest, floats past. She turns to me and smiles.

I wake up.

Tuesday's weather was even worse than Monday's. I guessed that Frank could only wait till about four p.m. before calling me. I had breakfast, read the *Toronto Star*, and did the crossword. At ten, I took the subway downtown to the museum. Afterwards, I walked to a diner off Yonge Street for lunch.

Sitting in a booth by the window, I watched pedestrians shuffle past. The diner was near where we'd found the dying girl. I tried to ignore the memories it brought up.

I was soothed by the rumble of conversation and soft chatter. The radio played syrupy music—Dionne Warwick or Burt Bacharach or something. I settled into my booth, enjoyed my soup, and read my newspaper. Life felt normal.

Out of the corner of my eye, I noticed activity by the till. I paid no attention, until I heard raised voices.

"You're full of shit, asshole!" one voice said, a thin, shaggy youth in torn denim bell-bottoms and a floppy hat.

"Hey, get out of my restaurant!" growled the other, a big bald man in a navy sweater.

"Screw you!" yelled the youth. He threw a flying kick into the man's chest.

The large man staggered backwards and fell. My head snapped up instinctively. I stood and felt for my warrant card.

The youth scooped money from the cash register. He had a desperate look. He was tall, gangly, and moved jerkily. He was on something. I didn't know what, but he was obviously high. I got to him as he turned for the door. He glowered at me and pulled out a small knife.

"Back off, asshole!" he screamed.

I shook my head and patted the air in front of him. "Wrong move, kid, wrong move. You don't want to do this. Drop the knife."

He took a deep breath and thrust it at me. I blocked his swing with my left hand, pulled his head down with my right, and tucked his arm behind his back. The knife fell automatically to the ground.

I was still silently furious about the murdered girl and the injured boys. That anger came out now against this thief—his bad luck. I pushed him back onto his butt.

I let him stand up; I knew what he'd do next. He tried to kick me, as he had the bald man. I moved left; his leg sailed past me, and I swung a right cross into his jaw. He dropped to the ground face-down, dazed. I enjoyed that punch, but I calmed down.

He tried to get up, so I bent his leg and sat on his calf. He howled in pain and tried to raise his head. I pressed my hand to his temple, pinning him to the floor. The bald man came over, rubbing his stomach in pain.

"Thanks, mister," he wheezed. "You want I should call the cops?"

I pulled out my warrant card with my free hand. He bent down and looked at it.

"Jeez, you guys are fast," he gasped.

Twenty diners roared with laughter.

The waitress had called the police from the kitchen, she told us. Two minutes later, a yellow cruiser slammed to a stop out front, and two large uniforms stormed in. I was still on top of the thin man. He was swearing at me, trying to pull my hand away. I pushed my thumb into the back of his ear and he gasped, gurgling in pain.

One constable nodded at my badge; he grabbed the thin man's shoulder and lifted him up with one meaty hand, and the man kicked like a landed trout.

"Albert, you want to lay charges on this one?" he asked the bald man.

"Hell yeah," the man grumbled, rubbing his stomach.

The constable turned to me. "Got it from here, Detective. We'll do the collar, you can sign off later." The officers lifted the man up by the armpits. He whimpered, looking back and forth between them.

"It was a mistake! He's my buddy! Ask him! It was all a mistake! Ask him!" he squealed as they carted him out to the cruiser.

One constable opened the back door, threw him into the cruiser, and sat beside him. They drove off. The bald man watched in fascination, then turned to me.

"Thanks so much, Officer. Anything you want, please, it's on me. Anything."

I shook my head. "I can't. Thanks, sorry, but I can't." I left a two-dollar bill, grabbed my coat and left.

Twenty pairs of eyes followed me.

I got home around three. I wanted to make the carrot cakes and let them sit.

Three forty-five. I made the frosting.

The phone rang at five to four. Frank wasted no time on pleasantries.

"You're a hero now, huh?"

"Excuse me?" I asked.

"You stopped a burglar. You tackled three armed men, so they say."

"One man, and it was a knife," I corrected.

"You know," he said, "time was that would get you laid."

"Thanks, Frank, but you're not my type. How did

you hear about it?"

He laughed. "It was on the air, kid. Don't you listen to CHUM radio?"

I sighed. "Not really. Did they at least get my name right?"

Frank snickered. "They called you Officer McBarr. You're still incognito, kid. On to important stuff—how's the cake coming?"

"That's not why you called."

He got serious. "No, course not. The boy who died in Italy—I did some checking."

"As part of being on vacation."

He paused slightly. "Yeah, vacation. So, he drove off a road between two villages in Tuscany, in the middle of nowhere. Near Assisi; know where that is?"

"It's near Florence. Francis of Assisi was the saint who was kind to animals," I said.

"Whatever. Anyway, I got out my atlas. The kid drove off an inside curve. Weird, huh?"

"Please explain that in English," I said slowly.

He sighed. "So, he's heading along this road, and it curves left. There's a cliff drop-off to his left and a sheer wall on his right. But he doesn't hit the wall. He goes off the cliff."

"Still not getting it, Frank."

"Look," he said with a sigh, "you doze off, or you're drunk, you just drive straight, yeah? But he steered hard left off this cliff. Doesn't make sense. The cops checked for skid marks, and it looks like he just turned left and drove off."

"Was he suicidal?" I suggested.

"Doesn't seem like. He was heading for a quick howdy-do with some girl and never made it. She got worried because he didn't show."

"So she reported him missing?"

"She did. They also got a call from a witness who saw him go off the road."

"So now will you go on vacation?" I asked.

"Maybe. Enjoy your evening. I'll see you tomorrow with the cake."

"OK," I answered. "By the way, are you sure you want a second one?"

"Is the Pope Catholic?" he chuckled. "Of course."

I'm in a hotel room. A radio plays "Nights in White Satin." A young girl is in the bed beside me, covered in blood. She turns and smiles at me. Her teeth are yellow, some are missing, and her mouth is full of blood. She sings along with the song, then tilts her head back and gurgles as the gash in her throat spews bloody foam.

I wake up.

Wednesday made Tuesday's weather look good. Overnight, it had snowed in earnest, making the roads slick. I gingerly loaded the carrot cakes into my car.

The Fury spun its tires, fishtailing up Silverthorn's cobblestones.

Frank had thoughtfully salted a clear path to his door. I climbed the steps, holding a cake in each hand. Helen opened the front door as I reached it, Frank's voice bellowing through from the living room.

"Cake! Did he bring cake?"

Helen rolled her eyes. "No. He's here to take me shopping."

Frank bellowed again. "What? Why, that . . ." He rushed up, feigning irritation, looking directly at the foil-covered dishes.

"Oh, good. I was worried there." He smiled. "Come look at this, kid. Helen, can I get coffee, hon? And cake—lots of icing?" He headed back to the living room, absorbed by whatever he wanted me to see.

I put the cakes on the kitchen table and strolled in after him.

Frank had scattered books, papers, and maps across the floor. He was crawling over them like a child planning a tree house, pulling at papers and matching up notes.

"What is all this?" I asked, incredulous.

"Accident report on the older Palumbo kid. The Italian police sent it last year." A pencil stuck behind his ear wiggled as he spoke. "Look at this." He pointed at two maps with both index fingers. "The kid is driving along this road, and he veers down the cliff. The witness says the boy's car just missed him."

I looked at his penciled squiggles on the margins.

"Yeah, so?"

Frank shook his head. "The witness was driving from—" he looked down, "—Foligno to his hotel outside Perugia." He pointed up. "But the witness wasn't on the main road. He must have detoured over ten miles to drive along a back road. Why?"

I shrugged. "See the sights? Pretty country, I hear."

Frank shook his head. "He called the cops at ten at night. It was dark way before he left Foligno. I spoke to a guy in Traffic who's from the area. The accident was in March. He says the fog at that time of year gets brutal. He wouldn't drive that route unless he had a good reason."

"Like shagging the girlfriend?" I asked.

Frank nodded. "That explains why the Palumbo boy was there. But why was our witness there? Did he set up the accident, maybe?"

"You think this guy might be our Impala driver?"

Frank shook his head. "Long shot. Anyway, Gary can't identify him. TV repair idiot."

It wasn't meant as an insult. I mulled this over. "This guy doesn't know that," I said. "Might he still worry that Gary can recognize him?"

"Right. I've asked the patrols to be extra heavy this week."

"Then why am I here?" I asked.

"You brought cake."

Frank stole cake from Helen's plate while she pretended to not notice. He finished his and went to the kitchen for more.

"Who was the witness?" I called.

"*Mff?*" he mumbled through frosting. He came back with a slab of cake on his plate.

"Who called the police?" I asked again.

Frank put his plate down beside me and went to the pile of papers. He turned and pointed sternly at us as he walked. "I know EXACTLY how much is on that plate." He returned a moment later with a handful of scribbled pages. "Wally Carpenter," he read, "art student from Hartford, Connecticut, in Europe for three months, doing the big tour. He hung around for two days then said he was going on to Spain. Spoke Italian, but poorly."

I ogled Frank's cake. Helen smirked and brought me another slice. She sipped her coffee and turned to Frank.

"What kind of car did he drive?" she asked.

Frank squinted, reading. "A red Alfa Romeo sedan, a real car, that. Not like some dinky Fiat convertible."

"Hey," I protested, "I love my Fiat."

"Funny thing, that," Helen said, thoughtful. "We rented a car on our honeymoon in Paris, remember? It was very expensive. I can't imagine that an art student could afford an Alfa, especially for three months."

Frank frowned. "Maybe he only rented it for a weekend, or bought it to sell after." He didn't sound convinced. She shook her head.

"That would be very risky. If it was stolen he'd be out of luck. Friends of mine in Italy took trains everywhere. Nobody drives there if they don't have to, not like here."

"So?" Frank asked, suddenly attentive.

She shrugged. "If the Impala was stolen, maybe the same guy stole the Alfa?"

"Wouldn't the police notice if they talked to a guy in a stolen car?" I asked.

Helen shook her head. "Only if the owner knew it was stolen."

Frank stared, silent. I planted a kiss on Helen's forehead.

"You want a job with us?" I asked.

I left Frank's house around two. A retro theatre was showing *The Five Pennies*. I had a choice between seeing that and buying a Muddy Waters LP. I decided on the LP.

The streetcar stopped across from my building, and I jogged to my front door, the LP tucked under my coat. I cued up the reel to reel and set the record on my turntable. Muddy Waters filled the living room as I recorded it onto tape. I played most records only once, then just listened to the tape.

I had an urge to make chicken for dinner, with salad—a second trip to the grocery store. I bundled up and went back out. Go left, pass five doors, left again into the store.

The street was nearly deserted now; the cold had forced everyone indoors. Drifting snow and a brisk wind kept me close to the buildings. I squinted, counting doors to the store.

The store was warm, but also deserted. I picked up some chicken and salad fixings, then on a whim some Italian bread.

I squinted again, counting doorways heading home. Go past five doors, then turn right.

I'd passed two buildings. A small child stood at the doorway to the third. He looked to be three, maybe four years old, well dressed, waiting for someone. He hopped up and down on his front step, looking around and shivering in the cold. He saw me and smiled.

"Man, man. Mister. Hi?" he said. I stopped. "Mister, are you a doctor?" It seemed like a casual question.

"No, I'm not." I smiled and kept walking. He looked down the empty street again. That seemed wrong. I turned back. "Why did you ask if I'm a doctor?"

"My mom got a boo-boo." He patted his head. "She went *ow*."

"Where is your mom?" I asked urgently. "Show me."

He grabbed my hand and led me into the building. He had to lift his legs almost to his chest to scale the stairs, but he climbed eagerly.

"What's your name?" I asked.

"Ethan."

We stopped at the second floor landing. Four doors faced me; one was open.

A woman lay sprawled on the floor beside a sofa, face down. I rested my groceries by the front door.

"Wait outside, Ethan, OK? I want to check on your

mom."

He stood at the doorway, peering in gingerly as I approached her.

"Some vacation," I grumbled. I bent down to check her over.

She could have been sleeping, but for a gash on her forehead that said otherwise. She had obviously tripped and hit the coffee table, then bled onto a rug under it. A pool of red, the size of my hand, oozed over the rug and onto the wood floor. I turned her over.

"Ma'am, are you OK?" I asked. Stupid question—of course she wasn't OK. I felt her hands—they were warm, and she wasn't clammy.

She started to moan softly. I picked her up and lay her gently on the sofa.

"Ethan," I called. He walked in slowly, hands behind his back. "Where is your phone?"

He shook his head. "We don't got a phone."

I sighed. "Stay here, OK, Ethan? Make sure she doesn't fall off the sofa."

I went to the nearest apartment and pounded on the door. No answer. I was deciding which one to try next, when one of the doors opened a crack. A gray, wrinkled face poked out at me. I held out my warrant card.

"Police: do you have a phone?"

The face faded back, and I walked in. The owner of the face, an ancient man in a plaid shirt and suspenders, pointed to a black phone on the wall.

"Thank you," I said. He smiled silently.

I got the ambulance operator, gave her the information, and told her I'd wait. The old man watched me, wordless.

"Thank you," I said again.

He whispered something in a language I didn't recognize, and nodded.

The woman was still unconscious, but now groaning restlessly. The boy was patting her hand comfortingly.

"Ethan," I said, "Would you please wait out front? An ambulance is coming, and they need help finding your apartment." He smiled and ran back downstairs.

I moved the coffee table and slid the bloody carpet aside. It was my first chance to get a good look at this woman.

She was very pretty, in her twenties, with curves in all the right places. Her hair was shoulder-length and auburn; her makeup was subtle but flattering, and she had no rings or bracelets, but she did wear dangly earrings. She was tall and slender, with the legs of a dancer. Her face was oval, with a slightly bulbous nose and high cheeks. Not quite centerfold material, but very far from unattractive.

I realized I'd seen her before, on the street. She'd been with the boy, so I didn't approach her—I figured she was married. I hadn't seen her close up before. I did remember seeing her walk away, watching her hips sway. She had on a navy skirt and a white blouse. Too cold to walk in today, I thought.

I found a coat and a shoulder bag hanging behind the door. I checked the bag and found her wallet; one door key, three dollars, a subway token.

The coat pockets were empty, except for some gum and a transfer from Union subway station, issued an hour ago. So, she worked downtown somewhere, and she had a son.

A pounding of footsteps got my attention. Two men in white pants and heavy white jackets clogged up the stairs, lugging a first aid kit and an oxygen tank. I called to them from the sofa. They raced in and squatted beside me.

"We'll take it from here. Stand back," one said. He had a baby face, curly red hair, and freckles to match. The other, somewhat older, had collar-length dirty blond hair. A stethoscope dangled from his neck.

The older one took the woman's pulse, checked her for fractures and looked into her eyes with a flashlight. He poked his chin out.

"Your wife have an accident?" he said with a sneer.

I pulled out my ID. "I was passing by. Her son stopped me."

He read the warrant card. "Oh, jeez, sorry. I didn't mean . . ." his voice trailed off. He looked at my badge again, then smiled at his partner. "Hey, Carl. Remember the news—that cop and the restaurant robbery?"

His partner looked up. "Yeah?"

The first one nodded at me. "This is the cop."

"Really? You're Officer McBarr?"

"No," I corrected, "I'm Detective McBriar."

They seemed suitably impressed. The red-haired one bandaged the woman's forehead while the blond one ran to the ambulance and radioed the hospital. He came back a minute later, winded from the stairs. They spoke quickly in medical jargon, indicating that she was not badly hurt.

The woman had woken up by now. She looked around, bewildered. She tried to get up, flailing at the coffee table to roll upright.

The redheaded one put his hand on her shoulder. "Listen, honey, you fell and hit your head. Do you know where you are?"

She nodded.

"Where are you?" he asked.

"I'm home. Who are you? Where's Ethan?" she sat up fast and staggered back, woozy.

"He's fine. He's right here." The blond one checked her pulse again and nodded, satisfied.

"What day is it?" he asked.

She thought for a moment. "Wednesday."

"What's today's date?"

"March seventh, nineteen seventy-three." She was angry now. It was a sexy look.

The blond one nodded and turned to me. "Listen," he started, "I called the resident on duty: she just has a mild concussion. We can take her to Branson, but the ward's full and she'll sleep in the hall. If someone can check on her here, we can leave her home."

I turned to the woman. "Do you want to go to hospital?"

She shook her head. "No. I'll stay home. I'm fine."

"Do you have someone who can watch you?" I

asked.

She shook her head. The blond one looked at his partner.

"We'll bring up the stretcher and take you, then."

"No!" she yelled. "I do not want to go to any hospital."

He bent down and glared at her. "We can't leave you here alone."

The woman stared at me, another sexy, angry stare. "Who are you? Why are you here?" Now she was alert and indignant.

I showed her my badge. "You hit your head. Your son stopped me; I called the ambulance."

She looked at me with less suspicion. I smiled.

"Is your husband here?" She shook her head. I got a small thrill at that.

"Anyone else live with you?" She shook her head.

I sighed. "Do you have a relative that can come over?"

Again she shook her head. Don't say it, I told myself. Don't say it.

"If you like, I could keep an eye on you until tomorrow," I said, the words rushing out.

She shrank back a little, hesitant. Even that was attractive. "I—OK, fine, yes, thank you." She glared at the attendants. "OK. That's cool. Thank you. He can watch me. I'll stay home."

One man wrote a report as the other packed up. She told them her name: Karen Prescott. It had a nice ring to it. I realized I was very strongly attracted to her. I wasn't entirely sure why, but I could feel I was. The man finished his report, then handed me an invoice for the call out.

"Wake her up every three hours and make sure she's coherent. Call an ambulance if she's unresponsive, delirious or confused, or if she starts to vomit." The redhead said mechanically. They left, plodding slowly down the stairs. I turned to the woman.

"I apologize for intruding, but you were in trouble there."

She smiled, which warmed me up inside. "That's OK. You were a real help tonight." She stood, unsteady on her feet. She squinted. "Do I know you?"

I smiled. "I live around the corner. Are you sure you're fine?"

She nodded, hesitantly. "Yes, I'm fine. Sorry, can I get you a coffee or tea?" She looked at her watch and tsked. "Six thirty. Ethan, do you want dinner? We have SpaghettiOs, and we have soup . . ."

I cringed at the menu. She misunderstood the expression.

"Oh, I'm so sorry; can I make something for you, too, Officer?"

I grinned, elated. "Tell you what. How about if I cook dinner for you? And the name is Ian."

She smiled. "Sure, yes. I'd like that." The smile lit up the room.

I retrieved my groceries from the hall. Ethan stood on a dining chair, watching in fascination as I butterflied chicken breasts. We chatted about nothing—small talk.

She worked in a bank building on Front Street. The branch downstairs had been robbed once, and it's probable I was one of the investigators who responded to the call. I didn't remember meeting her. I assured her I would have. She blushed.

Karen set her table, a small square one in the kitchen, with paper napkins and a faded white tablecloth. I sliced up cucumber and tomatoes for Ethan to snack on. He sat on the counter, eating happily from a Tupperware bowl. Karen smiled at him.

"How is it?" she asked. He nodded and rubbed his stomach.

The chicken would be done in thirty minutes. That gave me time to clean up. We lifted the carpet off the floor and washed out the blood stain in the tub.

I was puzzled by a hissing sound beside me. Karen read my expression.

"We have a noisy toilet," she said apologetically, "and the tap leaks. I called the super a dozen times, but he's always busy."

"Mind if I look at it?" I asked.

She shrugged. "It's not a big problem. You don't have to."

"It would be my pleasure."

I lifted the cover off the toilet tank. The copper float was half full of water, letting a trickle run from the overflow into the bowl. A wiggle confirmed that the washer in the hot water tap was loose. I got my coat.

"Tell you what; I need to grab some things. I'll be right back."

Ethan ran up and grabbed my leg. "Don't go, don't go. Stay, please?" he pleaded.

I looked at his mother with embarrassment. "I'll be back in no time, I promise. And you can help me out after we eat, OK?" He giggled happily. I turned to Karen again. "By the way, do you want wine with dinner?"

She smiled and nodded. I warmed up again.

"And dessert?" I added.

Ethan jumped up and waved his arms in the air.

The walk home was far more pleasant than it had any right to be. I'd often had this feeling when I dated Melissa. Now it felt the same, only more so.

I pulled my tool bag out of the closet, put a bottle of wine in the bag, and ran to the store before it closed. I bought some pastries, then raced back to Karen's.

Ethan opened the door, straining to reach the knob. He grinned at seeing me again. I gave Karen the wine.

"Keep this cool, if you would," I said with a smile. I placed the pastries on the kitchen counter and handed Ethan my tool bag. "Listen, sport, can you put this in the bathroom? Thanks."

He struggled with the straps, dragging the bag along the floor to the toilet.

The smell of baking chicken and tomato sauce filled the apartment. Karen and Ethan watched, fascinated, as I rinsed the lettuce.

"Do you eat many salads?" I asked him. He shook his head. "Do you like salad?"

He shrugged.

I looked at him slyly. "Do you eat worms?"

He laughed.

Karen smiled. I smiled back.

As I shredded, she picked at random bits of lettuce on the counter.

"Where did you learn to cook?" she asked.

"I worked in my dad's restaurant till I moved to Toronto."

"What made you move from . . . where'd you move from?" she asked, curious.

"Esterhazy, Saskatchewan. Not the center of the galaxy. I wanted to see the big city."

"Do you ever miss it?"

"Not the place. I miss family. We lost my mom, but my dad's still there."

"Any brothers and sisters, a big family?" she asked, picking lettuce from the bowl.

I shook my head. "One older brother. He went to Montreal to be in a jazz band."

"Don't you have a wife or girlfriend at home?" She reached for wedge of tomato and I playfully smacked at her hand. She grinned.

"Just me," I said.

She frowned. "Why the police force? Did you always want to drive a squad car, what?" She seemed amused by me now. The bandage on her forehead seemed almost invisible. It was all I could to stop from bending down to kiss her. I shredded lettuce, looking away.

"I was studying to become a priest." I almost mumbled it.

She put a fist in front of her mouth to stop from giggling. I frowned.

"Yeah, I know. Me, a priest?"

"So, what happened?" she asked.

"I came to St. Augustine's Seminary in Toronto. I figured I'd be a parish priest or run a soup kitchen or cure polio." Stop talking, I told myself. Just stop talking, stupid. "My mom was killed by a drunk driver. He blasted past our house as she crossed the street. My faith said I should forgive him, but I only wanted to kill him. I realized then that I wasn't cut out for a pastoral life, so I became a policeman."

Karen put her hand on my arm and looked sadly up at me. "I'm so sorry," she said.

I felt a warm rush.

Ethan ran up, smiling. "When can we eat?"

Karen sat at the table, Ethan beside her on a thick pillow. She poured wine for us and milk for Ethan, while I served dinner. She ate politely, but heartily.

Ethan was not so subtle. Tomato sauce covered his face, and lettuce stuck to his bib like medals on his chest.

We talked between forkfuls of food and sips of wine, pleasant nothing conversation. After dinner, Karen made coffee, apologizing that it was instant.

"That's OK," I lied. "I like instant coffee."

I set out the pastries. Ethan scanned the treats.

"What's that?" he asked, pointing to a cannoli.

"Well," I started, very serious, "you know some spiders make tubular nests?"

He nodded, not knowing at all, but agreeing anyway. I held the cannoli up.

"This tube is the nest from the Amazonian cannoli spider. They find these in the Amazon jungle, kick the spider out, and fill it with mascarpone cheese and spider venom." I nodded sternly.

He stared for a moment, then laughed loudly. "No! You're fooling!" He laughed again. Karen was smiling at us.

"You're very good with children," she said.

"You've met my partner?" I answered.

Ethan decided he would brave the spider venom and eat a cannoli. He also wanted to help with the plumbing repairs, so he dragged my tool bag out. I replaced the toilet float, and the noise stopped. I repaired the hot water tap. This fascinated Karen.

"Now I can take showers without the whistling," she said.

I felt another rush as I imagined her bathing. Ethan helped me pack up. By now, it was after his bedtime, and he was tired.

Karen excused herself to put him in pajamas. They

came out of the bedroom a minute later, and Ethan wrapped his arms around my neck to hug me.

"Thank you for dinner," he said politely. Karen nodded her approval. "Can you make food for us again?" he asked. His mother gasped, embarrassed.

"I guess that depends on your mom." I looked up at her.

"Let's ask Mr. McBriar next time you see him, OK? Say goodnight."

The words "next time" gave me a shiver. Ethan staggered off to bed.

Karen closed the bedroom door and sat beside me on the sofa. "I really want to thank you. But, you don't have to stay, honest. I'll be fine. Besides, I'm sure you have to work tomorrow."

It sounded like a plea to prove her wrong. I smiled softly. "I promised to watch you, and no, I don't have to be anywhere," I said. "I'll sleep on your sofa. Give me an alarm clock. I'll check on you every few hours."

She studied me, deciding something. "OK," she said, "but no funny stuff."

I held up three fingers. "Scout's honor."

We chatted until after eleven o'clock. She disappeared into the bedroom, returned with a blanket and pillow, and wished me a good night.

I lay on the couch, wide awake, wondering just what I was getting into.

CHAPTER FOUR

The young woman is standing in the window of her hotel room, staring out at the evening sky. I walk toward her. Her arms and legs are bloody. She smiles.

"I want to go home," she says. "To Sudbury." An alarm clock on her dresser goes off. She puts a finger to her lips. "Shh . . ." she says. "Shh . . ."

The alarm woke me with a start. I went quietly into Karen's room and listened to her breathing for a minute.

She was wearing a pink t-shirt. It may as well have been a silk negligee; it showed the curve of her bosom, and my eyes followed every inch.

Ethan was asleep in a small bed beside her. I shook her gently. She opened one eye.

"I'm fine," she whispered. "Go back to sleep."

"What day is it?" I asked.

"It better be Thursday," she grumbled.

"OK. Go back to sleep," I whispered. I headed back to the sofa.

"Hey," she hissed, "do you cook a great breakfast, too?" I heard her snicker as I left the room.

At six in the morning, I was wide awake. I opened the fridge. Nothing there that I wanted. I wrote a quick note—"back in ten"—and headed home.

I grabbed some staples—bread, bacon, eggs—and rushed back.

By six thirty, I had a full-scale meal going: bacon sizzling, coffee brewed, and eggs ready to scramble. I heard a noise from the bedroom; Ethan came out, dragging a blanket.

"Good morning champ." I smiled. "Want breakfast?"

He ran toward me, dropping the blanket. I squatted to give him a hug. It seemed natural. He wrapped his arms around my neck and kissed my cheek. I stood with him stuck to me like a limpet and sat him on the counter as I made breakfast.

"So, what are you doing today?" I asked.

"I go down to Mrs. Waleski's. I play with Tommy and Kristen till mom comes home."

"Does she watch them too?" I asked, the detective in me emerging.

He shook his head. "Mrs. Waleski is Tommy's mom. Mrs. Matesla is Kristen's mom. I like them. They gots a TV. We don't got a TV."

"Who's Mrs. Matesla?" I asked.

"She's Mrs. Waleski's sister. They're sisters, but old."

I was vaguely aware of someone behind me. I turned, a bowl full of beaten eggs in my hand, to see Karen, in a thick flannel robe, watching us, amused.

I smiled. "Good morning. I hope you're hungry."

"Good morning. Famished." She shuffled up to Ethan, her slippers buffing the floor. "Good morning tiger. Sleep well?" She rubbed his head.

He nodded. "Ian's making breakfast."

She smiled. "What are you making?" she asked me.

I held up an egg. "Amazonian spider omelets."

The snow fell in earnest now, and the streets filled with people rushing from one warm doorway to another. The slush in the sewers was gone, replaced by a dry, powdery snow-and-ice mix.

The first light of morning poked through the kitchen window. The kitchen looked out to a lane, then across to a red brick building on the back street. Light peeked between two buildings, thin and tentative.

The apartment was extra drab in this light. Karen

excused herself to get ready for the day. She had to be at work in an hour, she said. I had another coffee and stared out the window, my mind blank. She came out in a smart skirt and sweater, with Ethan in jeans and a shirt. Her bandage was replaced by a flesh-toned Band-Aid, which made the injury nearly invisible.

"When do you have to be at work?" I asked.

"Front and Yonge by eight thirty, but I have to get Ethan downstairs first."

"Would you like a ride to work?" I couldn't stop the words from leaving my lips.

She looked hard at me. "Look, I mean, you're a nice guy and all, but . . ." She waved at the air.

I was crestfallen. She's at least brushing me off gently, I thought. "Not your type? I'm sorry—pushing too hard. Sorry." I shook my head.

Her eyes widened. "No, not at all. That's not what I was, I mean, oh, shit." She ran both hands through her hair and looked down at her shoes, then flipped her head back. That set my pulse racing. "Look, I'm not great-looking, no money to speak of, raising a son . . ." she trailed off, then sighed. "Why would I dream that you'd be interested in me?"

My heart skipped. "Are you kidding? You're the most exciting woman I've ever met. I can't imagine you liking someone like me."

She beamed. The room lit up again. "Really? Do you really mean that?"

I nodded. "So, would you like a ride to work?"

I introduced myself to Mrs. Waleski, handed her my card, and told Ethan I'd see him later. He raved about his new friend the police officer.

Karen and I walked to my car, arm in arm. I held her hand as we stepped over slippery patches, let her in the passenger door, and headed downtown.

"Ever been in a police car before?" I asked casually.

"How do you mean, in the front seat?" she answered with a smirk.

I realized how that had sounded, and laughed. I

picked up the radio mike, mostly to impress her. "Fifty-two four-eight, to dispatch," I droned.

The speaker crackled. "Go four-eight."

"Four-eight, any messages?"

"Four-eight. Call Sergeant Burghezian at home ASAP."

I raised my eyebrows. "Ten-four. Four-eight out."

Karen looked me over, curious. "Are you in trouble?"

I shook my head. "Worse. My partner misses me."

We stopped outside her office building.

I was right, I told her. I remembered going there after the bank downstairs was robbed. Back then, I was a fresh face in the "blue suit club," and wanted to prove that a Métis kid was just as good as the rest of the force.

Karen grabbed the door handle and smiled. "See you later." It was a statement. She kissed me on the cheek. Then she paused, grabbed my chin, and kissed me passionately on the mouth. "See you real soon." She smiled again. My pulse raced. She headed up the stairs, swinging her purse. She turned back and waved. My hand went weakly up. She disappeared into the building.

I took a minute to compose myself and find a phone booth. Frank answered on the second ring.

"Hello?" he snapped.

"Hey, Frank."

"Where the hell are you?" he barked. "I kept calling till midnight."

"I spent the night at a woman's apartment," I answered smugly.

"Oh, really," he snorted, then his voice changed to a purr. "Oh, *really*? Tell me more."

"None of your damned business, Frank."

He snickered. "Film at eleven, then. Meanwhile, any word from the patrols at Gary's house?"

"I'll check the logs. Then I'll check if he's spotted our mystery man."

"So," Frank teased, "do I sense that your voice is deeper this morning?"

"No, but hope springs eternal. Talk to you later."

He roared with laughter and I hung up.

I pulled into the 52 Division lot, and sauntered into the back office. Frank was already there, finishing a joke.

"So the guy says, 'Listen, keep the money. I just can't take another sixty-seven of those.'" The detectives all guffawed.

I sat down; Frank leered and faced me. "Tell me, what's she like, this girl?" Frank made a Coke-bottle shape in the air then punched it slowly at waist level.

"Been playing hide the salami, have we?" said an officer named Parker, grinning.

I frowned. "It's not like that. She's a nice, very good woman."

Parker nodded, solemn. "Inflatable?"

They all laughed.

I was irritated, but only briefly. The novelty passed, and they went back to work. I read over the patrol logs. A shadow appeared; Captain Van Hoeke glared, angry.

"Hey, Captain," I piped up. "I just came by to look for . . ." I grabbed a pen. "Wow! Found it. My lucky Bic. Now I can go home." I stood up.

He motioned me back down. "Where's the back half of the pantomime horse?" he growled.

Frank sauntered in, reading something, and looked up quickly at Van Hoeke's voice. "Hey, Cap. Is it ever great to run into you. We have lots to report, don't we, Ian?"

Van Hoeke pointed sternly at him. "My office. Now."

I sat across from the Captain. Frank sat on the edge of the desk, defiantly.

Van Hoeke poked a finger at me. "The door," he barked.

I pushed it shut.

His voice lowered to just a whisper. He leaned forward. "I hoped you'd show up this week. Someone in the back room is letting Palumbo know what we're doing." He nodded at Frank. "You took out the Italian police reports on the Palumbo accident last year. Palumbo has been asking about those reports. Have you told him anything?"

Frank shook his head.

"I didn't think so." Van Hoeke leaned back. "Look; stay under the radar. Work from home the next while, OK? Tell nobody what you're doing. There's a rat in the office, OK? Go."

I dropped Frank home, and he asked me to check on Gary.

Gary peered slowly around his door, then opened it gingerly. "Yes?" he whispered.

"Gary, do you remember me?" I pulled out my warrant card.

He nodded, not looking at it. "You're Detective Constable Ian Stuart McBriar."

I smiled. "Very good. Is everything OK?"

He nodded. Dixie wagged her tail at me. I bent down and scratched her head. She licked my hand.

"Have you been able to work and get food OK?" I asked.

He shrugged. "I can work fine. They always deliver my groceries. No problem."

I took a breath and looked him in the eye. "Gary, do you ever fix TV sets, but people don't want them back?"

He nodded. "All the time."

"Do you have one I could buy from you?" I asked hopefully.

"Yeah. What do you want?" He wandered back to the bedroom. I followed him. A dozen TVs, stacked like wood, sat against one wall. Gary pointed at them. "These work, but people didn't want to pay. They said to keep them." He shrugged.

"They work fine? It's not for me, it's for a friend," I explained.

He pointed at a nearly new set with *Philco* emblazoned in plastic across the front. "This set is color. It works good. I changed the picture tube and flyback."

It was all Greek to me, but I nodded anyway. "How much do you want for it?" I asked.

"I had an old tube, and the flyback cost me six fifty.

I dunno, thirty dollars?"

"Would you take forty?" I asked.

Gary smiled. "I thought I was the retard."

I laughed out loud. "That was a very good joke, Gary."

He grinned broadly, proud of himself. We plugged the TV in. Gary turned the knobs through the stations, checking the reception. It looked great. I peeled off four tens and loaded the TV into my Fury.

"Do you still have my card?" I asked. He nodded. "Have you noticed the police cars driving past your house?" He nodded again. "Keep us posted if you see or hear anything, OK? Bye."

I stuck the TV in my living room and headed back out, racing toward downtown. Eleven forty. I parked at Karen's bank, placing a faded *Police Business* sign on the dash. In the lobby was a reception desk by a bank of elevators, where a gray-haired man in a security uniform sat, reading a newspaper. I walked up and waited for him to notice me. He didn't.

"Hi," I started pleasantly. He looked up, irritated.

"Yeah?" he grunted.

"Where can I find Karen Prescott?" I asked. He smacked the paper down, irritated. He sighed, picking up a clipboard.

"You got an appointment?"

I shook my head.

"Well, you got to make an appointment." He tossed the clipboard down and reached for his newspaper.

"Can you tell her I'm here? I'm a friend of hers," I asked, trying to stay polite.

He looked me up and down, disapprovingly. "Sure." He picked up the telephone handset and rested it on his shoulder. He sneered at me. "What's your name, Chief?"

The "Chief" was clearly an insult. I'd had enough. I pulled out my badge.

"Tell her that Detective Constable Ian McBriar would like to buy her lunch." I stared at him.

He shrank about six inches. He picked up the clipboard and hurriedly looked up a phone number.

He dialed it and spoke in a soft voice. "A detective is here to see you, for lunch?" He listened. "Oh." He sighed. "OK, I'll tell him." He looked down sadly. "Bye." He hung up softly.

My heart sank. I had read far too much into the kiss. I thought of the scene in *Casablanca* where Humphrey Bogart realizes he's lost Ingrid Bergman. The theme music, "As Time Goes By," went through my head.

The guard looked up. "If you'll take a seat, sir, she'll be right down."

My heart pounded. I sat down, barely touching the seat. I waited. And waited. For about four minutes, though it seemed forever.

The elevator opened. I stood up. A man with a briefcase got out, and the door closed. I sat down. A second elevator opened. I stood up again. Three men got out, discussing stock prices. I sat down again.

A moment later, Karen walked out of the same elevator, putting lipstick into her purse. She puckered, then smiled broadly as she saw me.

"Hey, you." She took my arm and pulled me close.

The guard nodded meekly.

"Where would you like to go? It's on me," she said.

We walked to a concourse by her building. I felt a flush of emotion. She smiled.

"What?" she asked, curious.

I looked around. Nobody close by. I bent down and gave her a kiss. She smiled again.

"I have to ask you something," she started, hesitant.

"*Hmm?*" I asked. My mood was beyond elated.

"You were going to be a priest. They take vows of celibacy, right?"

"Yes," I answered. "That was a problem."

She giggled, looked down, and got serious. "Look, I have not had great luck with men. Ethan's dad walked out on us. Before that . . ." She sighed. "I need to know if you're always like this."

"Like what?" I smiled.

She waved her hands, searching for words. "Are

you an angry drunk? Do you get into bad moods, do you hit women?"

I stopped dead. The look on my face must have said more than words could. She blushed, shaking her head.

"OK, that was wrong. Never mind. I'm sorry. Forget it." She shook her head again.

"For the record," I said, "I had one glass of wine with you yesterday. That's a night of heavy drinking for me. That's who I am."

She smiled and hugged my arm tighter. We went on to a nearby coffee shop.

"Also," I added, "if anyone is ever mean to you or Ethan, it won't be pleasant for them."

We ate something—I forget what—and talked about nothing special.

I cleared my throat. "Now, I have a question for you."

She went *hmm?* and sipped her ginger ale.

"Would Ethan like his own TV? I've got a color one I don't need, and he said he has to go downstairs to watch TV, so would he like one? Or, like, would you? Like, maybe you can watch TV? If you two wanted to watch, watch TV, you know?" I was rambling, I realized, and I thought the best thing I could do was shut up. I took a sip of her ginger ale and stared out the window, trying to act casual.

Karen looked at me, a faint smile on her lips. "You just bought one," she said simply.

"Me? I, no, well, I, uh, know this guy who . . ." I sighed, defeated. "Yes. Yes, I did."

She beamed. "That's lovely. Thank you very much. Ethan and I will love watching TV." She touched my hand. "With you." She smiled again and sipped from the same glass, leaving a smudge of lipstick.

We walked back to her office, holding hands.

"Listen," I said, "how about if you and Ethan come for dinner tonight?"

"We'd love to. Should I bring anything?"

"An appetite. Nothing fancy, but at least you can see my place."

She smirked. "Bachelor heaven?"

"Wait and see. Incidentally, would you like a ride home?" I asked hopefully.

She smiled, pulled my face down to hers and kissed me. "See you at five," she purred. She went back into the building, again swinging her purse.

I fairly skipped back to the car. People did double-takes as they passed me. It didn't register until I got in the car. In the rearview mirror I noticed a large smear of orange-red lipstick on one side of my mouth. I wiped it off, reluctantly, and drove home.

I strolled to my grocer's, deciding what to make for dinner. The grocer, a small, thick man with a pronounced limp, wiped his hands on his apron.

"Special night?" he asked. I nodded. "New girlfriend?"

"How did you know?" I asked.

"I know the look." He held up a fat palm. "How about shepherd's pie, Caesar salad, ice cream?"

I agreed and collected the fixings for dinner.

As I put the food in the fridge, the phone rang.

"Hey, kid," Frank's voice said. "What are you doing for dinner?"

"I have company." I smiled. "Female company."

"OK, what about after? Can you put your pants back on?"

"Why?" I asked. "What's on your mind?"

"Helen wants to meet this girl. Bring her over for coffee—about seven thirty?"

I thought for a second. "We would also be bringing a four-year-old boy. Is that OK?"

He chuckled. "Another child beside you? Sure, why not?"

At five after five, I paced the sidewalk outside Karen's office. She sashayed toward me seductively.

"Hey, mister, want a good time?" she drawled.

I wrapped an arm around her waist. "Watch it, lady, I used to work Vice," I joked.

Light snow fell, interspersed with soft rain,

smearing the car's windows. We chatted as the buildings rolled past. I had a question I needed her to answer.

"I have to ask you. You mentioned Ethan's father. What happened to him?"

She looked out her window, her face stony, and said nothing.

I drove up University Avenue, Queen's Park and the government buildings off to my left. Karen still stared off, silent.

I've really blown it, I thought. I felt truly dumb. Just like in *The Bad and the Beautiful*, where Kirk Douglas said something hurtful to Dick Powell. Nice going, stupid, I told myself. Finally, she inhaled softly.

"I was at school. I was twenty years old and got swept off my feet by someone old enough to know better. Right after Ethan was born, he went from being Prince Charming to the Prince of Darkness. He found some other gullible girl after that." She smiled sadly. "That's why I asked how you were. I won't expose Ethan to anything like that. Does that change anything?"

I stopped at a light and looked at her. "Not a bit."

She gripped my arm and smiled, holding on till we got to Mrs. Waleski's.

An angular, tall face in a kerchief poked through the door. The smell of sausage, cabbage and pine cleaner wafted out with her.

"Yes?" Mrs. Waleski barked. She recognized me and waved us in. "Ethan say he like you." She pointed at my chest. "You be good friend."

I leaned over to Karen. "Is that an order?" I whispered. She giggled.

"Come," Mrs. Waleski commanded.

We all went through to a room filled with toys; three cots lined up on one wall held a blanket and pillow each. Against another wall sat an old console TV, its screen dark.

Ethan was on his knees, pushing a Hot Wheels police car through a cardboard tunnel. Another young boy, about the same age, played with toy blocks.

That would be Tommy, I told myself. As he saw us,

Ethan ran over and tackled me.

I staggered back at the assault; he pulled me down to see his Hot Wheels cars.

Karen, sitting with Mrs. Waleski, looked on in amusement. They talked about their sons, the weather, and how difficult it was to get around in the snow.

Ethan had built a small cardboard ramp, and raced cars down it toward the cardboard tunnel. I crouched down beside him and played along.

After a few minutes of playing, I asked, "Hey, are you getting hungry?"

He nodded. "Yup."

I tipped back onto my knees. "Want to come to my place for dinner?"

He jumped up. "Yay!" he yelled, and leapt on me, knocking me back.

Karen gasped. I lifted Ethan up in the air, in mock menace. "Oh, yeah?" I tickled him until he giggled, then brushed myself off.

We headed out, Ethan walking between us on the sidewalk, shielded from the wind. An older man leaning on a cane neared us, bundled up in a long coat. We lifted Ethan up in unison, sailing him over puddles and back down again. He chortled with joy. The old man, amused, smiled at us as he approached. He nodded politely. I nodded back.

"You have a lovely family," he wheezed, and continued down the street.

I was mildly embarrassed at the implicit lie. I glanced over; Karen's eyes were wet.

"What?" I asked stupidly.

"Do we really look like a family?" she sniffed.

I smiled. "Frankly, yeah, we do."

She sniffed again, blinking tears away. "Yeah, we do."

Ethan, oblivious to this, just swung between us. He tilted his head back, bending backwards to catch snowflakes. Karen wiped her eyes.

"Oh!" I said, remembering. I turned and walked backwards, facing her.

"My partner and his wife are having a coffee evening after dinner."

She smiled. "That's OK, Ethan and I can amuse ourselves."

"No," I explained, "the invitation was for all three of us. Would you mind coming?"

"We'd love to," she said, beaming. "How will you introduce me?"

I smiled sheepishly. "How about as my main squeeze?"

"Main squeeze. I like that." She grinned.

My apartment, like Karen's, had a living room, one bedroom in back, and a kitchen that faced the lane. Ethan went straight for the TV. He was thrilled at the color set, instead of the black and white at Mrs. Waleski's. He sat cross-legged, mouth open, watching Lucille Ball in some escapade.

Karen, sipping a glass of wine, watched me prepare the salad. "So do we really look like a family?" she asked casually.

I glanced at Ethan, mesmerized by the TV. I nodded. "As much as I could imagine," I answered honestly.

She took a sip and lifted the glass, looking through the deep red liquid at me. "You think smooth talk will help you get lucky?" She was serious, but joking.

"A man might dream," I mumbled. I sat on the sofa beside her while dinner warmed up. "Now, I have to tell you something," I started. She leaned back, worried. "No, nothing bad." I smiled, then inhaled deeply as I collected my thoughts. "I was dating this girl until about six months ago. I thought we had a future, but apparently it didn't include me." I sighed. "I feel . . . I'm not just picking you up on the rebound. Can we see where this goes, at its own speed? Does that work for you?"

Her head rested in her left hand. She smiled. "That works just great for me."

"Also," I continued, "I work long, strange hours. You may not see much of me for a couple of days at a time."

"Absence makes the heart grow fonder." She playfully touched my nose.

Karen was afraid that Ethan would be a picky eater, but he devoured his pie and ate his salad all by himself, to her obvious pride.

Ethan was fascinated by my hi-fi; the push buttons on the tape player were particularly tempting, but he was very good about not touching the controls.

We told him we were going to visit my friends, and he reluctantly turned off the TV.

"Have you ever been in a police car?" I asked him. He shook his head. "Would you like a ride in one?" He nodded excitedly.

We walked him across the lane and sat him between us on the front bench seat. He ogled the police radio and magnetic gumball with the same look that children give to wrapped Christmas presents.

We slid up the icy cobblestones of Rogers Road and then right on Keele Street. Karen opened her purse and composed herself in her compact mirror. Ethan asked me all sorts of police questions. I enjoyed the conversation. This is what I always wanted in a family all right, I thought to myself.

All too quickly, we arrived at Frank's. Karen sighed deeply.

"You'll be great," I assured her. "But watch Frank. He likes brunettes."

We were barely at the front door when Helen opened it. Karen held out her hand.

"Hi, I'm Karen. This is Ethan," she said, a hand on his head.

Helen ignored the hand, giving Karen a hug and a kiss on the cheek. "Welcome," she said warmly.

Frank thundered through from the living room. He stopped dead when he saw us. Karen, in heels, stood a good three inches taller than him.

"Hi, I'm Frank," he cooed. Karen repeated her name. Frank nodded slowly. "You got a sister?" he asked.

Helen giggled and smacked him.

We all went in. Helen set out coffee and carrot

cake.

"Wow! My favorite," I gasped.

Helen explained the joke, and Karen looked slyly over at me. "First aid, dinner, plumbing, dessert. What don't you do?" she asked.

Frank snorted. "Paperwork."

The evening flew by. Ethan and Frank got along like best buddies. Frank pulled out his army uniform, explained his service medals, and let Ethan wear his green beret.

Karen and Helen chatted nonstop, Helen explaining how Frank and I leaned on each other. I went into the kitchen for more coffee. From the living room, Helen excused herself and walked up to me. She looked up with a hard expression I was not used to seeing.

"How do you feel about this girl?" she hissed.

I stammered something.

"You damn well better do right by her," she snapped. She instantly smiled sweetly and took coffee through to the living room.

By ten, Ethan was exhausted, and we were all tired from talking and laughing. Karen and Helen traded phone numbers. Frank waved me over.

"Sit tight till Monday," he ordered. "At this point, nothing more we can do."

"I'll check on Gary from time to time?" I asked. He nodded. We said our goodbyes; Helen and Karen hugged like old friends.

It snowed softly now, a dusting of white marking our steps to the car. Ethan raved about the U.S. Army, and Vietnam, and Frank's ceremonial dagger. Thirty seconds later, he was yawning deeply. By the time we hit Rogers Road, he was asleep.

"I like Helen," Karen started. "Ethan loves Frank. I see why you and he get along."

"Two nuts in a bowl," I agreed.

We parked out front of Karen's apartment. I slid the sleeping Ethan out, flopped him over a shoulder, and carried him upstairs.

Karen unlocked her apartment door. I reached for

the light switch, but she pulled my hand away, went into the bathroom, and turned on that light.

The apartment was now lit by a soft indirect glow. Shadows of furniture, magnified in the light, danced like fuzzy gray giants on the wall. Ethan was still over my shoulder, limp and heavy.

"Wait here," Karen whispered. She went into her bedroom and came out with blankets.

She laid them on the sofa and made up a bed for Ethan. I rested him gently on the sofa, and Karen covered him up. He rolled over to face the back cushion and started snoring softly. Karen watched him for a minute, made sure he was fast asleep, then grabbed my arm.

She pulled me into the bedroom, closed the door, pushed me onto the bed, and slid her hands up under my sweater, trying to peel it off.

Finally, stupidly, it dawned on me what was going on. "Uh," I said hesitantly, "are you sure about this?"

She gave me a sinful smile. "Shut up, you." She threw herself on top of me.

CHAPTER FIVE

I woke up at five a.m., warm and cozy under the covers. I was aware of breasts pressing against my back, and an arm over my waist. Despite the previous night, I became very aroused.

Karen's arm moved down and touched my crotch. She pressed closer.

"Someone is perky this morning," she whispered. I rolled over.

At six fifteen, we put Ethan, still sound asleep, back into his own bed.

The snow fell heavier now, a fluffy, colder snow, resting on the windowsill like an inch of soap flakes. We showered together, hugging and kissing until we almost fell.

I made breakfast. Karen was in her bathrobe, open to the waist. Even after seeing her naked in the shower, it was exciting to peek down her robe. She stretched, watching me with amusement.

At seven thirty, Ethan woke up. I made toast for him then asked if he wanted to do something. He shrugged.

"Have you two ever been to the Ontario Science Centre?" I asked.

Karen shook her head.

"We could do that. Want to go?" I asked.

"I can't. We've got financials; we need 'all hands on deck' apparently." She sighed.

"Tell you what, big guy, how about we drive your

mom to work then go and have fun."

Karen liked that idea. We told Mrs. Waleski about our plan and drove Karen downtown.

Ethan had rarely been in a car before, so everything was new and exciting to him. I offered to buy him a snack, but he just wanted to listen to the police radio and look at the tall buildings, so I gave him a tour of downtown before going to the Science Centre.

We drove along the Don River, under the Bloor Street Bridge. Ethan loved being under the bridge; the wrought iron formed a moving sculpture of angles and curves. He pressed his face against the window and stared up as we headed north.

The radio spat out constant alerts, a running commentary on city life. An accident in Scarborough, an alarm in a jewelry store—mental popcorn.

One call got my attention: an abandoned car at Pine Hills Cemetery. The dispatcher asked for a description. The responding officer paused.

"Ah, it's an Impala, sixty-five, sixty-six, two-door, brown, no plates."

I grabbed the microphone so quickly that Ethan jumped. "This is fifty-two four-eight, to the car at Pine Hills, over."

The officer answered casually, "Go four-eight."

"Can you secure the Impala? It may be evidence in an assault, over."

A long pause, then, "Detective McBriar? Ian?"

The voice was familiar. "Tom? Tom Wheeler."

"Yeah. It's been a while, man. Do you want to meet me at the vehicle?"

"Ten-four," I answered. "Thanks, man. Be there in ten."

"East entrance off Kennedy Road," he directed.

I turned to Ethan and smiled. "Watch what happens when I turn on the siren." I planted the gumball on the roof. Cars behind me suddenly backed off. I hit the siren.

I made a U-turn and headed south. I blipped the

siren through intersections and kept the gumball flashing. Several zigzags later, we stopped at Pine Hills Cemetery.

It had taken exactly nine minutes to get there.

Tom Wheeler climbed out of his cruiser and stretched out his hand. He looked like a farm boy—burly, tall, with a movie star smile and a Humphrey Bogart voice. We had gone through the academy together. We had patrolled together. He came from three generations of beat cop. That was what he'd always wanted to be, and his parents were proud that he'd followed in the family tradition.

"Tom. How's life?" I asked.

"Doing great. Frank driving you crazy yet?"

I shrugged.

He looked behind me, amused. "The academy's taking them awful young, huh?"

I swiveled to see Ethan, grabbing his zipper.

"I gotta pee," he moaned.

The receptionist in the cemetery office let him use the washroom. He went all by himself, and we walked back to the cars. Tom smirked.

"So, who's the rookie?" He bent down and stuck out a big hand. "Nice to meet you, son."

Ethan took it, smiling.

"This is Ethan," I said. "I'm dating his mom."

Tom raised an eyebrow. "Really? Far out."

We walked around the Impala; the driver-side door was open a crack. Snow had settled in the doorsill, indicating it had been there overnight. Tom pushed the door open with his nightstick and peered in. There was no trash in the car, no marks or decals or parking tickets or anything. Two license plates sat on the front seat.

"Someone left it clean," he commented.

Ethan looked, but obeyed my instructions to not touch anything.

"Ethan," I said, "would you stay with Constable Tom? I have to make a phone call."

The same receptionist let me use a phone.

"Yes?" Frank's voice barked immediately.

"Hey. How are you doing?" I started.

"This better be important. You know how rare it is to get Helen naked before noon?"

"There's an image that will haunt me," I said. "No, really. I think we found the Impala."

"No shit? Where?" He was serious now.

I described the find.

He went *uh-huh*, then inhaled deeply. "I'll tell forensics to check it out. You enjoy the day. Tell Tom that he can have it towed. He gets brownie points for this one."

Tom had Ethan sitting at the wheel of the cruiser as I returned.

"Frank says hi. He asked you to wrap this one up. It's a gold star for you, apparently."

Tom grinned a Gary Cooper smile. We shook hands, and I took Ethan back to the Fury.

Ethan loved the yellow squad car, he said, with the radios and switches and all. He was disappointed that we didn't use the siren and light again as we drove.

At the Science Centre, Ethan stared out the window, incredulous.

"Is the fun place in there?" he asked, pointing to the long building.

I smiled. "It's the whole building. We can spend the whole day there, OK?"

We went through the funhouse mirrors, the dinosaur models, the paper airplanes, the chemistry exhibits, and the "How a camera works" lab. At noon, we stopped for lunch. I found a pay phone. A businesslike voice said, "Karen Prescott."

"Hi," I mumbled. "I believe you left your son with a strange police officer?"

There was a gasp, then she laughed. "How is he?"

I chuckled. "He's fine. I'm exhausted."

She started to laugh. "OK," she purred. "I hope you're not *too* exhausted."

I glanced at Ethan. Hot dog in hand, he waved at

me. "Not a chance. See you later?"

"See you at five," she answered.

Ethan went for a second trip through all the exhibits. He raced through everything at breakneck speed, not wanting to miss a thing. He was soon tired; we left and joined the line of cars heading downtown.

Friday afternoon. I was looking forward to being with Karen, spending the weekend together. It was not something I could tell Ethan about, but I felt a glow just knowing he was connected to her. He looked out his window at the traffic.

"How did you enjoy the day?" I asked him.

"It was fun," he chirped. "Can we take mom next time?"

"We could. Let's see if there's anything else she'd like to do, though," I said. My father had said those same words to my brother and me a hundred times. I was turning into him. The thought tickled me.

Ethan yawned, leaned against the passenger door, and fell fast asleep.

I got to Front Street at five to five. The snow, now big white corn flakes, floated and drifted with the breeze. The sky went from a soft white to a darker gray as I waited.

A familiar profile came toward me. Karen waved and walked faster.

Ethan was asleep. I stepped out. All six feet two of me sauntered slowly up to greet her.

I was aware of a broad shadow behind her—four women, jockeying to get a good look. Karen looked sheepishly at the welcoming committee. She waved at them, then skipped toward me. She sighed.

"Say hi to the girls."

I waved at the women and gave them my widest smile. They giggled and waved back. Karen slid into the car, with Ethan between us. Instinctively, I leaned over him and kissed her softly.

"What?" she asked.

I was searching for words. "A man can't kiss his best girl hello?" I mumbled lamely.

She looked right through me. "That's not what that kiss was for," she said.

I glanced over at her. "How do you do that? No, that's not what it was for." I pulled into traffic. Karen reached over Ethan and scratched my leg playfully.

This feels right, I told myself. This feels like I always expected it should feel. At the same time, a small voice told me that I had known this woman for about two days, I knew almost nothing about her, and I was jumping to conclusions.

"So?" she asked again. "Why the kiss?"

I collected my thoughts. "Ever imagine, when you were a kid, what it would be like the first time that you drove a car, or made love, or flew in a plane? What you would be like as a parent?"

She shrugged. "Sure, everyone does, don't they?"

"I always wondered what it would feel like to fall in love."

She just stared at me, hard. I couldn't read her expression. "So, do you know the feeling?" she asked softly.

"I thought I did. Now . . . it's completely different." I hit a red light, turned, and faced her. "This feels like I always thought it should feel."

She was still staring, but the hardness had evaporated. "So, you really think talking like that will get you sex, huh?"

I smiled.

Ethan stirred. She hugged him tighter.

"How was he today?"

I glanced down at him. "We went on a police chase. He had fun."

She opened her mouth silently. "Please tell me you're kidding. You are kidding, right?"

I laughed. "Mostly. I stopped off to check out an abandoned car. Ethan met a patrol cop. Then we went to the Science Centre. He had a blast."

She stared wide-eyed. "Abandoned car? Was he in any danger? No, you wouldn't do that, right?"

I shook my head. "No way, no. Now, we have a whole weekend together. What would you like to do?"

Ethan woke up. He told her how he went to the Science Centre and played with real dinosaurs. Karen smiled approvingly. Ethan talked nonstop about the siren-and-light run to the cemetery, which Karen was not happy about, then the telescope exhibit, then about the brown car again. We were almost home. Ethan patted my arm.

"And Ian said stay with the policeman when he used a phone, and he said don't touch anything, and I didn't touch the gun."

I smiled. "Officer Tom's gun?"

"No," he corrected. "The one in that car."

Karen looked at him, frozen in shock. I pulled over.

"Ethan, this is very important. Where was the gun?"

He pointed to my floor mat. "It was under there. But you said don't touch, so I didn't. "

His mother turned pale.

"OK, Ian's getting a beating," I mumbled.

I got everyone upstairs. Karen was silent. Ethan just thought it was a tremendously fun day.

Nobody was very hungry, so we agreed on vegetable soup for dinner. This also made my Friday meatless. I put soup on while Ethan watched TV.

I called Frank.

"Hello," he sang.

"Frank, got some news for you," I started. "Ethan was looking under the seats of that Impala. Apparently, he saw a gun there."

Frank was quiet for a moment. "Hmm . . . was it a nickel-plated Beretta M951?"

I sighed with relief. "You found it."

He laughed. "Tell Ethan he's earned a detective badge. By the way, Helen would love to have you three over for lunch tomorrow. About twelve thirty, OK?"

"Hold on." I asked Karen if she'd like that. She nodded, still silent.

"See you at twelve thirty, then."

The soup warmed on the stove. Ethan, cross-legged on the floor, watched the news.

I felt idiotic that I'd dragged him along on the call,

doubly so that he'd found a gun. I washed dishes. Karen came over, wrapped her arms around me and leaned up to my ear.

"If you *ever* put my son in danger, I'll kill you with my bare hands," she whispered.

I smiled with relief. "Deal." I kissed her.

Ethan ate his soup, floating bread in the bowl and scooping it up with a spoon. We had coffee on the sofa, watching TV.

It was the first time in years I'd owned one. I didn't really want it, but I was glad Karen enjoyed it. Ethan was on his stomach, watching *The Brady Bunch*. Karen had her feet in my lap, watching Ethan. She saw me looking at her and smiled.

"What?" she asked.

"Feels right," I answered. "Us, warm home on a snowy night, just feels right, that's all." I closed one eye, and said, conspiratorially, "Wait a sec, now there's something I need to ask you."

"Hmm?" she smiled. "Is there a problem, officer?"

"Sure is. I realize I don't know anything about you. You're here, using me for sinful purposes, and I know next to nothing about you."

She glanced over to make sure Ethan was still mesmerized by the TV. "What do you want to know?" It was an open question, with no hesitation.

"Where are you from, where did you go to school, your favorite color, everything."

She sat up and crossed her legs. "I was born in Kingston, grew up in Ottawa. My father worked for the Ministry of Transport, then he opened a bookstore. My mother is a housewife, always was. I went to Carleton, studied business, and left after a year to have Ethan. My favorite color is dark blue. Ethan's is green. Anything else?"

"Brothers and sisters?"

"Only brat. It made it easier. My parents were very good about me keeping Ethan."

I thought the last sentence over. "He never married

you."

She looked at me softly, her dark brown eyes fixing me. "Does that bother you?"

I pressed my lips together, choosing my words, then said, "You deserve better. So does Ethan."

She leaned forward and nibbled my earlobe. "That'll get you special treats," she said. "I was wondering—what do we do? He can't sleep on the sofa again tonight."

I smiled. I'd thought that one out. "Ethan, have you ever been camping?"

He shook his head.

"Would you like to go camping tonight?"

He nodded vigorously and went back to watching the TV.

I set up my old pup tent and folded out my sleeping bag. At ten o'clock, Ethan gleefully climbed into the tent for a camp-out. His eyes closed in no time, but we waited until we were sure he was asleep.

Karen led me to bed, unbuttoning her blouse and walking backwards.

Around midnight, I went for something to drink and checked on Ethan. The ice in the glasses clattered noisily in the quiet living room, but he slept soundly.

I sat nude on the edge of the bed, and handed Karen a ginger ale. She propped herself up against a pillow, bare from the waist up, and sipped quietly. She rolled the glass between her hands, thinking.

"Do you wonder how often I do this—run off with strange men?"

I shook my head.

She looked up at me. "Like I said, I've been alone since his dad left. And I do mean alone."

"I know the feeling."

She leaned forward, a mischievous look in her eyes. "So, what happened to Melissa?"

"You talked to Helen," I said, grimacing theatrically. "It was terrible. She taught English in New Guinea and ran into a tribe of head-hunting cannibals."

Karen snickered.

I nodded, frowning. "She said 'Good morning' to the chief, but in their language that means 'I am delicious.' It was a tragedy."

Karen laughed into her knees, trying to not wake Ethan. I looked down at my glass.

More serious, I said, "Melissa is a good woman, a pediatrician. She always wanted to be a doctor, but never a cop's girlfriend. 'Change jobs or change girlfriends,' she said. I stayed on the force."

"What if your mom hadn't died? Would you still have become a priest?"

"I've wondered that a thousand times. But then, I figure that God has his plan for us, and all we can do is to follow it."

"So, maybe it was meant to be. Keep the job, lose the girlfriend, find me?"

"When we lose one blessing, another is often most unexpectedly given in its place."

I'm in bed with a young woman I don't know. She rolls over and looks at me; her face is cut and bruised. Her teeth are smashed in, blood is gushing from her neck, and her arms and legs are slashed, too. She sits up and opens her mouth to scream. Nothing comes out.

I sit up with a start.

As my eyes cleared, I could read the clock: four forty-five a.m. I worried I might have hurt Karen if I flailed in my sleep. Her eyes were open, looking at me with worry, but no fear. A wave of relief drained me. I lay back.

"Does this happen often?" she asked softly.

I shook my head. Nausea swept over me. Deep breath, I thought, deep breath. "Three weeks ago, we were investigating a series of assaults on call girls. This young girl, fifteen, came down from Sudbury." I huffed, breathing hard to fight the nausea.

"There are these newspaper ads promising jobs as models and stewardesses, but they come here, and they find it's all a sham." More huffing. Deep breath, deep breath.

"There are no jobs, and they're in debt to the scum that brought them here, and they have to turn tricks to pay their way back." I moaned, almost weeping.

"This john enjoyed beating up girls, but she didn't want to get beaten up. We were already after him. She fought, scratched his face, and broke his nose. He sliced her up. Another girl found her." I took a deep breath.

"We arrived before the ambulance—we were canvassing the building. The medics did everything they could, but she died five minutes after they got there."

Karen looked at me with deep sorrow. She pulled my face to her chest. I cried.

At six in the morning, I showered and woke her up. She slipped on my old plaid bathrobe. Even that looked alluring.

I made coffee. She looked into her cup, thoughtful.

"Are you feeling bad about how you were there?" she asked gently.

"You mean crying?" I shook my head. "I feel like the weight of the world was lifted from my shoulders."

"How does Frank deal with it? Does he have the same nightmares?"

"Dunno. Ask Helen at lunch."

I suggested going out for a pancake breakfast. Ethan was torn between pancakes and watching cartoons, but pancakes won out.

We drove past the U of T, east along Queen Street, down Bathurst Street to Lake Ontario. The snow had melted and turned to slush, slipping away into the sewers like a bad dream. The grass, hidden since December, poked through in places, brown and thin.

It stretched weakly up in the hazy sun, soaking up the thin rays as they struggled to push through the overcast.

Karen pointed out landmarks to Ethan. He nodded without understanding.

At Old Fort York, he got excited. He wanted to see if any cowboys were there, fighting Indians. Karen shot me a quick look. "Not today," she said. She sighed, puzzled. "Where exactly are we going?" she asked.

"Ah," I answered theatrically. "Somewhere special."

I parked at the Toronto Island Ferry terminal. The ferry was just loading; Ethan was giddy with excitement for the five-minute trip to Toronto Island.

The ferry was a barge, big enough for a handful of cars down the middle of the single deck, with covered seating areas to either side and open railings outside of that.

Ethan stood on my feet, watching waves splash the hull, while Karen held his hand. Lake Ontario on this cool March day smelled like I imagined the sea would.

Once we docked at the island, Ethan looked around in wonder, excited. We took a short walk to the terminal building for Toronto Island Airport.

Inside that, a small coffee shop faced the runways. A sign read *The Left Seat Diner*. We sat at a booth, Ethan kneeling, nose pressed against the glass, as a small plane prepared for takeoff. The diner's owner, Barry, a slight, young-looking man with curly hair and an Errol Flynn mustache, came over.

"Hey, Detective," he called. He handed us paper menus. "Long time no see." He glanced at Karen. "Ma'am." He turned back to me. "What can I get you?"

I asked about his pancakes.

He nodded. "Let me take care of it. This one's on me." He strode to the kitchen.

Karen smiled. "Friend of yours?"

"I stopped a robbery here, years back. I'm finally taking his offer of a free meal."

"Why now?" she asked.

"Hey," I teased, "you're an expensive date."

A small Cessna came in for a landing. Ethan was hypnotized.

Barry brought coffee in sky-blue mugs, and milk for Ethan. Karen sipped her coffee and watched her son. A twin-engine plane sat at the end of the runway, spooling up its engines. It disappeared behind the control tower and reappeared a moment later, a few feet off the ground. Ethan watched it till the food came.

Karen cut up his pancakes. She stopped to look at me. "Who was your partner then—Frank?"

"Tom Wheeler. Ethan met him yesterday. I'm sure Tom did take the odd free meal though, knowing his appetite."

We thanked Barry for the meal. I hid ten dollars under a plate and led Karen down the tarmac to a large hangar. I told Ethan I had a surprise for him.

We entered the hangar. A young man in overalls sat on a low stool, swiveling across the underside of a Learjet as he inspected something.

"Ian!" he bellowed. "Good to see ya, man." He reached his hand out.

I shook it. "Wolfgang, nice to see you too." I did the introductions.

"What brings you to the Island?" he asked. I put a hand on Ethan's shoulder.

"He wants a job as a pilot," I joked. Ethan shrank back and clung to my pants.

Wolfgang crouched down and looked him in the eye. "You like airplanes?"

Ethan nodded cautiously.

"Well, let's see how you fit in the pilot's seat. Come with me." He walked to the right side of the Learjet; a door folded down to form a stairway. He lifted Ethan inside. Karen gave me a look—proud and puzzled.

I whispered, "Wolfgang was a cop, but he prefers fixing airplanes."

The cabin of the Lear had three rows of plush leather seats, plus two seats for the pilots. Wolfgang led Ethan to the left pilot's seat and described the controls.

"Ah," Karen said, "The Left Seat Diner. I get it."

Wolfgang winked and turned back to Ethan. "This wheel lets you turn left and right. This makes it go up. That makes it go down. This is the throttle. It makes the plane go faster." He explained for a few minutes.

Karen reached into her purse and pulled out an Instamatic. She fumbled with the flash, then took three pictures. Ethan beamed.

I checked my watch and made a letter T with my hands; Wolfgang blinked OK. He said he had to work now, but asked if we would like to visit again.

We climbed out and Ethan stood, gaping at the pilot's seat through the window. Karen took more photos. I thanked Wolfgang.

"Listen, man. This was a huge treat for the little guy. I really appreciate it."

"Glad to help a buddy. I hear you're on the Palumbo case. Any leads?" He seemed too earnest, too helpful.

"Not yet. What have you heard?" I asked, smiling.

He shrugged nervously. "Just grapevine stuff."

I shook my head. "If I hear anything, I'll let you know," I lied.

We skipped back to the ferry, Ethan between us. He was as thrilled by the boat ride back as he had been by the airplane. He chattered nonstop.

There was something I couldn't quite remember; it nagged me as I drove. Karen was amused, watching me stare off. "Are you going to visit our planet soon?" she asked.

I smiled. "Frank and I are on the case of the kid that got hit by a train. From the news? His older brother died in a car crash in Italy last year. Their sister married a man called Zimmerman, also a German name."

Karen frowned, trying to follow my thoughts. "Wolfgang, Zimmerman. German names?"

"The witness to the other Palumbo son's accident was a man called Carpenter."

She was curious now. "Yeah, and?"

"The German word for carpenter is *zimmerman*."

She nodded. "Do you think this Zimmerman is actually the Carpenter fellow?"

I shrugged. "It's a thought. Helen had the same thought. Right now, I need to check on a friend."

Gary opened his door reluctantly, eyeing us as though we might be rabid. Ethan squatted down to pet

Dixie. She hunched away, then crept slowly forward as he cooed softly to her. A minute later, he was gently stroking her back. He sat on the floor, straight-legged, while Dixie licked his face.

Gary was animated, blatantly ogling Karen. She told him we enjoyed watching his TV. We declined tea; we were due at Frank's. He invited us back anytime, still staring at Karen till we got in the car. Karen smiled.

"Well, it seems he likes girls," she quipped.

I grunted. "You think?"

She gasped, incredulous. "You're jealous! Of poor Gary? You have got to be putting me on!"

I grumbled and drove off. Karen laughed and hugged my arm.

Frank greeted us in a bowling shirt and slacks. The smell of spinach tarts and lamb filled the house. Karen and Helen hugged, then talked in tag-team sentences, ending each other's thoughts.

Ethan tackled Frank, giving him a big hug around the neck. Did Ethan want to see a train set, Frank asked. Of course he did.

"Where were you?" Frank asked me. "I tried to call you."

"We went out for breakfast, then checked on Gary."

"Good. He's OK?"

"Yeah."

Ethan grabbed Frank's leg. "C'mon, Uncle Frank, show me your trains."

Frank smiled. He picked Ethan up with one arm. "Right away, sport." They headed for the basement

I was left alone in the living room. Frank had put away the case files, but the *Toronto Star* was out, open to the local news section. A prayer service for Nick Palumbo, at Immaculate Conception Church, was circled; I knew the church well.

The announcement thanked the people of Toronto for "thinking of our son at this difficult time." It also listed the reading of scriptures. Frank came back upstairs, looking for something.

"Where's Ethan?" I asked.

"Running the trains. What's up?"

I pointed to the list of readings. "Psalm 109; not a usual reading at a service. It's a call for punishment of the wicked."

Frank re-read the announcement. "A message? A warning."

"Yup. He's telling the guy who did this, 'I'll find you and get you.' By the way," I added, "The witness in Italy—Carpenter? Palumbo's daughter is married to someone or other Zimmerman. Zimmerman is German for carpenter."

Frank gasped and put his hands on his cheeks.

"You knew." I sighed.

He smiled. "Yeah, we checked. Her Zimmerman was in New Jersey when the older boy died."

"What do you do when you're not on vacation?" I asked.

"Keep your ass out of trouble." He faced the kitchen. "Helen, lunch?" he called.

She yelled, "Ten minutes." Frank barreled back to the basement.

I followed him down the stairs. Frank had built a diorama on two raised sheets of plywood, with hills, tunnels, bridges, and scenery. From a distance of ten feet, I could blur my eyes and believe it was real. A tiny sign read *Confluence, Pennsylvania.*

"Homesick, are we?"

Frank shrugged. "Sometimes I miss the place. It looked like this in '59, but it's different now."

"Never went back to visit your folks, school buddies?" A locomotive clattered along, pulling flatcars loaded with scribble pads—Ethan's work.

"No point in reliving the past." He left it at that.

Helen called down that lunch was ready.

Ethan sprinted up ahead of us, raving about airplanes, trains, the man with a funny dog, and really good pancakes.

Helen hung on his every word. She had set an elegant table; her good china, silverware, even napkins folded into fans, standing by the plates.

"Gee," I mumbled, "how come I never got this fancy treatment?"

Frank grunted. "You're not fancy. Karen is. So is Ethan, aren't you, big fella?"

We ate, drank, and talked shop till almost five. Helen wanted to know more about Karen's family. Frank and I spoke softly, avoiding details of the Palumbo case. Frank told Ethan stories about being in Vietnam. Ethan said it sounded like fun, but Frank explained how hard it was to see friends get hurt and how it was not fun always being wet, hungry, tired, and scared.

Helen popped her head out of the kitchen and said something about the basement.

"Hey," Frank said to Ethan, "would your mom like to see the train set?" He ordered Karen and Ethan downstairs. Helen asked me for help. I sensed a setup. I walked meekly into the kitchen and playfully bumped her hip.

"So, why this meeting?" I asked.

"Were we that obvious?" she said matter-of-factly.

"Yes. I assume this is about me and Karen."

She glanced at me sideways. "What do you know, you *are* a detective." She put her towel down and leaned against the sink. "How do you feel about this woman? I mean it. Are you serious, or what?" She was earnest, but I felt like having some fun with her.

"I dunno." I shrugged. "I mean, she's cute and all, but I think I could do better."

Her face dropped, then she picked up her tea towel and thwacked me angrily. "You bastard!" she barked. "You enjoyed that!"

I laughed.

She hit me again, slammed the towel down, and poked my ribs. "This woman is the best damned thing you've ever had happen in your life."

By now I was biting my lip, trying not to laugh. This infuriated her even more, and she faced the sink, fuming. I put my arm over her shoulder and gave her a hug.

"If it's any consolation, I feel the same way about her," I said. "But why are you and Frank so interested in my love life suddenly?"

She looked up. Her eyes were wet. "Frank is a baby. He sees Ethan as—" she paused, "—the little brother he never had. Inside that grumpy thirty-five-year-old man is a six-year-old child."

"Sure," I said, "but he's a grumpy six-year-old child."

Helen sniffed and laughed. She looked at me, serious again. "I love you like a brother. You know that. I just want what's best for you." She stopped and sniffed again.

"So you're telling me to stop dating the other women, huh?" I teased.

Helen had a wicked backhand, and she unleashed it.

Helen and I came down the basement steps. Frank and Ethan were coupling a line of boxcars to a train. Ethan worked the throttle, backing the locomotive gently into place and picking up cars from a spur line. He turned the control the other way, and the entire train moved slowly onto the mainline. He squealed with pride.

Helen whispered into my ear. I nodded. "Say, Karen," I started, "I was thinking we should have Frank and Helen over for dinner tomorrow night. What do you think?"

Frank popped his head up. "You making lasagna?"

"Wasn't planning on it," I answered. Helen elbowed me. "You know, now that I think of it, lasagna sounds good after all." I turned to her. "Yes, I'll make two, one for you to take home."

Karen shook her head. "I don't see how you read each other's minds like that."

"Just as well," Frank smirked. "You'd slap him out."

Helen gave me a goodbye peck on the cheek. Frank hugged Karen and tried to hug Ethan with one arm, but

Ethan knocked him back, giving him a big kiss on the nose. Ethan left clutching an engineer's cap, a souvenir from the afternoon. Frank waved as we drove away, his arm around Helen.

"They really love each other," Karen said. Ethan was asleep by the time we hit Rogers Road.

"Funny," I said, "Helen said that about us."

Karen was silent. I shut up, not wanting to break the spell, to hear I'd said the wrong thing. That was a dumb statement, I thought. I was moving way too fast.

"You know," she smiled, "we should find a bigger apartment."

I sighed, delighted. "Yes, we certainly will."

I carried Ethan upstairs, dead weight and all floppy. Karen put him to bed and closed the door. He would sleep for a good hour.

We made love on the carpet, rushing to finish before Ethan woke up.

I made dinner. Ethan stood on a chair, watching as I cooked pasta in sauce. After dinner, Ethan played with his Hot Wheels as we sat on the sofa.

"In a bit, I'll go get my tent," I said.

Karen smiled and rubbed her foot playfully into my thigh.

"You know," I said, "sometime soon I'm going to want a full night's sleep."

She grinned. "Not tonight."

I headed back to my place for my camping gear and a good suit for church.

On a hunch, I called Frank.

"So, you're vertical again, are you?" he asked, bluntly.

"None of your business, Frank. Dinner around six?"

"Sure." His voice was soft. "Say goodnight to Karen and Ethan."

"How do you know I'll see them later?" I asked defiantly.

"C'mon, how stupid am I?" He said with a laugh. "Six p.m., lasagna."

I chuckled and said goodbye.

I set up my tent in the living room; we built a "campfire" with drinking straws and played till Ethan was ready for bed.

Karen sang him a lullaby as he got sleepy. I could hear it, muffled, through the door. I rolled out my sleeping bag and slid in. A thin strip of light under the bedroom door rippled as Karen walked around. It abruptly went dark; the door opened, and I heard a patter of feet.

In the soft light, I saw Karen, wearing an undershirt and a pair of pink briefs. She slid into the sleeping bag beside me, rubbing against me with deliberate force. I slid my hand up her back and pulled her close.

"I have a question for you," I said.

"Really?" She propped herself up on one elbow, amused. She was smiling.

"Helen thinks you love me," I said. There was a long pause. Her smile had faded.

"And?" she asked quietly.

"I love you, too," I whispered.

CHAPTER SIX

At four in the morning, I woke up. I caressed Karen's leg, stroking slowly up the inside of her thigh. She wriggled and turned her head the other way, still asleep. I wrapped my arm around her, pulled her close and fell back to sleep.

At six, I was in the shower. I heard a noise and poked my head out. Ethan looked up at me.

"Hi, sport," I chirped. "Are you okay?"

He nodded. "Where's mommy?" he asked.

From the living room I heard "Oh shit!" and a scramble of activity. A minute later, Karen ran into the bathroom, tying up a robe. She ushered Ethan out, poked her head around the curtain and smirked.

"Happy to see you, too," she joked.

I got dressed for church.

The early mass at Immaculate Conception was rarely busy; today was no exception. Easter wasn't for another month. We were between feast days, so this one was sparsely attended. I sat to the back, on the right side of the aisle.

The regulars, mostly old people, took their usual seats. I opened my prayer book and read quietly. An old man in a poorly fitting suit walked out from the vestry, turned to the altar, and bowed. He walked to the back of the church and dipped his hand in holy water. He made the sign of the cross, bowed again, then exited the back door.

A moment later, in came Palumbo, arm in arm with his mother. A man followed them. He looked like a small truck; massive, burly, good suit, but clearly not here for the mass. Palumbo helped his mother to her seat and whispered something. Without a word, he sat beside me. He looked me square in the eye, a look that compelled me to say something.

"Mr. Palumbo," I whispered, "I'm again very sorry for the accident."

He bowed his head, accepting my sympathies. "Why are you here, Detective?"

I held up my prayer book. "I'm Catholic. This church is close to home."

He nodded, analyzing my response. "Is there any progress in my son's case?"

"How do you mean?" I didn't want to say anything revealing.

"Are there any further developments in Nick's accident?"

I realized I'd been thinking about the older boy's accident. I was glad I'd said nothing. Palumbo studied me.

"Which accident are you investigating?" he asked.

That took me aback. "We are actively investigating Nick's accident. That's all."

He thought for a moment, stood up, and stretched out his hand. "It's a pleasure to see you in God's house. Perhaps we can speak again?"

I stood, shook his hand, and sat back down. He ignored me for the rest of the mass. At the end of the mass, the priest gave a final blessing, and we all turned to leave.

The "small truck in a suit" glided over to me. For someone that large, he was smooth on his feet. He opened his mouth, and a sound like rolling thunder poured out.

"Mr. Palumbo thanks you for your efforts at this difficult time," he growled. I imagined him saying "pay or else," and making it stick. He handed me a business card, fine, smooth paper with embossed printing. "Mr. Palumbo requests your company for dinner. Of course, your friend is also invited."

I kept my composure. "My friend?"

"The young lady." His eyes, hazel and dead, said, "We know about her." He didn't wait for an answer. I supposed people didn't often say no.

I walked into my apartment. Karen frowned as she saw me.

"What is it?" she asked.

I told her about the invitation. She giggled.

"I get to eat with a Mafia boss? Far out. And as your moll?" She slid up to me. "I can wear opera gloves with a dress slit to the hip and a long cigarette holder . . ."

I smirked. "I could get you a little pearl-handled pistol for your garter."

"Sounds like a blast. When are we going?"

"Not sure. But I have an outing planned for today."

We took the subway downtown. Ethan loved the ride, blasting underground at high speed. We walked down Bloor Street, past the museum to the domed building next door.

"Ethan," I said, pointing, "that is a planetarium."

Ethan went through the planetarium exhibits with the same wonder he had at the Science Centre, touching everything and asking questions.

We lined up for the show; I warned Ethan that it would get dark, but his mother and I would be with him, and he could ask questions in a whisper. The lights dimmed; the ceiling turned from a sunset gold to an inky black, then filled with stars. Ethan gasped.

The presenter put a lot of emotion into the show, talking about things one sees in a night sky. The full moon sailed past. In the dim light I saw Ethan lean back, mesmerized.

I settled back to think. Palumbo wanted to talk to me. Not officially, though, or he'd have called me at the station. Why me? Was it a common thread? Both Catholic? Think about it later.

Jupiter loomed overhead, a beige ball. Ethan gawked at the display. Karen leaned over him and stared at me.

"Good of you to rejoin us," she scolded.

I smiled meekly. The show went on for another twenty minutes. I tried to concentrate, but something nagged me, and I couldn't put my finger on it.

The dome went dark, the house lights came on, and everyone left. Ethan raved about the cool stars inside the building, and how it looked like being outside. I nodded and smiled, still nagged by whatever I couldn't think of. We stepped back into the bright street. Karen looked around, puzzled.

"What?" I asked.

She shook her head. "I'm sorry. I got so used to being in your car, I forgot we took transit."

A puzzle piece clicked for me. I hunched over and groaned, frustrated with myself.

"What's wrong?" Karen said in alarm, clutching Ethan tight.

I shook my head. It made sense now. "Transit! That's it! Thank you, Karen. Thank you, thank you." I kissed her hard.

She gave me a sly smile. "If you wanted a kiss, you just had to ask."

I stood up straight. "Let's get some groceries." I smiled. "It's going to be an interesting evening."

We found an open Dominion store. Karen ignored my outburst until we were in the store. I pushed a cart, Ethan standing in it like Ahab on the prow of the Pequod. Randomly, Karen pestered me for an explanation.

"Transit?" she prodded several times.

I just smiled. "Watch Frank's reaction," I finally said. "He'll say he already thought of it."

"You're not going to tell me?" Now she was irritated. I smiled again.

By four o'clock I was assembling dinner. Ethan fell in front of the TV. Karen rubbed up against me.

"That is very distracting," I said, not at all upset.

"Glad to see I haven't lost my touch." She nuzzled my ear. "Transit?" she purred.

I shook my head. She huffed and watched TV with Ethan. I made two lasagnas, set them aside, tossed a salad, then set that aside, too.

Four thirty. An hour and a half till dinner. I had a special old bottle of Chianti; this seemed like the ideal time to open it.

This was the first time I'd had more than four people at dinner. Frank and Helen had come over exactly twice to eat with Melissa and me, then dashed off quickly both times.

Karen placed fresh flowers on the table. I chose some music: Milt Jackson seemed right. I set the reel to a mellow track, perfect for quiet conversation.

At five to six, I heard a knock. Karen got the door while I sliced French bread. After the standard hellos, Frank sat down to play with Ethan. Helen came into the kitchen and gave me a kiss on the cheek.

"Hey, handsome." She hugged me warmly.

"To what do I owe this honor?" I asked.

"Let's just say that Frank has been easier to live with lately," she said.

"Really?" I smirked. "Tell me more."

She blushed and giggled. "You."

We ate to Thelonious Monk. Frank wolfed down his lasagna, mumbling soft praises.

Karen commented, "Now I see why you had to make two of them."

"Oh, right," Frank grunted. "One for me to take home?"

I nodded.

"Cool," he said. "You get to keep your job."

I put my fork down. "In that vein," I started. "I wondered why that Impala was at the cemetery. I think I know."

Karen looked up, curiosity eating her.

"*Hmf?*" Frank said. Karen stopped eating.

"Transit," I said simply.

Frank patted his mouth with a napkin. "Transit?" He looked up, thoughtful. "Warden Station, very good," he mumbled. "That says it all, of course, Warden."

Karen shrugged. Helen shook her head. I explained. "You dump a stolen car, you don't ditch it near where you live."

"If you are doing this with someone," Frank said, "they drive behind you, and you dump the car at the airport—somewhere nobody pays any attention—then you leave in the other person's car. But if you're alone, you dump it near transit. From where the car was dumped, this guy just walked to the subway." He nodded. "Good work, kid, I knew you'd get it too."

I laughed. "Damn you, Frank, that did *not* occur to you."

He shrugged nonchalantly. "Same idea. More salad?"

Helen gazed off, thinking. "Is that what happened in Italy, only backwards?" she asked.

Frank frowned. "Explain."

"Well," she started, "if the older Palumbo fellow was murdered, then someone pushed him off the road, right?" We all nodded. "Then if that person, alone, attacked the younger son, maybe they were alone when they killed the boy in Italy." She leaned forward. "So, how would you get to the place where he goes off the road?"

"He had a car, an Alfa Romeo," Frank said softly.

Helen nodded. "But the boy was in his own car, right? You'd have to run it off the road where it would be fatal. Otherwise he might just wake up with a bump on his head and call the police."

We all sat, silent.

"Go on, hon," Frank said warmly.

Helen shook her head, moved a glass, and placed a fork beside it for clarification. "You park the Alfa where you want the accident to happen. You take a bus to the town where the boy was—Foligno?" We all nodded. "Then you get him drunk and drive him back in his own car. You put him in the driver's seat and push him off the cliff. Remember in *North by Northwest*, they did that to Gregory Peck?"

"Cary Grant," I corrected. "Whatever. Go on, Helen."

"Cary Grant. But he didn't crash in the movie. So you drive the boy off the road. Then you call the police, and they just assume he's an unlucky drunk."

Frank looked at Helen, his mouth open. "Right on," he mumbled.

"Ditto." I nodded.

The rest of dinner, we kept the conversation light. Frank turned to Helen at one point and asked something cryptic. She raised her eyebrows and nodded. Frank turned to Karen.

"Listen," he said, coughing, "we wonder if Ethan would like to spend a weekend out with us. Helen's cousin has a farm in Barrie. He could pester goats and chickens all day. What do you think?"

Ethan bounced up and down. Of course he would like that, I told myself. That also meant an entire weekend with Karen.

"Then it's set." Frank leaned back. "We'll pick him up Friday night and bring him back Sunday night. How's that, champ?"

Ethan jumped off his chair and gave Frank a bear hug. Frank blinked away tears.

By nine, we were all sleepy. Ethan watched *The Wonderful World of Disney*. Helen and Karen had coffee on the sofa. Every so often they'd look our way and giggle. Frank pulled out his Moleskine notebook and read his notes.

"We took Ethan to the Island for pancakes," I said.

Frank nodded. "The Left Seat Diner? Love their pancakes."

"We ran into Wolfgang. He asked how our investigation was going."

Frank frowned. "What did he know?"

"He was fishing. I said no leads, but I'd keep him posted."

"Good call. What else?"

I shook my head. "Can't surprise you. I ran into Palumbo at church. He invited me to dinner."

Frank smiled. "His bruiser dropped by our house yesterday. He doesn't leave much to chance." Frank pulled out Palumbo's business card. I pulled mine out.

"Snap," I said. "I figure Wolfgang was talking to Palumbo. The big guy at church said Karen was invited as well. 'The young lady,' he called her. How else would he know?"

Frank agreed. "Last thing," Frank said. He cleared his throat. "We've been asked to help with some parts thefts. Two Mohawk kids from Temagami. We need their help to get higher up the food chain." He looked at me expectantly.

"No, no, no," I said, shaking my head. "Not the rainbow Indian."

Frank leaned back, smiling to put me at ease. "Hey, it's for a good cause. Think of the brownie points if we crack them."

I shook my head. Karen and Helen stopped talking and watched us.

"How about something I can do for you? Quid pro quo?" Frank asked.

I waved my hand in front of him.

"*De minimis non curat*, Frank."

"Damned Latin students," he huffed, scowling at me. He thought for a moment and grinned, triumphant. "You can drive Karen to work for a week."

I groaned. "Damn you Frank, dirty pool."

He grinned, satisfied.

"What?" Karen asked, puzzled. "What did I miss?"

Frank and Helen went home.

I put fresh clothes, my gun and badge in a gym bag. Ethan asked about Uncle Frank's farm and the animals, like farms on TV. Karen explained that there might not be many animals, but he would have lots of fun anyway. We walked back to Karen's apartment. She was smiling at us.

"What?" I asked.

"Ethan and you, you're both such kids."

"How so?"

"You have this kid attitude. I don't know, like you'd have fun swinging from trees."

"Is that an Indian crack?" I teased.

She scowled and tried to kick my leg. I laughed, jumping away. She shook her head.

"Great. I have a four-year-old and I'm dating a five-year-old."

We put my toiletries in the bathroom, opposite hers. She liked the arrangement. I imagined it becoming permanent.

I promised Ethan eggs for breakfast, rolled out my sleeping bag, and Karen got him ready for bed. My gym bag was out of reach on a high shelf, my gun locked and the key in a pocket.

By ten, Ethan was asleep in his bed. I got into the sleeping bag and waited patiently. Karen was in the bedroom. A minute later, she came out, slid into my sleeping bag, and wrapped her arms around my neck. She kissed me, very slowly.

"That was a lovely dinner," she said. "I like being around Helen. Ethan and Frank get along terrific, too."

I stroked the small of her back. "You mean the two boys?" I joked.

"You make me laugh." She smiled, wrapping her arms tighter around my neck.

"Not too tight," I gasped. "I need some blood flow, after all."

It is a warm, sunny September day. I am seven years old. In the field behind my school, my friends and I are playing with a kite. The wind is light, but strong enough to lift the bright green fabric diamond into the air.

Its tail, bowties made of old bed sheets knotted at intervals along a thin rope, keep it pointed skyward. It wobbles and struggles up, catching gusts of wind and dipping, but it stays aloft. I am concentrating on the kite; my brother, three years older, pats me on the shoulder and points away, down the road toward town.

In the distance I see someone; a figure in a green uniform, limping slowly toward me.

We run away from the kite fliers, toward my father.

I wake up.

Five a.m. Karen was curled up, facing away from me in the sleeping bag. My arm was over her waist, my hand absentmindedly caressing her breasts. She rolled onto her back and opened her eyes sleepily.

"You were snoring," she whispered. "Not a lot. And you talked in your sleep." She slid partway out of the sleeping bag and sat up, outlined in the dim streetlight.

"What time is it?"

I picked up my watch. "Just after five."

She slid back down. "Do you always wake up this early?"

I nodded.

"That might take getting used to."

I wrapped my arm around her. "Get used to it. What was I saying?"

"Hmm?"

"In my sleep."

She furrowed her brow. "Pat? Pot? I couldn't tell. Something like that."

"Pops. My father. He got demobbed after Korea and walked to our school in his uniform to see James and me."

She smiled, sighed, and fell back to sleep.

Seven a.m. Karen showered, singing through the streaming water. She came out in her robe, rubbing her hair dry, and stopped dead.

"What are you wearing?" she groaned. "You look like a rodeo clown."

I sighed. I wore a lime green polyester jacket, bright blue pants, and a gaudy tangerine tie. "Remember I didn't want to do the rainbow Indian? This is the rainbow Indian."

She gave me the look you give someone who's fallen into manure. "Why?" she whined.

"Tell you later." I sighed. "I'll be well dressed when I pick you up."

She nodded, satisfied. "The girls in the office want to meet you. I'd hate them to meet you like this."

A freak snowstorm had blanketed the area north of Toronto, but we only saw a dusting in town. Karen dropped Ethan at Mrs. Waleski's, and we walked to my car. We sat in the Fury for a minute, clearing the windows. Karen leaned over and kissed me.

"What was that for?" I asked, not really caring why.

"Wearing ugly clothes for me." She kissed me again.

I parked downtown. She asked me to stop by her office later, but insisted I could stay in the car if I was still dressed like this. I went to work.

The staff did a quick double-take when they saw my clothes. The receptionist had the jazz LP I wanted to borrow. Frank was telling a joke.

"And the third guy says, 'So I was hiding in this fridge.'" They all laughed.

Frank turned to me. I held my arms out at shoulder height, displaying my wardrobe. Parker handed him a five-dollar bill.

"Betting on my attire again?" I asked.

"Let's get these guys," Frank said, grinning. "They're in room three, and they're antsy."

"How do you want to play it?" I asked. "Spade and Tonto?"

Frank nodded. "Sure. I'll do the opening act. Who are you?"

I thought for a moment. "Nathan Littlefeather, from the . . . Reserve Policing Initiative Program. And I live in—" I looked around for inspiration, settling on a shiny ashtray, "—Chromium Lake, Alberta."

"That a real place?"

"No idea. Let's do this."

Parker, Frank, and I headed to the interrogation room. As we walked, Frank filled me in. A nineteen-year-old, Scott Henry Joseph, had been caught driving a truck full of stolen car parts. He had a sixteen-year-old buddy simply called Dwayne. We didn't know who was paying them, but I was to find out. That was why I was "dressed like a rodeo clown," as Karen put it. We stood back from the interrogation room door. Frank stormed in, and we listened.

Parker nodded at my outfit. "I feel for you, man," he soothed. "You got some guts to do this."

We heard Frank yelling through the open door,

threatening them. There was little sound from the youths. It was all according to plan. Frank's voice boomed out.

"You think this is a picnic?"

"Picnic" was the first signal. Parker winked at me and marched into the room. He bellowed at Frank.

"I told you, I want Nathan to interview them! What the hell are you doing?"

Frank answered, pleading. "Captain, let me work on these guys. I can crack them."

Then Parker again. "Out! Now! I want Nathan in here! That's an order, Detective!"

Frank stomped out, smiling as he joined me. We heard Parker lecturing the two, saying that a Native officer would interview them now, and he didn't screw around.

"Screw" was the other signal. I inhaled deeply and lumbered stupidly through the open door. Parker patted my shoulder, grunted, and left. I sat across from the two youths. The older one, Scott, was slight, short, and cocky. He had a cross tattoo between his left thumb and forefinger—a Juvie souvenir. He wore a ripped denim vest, a black shirt, and striped bell-bottoms frayed at the cuffs. He had the sneer of someone who doesn't want the world to know he's scared to death.

His buddy was somewhat taller, chubby, with greasy hair falling over his ears and a slightly puzzled look. His mouth hung open, which told me he was out of his depth.

"Hey, how ya doin'?" I started, in the staccato speech of TV Indians. "My name's Nathan Littlefeather, eh? I come to work wit the Toronto cops, an they toll me to interview you guys." I extended my hand. The older one just smirked at me.

"Shit, are you for real, man?"

I stared blankly back. I had no expectation of turning him. I was betting on his friend. "Oh, yeah," I gushed. "I got this job, ya know, wit the RPIP. The . . ." I paused and thought hard. I spoke slowly. "Provincial, no, Reserve Policing Initiative Program."

The older boy whispered something to the younger

one. Both snickered. He smiled. "You are one dumb shit, you know?" I just looked at him. He leaned forward. "You are being used by these pigs, asshole. That's why you're here. They think we'll talk to a Chug, cause we won't say shit to them."

It was all I could do to not smile. "No, man, like, they let me do work for them and stuff. Like, I can use the Xerox machine, and I get to ride with them to get pizza and stuff." I nodded solemnly, borrowing Gary's mannerism.

He rolled his eyes and leaned back. "Look, we're way smarter'n you'll ever be. You should wish you was us."

I showed surprise. "Doing what?"

He opened his mouth, then shook his head. "No, man. No way."

I waved at the room. "What job's better'n this?"

He shook a finger at me. "You're smarter than you look. I ain't falling down that hole." He smiled.

I knew then I'd won. I leaned back, my expression and voice now normal.

"Thanks, that's all I need." I opened my folder and made notes in the margins. The younger one sat up.

"Why? What did he say?"

I shook my head and kept writing meaningless notes without looking at the pair. "I have enough to send you both to jail for a long time. Thank you." I turned to the younger one. "You ever been to jail, kid?" He shook his head. I turned to the older one. "Smile."

He bared a mouthful of white teeth.

I smirked. "Say goodbye to those."

His face dropped slightly. "Why?"

"First week in jail, they'll knock out your front teeth. That way you won't bite down on anything they stick in your mouth." His friend turned pale. "Also," I said, "you can say goodbye to constipation. Same day, different cellmate."

The older one sneered again. "You're bullshitting me. No, it's bullshit." He looked off at the wall. That told me he didn't want to face the danger.

I nodded. "Tell you what. We'll put you in the Don

Jail for a week. Then we'll feed you to the wolves."

That got him.

"What do you mean?" he asked, suddenly cautious.

I smiled. "You like steak? I'll make sure you get steak, gravy, dessert, all sent to your cells."

Now he was really worried. "Why?"

I leaned forward. "We will roll a food cart past all the guys living on mashed potatoes and stew. When they ask, and they will, we will tell them that you are getting special treatment because of the help you gave us. God help you, though, when you get out. Your bosses will be very interested in what you said." I scribbled more notes and waited a moment, then I closed the file folder and stood up. "Bye now," I said.

The older one swatted the air. "You're just shitting me, right?"

I smiled. "You'll find out. If I'm lying, you can say 'I told you so.'"

He glanced at the younger one. I'd found my weak spot.

I pointed to the taller boy. "Enjoy wearing denim, kid. It'll make life more pleasant." I turned to leave.

The younger one broke, as I hoped. He wanted to deal, he said, and he wanted to get away, while the older one yelled, "Shut up, stupid, they're bluffing!" He offered to name the people moving stolen goods into Quebec. From there the goods were spirited across into New York, he said, and distributed around the United States.

I offered him a "one time only" deal if the information proved good. The older one decided to join in: he opted to sweeten the deal. He had a list of who's who in exchange for no jail and a head start. We ironed out an agreement and called four uniforms to escort them back to lockup. The sight of two uniformed men for each of them cinched their decision. As the boys were shuffled off, Parker and Frank reappeared, pleased with my work.

"Good stuff, kid," Frank said.

Parker wrinkled his nose. "Chug? Why did he call you a Chug?"

"It's a derogatory term for a Native," I mumbled.

"What does it mean?"

I sighed. "When you guzzle beer, you 'chug' it. So, a Chug."

Parker nodded, embarrassed. "Sorry, man. Thanks, no offence."

I went back to my desk. Forensics had left me some photos in an envelope. One was of a disassembled Beretta pistol. Black dust revealed no fingerprints. Frank walked over.

"Hey," I said. "Nice tag team. They're guilty and scared. You still owe me, though."

He sat down. "I checked the subway schedule the night the Impala was dumped. From the snow in the car, we figure it was ditched between ten and one at night. The last subway ran at one thirty, and the buses stopped at one. I figure he walked to the train—fewer witnesses. One uniform said it took maybe ten minutes at a stroll."

I held the photo of the Beretta. "Why leave the gun? Was it on purpose, or a mistake? I mean, he wiped it. He even cleaned the bullets. I can't believe he'd leave it behind by mistake."

Frank stared at the floor. I watched his mind working, the same look he'd had when he retraced the boys' actions back at Gary's. He looked up. "What was the weather last Sunday?"

I checked my notes. "Light flurries, cold. Some wind."

He nodded. "You are sitting in a car, waiting for the kids. You don't run the engine, because that would draw attention. But that means you get cold waiting."

I continued the train of thought. "You planned to shoot the kid. You wear gloves because it's cold, but they make it hard to hold a gun, so you change the plan. It works even better than you hoped. It looks like an accident. You stash the car, wait a week, then ditch it. You realize you forgot the gun, but by then the car's in impound."

Frank nodded. "Can we make him pop up—say something to the press?"

"Like what? 'Hey, did you leave a gun in a stolen

car? Come get it.'" I shrugged.

"Right, forget it." Frank shook his head.

I flipped through my file folder. Something Helen said came back. "Frank, the dead boy in Italy; the witness was driving an Alfa. Remember what Helen said? Maybe he stole the Alfa, like he stole the Impala. There would be a stolen car file. And not far from where the accident happened."

"Why?"

I repeated Helen's comment. "The same as the other boy, only backwards."

He smacked his forehead. "You don't want to drive far in a hot car. You steal it, leave it at the accident scene, kill the Palumbo kid then call the cops. They concentrate on the dead kid, and you hang around being a Good Samaritan until you're sure he's dead. Then head to wherever."

"Spain," I said.

"So he says. Maybe Paris, or Toronto, or Timbuktu. Who knows?"

I looked through the Italian police report again. "There is nothing about a stolen Alfa. Why is there nothing about a stolen Alfa?"

Frank's eyes widened. "They didn't tie the events together. Why would they? To them, it was just an accident. Hell, *we* don't know for sure it wasn't an accident."

I grabbed a steno pad. "We need to know if any local Alfas were reported stolen."

We filled out the telex request and went down the street for lunch.

I'd changed my ugly tie for a gray one I kept in my desk. That helped some, but only some. The waitress at our local diner, a middle-aged woman with Catwoman glasses and a beehive hairdo, eyed me like I was a spilled milkshake.

"Selling used cars now, Detective?"

Frank howled with laughter. I made him buy lunch. On the walk back to the station, Frank stared at his shoes, thinking.

"Penny for your thoughts?" I offered.

He shrugged. "Could we be all wrong? Maybe the kid just drove off the road. Maybe Palumbo is just unlucky. But the two events are a huge coincidence. I don't believe in coincidences."

"What if I hadn't happened by when Karen hurt her head? That was coincidence."

He grunted. "No, that was fate. By the way, did I mention she has a really great butt?"

"Thanks, I'll pass that on."

"But why *didn't* they connect the dead kid to a stolen Alfa?"

I shrugged. "Unless," I said, "it was never reported stolen."

Frank smacked his forehead. "Because the owner was dead."

CHAPTER SEVEN

We sent another telex to the Italian police. It would be a day or two before they could give us the information we wanted. Thursday, then, things would come together. Before then there was little we could do.

Captain Van Hoeke called us into his office. "Any developments?"

Frank shook his head. "We haven't said anything to anyone. Ian here says that Wolfgang, our old friend from Toronto Island, was asking where we are. Also, Palumbo asked me and Ian, separately, to have dinner with him."

Van Hoeke leaned back, resting his head on his wrists. "Really?"

I nodded. "He also knew I was seeing someone. I have no idea how."

Van Hoeke grinned. "She cute?"

"Piss off, sir." I smiled.

He smirked. "Will you be going? I think it's a good idea."

"I agree, but I wanted you to know about it first."

Van Hoeke smiled. "I appreciate that, Ian. You're working toward your Sergeant's badge. Keep this up and you'll definitely get it this year."

I blushed. The status, higher pay grade, and title were what I wanted. I could almost taste it.

We had two stops to make before I picked Karen up. First was Northwestern Hospital. We went up to visit Victor, the first injured boy. From several doors away, we could hear talking; adults, cheery and solicitous, and the soft weeping of a child. Frank barged forward. I hung back. He strode into the room, announcing himself to everyone. The adult voices stopped. Then the weeping stopped. I heard Frank's voice boom through the ward.

"Hey, Victor, buddy, how's it going?"

I came around the corner; Frank was squatting on the near side of the bed, eye to eye with the young patient. His parents, I guessed, hovered around the bed, looking artificially cheery. They backed up as Frank talked, happy to have a distraction.

The boy raised a bandaged hand, his lower lip trembling. "They cut off three fingers," he whimpered. "I can't write or nothing."

Frank leaned over and picked up the medical clipboard. He read it, wrinkling his forehead. "I don't understand," he mumbled. "Says here you were supposed to lose five fingers." He flipped some pages. "And a nose."

The boy stared, incredulous, then laughed out loud. His mother seemed ready to faint. He got sad again.

"I wanted to be a policeman. Now I can't."

Frank leaned in again. "You told me your favorite TV shows. *Rocketship 7, Columbo, Adam-12*? How about *Longstreet*? Ever watch that? Or *Ironside*?"

The boy shook his head.

"Well, one is about a blind detective, the other is a guy in a wheelchair who solves crime. You're way ahead of them. Three fingers gone is no problem for a detective. We have police dogs with two wooden legs. Then again, we do spray them for termites."

The boy giggled. His mother managed a weak smile.

Frank stood up. "Victor, when you went off with Nick, did you see anyone sitting in a car?"

The boy frowned, thinking. "There was a guy in a car. He stared at us."

"Can you describe him?"

Victor shook his head. "I don't remember."

"How about his car?"

Victor looked down, thinking. "It was big. It was gray or brown, I think. It made a noise."

Frank smiled at me, then looked back at Victor. "What noise?"

Victor bared his teeth and hissed.

"How long did you hear the noise?"

Victor thought for a moment. "I dunno . . . When we were walking to the house with the dog?"

Frank smiled. "That's good, good. We'll keep you posted."

We shook the parents' hands. Frank reminded them his business card was behind the badge he'd given Victor. The boy's mother checked that the card was still there and thanked us. We left.

Our next stop was Gary's house. Dixie bounced happily up and down, hoping to see Ethan, I imagined. Gary talked with us for just a while. He was busy with repairs, he said.

We said that the patrols would be less frequent now. We still wanted him to tell us if he saw the mystery man from the railroad track.

I thought about Victor's comment in the hospital, that the car made a hissing noise.

"Follow me, Frank," I said. I walked to the spot where Gary had seen the Impala, and found what I hoped to find. On the ground was a partly dried pool of antifreeze. It had seeped into the asphalt, oozed into the cracks, but had left a small puddle near the curb.

I squatted down. Frank stooped beside me and poked it with his pen.

"He had a leaky radiator," he said. "That was the noise Victor heard. Very good, almost-Sergeant."

I drove Frank home and changed into my "court outfit," a stylish three-piece gray suit that made me look like a lawyer. I combed my hair, brushed my mustache, and gargled. I made sure to wear my shoulder holster a little loose, to impress the civilians. I even wore my dress watch with the black leather strap and the gold face.

I waited outside Karen's building for a few minutes. I didn't mind being the object of her show-and-tell, but not for too long. At four forty, I walked into the lobby. The same gloomy-faced old security guard was at his desk, reading a newspaper. This time he sat up and smiled; nicotine tinged crooked teeth greeted me.

"Good afternoon, Officer," he creaked. "You're here to see Miss Prescott? She's expecting you, sir. Twelfth floor, mortgages."

I took the elevator to the twelfth floor. I hate elevators. They're too confining. I stepped out on the twelfth floor into a dim, narrow hall with dark walls. Mild panic gripped me. I hate enclosed spaces and dark spaces. This had both. I felt claustrophobic—one of my private shortcomings. I started panting.

At the end of the hall were three black doors, labeled with brass plaques. The rightmost one said *Mortgages and Loans*. I moved quickly toward it, took a deep breath, and opened the door.

Inside was a bright waiting area, with three swivel chairs around a Formica coffee table. I immediately relaxed. Scattered on the table were financial magazines, showing happy gray-haired couples sailing and riding bicycles. A high counter blocked a doorway to the back office.

A chair behind the counter swung slowly back and forth, its owner having just left. The sound of heels got close; a handsome, well-dressed woman walked through the doorway and stood behind the counter. She did not notice me at first, then she looked up and smiled broadly.

"Can I help you?" her voice was sharp honey— smooth, firm, and practiced all at once.

I smiled. "Hi. I'm here to see Karen Prescott."

She laid her forearms on the counter, like a cat watching a sparrow across the lawn. "You're Ian." More honey poured out.

"Yes." I smiled again.

She patted the countertop. "Wait here." She disappeared through the doorway.

I waited about thirty seconds. A cavalcade of heels tumbled into earshot. Seven or eight women, of various shapes and sizes, filled the area behind the counter. I imagined this was how prize bulls must feel at a fair. I walked up and introduced myself.

I decided to play up the occasion. I leaned on the counter with my left palm, letting my shoulder holster hang loose and visible. They all stared.

One spoke. A middle-aged woman, plump and wide, who had a housewifely look about her. She stuck a pudgy arm out. "Hi, I'm Millicent—Millie." She giggled.

I shook her hand then held onto it with both of mine. "Karen never told me about you. Now I see why."

Millie sucked in a lungful of air and turned bright red. I smiled, and she giggled again. The rest clustered closer, introducing themselves. I smiled politely, repeated their names and answered the usual questions. It seemed to last an eternity.

Karen came out from behind them and pushed to the front of the group.

"Hey, you. I'll get my coat and be right out." She looked around, amused. "I see you met the girls." She disappeared into the back area again.

One of the women looked at me dismissively. She spoke up loudly. "So you're a cop."

I smiled politely. "A detective, actually."

"I hear you're also an Indian."

I kept the polite smile. "Only part, mostly Scottish-French."

She raised an eyebrow. "Oh, only part?" she repeated, mocking.

I leaned close. "Only part. I haven't scalped anyone in months."

She jumped back, frowned, and stormed off. The others laughed.

Karen appeared on my side of the counter and pulled me toward the door. I turned back and waved.

"Ladies, it's been a pleasure." I pointed to the plump woman. "Millie, I'll call you?"

Millie giggled once more. Karen elbowed my ribs. We got an empty elevator. She pulled my lapels down and kissed me hard.

"Hello to you, too," I said. "How was your day?"

"Long. The girls thought I was making you up."

I looked down. "Really? Couldn't you have invented

someone better than me?"

She smiled. "Not possible."

On the drive home, we discussed the rest of the week. Ethan would sleep over two nights at Mrs. Waleski's, if he wanted. Her son Tommy wanted a friend for a sleepover.

Karen looked out at Bloor Street, the stores now brighter than the fading sunlight.

"I asked about apartments in my building," she said in a whisper.

"And?" I asked.

"There's a two-bedroom, but it's one eighty five a month." She sounded apologetic.

"What's the problem?" I asked.

"I couldn't afford that on my own."

"You wouldn't have to," I said. "I'd pay what I pay now, you just pay the difference."

She looked at her purse, composing her thoughts. "What if we don't work out? I'd be in a place I can't afford. I have to consider Ethan."

I parked abruptly, swiveled in my seat, and glowered at her. She leaned back, fearful.

"Look," I said firmly. "First, I have no intentions of turning nasty or running off. That was him, not me. Second, I would not do anything that would hurt you or Ethan. If I did, Frank would shoot me. Third, I don't do asshole stuff to people I love." I was almost yelling by now.

She was smiling.

"What?" I barked.

She looked out the windshield. "I want a bigger bed." I started driving again.

"And a bigger sofa," I added gruffly.

She hugged my arm. "Dumbass," she said sweetly.

Tuesday morning, it felt like spring might actually arrive sometime soon. An aquatic symphony of melting snow fell on the roof outside my kitchen, like Gene Krupa playing drums in the distance.

I tiptoed past Ethan in the sleeping bag, and brought a mug of coffee into the bedroom. Karen sat up, ran her fingers through her hair and gratefully took it from me. I offered to make breakfast, but she suggested I shower and let her sleep some more.

I was dressed in twenty minutes. She was asleep, the unfinished coffee on the nightstand beside her. I kissed her and she sat up, stretching.

For the first time in days, clear blue sunlight streamed through my kitchen window. I made oatmeal. Karen padded into the kitchen and wrapped her arms around me.

"Hey, you," she said. I caressed her fingers, interlocked around my waist.

"Hungry?" I asked.

"Starved." She nuzzled my neck.

In the living room window I saw our reflection. Karen was on her toes, in a t-shirt and briefs, her midriff bare. I reached back and rubbed her back under her shirt, then slid my hand down and patted her bum. She bit my ear playfully.

"When do you want to do our Mafia dinner?" she asked.

I turned around and patted her bum again. "How about when Ethan is at Mrs. Waleski's? That way, we can make an evening of it."

She squeezed my waist tighter. "I have a half-day off this Thursday. Would that work?"

"Sure." I kissed her.

"How will we do this when we're old and gray?" she asked.

"Take our teeth out first."

By eight thirty, we were out front of her office. Karen looked down, thoughtful.

"What's wrong?" I asked.

She looked up into my eyes. "Do you love me?"

I was puzzled by the question. "What?"

She shook her head. "I'm serious. You care about me, and I need to know why."

I was confused. "Is there something you're not telling me?"

She glared at me. "Answer the question, damn you. It's a simple, straightforward question. Why, out of all the women on this whole damned planet, did you pick me?"

I was totally confused now. "Are you angry at me for caring about you?"

She rolled her eyes and groaned. "Jesus, no. You just don't get it, do you?" She sighed. "Look, I've got to go. See you later." She walked off. No kiss, no looking back.

I got to Frank's house by nine. Most of the snow was gone, and a soft rain had started. It was warmer than it had been in months, a sign that spring was on its way. The grass poked through the few patches of snow, as if it knew it that winter had ended.

Helen had made muffins. Frank and I had some as we discussed the day's plans. We decided to visit Palumbo's daughter, and planned our strategy. Frank stared at me.

"Something on my nose?" I asked.

"Trouble in nookie land, huh?" he asked.

"Adult stuff. You wouldn't understand."

He smirked and sipped coffee. "Women," he mumbled. "You can't live with 'em, you can't take them to the pound."

Helen called through from the living room. "I *heard* that!"

Frank yelled back. "Not you, sugar plum."

I shrugged. "She wanted to know why I picked her, out of all the girls in the world—her words. When I asked if she was angry at me, she got angry."

Frank leaned back. "Helen! Help here, please!"

Helen came through and I repeated what I'd told Frank. She smirked. "Three years ago, you kids were paired up by Captain Van Hoeke," she said. "Do you remember what you each said?"

I nodded. "He said, 'Why would I spend my time with an outcast from a reserve?'"

Frank smiled. "You said 'Why should I babysit a draft-dodger?'"

Helen nodded. "Frank told me. He said you were about ready to beat each other up. It took a week so you could stand being in the same room."

I smirked. "And here we are, married."

"If that makes you two happy. Karen wants to know she's important in your life, that's all. Just like you two needed to respect each other."

Frank stood and got his coat. "Ready for work, darling?"

I stood, too. "Right with you, sweetheart."

Finch Avenue East. A sterile, bleak suburban hell. Pale gray high-rise buildings climbed away from the street. Strip malls and industrial buildings crowded the bare sidewalks. The weak attempts at landscaping did nothing for the area.

At the entrance to one nondescript mall was a large sign with the exuberant name *Shoppers' Mecca*. The buildings were in a U-shape, wrapping around a parking lot. Inside the U was a patch of brown grass, a rusty child's slide and a dusty park bench. The businesses in the mall sold auto parts, plumbing supplies, and cheap housewares.

One building, painted a dark-putty color, had a glossy green sign that read *Zimmerman of Toronto—Fine European Furniture at Everyday Prices*. Through the window I saw Swedish modern tables, gaudy rococo armchairs, and black leatherette La-Z-Boys.

Frank shook his head. "Looks like Liberace had a garage sale," he mumbled.

We entered, assaulted by loud classical music and the aroma of burning candles. It was dim inside, giving the drab space the feel of a dungeon. I steeled myself against panic from being in the darkness.

A gaunt woman in a black dress and streaked gray hair wafted toward us. "Hello," she enthused, smiling broadly. "Welcome to Zimmerman of Toronto Fine Furnishings. How can I be of assistance?"

Frank pointed up. "Turn down the Mozart?"

The smile faded. "I'm sorry?"

"We're here to speak with Maureen Zimmerman." Frank held out his warrant card.

"I see. Please wait here." She glided to an office door at the back of the building.

"Vivaldi," I said.

"Hmm?"

"Vivaldi's *Four Seasons*."

He shrugged. "What's the difference?"

I stared at him. "Vivaldi was Italian, Mozart was Austrian."

He grunted. "Sort of like Palumbo's daughter and her husband."

"Sort of."

A light glowed briefly as a door opened, and a figure walked toward us. A young, tall version of Palumbo's mother walked up.

"Hello, I'm Maureen Zimmerman," she said. Her voice was strong and confident.

We made the usual round of introductions and expressed our best wishes for Nick. Frank handed her a business card. She nodded.

"My father said you'd be by this week." Her voice trembled slightly. "He's visited Nicky in hospital every day. The doctors say he may never get out of the coma, but they aren't sure."

Frank glanced at me. I would be the likeable one and he would be the gruff one. He lifted his notebook up almost to his chin. "Has anyone suspicious been around, someone out of the ordinary?"

She shook her head.

"Had anyone in your family had threats of any kind?"

She rolled her eyes. "You've met my father. Figure it out."

Frank wrote eagerly.

I smiled. "Where do you find these pieces? I've never seen pieces like them," I lied.

She nodded. "My husband travels to the U.S. and Europe. We buy from manufacturers in the U.S., Germany, and Sweden."

I turned to Frank. "I thought these pieces were Danish, but they're Swedish. Who knew?" Then back to

Maureen. "Your husband is German, isn't he? It must help for him to speak the language."

She tucked the clipboard under her arm. That told me she was lowering her guard. "Actually," she said, "he's Swiss."

Frank kept scribbling. "Anything else you can tell us? Anything at all?"

She shook her head. "Nick is a great kid." Her voice broke. "Why would anybody want to hurt . . ." She slumped on a sofa.

I squatted beside her. "I'm sorry. Is there something I can get you?"

She shook her head. "Dad has so much on his plate, he doesn't need me bringing him down. He has so much love for Nicky, and this kills him so much."

"A burden shared is a burden lightened. I think it would help to talk about how you feel."

Frank stood behind her, rolling his eyes at my performance.

"Would you like to talk some more?" I asked. "Your father invited me to dinner."

She looked up at me. "Really?"

I nodded. "Sure, I would be honored."

She shrugged. "Any night is good." She dried her eyes.

I smiled. "Thursday, then? He asked me and my girlfriend."

She nodded. "That would be very nice. Thank you."

The rest of the day we concentrated on the gun and the Impala. The Beretta pistol had originally been sold in the United States. Beyond that it got hazy.

The Impala was registered to a W. Abernathy. The report said he hadn't noticed it missing because he rarely drove. We had lunch, then I called Palumbo.

The man with the voice like thunder picked up the phone. "Yes?" he said simply.

"Hello, this is Ian McBriar. Mr. Palumbo asked me to join him for dinner."

"Yes, Detective?" He didn't sound like he expected me to say no.

"How does Thursday work?"

"Six thirty," he answered immediately.

"Six thirty," I repeated.

"Thank you. Will we see you both?"

I paused. "Yes. I will be bringing my girlfriend. Thank you."

"See you then. Goodbye." He hung up.

Frank looked up from a report he was reading. "Free food?"

I shrugged. "I want to find out from whom he's been getting information."

Frank snickered. "Whom."

I sneered. "High school dropout."

We processed the two Mohawk kids. The older one got his wish; we gave him bus fare, a hundred dollars, and a two-day head start before we arrested his employer. The younger one walked out and I never saw or heard from him again.

Still no telex from Italy. We called it a day, and I drove Frank home. I stopped out front of his house. He looked out the window, preoccupied.

"Penny for your thoughts?" I prompted.

"Tell Karen that you love her," he said.

"OK . . ." I started. "Because?"

"It's true, isn't it?"

"Yeah, so?"

"She needs to know she's important to you. That's what it was about this morning."

"Thank you, Dear Abby. What other advice do you have?"

He frowned. He poked his finger at me. "What do you know about my past? My grandparents survived the Armenian death march in 1915. They carried my father out of Turkey in their arms when he was four years old. Every day, every single day, they were grateful just to be free. My grandfather worked in a Pennsylvania steel mill till he died. He was the proudest damned American I knew.

"My father worked on the Union Pacific Railroad. He still remembers walking through the desert in 1915, pushed on by soldiers. In the war he was a tank driver in North Africa—it was 1915 all over again. He fought with an anger that scared the shit out of his men." Frank faced me. "He felt he had nothing to lose. Don't lose what you have. Tell her you love her."

I nodded. "Are we talking about Karen, or Helen?"

He smiled. "None of your damned business."

Five o'clock. The sky was still blue near the western horizon, and puffy white clouds dotted the sky. I watched people stream out of Karen's office. Finally, she walked out, straightened her coat, and shuffled toward me.

I had my hands behind my back. As I brought my left hand around I handed her the bouquet, wrapped in brightly colored paper. She held it like it might explode.

"What's this for?" she asked, puzzled.

"You were angry this morning. I'm sorry if I upset you."

She looked down at the flowers. "That's the sweetest thing." She tiptoed up and kissed me.

"C'mon," I said. "Let's get Ethan."

"Actually," she said, softly, "I asked Mrs. Waleski if he could stay over tonight."

I smiled. "I hope he has fun."

At five thirty a.m., I woke up. Karen's arms were around me, one leg over me. I caressed her from her neck down to the back of her knee. She didn't stir.

I moved to the back of the other knee and caressed back up to her neck. She moved her hand onto my face.

"That tickles," she whispered.

I stared down at her breasts. She sat up and propped a pillow in front of her.

"Doesn't help," I said. "You're still making me horny."

She laughed. I pulled the pillow slowly away, but she snatched it back, playfully.

"How about breakfast in bed?" I offered.

We sat propped up on pillows, with a tray of coffee

and buttered rolls between us. I decided to bring up a subject I'd been avoiding.

"When I drove you to work yesterday," I began, "you asked why, of all the women in the world, I picked you."

She nodded *uh hum* through a mouthful of coffee and jam. She put her coffee down, fixing me with her large brown eyes. "And the answer is?" she asked quietly.

I thought of Frank's advice to "hold on to what I have."

"I have no idea," I answered truthfully. "I can't make up something glib and smarmy. I just know that the room lights up when you come in. The sun shines when you smile. My heart skips when I see you walking toward me. That's all. Period."

She jumped over the tray and smothered me with kisses.

I tilted my head back. "Right answer, I guess?"

CHAPTER EIGHT

I walked into the detective room. Frank was telling his morning joke.

"He says, 'Nice body. Where do you want the blinds, sister?'" They all laughed. Frank smiled like a kid with a new toy. He crooked his finger and waved me over. He waved a scrap of teletype paper. "Guess what?" he grinned.

"Love letter from Sophia Loren?" I asked.

"No, better. OK, no, not better at all, but good, still good." He thrust it at me. "There were three suspicious deaths in the area at the same time as the Palumbo kid died. Two women, one guy."

"Really? That narrows it down."

He nodded. "It gets better. Of the three, two were solved—the two women. One was a suicide. Sick old lady, dying of cancer, sleeping pills. The other was a bad robbery. They caught the thief trying to sell some of the victim's jewelry. That leaves the guy." He smiled like the Cheshire cat.

"And?"

"He drove an Alfa Romeo—a red sedan."

"OK. How did he die?"

Frank grinned. "Nine mil to the chest. Want to guess about the bullet? Six grooves, right-hand twist, consistent with . . ." He held his palm out.

"A Beretta M951?" I asked.

"Bingo."

"We need that bullet, Frank."

He held up a different teletype page. "On its way. Should be here Friday."

I tried to concentrate, but Karen was on my mind. Frank sat across from me, like Joe Friday and Bill Gannon on *Dragnet*. He stared at me for a long time.

"What?" I asked.

"You get laid in the shower this morning?"

I blushed a deep red.

He smacked the desk. "You did, you lucky bastard! Hah!"

By that afternoon, we'd decided how I should proceed at Palumbo's dinner. I'd be forthcoming about a link between the two boys' deaths, but only if asked directly. Palumbo wasn't stupid, and he'd find out anyway, even if I didn't tell him. This way, at least, I could be seen as working with him.

We dropped by the impound yard for a quick look at the Impala. The forensics boys were very good, but I wanted to see the car for myself. Frank sat in the driver's seat, frowning.

"John, come over for a sec, will you?"

A small, middle-aged man with wispy gray hair and glasses came over. Frank pointed at the dashboard.

"Has anyone moved the seat forward or back?"

The man shrugged. "We took it out, but we marked it and put it back in the same place."

Frank nodded. "Thanks, man." He got out of the car and pointed at me. "Sit in here, will you?"

I got in. It was a tight fit.

"I'm about five eight, you're six two. The seat is set for someone taller than me but shorter than you."

"Average height. Does that help us?"

He opened his notebook. "He waited in the cold car. He had the engine off, but the rad was hissing. So, he couldn't have been waiting long. He ran after them. He *ran*." He frowned, thinking. "How old was he? A guy over forty wouldn't run. A guy under twenty wouldn't wait. And he had to know the car was not used often, so he could hang on to it without it being reported stolen right away." He shrugged. "Let's talk to the owner."

*

Downtown Toronto was a hodgepodge of architecture. The ultramodern New City Hall twin towers were reflected in the glass office towers across Queen Street. Just east, on Bay Street, the neo-Gothic Old City Hall, now a police building and courts, looked like a castle from a Dracula movie.

A few blocks west, surrounded by decaying old houses, was Trinity Bellwoods Park. In the winter, the city flooded a skating rink. In summer, families would picnic and fly kites.

Bellwoods Avenue was intersected by a short street called Bellwoods Place. The Impala's owner lived down Bellwoods Place. On one side of the street was a string of two-car garages with battered wooden doors. On the other side, low brick buildings were once factories, but long ago they had been chopped up into cheap apartments.

We headed down a set of wooden stairs along a damp brick wall, to a dark basement unit. The Impala owner was expecting us. Frank knocked on a thick wooden door. A moment later, the muffled clatter of moving furniture told us he was home.

I heard a voice, defiant but weak, call, "Hello?"

Frank announced us. A chain slid noisily, then the door opened. Frank stood still and held his warrant card out. A face peered out, Henry Fonda at eighty. He was taller than me, gaunt, with pale gray eyes.

"You're the police?" he asked, his parchment voice thin from age. He invited us in. I sat in a crackled leather armchair. Frank sat on a wooden chair, as did our host.

"As you know," Frank began, "we found your car. We are holding it at our impound yard, since it may have been used in a crime." He was talking slowly, deliberately.

The old man sighed. "Y'know, I'm just old, not stupid. You can talk faster."

Frank smirked. "Sorry, sir. Where was the car parked when it went missing?"

The man leaned back. "Call me Walter. It was across the street, where it always is. At least, till it gets stolen."

"Thanks, Walter. When was the last time you saw the car?"

"About three weeks ago."

"Where did you drive it, three weeks ago?"

"I got some gas, and I drove to Scarborough. My buddy brews beer. I brung some home."

"You know the radiator leaks? When did this start? I mean, how long has it been leaking?"

"Few months," Walter said. "Top it up when I drive, it's fine." He looked around. "Would y'all like coffee and biscuits? Got some here somewhere."

We thanked him and said no. He had an accent I couldn't place.

"Excuse me, sir—Walter," I said. "Where are you from originally?"

He smiled. "Born and raised in Raleigh, North Carolina. Moved north for a woman. Ain't that always the way, though?"

"What do you do for a living, if I may ask?"

"Used to be a welder. Now, I just pick up the odd dollar paintin' houses for folk."

"Do you live alone, Walter?" Frank asked.

"Yup, ever since the old lady passed."

"Ever considered going to a home? Be around other people your age?"

He shook his head. "God's waitin' room? No, thanks. When I leave, I'm goin' alone."

Frank stood up. "Mind if we see your garage?"

Walter stood, slowly. "Sure. Let's go."

We followed him across the street to one of the wooden garage doors. Walter fumbled through keys on a ring then opened the padlock.

It was empty, except for a small stack of paint cans, brushes soaking in turpentine, and neatly folded canvas drop cloths. Frank squatted down and touched a small puddle near the front of the garage. Walter looked amused, like a child caught sneaking out of class.

"What kind of antifreeze is this?" Frank asked.

Walter fidgeted. "Antifreeze costs a lot. I just use the windshield stuff. Works OK."

Frank smiled. "Thanks, Walter. That should actually help us track the thief down." He tapped the puddle. "Windshield washer fluid. It doesn't mix well with the GM stuff. This mixture will be unique, almost like a fingerprint if we find more puddles."

I looked around the shed. It was stark, with no other belongings except for the paint supplies. Yet, the Impala was a relatively fancy car, too fancy to just haul paint.

"Walter," I asked, "why did you buy an Impala?"

"The old lady wanted it. Said it was a plush car to be in. Dunno why, she didn't drive."

Frank opened his Moleskine. "So, it was really her car, not yours?"

Walter nodded. "Yup. Her baby. It were OK, but ain't nothin' special to me."

Frank closed his book. "Thanks. Can we call you if we have any other questions?"

"Sure, glad to help." He smiled. "Hope you wash it this time, too."

I looked at him blankly. "Sorry?"

He looked puzzled. "Last time they stole it, 'bout a year ago. When I got it back from you folk, it were all washed and vacuumed inside."

Frank's face dropped. "When was this?"

"'Bout this time. March, April, I think."

"Where did they find it?"

"Islington Station. By the subway."

We stood, stunned. Frank handed him a business card. "Walter, if you remember anything else, call us."

Walter put it in a shirt pocket.

I stretched out my hand. "Thanks, Mr. Abernathy."

Walter smiled. "That were the old lady. She never got divorced from her first, so she kept Abernathy."

"Sorry, Walter. What is your name?"

He grinned, crooked brown teeth in a red mouth. "Carpenter. Walter Carpenter."

Frank fumed all the way back to the office. "How the *hell* did we miss that?" he growled. "So *stupid*. It was *right there!*" He pounded the dash, beating on the padded vinyl with all his might.

"Frank," I soothed, "how could we know? The car is registered to W. Abernathy. The phone is in the name of W. Abernathy. We thought that was Walter, not Wilma. It's a reasonable assumption."

He rubbed his face and pulled out his notebook. "OK, let's figure this out." He let out a sigh. "So, I want a car. I grabbed it a year ago. I get the owner's name, Walter Carpenter, and call myself that in Italy when I bump off the Palumbo kid." He stared out the window. "After that, why do I steal the same car a year later when I sock the second kid?"

"I don't suppose the old guy went to Italy and did it?" I mumbled half-heartedly.

Frank shook his head. "And tells the police he's an art student? No."

"Why use that name?" I asked. "You steal a car in Toronto, then you steal one in Italy. Maybe we're blowing smoke on this one. But then, why travel using the name of the guy you stole the car from?"

Frank frowned at the retracting spongy dents in the dashboard. "Your car is registered to the Toronto Police. His car was registered to his wife."

"So?" I asked.

Frank flipped through some papers in a folder. "Shit. Co-owner is R. W. Carpenter—Wally. We didn't look far enough down the page."

I smiled, understanding the reason the car was chosen. "I get stopped for speeding and they run the plate. My ID says Wally Carpenter. The ownership says R.W. Carpenter. The old guy rarely drives. I can drive for weeks before it's reported stolen."

Frank grimaced. "Better yet, even if it is reported, you have ID saying you're him, and say it's a mistake."

I shook my head. "Brilliant. So, who is our fake Wally Carpenter? I mean, he spoke to the Italian police, didn't they say 'Show us some ID?'"

Frank nodded. "Even if they didn't ask for ID, he'd carry some in that name, just in case."

I had a thought. "Our driver's licenses don't have

pictures. I could fake one up with any name I want and have foreign police think it's real, if they don't see many Ontario driver's licenses."

Frank sighed. "The witness told the Italian police he was an art student from Hartford. Connecticut has pictures on their driver's licenses. He could get one made up with a photo on it, and it might look real to the Italian police. I wouldn't recognize a fake Italian driver's license."

I nodded. "He would also want a passport in that name, wouldn't he?"

Frank leaned forward. "Go on."

"He has a passport for Walter Carpenter. Where did he get it? Not a forgery—too hard to make. It was real, or at least, belonged to a Walter Carpenter. Do you steal one?" I threw the last thought out.

Frank shook his head. "If that was reported, you'd be really screwed."

"Kill the owner and steal it?"

"Maybe, but how many people do you kill? Besides, it has to have *your* photo on it." Frank tapped his pen, thinking. He smiled. "Tombstoning."

"Got me. What's that?"

"You're what, twenty-seven, twenty-eight? You check the death records for an infant who died around the time you were born. They never paid taxes or bought a house, but they existed. You go to vital statistics and say, 'I need my birth certificate for a passport. My name is Walter Carpenter.'"

"Don't they cross reference deaths with births?"

Frank smiled. "No, they don't. We had a seminar two years ago. That was a hole in the system. They still haven't plugged it."

"Where would he get the birth certificate?" I asked.

"He told the Italian police he was from Hartford, maybe he got a name from there."

I nodded. "So, he's young. Must be to pull off the 'I'm an art student' bit. We can have Connecticut check vital statistics for dead infants named Carpenter in the last twenty or thirty years."

Frank grinned. "Still pushing to become a sergeant,

huh?"

We sent the vital records request to the Connecticut State Police. Frank stayed at work to run down some leads. I headed downtown to pick up Karen.

I sat in the car, thinking. I was involved with a young single mother. I was prepared to move in with her. Helen thought we were meant for each other. Frank adored Ethan. Helen loved Karen. I was looking for a fly in this ointment, and there was none. I got out and leaned against the car, still thinking.

A blue pantsuit headed in my direction. Karen. She saw me and walked faster. I ran up the stairs and threw my arm around her waist. She smiled.

"Hey, you." She clung to my arm as we walked back to the car.

I smiled. "Not bored with me yet?"

She shook her head. "The girls are asking how serious we are. They've noticed a big change in my attitude. They want me to keep it up."

I opened the passenger door and patted her bottom as she slid in. I got in my side. She stared at me.

"What was that for?" she asked, puzzled.

"What?"

"The pat on the bum. How come?"

"I like touching you. You're very . . . touchable."

She studied me for a moment, smiling. "Touchable. I like that."

We ate at my place. Ethan sat glued to the TV, watching something inane. I was on the sofa, my head in Karen's lap.

"Tomorrow night's the dinner," I reminded her.

"Right. What should I wear?"

"Something subdued. He's worried, after all."

She thought for a moment. "Right. Something in black or dark blue?"

"Yeah. This is more business than social, but I'd still like to show you off."

She stroked my hair and smiled. "Smooth talker, you."

*

In the morning, I stared out the window, sipping coffee. I heard a soft patter of feet behind me. Karen was in her flannel robe, bundled up against the cold.

I whispered, "Good morning," and glanced over at the pup tent. Ethan was asleep, on his back, mouth open.

Karen kissed me softly. "Hey, you," she said. I handed her the coffee. "Hmm. Good." She took the cup and headed back to the bedroom.

I looked out the window again, deciding something irrevocable.

She was sitting on the edge of her bed, getting clothes out for the morning. "Remember, I have a half day today," she said.

"I've made a decision," I said firmly.

"Oh?" she asked, rummaging through her drawer.

"We're not going to take that two-bedroom apartment." I frowned. I thought she might cry or complain, but she just smiled.

"Go on."

I grabbed her coffee. She looked as though I'd taken away a favorite toy. I cleared my throat. "There's this rental house, near Frank's place. It's a nice house. I thought it would be better for Ethan to have a yard, you know, and, like, it would be close to Frank's, and you could still take him to Mrs. Waleski's, and you could visit Helen whenever you want, and it's near a schoolyard. And it's nice."

Karen smiled, wider and wider.

I sipped her coffee and put the cup down. "I mean, it needs some work, and we'd have to buy a lawn mower and a new stove and fridge, but it's really pretty, and the street's quiet, and it has a garage . . ." I sighed. "I'm rambling here, aren't I? Do you want me to shut up yet?"

She crept forward and wrapped her arms around my neck. She kissed me, very softly. "Shut up, you."

We dropped Ethan at Mrs. Waleski's, reminding her we had a dinner and he would be sleeping over. Tommy had new Hot Wheels, so they could play till bedtime. Karen threw on a heavy coat, and we walked to the car.

She hugged my arm tight. "Why'd you think of renting a house, you nut?"

I pulled her closer. "You need security. Ethan needs to grow up with a real home."

She looked up at me, serious. "What do you need?"

I had never been asked that before. "Pardon?"

She stopped, faced me and said it again, with emphasis. "What do *you* need?"

I looked off, thinking. Nothing came to mind. Yes, it did. "I need you." I sniffed, the cold air stuffing my nose.

She wrapped her arms wide around me, pinching my arms to my side, and squeezed hard. We went on, holding hands. I was floating, elated. She was almost skipping.

She smirked. "That's what I get for wearing a short skirt, huh?"

I snickered. "You bet. Wait till you don't wear a bra."

We got to her office in good time. She kissed me and waved a finger.

"I'm off at twelve thirty. See you then."

I hummed softly as I walked into the detectives' room. Frank was sorting through some papers. He sneered. "Another exciting shower?" he asked loudly.

I smiled. "Even better. She has a twin sister." I winked.

Frank's face froze. It took him a minute to recover. "You bastard! Had me going, there." He scowled. "No, really, does she have a sister?"

I shook my head. "A gentleman doesn't tell, Frank." I sat down.

He walked over, pretending to be miffed. "My turn for interesting news." He put a sheet of paper on my desk. "A kid named Walter James Carpenter, two years old, born in Waterbury, Connecticut, in December of forty-six, died of pneumonia."

I picked the paper up. "He got a driver's license afterwards. Pretty remarkable."

Frank nodded. "We're waiting for the license photo. Should be here any time."

I smiled. Frank sat on the corner of my desk.

"You can tell me," he said.

"What?"

He nodded suggestively. "You know. Does she like to be soaped up, or scrubbed all over, or what?"

I leaned forward, serious. "Well, first, I take a towel and some soap, and then—" I looked at my watch, "—oops, got to go. See you." I headed for the toilet to pee. His mouth hung open.

He yelled after me. "Not funny, Ian! Not funny! I got feelings, y'know!"

I grinned as I peed; Frank deserved that one. I imagined moving in with Karen. A familiar figure appeared beside me. I nodded. "Captain."

He grunted. "Palumbo is having you to dinner tonight? Do us proud, son."

I zipped up. "Not to worry, sir. I will."

He nodded his approval.

Frank was still acting annoyed as I came back. I read through some paperwork; the girl from the telex room handed Frank a glossy sheet of paper and a teletype sheet. He looked at the glossy paper, furrowing his brow.

"Apparently, Walter Carpenter looks like Chico Marx." He passed it to me.

It was a black and white photo, dated a year and a half ago. The person in the photo was a chubby white man with a stubby, light Afro. His eyes were dark behind thick black glasses, and his skin was mottled.

Frank read the teletype sheet and rested his elbows on his desk. "Know how he got that license? He showed his Ontario license as ID. That means there's an Ontario one for him in the system."

We almost ran down the hall to records. I had an idea what we'd find, and I was right. The Walter James Carpenter born on the date listed on the Connecticut license had never held an Ontario driver's license. The man in the photo therefore faked an Ontario driver's license, got the birth certificate of a dead infant, and with them applied for a Connecticut license.

Using that, he applied for an American passport,

and on that passport he went to Italy and probably killed the older Palumbo boy. But why all the subterfuge? Frank stretched back and looked at his watch.

"Early lunch?" he asked.

I glanced at the clock on the wall. Eleven forty-five. "Picking up Karen. If you wait, we can eat together."

"Great. Mind if Helen joins us?"

"Sure. See you soon."

I rode the elevator to the twelfth floor, took a deep breath and stepped into the hallway. I was instantly nauseous. I breathed deep, panting, to stay in control, to not vomit. I went through the *Mortgages and Loans* door and started to breathe normally again.

The woman with the silky voice was behind the high counter. She smiled; more honey oozed out.

"Hi. Karen told us you'd stop by. Be right back."

I flipped through a magazine. A number of women came by in ones and twos, pretending to look for something, then scurried away. I crossed my legs and kept reading, acting oblivious to the blatant ogling. Just before twelve thirty, Karen appeared.

"Hey, you," she purred.

We headed for the elevators. I pushed the button. The light didn't come on. I pushed it again. Again, no light. I breathed heavily, huffing. I walked around in a large circle, anxious.

Karen looked at me, worried. "Sometimes it takes a minute," she offered apologetically. She leaned forward and pressed the button. The light came on. A second later, the elevator door opened on an empty car. We got in, and I started breathing evenly again. Karen stared up at me.

She stared like Patricia Neal in *The Day the Earth Stood Still*, when she's stuck in an elevator with Michael Rennie and suddenly realizes he's an alien.

"Claustrophobia," I mumbled.

Her eyes widened, incredulous. "Really. You?"

I shrugged. "Not a problem in Saskatchewan. Big problem here."

She rubbed against me, chest to chest. "Helping?"

I smiled. "Sure is. I may get really claustrophobic later, too."

Frank and Helen were already at our diner, in a booth by the front window. We joked like teenagers. Our waitress, adjusting her glasses, passed out menus.

"You boys finally dating classier women?" she quipped.

Helen and Karen talked about work, Ethan, and life in general, in staccato sentences. Frank and I discussed the dinner; we finalized what I would and would not discuss. Frank grunted.

"Why would you bother getting an Ontario driver's license and a Connecticut one?"

Helen glanced at him. "Hmm?" she asked, sipping cola.

Frank sighed. "Guy gets a birth certificate in the name of a dead infant from Connecticut. He fakes an Ontario driver's license. With the ID from the dead infant, and the fake Ontario license, he gets a real Connecticut driver's license and a U.S. passport. Why bother doing all that?"

Helen looked up. "You would need a current license to show at the DMV—that's what they call it in the States—for a new Connecticut one. Otherwise you'd have to go in for tests and stuff."

Frank nodded. "I thought of that too."

She leaned forward. "The Ontario license would let you cross the border, though. A lot of people don't have passports, but they have driver's licenses. We went to Buffalo with just ours, remember?"

Frank was attentive. "Couldn't you use the U.S. passport to cross the border?" he challenged.

Helen thought for a moment. "But they keep records of American citizens returning, don't they? If you said you were just going over on your Canadian license, they don't record that, do they?"

I shook my head. "God, Frank, she should work for us, shouldn't she?"

He smiled lovingly at her. "Take my damn job, she

would."

After lunch I hugged Helen and said I'd call Frank after the dinner. Karen sat quietly in my car, thinking.

"That house for rent, can we see it?" she asked.

I smiled. "Let's go."

Trowell Street was a short, quiet road of brick bungalows, facing a schoolyard. Maple trees shaded the sidewalk. It was a street where children tricycled and roller-skated up and down, where you barbecued in the backyard and invited your neighbors onto the front stoop for a beer.

We parked out front of a small house with a flower bed bordering a narrow front lawn and a side driveway leading to a garage in the backyard. The garage was empty, the curtains open.

Karen walked ahead of me to the raised porch. She tried peeking into the front window, but the porch did not extend under it. I pulled out some keys and unlocked the door. Karen walked into the front hall, her footsteps echoing in the empty space.

The house was a typical 1930s layout; to the left from the front entry was a kitchen leading to a bathroom and on to two bedrooms. To the right were a living room at the front and a dining room behind, separated by a wide archway. The dining room led through another archway back to the kitchen. It was small, but cozy. A fireplace in the living room, even unlit, suggested warmth.

Karen wandered back and forth, mouth open, pacing every square foot of the upstairs.

"There's also a basement," I said finally. "It's finished, and it has a fireplace in the den."

She stopped suddenly and looked at me, her mouth open. "Why do you have the keys?"

I shook my head.

She pointed at me, suddenly angry. "Who owns this house?" she walked toward me. I backed away.

"Whose house is this?" She grabbed my keys and held them up to my face. "*Is this your house?*" she yelled. She turned bright red and kicked my calf. "Damn you!"

I crouched down and held my sore leg. "What?" I asked, genuinely puzzled.

"You could have told me! You own a house? You could have told me!" She kicked my other calf. I fell down, nursing sharp pain in both legs.

"When?" I asked, wincing.

"What?" she asked. The anger vanished.

"When should I have told you? 'Hi, you bumped your head. I own a house.' How about 'Let's get naked, I own a house.'"

She paced back and forth, having an internal conversation. "Should have told me," she muttered. "What the hell else didn't you tell me?" She kicked my heel.

I struggled to my feet and threw her over my shoulder. She screamed, kicking at the air as her skirt rode up. She started to laugh, kicking and wriggling. I carried her down to the basement, gently spanked her backside, and put her down.

"Here we have the finished basement," I said, sweeping my hand out expressively. "Note the parquet floor, the third bedroom, the generous den with fireplace, and the laundry room." I was grinning, waving at the air like a carpet salesman.

She looked around, not absorbing anything. "Why do you own a house?"

My smile faded.

She repeated it quietly. "Ian, why do you own a house?"

I slid down to the floor, my back against a wall. "When my mom died, my dad said he didn't want anything from the insurance. 'Blood money,' he called it. He gave it all to my brother and me. I took my half and invested it."

Karen sat down and leaned against me. "And you bought a house."

"Yes. I still have about seventy thousand left."

She leaned back, stunned. "I'm not a gold digger. You do know that, right?"

I nodded. "So, do you wanna get naked?"

She laughed. "Idiot."

We walked through the backyard, over wet grass to

a small vegetable garden.

"Think Ethan would like this?" I asked.

She leaned against my shoulder. "Sorry about kicking you."

I patted her bottom. "It's OK. By the way, Frank says you have a very nice bum."

Love in the Afternoon. I never liked the movie—my mom was the Audrey Hepburn fan—but it perfectly described our time before the dinner.

I lay beside her, my hands behind my head, smiling.

"What's so funny?" she asked.

"Funny?"

"You're smiling at something. What?"

I sat up and looked at the far wall. "When I was growing up, I was, I dunno, seven, eight, driving with my parents. But I remember exactly where we were—just south of Melville, Saskatchewan. It was a glorious evening, the end of Indian summer, and we were heading home from a friend's farm. We had this '47 Dodge, all black and chrome. All of a sudden, my father stopped the car, and we all piled out. I thought we had a flat tire or hit a deer or something. He just stopped, not another car as far as we could see. We got out, and he pointed to the west." I held an invisible ball in my hands.

"The sun was just sinking. There was no wind, there were no mosquitoes, there was no heat or cold, it was perfect. The horizon was the color of polished copper, the sky overhead was an inky blue, and I could just see the first stars come out. I told myself, 'Remember this when you grow up, because you'll cherish these images.' Then my father pointed to the horizon, held my mother's hand, and said, 'Look, Miriam, what more proof do you need that God exists?'"

Karen smiled, her eyes moist. "What brought that to mind?"

I rubbed her shoulder. "This is the same feeling. I never had it with anyone else."

She draped herself over my chest, sniffling softly. "You're too sensitive to be a cop."

I hugged her close. She sniffled and punched my ribs.

"What was that for?" I cried.

She hugged me. "Should have told me about the house."

"Boy," I said, "then you'll really be pissed about the yacht."

She sat up, startled.

I snickered. "Kidding."

She punched me again.

Chapter Nine

We got to Palumbo's house just before six thirty. Karen wore a black knee-length dress; I wore my navy blue suit. We both looked very prim and low key.

The front door opened as we approached it. The man who looked like a small truck held the door, growled, "Good evening," and nodded us into the foyer.

Palumbo showed up a moment later, in a striped shirt and black slacks, his mother trailing behind at a discreet distance. He stretched out his hand.

"Ian, welcome again to my house. Please, make yourself at home."

I introduced Karen as my girlfriend—we'd agreed on that—and he shook her hand warmly.

"I see he's a great detective." Palumbo shook a finger at me.

Karen frowned. "Why is that?"

"It takes a great detective to find someone as rare and lovely as you."

She blushed slightly.

He smiled. "Please, come, let's eat." He ushered us into a formal dining room, with an oval dining table, an ornate hutch stacked with gold edged plates and outré wine pitchers; the collected memories of a lifetime, I thought.

Palumbo sat at the head of the table, with Karen and me beside him. His mother sat by me, her hands in her lap, and "the Truck," as I now thought of him, sat further down. It was carefully arranged to have me defend

Karen, and at the same time make me vulnerable by having the old lady near me.

A noise from the front door carried through. Maureen Zimmerman came through, followed by a slender, frail-looking young man. I stood up politely. She went straight to her father and kissed him on the cheek.

"Hi, Pappa, sorry we're late," she said. Palumbo grunted. She shook my hand. "We meet again, detective."

"Please, call me Ian. I'm here as a friend." I introduced Karen, and sat back down.

The thin man stuck out an icy hand and announced in a hoarse whisper, "Hi, I'm Bruno Zimmerman." Palumbo glared at him. Zimmerman turned to Karen and introduced himself.

"You've kept our guests waiting," Palumbo said, smiling, but with a voice as sharp as steel.

Zimmerman looked bashfully down. "Sorry, I was, I was busy at the shop."

Maureen sat to the far side of her grandmother. Bruno sat beside the Truck. The power structure was crystal clear.

Palumbo took a sip of wine and leaned back. He nodded to the Truck, who went to the kitchen. Palumbo's mother sat, silently, her hands in her lap, looking like a child left at school. I smiled at her.

"*Signora*," I said, "*Situazione terribile.*"

She looked up and said something I didn't understand.

"I'm sorry, but my Italian is rather limited," I apologized.

Karen leaned forward and spoke in Italian. The old lady instantly brightened up. I stared at Karen.

"You speak Italian?"

She shrugged. "A little. My grandmother was Italian."

"Why didn't you tell me?" I asked.

"Why didn't you tell me you own a house?" she asked defiantly.

I turned to Maureen. "You sell lots of interesting pieces. Where do you find them all?"

She nodded at her husband. "Bruno. Like I said, he deals with manufacturers from all over."

Bruno turned to Karen. "Have you always lived in Toronto?"

Karen put down her wine and shook her head. "Moved here from Ottawa three years ago. I like this city though. More to do."

The kitchen door opened, and three young women entered, carrying plates of food. Palumbo smiled. The women brought salad, bread, and more wine. They silently served food and filled glasses; we talked and ate.

Karen didn't mention Ethan—that would be a sore point. I skimmed over the case; Palumbo probed at first, then abandoned the subject when he felt resistance.

Karen had always wanted to see Italy; Palumbo described the Amalfi coast, the streets of Rome, and the countryside around Naples. She smiled, fascinated.

Palumbo's mother asked her a number of questions; I never understood what they said. Karen's Italian was halting, and she struggled with some words, but they got on well. Karen complimented the lasagna, shooting me a sly glance as she said it.

I stuck to ginger ale and water; Karen had wine. After the last course, the kitchen door opened, and the three women brought us demitasse cups of steaming espresso.

Palumbo opened a cabinet door, retrieving his brown bottle of grappa. He poured a small amount into his coffee. He proffered the bottle; I politely declined. Karen, feeling adventuresome, poured some into her coffee. She grimaced as the alcohol, warmed by coffee, filled her nose and burned going down her throat.

"Ooh," she whispered, "that sure wakes you up."

Palumbo chuckled. "It's an acquired taste. You either love it or hate it. I grew up on this stuff." He held the bottle, reading the label. He turned to me. "You studied religion. Why did you become a policeman?"

I leaned back, deciding what to tell him. "I also had a tragedy," I said. "This way I could be true to my beliefs and still have . . ." I searched for the right word. "Justice."

Palumbo stared, his eyes fixed on me. "You were going to say revenge."

The room went silent.

"It occurred to me. But that would have disrespected the person we lost."

He was still staring. "A parent? Your mother."

I smiled sadly.

"Was it an unfortunate—an accident?" he probed.

I shook my head. "Remind me never to play poker with you."

Palumbo scowled. "Imagine how you would feel if it were your child. You don't have children, do you?" I shot a quick glance at Karen, then immediately regretted it. "Ah, but you do, Miss Prescott."

Karen went rigid. "A son. Four years old."

Palumbo leaned back, nodding. "You understand."

Karen lowered her eyes. "You're right." She looked up. "I could not forgive."

The conversation drifted to other matters, unimportant things, and time passed. By ten o'clock we politely took our leave. Karen said something to Mrs. Palumbo; the old woman said something back and kissed Karen on the cheek. We all shook hands and left. I decided on a detour home.

"Where are we going?" Karen asked, curious.

"For a quick stop," I said. "Do you mind?"

"Am I being debriefed here?"

I smiled. "That comes later."

She chuckled at the joke.

"I do have to ask you," I started, serious. "Did you like his lasagna better?"

"It was different. Not better."

"That's an evasion."

She hugged my arm. "I don't sleep with him."

We sat by a window in a coffee shop, sipping weak coffee and nibbling toast, the cloudy sky reflecting the glow of North Toronto. Karen watched traffic in the distance.

I watched her, my head in my hands.

"What?" she smiled.

"You speak Italian. That fascinates me. You make me feel wonderful just by being in the room, and you can sit and eat with mobsters without batting an eye."

She leaned forward. Her dress bowed out, revealing cleavage. "What else do I do that fascinates you?"

"Keep doing that and I won't be able to stand up. What was Mrs. Palumbo saying?"

She nodded, serious. "They lost the older son a year ago, now the younger one got hurt. She wanted to know how the investigation was going, where you are in finding the culprit."

"And you told her what?" I was curious.

"I said if anyone could solve this, you could. I also said that if I heard anything, I would tell her. She's a tough old bird; her husband died years ago, when her son was just a teenager. They had saved enough to put him into private school, though, and she decided he would get the best '*mangiacake*' education she could afford."

I frowned. "*Mangiacake?*"

"It's a term my grandmother used for Anglo-Canadians. It means 'cake eaters.'" She leaned forward. "Mrs. Palumbo sent him to Upper Canada College. UCC is upper-class, white bread, blond, Anglo, Protestant, Progressive-Conservative territory. Imagine how it was to be an Italian Catholic dark-haired immigrant kid in that place. But he made it, and on his own merits."

"Sounds like you admire him."

Karen shook her head. "She has a blind spot for him. She thinks he's a solid citizen. But I did find out that someone hates him. There's a man called DiNardo—that's what she called him—who had a falling out with Palumbo forever ago. He has an import business in Etobicoke. That's all I know."

We got back to my place and fell over each other getting undressed. I carried her to the bed as I dumped clothes behind me.

Five thirty a.m. I put on the coffee. It seemed a good day for an omelet. At six, Karen pulled the sheets over her, still asleep. I brought her coffee. She sighed, opening her eyes.

"What time is it?"

"Still early. Want eggs?" I offered.

She nodded. "Do I still excite you?" she asked, from the bedroom.

"What?" I looked at her, incredulous.

"Really. Do I still turn you on? A girl likes to know she can still make her man happy."

I chuckled. "Any happier and I'd be on oxygen."

Ethan had enjoyed his sleepover. He ate breakfast, hugged Karen tightly, hugged me, then went back downstairs to play with Tommy some more. We drove downtown.

Karen pulled some gum out of her purse and popped it into her mouth, chewing loudly.

I parked and turned to face her.

"What?" she asked, chewing absentmindedly.

I sighed. "You've known me less than two weeks. I've intruded into your life, I've asked you to move in with me, I've dragged you to a dinner with a criminal, and I've taken cruel advantage of your body. To top it off, I'm not that great a catch, either. You said you were just a mom with no money. I'm just a cop, and I'm not even completely white. So, tell me, miss, what do you see in me?" I was leaning in now, eye to eye with her.

She took the gum out of her mouth and stuck it on my nose. "Shut up, you," she purred. She kissed me slowly, passionately. "Does that answer your question?"

I nodded. "Yup."

She kissed me again. "See you at five?" She slid out.

I leaned quickly toward her. "Hey, want to do something fun this weekend?"

She beamed. "Surprise me." She sashayed off, turning back to smile and wave.

I put the gum in my mouth, chewing as I drove to the station.

Frank was finishing a joke. "So the first guy says, 'Then why are you banging my wife?'" The detectives laughed. He looked over his shoulder at me. "Fun night?"

"None of your business," I retorted defensively. "Oh, you mean dinner. Yeah, went well."

He leered. "Forget dinner, tell me about the other part."

"Piss off, Frank."

He chuckled. "OK, fine. How was dinner?"

I nodded at the Captain's office. We went in and closed the door. Van Hoeke looked up.

"Dinner went well," I started. "Karen got along with Mrs. Palumbo. I was unaware that Karen spoke some Italian; she and the old lady spoke at length. One interesting bit: someone called DiNardo had a feud with Palumbo going way back. She figures if anyone wanted to do the family harm, he would."

Frank and Van Hoeke frowned at each other.

"What?" I asked.

Frank sighed. "Tomaso Onofrio DiNardo. We figure he's one of the major liquor smugglers in the area. Word is the New York families gave him the rights to everything from Mississauga to Oshawa."

"I'm told he has an import company?" I asked.

"He does. Actually quite legit. Italian food, china, stuff for people from the old country."

Van Hoeke pointed at me. "Talk to him. I want him to know we're looking at him. That should get him to pop out of his foxhole, if nothing else. So, you didn't tell Palumbo where we're at?"

I shook my head. "He knows we're investigating the younger boy's accident. I'm sure he suspects we've connected the dots with the older boy, but that's all. Nothing he couldn't read in *The Globe and Mail*."

Van Hoeke nodded. "Go see DiNardo. If you're going to become a sergeant sometime soon, you need the experience."

We left the captain's office. A small package sat on Frank's desk. The postmark read Florence, Italy. He yelled out at a passing secretary.

"Hey! When did this get here?"

She glanced at it. "Just now, Sergeant."

Frank opened the box. Inside was a plastic bag. In the bag was a dark, squished bullet. Frank held it up to my face.

"Now," he said, "the ball starts rolling."

We handed the bullet over to forensics, and asked them to radio us if it matched the Beretta. It might take a while, they said. We left to talk to DiNardo.

Someone once said that Toronto was a thousand neighborhoods acting as a city. Etobicoke was one such neighborhood, on the west side of town.

DiNardo had a warehouse in an industrial zone, like dozens of other warehouses in the area. A large concrete box surrounded by gravel. We parked in a spot marked *Valued Customers* and went into the office.

Inside, an immaculate linoleum floor was laid in a diagonal check pattern. A sofa and chair bracketed a coffee table, with a nearly full ashtray on the table. An empty reception desk stood opposite us. We sat and waited.

A minute later, the sound of heels on linoleum brought us to our feet; around the corner from a side hallway, a very tall, stunning blonde woman walked up to the reception desk, placed papers on it, and looked at us. She wore a short red silk skirt, red high heels, and a sheer beige silk blouse over a peach colored brassiere. Her voice was cold, professional, and direct.

"Yes?"

Frank moved forward. "We're looking for Mr. DiNardo."

She looked down at the desk and shook her head. "He doesn't see salesmen without an appointment. You'll have to write us."

Frank was unfazed. "We're not salesmen. I'm Detective Sergeant Burghezian, and this is Detective Constable McBriar, from the Toronto Police Department." We held out our warrant cards. She walked around the desk and studied them.

"What's this about?"

Frank smiled. "We'd like to ask Mr. DiNardo some questions."

She smiled coolly. "That's not what I asked. What's this about?"

"We have some questions about a suspicious accident."

She raised an eyebrow. "Really? Wait here." She marched off to the back of the building again, her footsteps fading slowly.

Frank's head leaned around the corner, watching her wiggle. "Built like a concrete crapper. Think she likes cops?"

I nodded solemnly. "Yeah, she could barely keep her hands off you."

He smirked. "I thought so, too."

The heels came toward us again, slower this time. She gave the smile a waiter gives a bad tipper. "Mr. DiNardo will see you now."

She led us down a hall, past a series of closed wooden doors. The last door was steel, with a small wired glass window buried in it. Inside was a plush office. A second door led out of it; I couldn't tell where it went.

That door opened, and a large man came in. He was balding, with a bushy handlebar mustache. His forearms, sticking out of his golf shirt, were a mat of black fur. He wore a large gold ring on his left hand and an immense gold watch on his left wrist. He held out a thick arm.

"Hi, I'm Tom DiNardo," he said in a Charlton Heston voice. "Please, sit down." He sat at the desk.

I sat in the more commanding swivel chair. Frank sat behind me. Frank pulled out his notebook. Another man came in from the same door. He looked like a version of the Truck at Palumbo's, only larger. He kept his hands down, but I noticed that part of his right thumb was missing. He stood, silent, beside DiNardo. DiNardo rested his arms on the tabletop and laced his fingers together.

"Now, what can I do for you?" he asked.

"We're investigating a serious accident," I started.

The men's faces didn't register guilt, panic, or anything. DiNardo threw one arm over his chair back. "Yeah? Who?"

"Nicholas Palumbo."

There was a pause, then DiNardo exploded with laughter. The man beside him smiled, silently.

Frank frowned. "Do you have a statement you wish to make?"

DiNardo wiped his eyes, and looked at us. "The injury to a member of our business community," he snickered, "is always a shock." He giggled. "I have great admiration for Nick Palumbo, and he will always be," he laughed out loud, "a valued friend." He roared with laughter, rubbing his eyes with the heels of his hands. He smiled at Frank. "That do it, officers?"

Frank was stony-faced. "Actually, it was his son, Nicholas Jr., who was hurt."

DiNardo stopped laughing. "What?" He looked at the other man, who slowly, imperceptibly, shook his head. DiNardo leaned forward, all humor gone. "What happened?"

Frank leaned forward too. "He was attacked while he was out with a school friend."

"When did this happen?" DiNardo made notes on a desk pad.

I spoke. "About two weeks ago. I'm surprised you weren't aware of this before."

He shrugged. "I was in Florida. I'm always there this time of year." He turned to the man beside him. "Call Nick. I want to send my wishes."

The blonde appeared, magically. DiNardo looked up, all business. "Judith, please send a large bouquet to Nick Palumbo. His son got hurt. He's—" he turned to us, "—eight? nine?"

"Nine," I said.

"Nine. Something appropriate? Thanks." She nodded and disappeared. DiNardo stared at Frank, his face stony, ignoring me. "What else?"

Frank raised his notebook, reading. It was blank, but they couldn't see that.

I spoke again. "What about this feud between you and Palumbo? How bad is it?"

DiNardo twirled a Zippo lighter between his

fingers. He sighed. "You'd find out eventually. We fell out way back, in '61, '62. His marriage had problems. We were friends, but I was a better friend to his wife, if you know what I mean. He never forgave that. Every chance he had after that, he screwed me over. Poetic justice, I suppose."

Frank leaned forward. "Does the name Walter Carpenter mean anything to you?"

DiNardo mentally went through names and shook his head.

"Anyone you know own a handgun?" Frank was fishing now.

DiNardo smiled and leaned back. "What kind?"

"A Beretta."

DiNardo smiled. "Maybe. Nickel plated?"

Frank nodded.

DiNardo glanced at the man beside him. "Yeah, I know someone who has one like that. Nick Palumbo."

Frank scowled on the drive back to the station. The dispatcher hadn't heard from ballistics. He tapped his pen against his notebook, furious. I was only thinking about the gun, not the bullet.

"What would Palumbo say?" I said. "'Hey, I had this gun, but now it's missing?' I don't think so. If he connected the dead guy in Italy to his older son's death, he'd tell us. Otherwise, why would he? It may not even be the same gun."

Frank got out before I got the car in park. I ran to follow him through the door, catching up by the forensics wing. He yanked the lab door open, almost hitting me. He grumbled an apology and stormed up to a disheveled man in a lab coat and glasses behind a desk. The man looked up from his work.

"Frank," he said. "Help you?"

Frank put his knuckles on the desk and leaned in close. "Have you tested that bullet against the gun we brought in?"

The man nodded matter-of-factly.

"And the answer is?"

The man shrugged.

"You won't tell me because . . ." He left the question

hanging.

The man looked around, furtively, then slid one hand into his coat sleeve and made a hook with his finger.

Frank pursed his lips, turned, and stormed out of the room. I followed at a sprint.

Captain Van Hoeke was at his desk. Frank burst into the office, unannounced, and closed the door behind us. He leaned over the Captain's desk. Van Hoeke went to stand up. Frank pointed at him.

"Sit," he ordered.

Van Hoeke sat, amused.

"Do I look like a mushroom, Martin?" Frank seethed through gritted teeth.

The Captain frowned.

"Keep me in the dark, feed me bullshit?" Frank sat down defiantly.

The Captain leaned back and grinned at me. "This is why he's a sergeant, son. He thinks two steps ahead."

I had no idea what was going on. Van Hoeke leaned forward. "We now know that the bullet that killed the man in Italy, yes, Frank, was fired from the gun you found. Now, if Palumbo asks you about it, we'll know who told him."

"Who?" I asked.

The Captain shook his head. "Baby steps, son. Walk before you run."

Frank studied him for a long, long minute. He stood back up. "I'm going to trust you on this one, Martin. But if you screw me, I'll crap all over you. C'mon, kid, let's go." He stormed out of the office.

We ate at the diner, silently. I spent lunch watching Frank stare out the window. I was bored, ready to do the crossword, when he turned to me.

"Dinner was OK?" he asked.

I nodded. Only after a moment did I realize he meant dinner with Palumbo.

"How's the husband?"

I thought about that question. "Right, you never met him. Not the mobster's-son-in-law type. Way too passive."

Frank seemed interested in that. "Go on."

"Palumbo hates his guts. I got the feeling that if the guy caught fire, he wouldn't piss on him to put out the flame."

That brought a smile. "Yeah? Any chance he's the Carpenter guy in the Connecticut Driver's License photo?"

I shook my head. "Too short, too skinny."

Frank sighed and looked out the window again. "Monday," he said.

"Monday?" I repeated.

He nodded. "Monday we'll get moving on this. Tonight we're taking Ethan to Barrie, remember?" He grabbed the bill. "Screw it, Ian. Let's go home."

We headed down Keele Street to Frank's house.

"By the way, kid, thanks for that lasagna. Helen says to tell you it was delicious."

High praise indeed, I thought. "We had lasagna at Palumbo's," I said.

"How was it?"

"Good. Karen said it wasn't better than mine, just different."

He nodded. "Interesting. I'll let you know after I go there."

"When are you going?"

"Monday night. Already set up," he said nonchalantly.

We got to Frank's. Helen made coffee, and we sat staring glumly into our mugs.

"Did your ponies die?" she asked sarcastically.

Frank looked up at her and smiled weakly. "Captain Hook knows the answer to something and won't tell us."

"Maybe he's hoping you find out on your own?" she offered.

Frank shot me a look. "Go on."

She shrugged. "Could be he wants to see if you can get the answer without his help. I do that with some of my students."

Frank frowned. "What's he got to gain by that, though?"

I thought for a moment. "We have a mole."

"Yeah?" Frank shrugged.

"If Van Hoeke tells the boys downtown who that is," I started, "it could be seen as sour grapes, or a personal thing. But if the mole gets ratted out by one of us, then it's genuine."

Frank smiled. "We're not the bait, we're the hunting dogs."

Just before five, I was at Karen's office building. I paced the lobby, chatted with the security guard, and waited by the elevator. She came out, surrounded by a handful of women from her floor. They saw me, giggled, and walked off toward the subway.

Karen clutched my arm. "Hey, you," she said.

I gave her a quick kiss, and when we were alone I gave her a proper kiss.

"What was that for?" she smiled.

"Just a sample for later," I answered.

By six o'clock, we'd prepared Ethan's clothes and toys for his trip. Karen wrote down the farm's phone number, read it back to Helen, and kissed Ethan goodbye as though he was going to the moon. She promised to phone in two hours. Helen drove as the Nova disappeared north toward Barrie.

Karen sniffled slightly. I felt sadness for her, as she watched the tail lights fade up the street. She stared down at her shoes.

"Hard to let go?" I asked.

She shrugged. "He's my baby. What do you expect?"

I wrapped my arms around her. "Come, I have something exciting planned."

We changed into jeans and sweaters, then drove to a small, dingy parking lot west of Chinatown. Karen stared, mouth open.

"Where are we going?" she asked warily. "This is not the best part of town, you know."

I nodded. "Trust me."

We walked south on Spadina, dodging the Friday night pub crowds, Karen behind me. The noise and lights of the strip joints and beer halls surrounded us. I turned abruptly right and up a set of brick steps, leading to a red painted door. The building had been a big rooming house before the First World War. Now it had an architect's office upstairs.

We went through an entryway, then down the stairs to a large basement with a jazz club. On a stage in one corner, four men in blue satin suits played horns at a dizzying volume. Behind them, a man on a Hammond organ and another on a bass played backup. I recognized the tune—Cannonball Adderley's "Mercy, Mercy, Mercy."

Karen gawked, fascinated by this side of my personality. I still held her behind me. I waved with my free hand; a thin black man in a bartender's shirt and apron smiled at me. We sat down. Silently, he brought me a bowl of pretzels and a glass of ginger ale.

He leaned down and yelled at Karen in a hoarse New Orleans voice. "What you want?"

She gave me a mischievous smile and yelled back, "Vodka!"

He came back a minute later with vodka and ice water. Within a half hour, she'd had two more vodkas, bouncing in her chair to the music. She stood and cheered when the band finished its set, hooting with the rest of the crowd.

"Like jazz?" I called. She hadn't heard me. I cupped my hands around my mouth. "Having fun?" I yelled.

She smiled and kissed me. "Yeah! Most fun I've had in years!" She looked around. "How did you find this place?"

I opened my mouth to yell, but the noise level dropped to a hum as the band left the stage. The man in the apron put a Chet Baker LP on the stereo, and the room went quiet. I took her hand. "My brother played here a while ago. Great sound, tight band."

She scratched my leg playfully, the alcohol kicking in. "Is he married?" she asked.

"Who?" I looked around, feeling a twinge of jealousy.

"Your brother—a wife, kids, all that?"

I shook my head and played with the ice in my glass.

She gave me an impish grin. "String of girlfriends?"

I smiled sadly. "Not for him, I'm afraid."

She looked at me for a moment, the vodka slowing her thoughts, then her eyes widened.

"Ah. I see." She looked down sheepishly, and sipped from my glass.

Around eight o'clock, I asked to use a phone. The bartender took us to the kitchen, where a small Oriental man in checked pants and a white t-shirt leaned against the tile wall, smoking a hand-rolled cigarette. He was talking to an equally small blonde, her hair in a net. She was washing dishes, mechanically stacking them on a rack.

I picked up the phone and dialed the number Frank had given us. Frank's voice came on a moment later.

"Right on time, kid," he gushed. "Wanna talk to the little squirt?"

I handed the phone to Karen, watching her as she spoke.

"You did?" She smiled. "A big cow? That's exciting. Uh huh, and the chickens make the eggs, yes." She listened. "I'd like that." She smiled and looked at me. "You can bring them home and Ian can make omelets." She nodded. "Can I talk to Frank? Thanks, sweetheart. Bye." She waited. "Frank, you take good care of him, OK?" Another pause. She smiled. "Fine, see you Sunday night. All my love to Helen." She hung up, looking at the receiver for a minute.

"How is he?" I asked.

"My little boy is growing up. He's having fun without me." She sniffed.

"That means you're doing your job well."

She hugged me and nodded. "Come on, I need another vodka."

We ordered food and ate, bopping to the next set. The band covered James Brown, Sly Stone, and Fats Waller. Within an hour, the brass guys had their jackets on the floor and dripped sweat; the crowd was on its feet, stomping to a rousing rendition of "Honeysuckle Rose."

The tune ended, and the band left for their next break, chased by a roar from the audience. Karen was giddy from the dancing, the clapping, and the vodka. She staggered, grabbed my arm, and held on.

"Time to get you home," I chuckled.

She giggled. "OK, you smooth talker," she slurred.

I paid up, and we headed back out onto Spadina Avenue. The evening had turned cold; a haze hung in the air. Misty car windows looked like frosted glass.

Most of the Friday night crowds had scattered. Everyone had gone to movies, dinners, and home by now. Even the street lights looked tired; the glow from the overhead lamps seemed soft, dimmer than it should be.

A small handful of people, shuffling against the cold, passed us. Three young men, slightly drunk, laughed and walked toward Karen, ogling her. One of them whispered something. He swaggered, leering, reaching toward her.

I stepped in front of her and stopped dead. I put a hand on the man's chest and glared at him. They all stopped laughing. The men looked embarrassed and continued down the street. Karen grinned.

"What?" I asked. The drinks were wearing off quickly.

"You told me something right after we met."

"Yeah?" I had no idea what she meant.

"You said that you'd protect Ethan and me if anyone tried to do us harm." She grabbed my arm tightly. "I thought it was just typical macho bullshit. I realize now it was the truth."

I smiled. "Yeah, well. I'm not just another pretty face, you know."

She stopped three feet from the car, tugged my face down and kissed me, softly. She tasted of vinegar and vodka, but her lips were warm.

I felt a rush of pure lust; I put my hands under her ribs and sat her on the hood. I wrapped my arms around her and we kissed passionately. I reached up under her sweater, rubbed her back, and smiled. "Let's go home."

*

At seven in the morning, I woke up. Karen was draped over me, her arm over my shoulder. I slid out from under her, reluctantly, pulled on a bathrobe, and poured myself a coffee before waking her. I brought a mug, wafted it under her nose, and set it on the night table. She opened one eye, looked around cautiously, and settled on me.

"Very subtle," she croaked. "I appreciate you not making a lot of noise." She tried to sit up, unsuccessfully.

I propped up two pillows and slid her against them. She waited, placidly, for the coffee. I leaned down and kissed her. She smiled weakly.

"What was that for?"

I raised an eyebrow. "You don't remember? Wow."

She opened both eyes, wide. "What? What did I do?"

"All I can say is, I never saw that side of you before."

She leaned forward, angry. "Ian, if you're screwing with me, tell me. I mean it."

I laughed. "Sorry. I couldn't resist. Yes, I'm messing with you. Mind you, last night was fun."

"Asshole." She shook her head.

Last night's drizzle was gone. Clear sunlight streamed in through the kitchen window. Karen was putting on makeup as the phone rang. I answered it and called her. "Do you know an Ethan Prescott in Barrie?"

She thundered through, wide-eyed, and grabbed the receiver. "Hello? Yes, is everything OK, sweetheart?"

I watched her, listening to the voice at the other end, the only other person in her world, talking to her. She smiled, relieved. She went *uh-huh* a few times, then looked at me. "I think he'd like that very much. You can tell him tomorrow, OK? Bye, sweetheart." She put the phone down softly. "Ethan has a gift for you—fresh eggs."

"I would love that. Thank you very much."

"He's having fun chasing ducks and cats around. Helen thanks us for letting him go."

"I'm just happy he's enjoying himself. He's a good kid."

"So are you." She kissed my nose. "Let's go choose colors for Ethan's room."

I have no understanding of women, or men, who voluntarily spend long periods of time shopping for clothing, shoes, furniture, televisions, or anything else. The same goes for choosing paint, carpets, and hardware. That said, I tagged along behind Karen as she wandered the local paint store, picking up color samples with names like "mourning dove" and "aspen breeze." To me, it was just blue and green.

She held a paper strip up, questioningly. I shrugged.

"It's blue. Looks nice."

She shook her head. "But, is it too *vivid* a blue? Should I go for teal blue instead?"

"Dunno, looks the same."

"It is *not* the same. This one's much more vibrant."

"OK."

"Are you just saying that, or do you mean it?" she huffed.

"Um, yes."

"No, not yes. Which one do you prefer?"

"That one." I pointed to a strip of paper.

"Why?"

"I dunno. It's nice."

"It's not too vivid?"

"I dunno." I shrugged.

"Make a decision, will you?"

And so it went, until I capitulated on everything.

We went to a burger place I knew near Frank's house. We sat at the only table, a small Formica two-seater in one corner. Karen leaned her head on her hand, slurping her milkshake. I grinned at her.

"Is there something on my nose?" she asked.

I shook my head. "There's a famous photo of Lana Turner drinking a milkshake at Schwab's Pharmacy in Hollywood. You look like her just now."

"Did you watch a lot of movies growing up?"

I swallowed a mouthful of burger and nodded. "My mom was a movie nut. She had all the old magazines. I should have kept them. They'd be valuable now, I bet."

She stared at me. "That's not why you'd keep them, though."

I smiled softly. "No, you're right. They'd remind me of her."

She leaned back, pushing the empty glass away. "What was she like?"

"Lana Turner?"

"You know who I mean. You don't get away that easily."

I sighed. "She was tough. I mean, my dad was a combat instructor, but she was a drill sergeant. She made us do homework, clean our rooms, stay honest. She made me who I am."

Karen stared down at her empty glass. "How is your dad?"

I hadn't expected that question. I sighed. "He is the mildest man you could imagine, very soft-spoken, very polite. When I was seven, eight, we were walking back from a movie, and two drunks picked a fight with him. He pleaded with them to walk away, but they were belligerent, determined to fight."

She winced. "Turned out badly, huh?"

"A broken jaw, shattered knee, broken nose. He felt bad about it for weeks."

She frowned; her eyes slowly widened.

"Ah. You thought *he* got creamed." I shook my head. "He isn't tall like me; he looks like a librarian, but as I say, he taught unarmed combat."

She looked out the window. The day was warm enough that people wore light jackets, strolling instead of shuffling stiffly. Spring was on its way.

"How was he when your mom died?"

I sipped my ginger ale. "My dad was very reserved about his feelings, especially outside the family. The only time I remember him showing real anger was once, right after her funeral. He was grieving, but holding it in. We were driving along, dad in his fedora and his overalls, smiling despite the pain.

"We were at a red light, talking about something, I don't remember what. The light turned green, and we were still talking. The guy behind us started honking, impatient that we were holding him up. And he was a big guy, a farm boy. My dad waved an apology and started to go.

"The guy passed us, yelling, cut us off, and threw something at us. I think it was a chunk of wood or a rock or something. Anyway, it chipped the windshield. So my dad snaps. It's the only time in my life I've ever seen him really angry. He speeds up and forces the guy to the side of the road. The guy jumps out of his car, really pissed off. He's big, really pissed, and he's carrying a baseball bat.

"My dad tells the guy he doesn't want trouble. The guy swings the bat, and my dad just decks him. Next thing I know, the guy is bouncing off the side of his car, and my father is punching the living hell out of him. The guy falls down in the road. My dad drags him onto the sidewalk and kicks the shit out of him. A crowd gathers, staring at us.

"Then the police show up; the officer looks at my dad and tells him to go home. The next day, we went to church, and he apologized to me for being so angry."

Karen looked at me for a long time. "How did you feel about what he did?"

"I'd have killed the guy. I told him so. He said, 'It's OK to feel that, but don't let your anger end a life. You can't take that back.' I realized that his sense of morality overrode his anger, even then. He could have killed the guy in a second. Instead, he simply made him suffer."

I looked out the window. The few remaining patches of snow, hiding in shady spots, were getting smaller. Sunlight streaming through the window made me sleepy. "C'mon," I said. "I want to take you somewhere."

"Sure. Where?"

"Your other boyfriend's house." I grinned.

We pulled up to Gary's place. His dog, Dixie, barked loudly inside, but Gary didn't come to the side door when I knocked. The dog started howling, an urgent, desperate howl. Something seemed terribly wrong.

I walked around to the back and peeked in at the kitchen window. Karen stayed by the side door, waiting for Gary to open it. She jumped back as I flung open the side door from inside the house and raced back to the kitchen. Gary was lying on the floor in a pool of blood. Karen followed me, stunned.

"Call an ambulance!" I yelled.

She froze, shocked at the sight.

"Now, Karen! *Now!*"

She ran to his phone and dialed zero, then, in a quivering voice, asked the operator to send an ambulance. She listened for a second, then turned to me. "What's wrong with him?" she asked.

"He's been stabbed!"

The ambulance arrived in five minutes. I phoned our dispatcher, and a cruiser arrived right after that. The two ambulance attendants raced in, pushed us aside, and talked in shorthand to each other, producing plastic bags and needles.

I identified myself and stood back, letting them do their job. They checked Gary for a pulse and worked feverishly to get an IV into him. Karen sat on a kitchen chair, her feet on a crossbar, as though the blood might splash up onto her. Dixie was curled up on her lap, whimpering.

One attendant came back with a gurney. "What was this, a robbery?" he asked.

I shook my head. "He's a material witness. I'll arrange protection for him in hospital."

They said "one, two, three" in unison and lifted him gently onto the gurney.

The other attendant nodded. "We're taking him to Sunnybrook—better trauma team. He's lucky. He'll be OK." They strapped him down and rolled out into the lane.

A small crowd had gathered outside. A dozen or so people, curious, milled about, whispering to each other. One woman pushed through the group.

"What happened to Gary?" she asked. She was slight, thin, and smelled of stale cigarettes.

I showed her my badge. "Ma'am, I'm Detective

McBriar. Do you know Gary well?"

She shrugged. "He fixed my TV last year. He's peculiar, but he's OK."

I addressed the crowd. "Did anyone here see anybody unusual in the area today? Someone you don't recognize?" Everyone shook their head. "Anyone see any strange cars? A vehicle you haven't seen before?" No response. I turned back to the woman. "Do you know anyone who could take care of Gary's dog while he's in hospital?"

She nodded. "Dixie? Sure, Gary had her with him when I picked up my TV. She's a good dog."

"Would your husband be fine with that?"

She grinned. "What if he's not? It's my house, not his."

I smiled. "Here's my card. Let me know what you spend on Dixie, and I'll get it paid."

She took it, reading my name slowly. "You're the one in that restaurant . . ."

"Yeah, yeah, that's me. Six armed guys and I fought them with a spoon."

She laughed. I got her particulars and shook her hand. Karen leashed Dixie and handed the strap to the woman. The dog jumped up and licked the woman's lowered hand.

The ambulance left, one man hunched over Gary as the other drove. The crowd opened up for the siren, moving together again as it drove north. The uniform took down names, searched Gary's house, and helped me lock up. We strung police tape over the doors and let forensics know they had work to do.

Everybody left. The sudden quiet was almost eerie. Karen was trembling, sitting in the Fury as gawkers walked past.

"You OK, hon?" I asked.

"Poor Gary," she said, looking down. "What did he ever do to deserve this?"

I shook my head. "Someone thinks he saw them hurt those boys. We'll set up a guard at the hospital, though. He'll be OK."

Karen started to weep softly, then her eyes welled up and she pounded the car door.

"How the *hell* can you be so calm? That poor man is in hospital. He almost *died*. Do you know how I feel? Scared *shitless*, that's how. Scared to *death*."

I sighed and faced her. "Do you remember what I told you two weeks ago?"

She shook her head.

"I work hard, and I work long hours. My job is to catch bad guys. I carry a gun, I wear a badge. But mostly I catch the guys who make you less safe." I pointed at Gary's house. "This is what I prevent. The man who did this to Gary killed two other people. I will stop him. I will find him, and I will put him in jail for the rest of his miserable life. I will also stop him from hurting anyone else. That's my job. Period. OK?"

She sniffled, reached into her purse for a Kleenex, and dried her eyes. She smiled at me.

I smiled back. "Look, I got there in time. Gary will make it." I repeated it, softly. "Gary will make it."

She stared at me. "This reminds you of that girl, doesn't it? From when we met?"

I nodded. "This time though, no bad dreams. I got there in time. I got there in time."

CHAPTER TEN

I warmed up packaged quiche and made a salad. Karen had two glasses of wine with dinner and fell asleep. I tucked her into bed.

I went through to the living room and unloaded my revolver. I removed the cylinder, firing pin, and trigger assembly. I wiped the parts down and oiled them. I reassembled the gun, spinning the cylinder to make sure it ran smoothly, and cleaned the bullets before reloading.

I then brought out a box of .38 bullets and a speedloader. I would not be caught without a loaded gun. I reloaded my gun, filled the speedloader, then put them both away. I climbed into bed.

Karen rolled over, pulling me close in her sleep. She looked angelic. I felt like the luckiest man in the world. I kissed her nose gently. "Goodnight, sweetheart."

She moved slightly and pulled me closer. She smiled in her sleep.

At six thirty in the morning, I made coffee and toast. Karen was asleep, but stirring. I brought coffee through and put the mug on the night table. Her eyes opened slightly, then she slid up and leaned forward, combing her hair with her fingers.

"Hey, you," she said. She smiled, grabbing the coffee.

"How's your head?" I asked.

"Fine," she said with a nod. She sipped, frowning at the hot mug.

"Want to shower together?" I asked.

She smiled. "Sure. Then what?"

"After that we're going to church."

We went to Karen's. She changed into a skirt suit and hat, and we were at Immaculate Conception Church by seven twenty-five.

I sat in the same pew I'd sat in before. Again, just before seven thirty, the same old man in the ill-fitting suit walked slowly down the nave, did a perfunctory bow, and walked out the back door. A moment later, Palumbo and his mother came in from the street, followed closely by the Truck.

Palumbo whispered something to his mother, and the Truck walked her to their pew. Palumbo watched to see that she was seated, then sat beside me. He nodded to Karen. "Miss Prescott, very nice to see you again. Ian, good to see you in God's house."

"I'm here to pray for a friend." I smiled.

He looked through me, reading me. "I hope your friend is not seriously ill?"

I shook my head. "He was assaulted in his home, but he'll recover."

Palumbo stared at me. Time stood still. He leaned past me and spoke to Karen. "Miss Prescott, would you excuse us briefly?" He stood and ushered me to the back door. The Truck stood to follow. Palumbo put his palm parallel to the ground, a subtle move nobody else saw, and the Truck sat back down.

We stood on the steps outside the church. The streets were empty, but Palumbo looked around constantly to see if we were being overheard. The morning was still quite cool, and Palumbo shivered slightly.

"What happened?" he asked sharply.

"The man who saw Nick's accident was attacked. Stabbed."

"The mental defective?"

I sighed. "He's autistic, not stupid. Anyway, somebody thinks he saw something he didn't see. Any thoughts on who that might be?"

"You make enemies." Palumbo shrugged. "When

you find the person who did this, I'll make it very advantageous for you to tell me first."

I decided to ignore the offer. "Is there something your older son had in Italy—some item—that was not returned to you?" I was reaching, but I decided to risk it.

He stared at me again. "Give me a clue."

"Something personal, a keepsake you sent him off with."

"Besides the gun you found? Nothing special." Did he not realize what he'd just told me? I decided to distract him.

"You know a Thomas DiNardo?"

"So do you," he replied. "Tom sent flowers after you spoke to him."

"Are you and he still at odds?"

"We're talking. We were friends once. Maybe again. Never say never."

I shrugged. "I've kept you out here for too long. Thank you for your time." I turned to go back in.

He grabbed my arm. "One second. The gun, where did you find it?"

"Did Peter have it in Italy?"

"Yeah, he had it for protection. He was a good kid. He was in university, in no way involved in my affairs. I was just trying to keep him safe. Now, for the last time, where did you find his gun?" His voice was almost pleading.

"Sorry, I can't tell you that."

"It was in that Impala, wasn't it?" He was angry now, a quiet fury.

"Who told you that?" I asked.

"Doesn't matter. So the guy who killed Peter also hurt Nick?"

"Looks like," I said.

"I repeat. Tell me his name, and you can retire tomorrow."

"You know I can't do that. But I'll let you know as soon as we have an arrest."

"He's dead either way. My way, you're rich."

I saw him now in a new light. I saw a man in

terrible pain, trying to hold it in. It reminded me of my own father before he beat up the driver. I felt pity for him.

"My dad once said that it's OK to feel the anger but don't let your rage take a life. You can't get it back. Let me do my job, and I will give you justice."

He glared at me, gritting his teeth, and nodded slowly. "Your father was a wise man. As I've told you, I am patient, but I want this dealt with." His face softened and he smiled again. "I'm so sorry. I've kept you from mass. Let's go back in, shall we?"

After the service, Karen and I bought pastries; she changed to jeans and a sweater. I flipped through yesterday's newspaper, deciding on whether to do the crossword.

"Hey," she called from the kitchen, "how's Gary doing?"

I sighed. I'd been avoiding the call. "I'll check and find out." I dialed the intensive care desk and identified myself.

The nurse on the phone recognized me; she had worked with Melissa at Northwestern. Gary was improving and asking about his dog, she said. I told her that Dixie was being cared for, and he could rest easier knowing that. She thanked me and hung up. That left the rest of the day to spend with Karen.

"Anywhere you want to go today?" I asked. "Anywhere at all?"

She leaned on the kitchen counter and smiled. "Let's go for a walk."

The phone rang. I jumped, still worried about Gary.

"Hello?" I grinned. "Karen, Ethan has a question for you."

She rushed through and took the phone, smiling. "Yes, sweetheart?" She opened her mouth to speak and closed it, opened it, and closed it again. "Wait, Ethan, wait a second, hon," she interrupted, laughing. "No, we don't have room for a cow. But I'm very happy to hear how much fun you're having, OK?"

I mouthed "Frank" and held up an invisible phone. Karen nodded. "Listen, sweetheart, we'll see you tonight,

then. Can you put Uncle Frank on the phone? Ian needs to
talk to him. Ok, love you too. Bye."

I took the receiver from her, and Frank came on.

"Hey, kid, what's up?"

"Someone stabbed Gary. We dropped by his place
on spec and found him on the floor. He's recovering in
Sunnybrook, though. He'll be fine."

He gave a long sigh. "Do you have a guard on him?"

"Yup."

"OK then. All we can do for now. Lucky timing. By
the way, Ethan is having a blast. You guys should come up
sometime."

"Thanks, Frank. I owe you one."

"On the contrary. He's a treat to be around. Thank
you."

"Good to hear, man. Talk to you after dinner
tonight then."

"See you around seven, Ian."

Ian. Not "kid." Interesting. I hung up and turned to
Karen. She was sipping coffee, reading my paper.

"Everything OK?" she asked.

I gave her a wide hug.

"What was that for?" she asked, beaming up at me.

"Can't a guy hug his girlfriend and tell her he loves
her?"

"Loves her? What brought this on?" She draped her
hands over my shoulders.

"You have a great son. You should be proud of
that." I wrapped my arms around her.

She gave me a long, sad look. "He needs a father,
even more than a house."

I felt very nervous again, very trapped. Karen
looked down bashfully. "I'm sorry. I got carried away. I'm
running off here," she said, her voice a whisper.

I suddenly felt angry. I grabbed her arm. "You
know what? I do love you. I told you that, and I mean it.
But we've known each other for about two weeks. I don't
want either of us making a dumb choice on impulse. That's
not fair to you or to Ethan."

She stared up at me. "I'm still on your short list,

though, right?"

I nodded sternly. "Yeah, you're still in the top three."

She wrapped her arms around me tightly. "Dumbass," she mumbled.

The first warm morning of March was full of promise. By that afternoon, it was almost short-sleeve temperature, miles away from the snow of the past week.

We walked around Grenadier Pond. Ducks and geese, returning from winter in the Carolinas, were still getting used to the cold ground and hard soil. Here and there patches of snow, protected from the sunlight, clung firmly to winter. I looked out at the pond.

"In summer, I come out here and rent a rowboat," I said. "It helps me think."

Karen looked out at the dark water. "Sounds lovely. I've never done that." She looked at her shoes. "Couldn't afford it. Had to think of Ethan."

I imagined myself living with her. "Think he'll like the house?"

She looked up. "Do you really want us to move in with you?"

I stopped, irritated. "Look, we've gone over this before. This is not pity, this is love. For the last time, it's not because I feel sorry for you, it's because I LOVE YOU!"

"So, what you're saying," she replied, seriously, "is that you love me?"

I shook my head. "Glutton for punishment, I am. I tell you, I could do so much better than this."

She bent over and laughed, a giggly, school-girl laugh. "No, you couldn't. No way."

"Now you're getting it." I reached behind her and patted her bum. "Dumbass," I said. She laughed some more.

Even though it was a warm afternoon, spending time in bed seemed like a good idea. Karen announced she needed to pee. She wrapped a sheet around her, shuffled to the bathroom, and sat on the toilet, the door open.

"How should we tell Ethan?" she asked, out of the blue.

"What?"

"About the house. What do we say?" She was looking down as she spoke.

"The truth. I have a house. Show it to him, ask if he'd like to live there."

"That's pretty straightforward. I'm sure he'll say yes." The toilet flushed, and she scuttled back to bed, her skin cool from being out. I wrapped my arms around her and warmed her up.

"There is another problem," I said. "Do you have a driver's license?"

"Sure. Why?"

"We'll be blocks from Mrs. Waleski's. You'd need to drive there."

She sat up, her breasts out in the cold. "But I don't have a car."

"I know. I could get you one."

She squinted at me. "Are you offering to turn me into a kept woman?"

"If you want. Then I could come home for quickies at noon and get rid of the other women on my list."

She poked me in the ribs and smiled.

"I'm just thinking of you," I said. "I can't pick you up and drop you off every day. Your bank has employee parking. It would work out best for everyone, that's all."

She frowned. Maybe I was assuming too much.

"Something wrong with that idea?" I asked.

She slumped onto my chest and caressed my mustache. "Never owned a car, that's all," she said softly.

"Really? Then that makes it special."

"What do you have in mind?" she asked.

"I dunno. Something small, a used Beetle, maybe a Vega or a Pinto?"

"My dad had a Beetle, deep blue." She smiled.

"Can you drive standard?"

"Like Jackie Stewart."

"A Beetle it is, then." I wrapped my arms around her. We ate a light dinner. The phone rang just before seven.

"Hello?" I sang, knowing perfectly well who it was.

"You decent?" Frank's voice came back.

"Depends on your point of view, Frank."

"Well, come pick up Ethan, will you?" He feigned irritation.

At Frank's, Ethan presented his mother with assorted gifts. He had chicken feathers, a corn cob, some straw, and a horseshoe in a paper bag. He also had boxes of eggs, which Helen carefully passed to me.

Karen sat at the kitchen table, Ethan on her lap, talking to Helen. I saw then that moving into the house was a very good idea. Helen and Ethan were holding hands as he talked about the fun he had with Aunt Helen and Uncle Frank. I realized how much I'd taken my own family for granted.

Frank and I went over Gary's stabbing and my conversation with Palumbo. We would talk more at our Monday meeting. "Tomorrow morning, man?" I asked.

"Don't be late."

Ethan was exhausted. It seemed natural to him these last weeks that he slept in his room while his mother and I camped out in his living room. He fell right to sleep. Karen and I had coffee and talked.

Tomorrow was the nineteenth. We agreed we'd show Ethan the house mid-week, and we'd give notice in time for May first, and take April to set up the place like we wanted. Karen curled up in my arms. She dozed off, and I carried her to her bed. I tucked her in and made sure she and Ethan were both sleeping peacefully, then headed back to my place for fresh clothes, my badge, and gun.

I came back quietly. I could hear Ethan breathing softly and Karen sighing as she slept. I laid my clothes out on a chair and settled onto the sofa.

In about six weeks, I would be able to openly share a bedroom with Karen, not behind Ethan's back. Meanwhile, the sofa wasn't half-bad. I was very tired, too.

Six in the morning: I was wide awake. I showered, dressed for work, then made coffee and eggs for Karen. I shook her shoulder gently. She opened an eye and smiled.

"Hey, you," she groaned sleepily.

I placed the mug of coffee on her night table and quietly kissed her good morning.

Ethan was asleep, knees in the air and mouth open. Karen slinked out of bed, pulled on a robe, and joined me in the kitchen. Over eggs, we discussed the best way to tell Ethan about the house and that we'd be sharing a room. We agreed that honesty was the only way to proceed. We would tell him later that day. We took him to Mrs. Waleski's, along with a gift of a dozen fresh eggs. Ethan was full of farm experiences to tell Tommy Waleski.

The day was mild, spring-like, and the smell of growing things was definitely in the air. We walked hand in hand to my car, like love-struck teens. I let Karen in and slid behind the wheel. I turned to face her, only to be attacked by a pair of lips. I pulled back for a breath, many seconds later.

"What was that for?" I gasped.

"Your first thought this morning was for Ethan. That's so sweet."

"Ethan. Ethan. Ethan. Ethan. Ethan. What will that get me?"

"Ask me later."

We got to her office early. "Come on up with me, we have lots of time."

I agreed. I wanted to spend as much time with her as I could. We got an empty elevator car and necked all the way up, pulling apart just as the doors opened. Karen led me to the reception area. The woman with the silky voice looked up at us.

"Good morning, Karen. And Ian, nice to see you again."

I smiled. "I actually just came up to see you."

"Liar," she chided. "But I'll take the compliment, anyway." She swooshed away.

Karen elbowed me. "It takes a lot to get her to smile like that. I'm impressed." Karen vanished, reappearing behind the high counter. She pulled some papers out and placed them on top of it.

"You're selling me life insurance?" I asked.

"That's my job, silly," she said with a giggle. "This is part of the mortgage process."

"I'd have to fill out all this?"

Something on a page caught my attention. Her face dropped. "Oh. I'm so sorry, I forgot." She shook her head. "I wasn't thinking. I'm so sorry," she kept apologizing.

"What do they mean, here?" I pointed.

"Look, I shouldn't have brought these papers out— your mom and all." She reached for them. I stopped her and held my hand up.

"No, I'm talking about police work here. The case I'm working on." I leaned my elbows on the counter. "If I take out an insurance policy and list you as beneficiary, would I have to tell you?"

She shrugged. "No, of course not." She got all business, serious and direct. "If I had a policy and made you beneficiary," she explained, "I wouldn't have to tell you. I could even just pick a name out of the phone book. No law against it."

I nodded. "What if I took out a policy on your life and listed myself as beneficiary?"

Her eyes widened, then she realized why I asked the question. "Oh, I see. If you could get my signature on the policy, sure, then pay the premiums."

"Just like in *Double Indemnity*." I grabbed the forms. "Can I take these?"

"Not trying to kill me, then?" she inquired, smirking.

"Only with love." I kissed her passionately. As I pulled back, I saw the woman with the honey voice in the doorway, mouth open. "You're next, sweetheart." I smiled at them both.

I parked at my usual spot in the police lot, the insurance papers under my arm. Frank was finishing his morning joke.

"So the first guy says, 'Doc says you're going to die.'" The men all laughed.

I slapped the papers on my desk and grinned at

him. "Guess where I've been."

He shrugged. "Horizontal?"

"Yeah, but besides that. I think I know why the Palumbo kid was killed." I handed him a form. "Look at paragraph seven. Accidental death: triple benefits."

He read slowly. "You think that's what happened in Italy?"

"Why else make it look like an accident? Didn't you see *Double Indemnity?*"

He shook his head. I sighed.

"Fred MacMurray, Barbara Stanwyck? C'mon, Frank. It's a classic."

He threw his arms up. "Old movie—whatever. How do we find out if the boy had a policy on him?"

"We ask Maureen Zimmerman."

"Getting closer to those three stripes, kid."

I leaned forward, lowering my tone. "Something else."

He leaned in close, pretending to write something on a pad. "Uh huh?"

"Palumbo was at church yesterday. He knew about the gun in the Impala."

Frank stopped writing and nodded toward Van Hoeke's office. The Captain looked up as we entered, and put his pen down. "Yes?"

Frank sat down. "Two things, Cap. First, Palumbo knew about the gun."

Van Hoeke's eyes widened. "Second?"

Frank showed Van Hoeke my insurance form. "Ian thinks the boy in Italy was killed for an insurance scam."

The Captain leaned back and cradled his head in his hands. "Scam Palumbo? That's taking quite a risk, I'd say."

"It's only a theory. I'll run it down today," I said.

"Good," Van Hoeke said. "Right after the chin wag."

"Also," I added, "why didn't you tell us the bullet from Italy matched our gun?"

Van Hoeke glanced at Frank and sighed. "No harm now. We were checking to see how Palumbo found out.

Now we know."

"How?"

Van Hoeke ignored the question. "Your reports will mention that he knew about the gun, yes? Once you file it, I'll be able to act on that information."

Frank smiled at Van Hoeke. "Martin, you're a devious little weasel. OK, who fries for this?"

Van Hoeke shook his head. "Don't be too quick to judge. You may be surprised where this leads."

The Monday meeting seemed anticlimactic. We reviewed the standard burglaries, accidents, and incidents, took notes, and gave opinions. I did it all on autopilot, not really thinking too much about it. Afterwards, we drove to Maureen Zimmerman's store.

The sales floor had been rearranged, now looking more like a series of conversation pits or room arrangements than rows of furniture. The space was still very dim, shadowy, and, for me, claustrophobic. Various tableaux were lit, but the areas around them were dark, making it look like a series of Gary Frost interview sets.

We looked around for Maureen, but didn't see her. The saleswoman from last week was talking with a customer, offering him fabric swatches. I nodded to her and discreetly stayed back. She smiled in appreciation. After a minute, the customer wandered off. She strutted over to us.

"Hello again," she said warmly. "Can I help you?"

Frank stepped forward. "Hi, is Maureen in today?"

She shook her head. "Not on Mondays. Mondays she works at her father's office."

"How about Mr. Zimmerman? Is he in?"

"Bruno's usually here around ten." She looked at her watch. "Any time now."

We browsed the store, waiting. Five minutes later, light streamed in as someone opened a back door. The sound of hard-soled shoes came closer. From the shadows, we saw Bruno Zimmerman walking in our direction, wearing a sharp blue-black suit and a red silk tie, a leather folio under his arm. He strode straight toward us, outlined by the glow from one of the displays.

"Good morning, may I help—oh, hello, Detective," he said, recognizing me. He shook my hand, a much firmer, warmer handshake than at Palumbo's.

"This is Frank Burghezian. He's coming to dinner this evening," I said, nodding at Frank.

Zimmerman wrinkled his brow. "Anything I can help you with? Furniture, table, chairs?" He smiled impishly.

I gave a plastic smile back. "We have a question for you, about why someone might have wanted to hurt Peter."

He gasped. "But, wasn't that an accident?"

I shook my head. "We don't think so."

He nodded solemnly. "Please, my office." He turned back, through the darkness, and we followed.

We entered a pure white office with an ebony Swedish modern desk sitting on a pure white shag rug. Posters on the wall showed mountains and ski resorts interspersed with advertisements from furniture manufacturers.

Bruno sat behind the desk in a swiveling white plastic egg chair, and we sat in a pair of paperclip chairs. It felt like being in an Ingmar Bergman movie.

"How would anyone benefit from Peter's death?" he asked, puzzled.

"Did anyone have an insurance policy on Peter?" I asked.

He shrugged. "We had them on each other. Maureen on me, me on Maureen, and one on Peter."

"Why so many policies?"

"It meant we would be provided for in case of calamity, that's all."

"Whose idea was that?" Frank frowned.

Zimmerman shrugged again. "Nick Sr. He decided it."

Frank made a note. "Did you approve of the idea?"

Zimmerman smiled. "What Nick wants, Nick gets."

I scratched my ear. "He doesn't like you very much, does he?" I made it sound as conciliatory as I could.

Zimmerman looked at me, calculating something. "I

think Nick wanted Maureen to marry an Italian lawyer. My degree is in Urban Design. That and my nationality bother him."

"The fact that you're German?" I asked, pretending to not know.

"Swiss. I'm Swiss," he corrected.

"I'm sorry," I said. "We've taken up enough of your time. One last quick question." I did my Columbo bit, scratching my head and pretending to think hard. "Did your policies have a . . ." I squinted as I thought, "double indemnity clause?"

"A what?"

"You know, where your policy pays out more for an accidental death?"

"Can't recall, don't think so. I'm pretty sure I'd have noticed that."

We smiled and stood up. "Thanks again for your time," I said, holding out my hand.

Frank shook Zimmerman's hand. "See you this evening. I look forward to seeing you and Maureen."

Zimmerman nodded. "It'll be our pleasure."

I looked at the travel posters by the door. "Whereabouts are you from?" I asked.

He frowned. "Swit-zer-land?" he said slowly, as though I were stupid.

"No. I mean, I've heard the scenery varies a lot from area to area."

"Oh. My family is from Lugano—on Lake Lugano. We went there a couple of times."

"Sounds lovely." I smiled. "Always wanted to see Europe. Thanks again." We walked silently back to the car. I gripped the wheel, thinking.

"You did very well there, kid," Frank said, looking at his notes.

"Thanks. He told me more than he thinks."

"How do you mean?"

"He's from the Italian canton of Switzerland. He could be the guy who the Italian police interviewed."

"Don't you mean *whom*?"

"I was trying to elucidate for you."

"Elucidate?" he snapped, feigning irritation.

I drove out onto Finch Avenue. "Yes, without being obsequious, didactical or expository."

"Now you're just showing off." Frank stared out the window. "But he was in New Jersey when the older boy died. Screw it, let's visit Gary."

Sunnybrook Hospital was a long, low connected series of brown brick buildings, spread out over a number of city blocks, along a wooded ravine. We showed our badges at the front desk and were directed upstairs to the recovery wing. On the third floor, a plump, black woman with a thick Caribbean accent directed us.

A uniformed officer sat in a chair outside Gary's room. He was grateful for the chance to stretch his legs. Frank stood back and let me go into the room alone.

"He's your witness, you talk to him," he said. He took the empty chair.

I nodded and went in. Gary was watching TV. An IV drip in his arm metered saline into him. A heart monitor flashed his pulse, silently drawing squiggly lines on a paper tape. A tray with a half-eaten bowl of oatmeal and a cold cup of coffee sat beside him on the night table.

"Hey, Gary," I said, "how are you feeling?"

He was clearly miserable. "I want to go home. I can't sleep. I don't like the food."

I nodded. "Gary, they saved your life. You barely survived. Despite that, you'll be home in a week. I think that's remarkable."

"Is Dixie OK?" he fretted. "I worry about her."

"She's fine. One of your neighbors has her. Now, do you know who did this to you?"

He looked at me, a pleading look. "They were bad men. They said they were policemen. But they were bad."

I sat back, shocked. "How many men were there, Gary?"

"Two men. They said they were policemen."

"Did they wear uniforms?"

"No."

"They were in plain clothes?"

"Yes."

"What did they look like?"

"I'm not good at people."

"Were they taller than you?"

"The fat one was. The other one was maybe like me, maybe."

"Did they tell you their names?"

He nodded. "The short one said, 'I'm Ian McBriar.' I said, 'No, I know Ian McBriar, I think you are fooling me.' Then he said, 'We need to ask you some questions' and they pushed me."

"Did the other one tell you his name?"

"He said his name was Officer Walter Carpenter."

"What did he ask you?"

"He asked me what I knew. I told him to go away. He said, 'Hold him,' and the big one grabbed my arms. I said, 'Leave me alone,' then the other one got a knife and stabbed me. It hurt a lot. I screamed, real loud, and they said, 'Shut up, stupid.' I fell down. Dixie started barking. I could hear them say, 'Jeez, the dog's crazy, let's go,' and they drove away."

"Did you see their car?"

"No."

"Can you describe the men—hair color, clothes, something?"

"The fat one was a clown."

"A clown?"

"He had curly hair. It wasn't real. I saw that on TV once, on a clown. It wasn't real. The clown on TV took it off. It was a hat." He patted his head.

"You mean it was a wig?"

"Yes, that's the word. A wig."

"What clothes was he wearing?"

"He had a jacket. It looked like mine, but black."

"A golf jacket?"

"I guess."

"How about the other one, not the clown?"

"He had a jacket and pants the same color. Like you."

"He wore a suit?"

"Yes, a suit."

"What color was it?"

"Dark. Dark gray, maybe black."

"Did he have a tie?"

"Yes. It was blue."

I sighed. "Anything else you remember, Gary?"

He smiled with a sudden flash. I got hopeful. "No. Will Karen come to visit me?"

"We can come by to see you tonight, if you like."

He managed a weak grin. "Yes, please."

"OK, save your strength, Gary. See you later."

The conversation had tired him out. He fell asleep. We waited outside Gary's room until the uniform came back from lunch. He hadn't seen anyone suspicious, and, after being there for a couple of days, he recognized most of the doctors by sight.

The squeak of rubber soles on linoleum had us all turn in unison; a volunteer nurse, in a candy striper red-and-white smock and tennis shoes, came up to us. She eyed me with suspicion.

"Can I help you?" she asked, sharply.

"We're interviewing this man," Frank said, showing his warrant card. "Has anyone asked about Gary?"

She shook her head. "His doctor asked me to keep an eye on him, since he's under protection."

"Thanks anyway," Frank said.

She walked down the hall, stopped, and turned back. "Wait. There were two men."

"Who? When?" I asked.

She pointed toward the elevators. "Now. They didn't ask about Gary, but they said they were reporters, at the desk."

I ran back to the elevator area. Frank yelled, "Stay here" at the uniform and followed me. I slammed to a stop against the desk. A doctor was talking to the nurse. I barged in.

"Two men just now—reporters—where did they go?"

The doctor put a hand on his hip and glowered at me. "I was talking," he growled.

I turned to him. "Shut up. The two men—where did they go?"

The nurse, clearly amused, pointed over my shoulder. "They just took the elevator."

I could hear the elevator car heading down. Beside the elevator shaft was a stairwell. I vaulted down the stairs, three at a time, sliding round the landing at the bottom of a run. It took just a minute to get to the main floor, and even less to get out to the parking lot.

Three vehicles were leaving as I ran out the doors: a white Chevy delivery van, a yellow Javelin, and a dirty navy LTD. I couldn't see who was in the vehicles. They were too far away, and I was too far from my car to catch them. They rolled out onto Bayview Avenue, and I lost sight of them.

"Shit," I cursed.

Frank was at the front doors, panting, out of breath. "Anything?"

"Squat," I spat. "Dick all. They got away."

He bent forward, his hands on his knees. "Too old for this crap," he wheezed.

"You should exercise more," I scolded.

"C'mon," he said, taking a deep breath. "I'll buy you lunch."

CHAPTER ELEVEN

We ate at our usual diner. The waitress had no snappy remarks; she read our faces and quietly brought us our food. Frank stared out at traffic.

"Why try to get at him in hospital? It's so stupid, so dangerous," he mumbled.

"Maybe we should ask Helen?" I joked. "She's good at figuring out this crap."

"Not a bad idea," he agreed.

I stared out the window, thinking. "Frank," I started, "what's the date that the older kid died in Italy?"

He pulled out his Moleskine and flipped to a page. "March 22; almost exactly a year ago."

"One of the insurance forms Karen had—it talked about the double indemnity clause."

Frank rolled his eyes. "That old movie thing again."

"It also mentioned that it might take as long as one year to pay out claims." I leaned forward. "If Gary tells us he saw someone trying to kill the younger Palumbo boy, then they might use that to hold up the older boy's claim. If, however, the death were ruled accidental, then they'd have to pay out. Double, if they had a double indemnity clause."

Frank leaned back, thinking. "So, they'll want Gary dead?"

"Or maybe lose half the payout. We still have to find out who benefits."

Frank smiled, satisfied. "I'll ask that tonight, then."

*

At five o'clock on the nose, Karen walked toward me. I rushed up the steps and wrapped an arm around her.

"Hey, you," she said, grinning.

"Guess where we're going," I said, pausing for effect. "We're taking you and Ethan to visit Gary in hospital, then I'm buying you dinner, then we're showing Ethan the house."

She stared, eyes wide open. "Got it all planned out, huh?"

"At least for tonight."

Ethan was fascinated by the hospital. We explained that Gary was feeling very sick, so we wouldn't spend a lot of time with him.

We got out of the elevator and headed toward the recovery wing. The officer at Gary's door had a daughter about Ethan's age; he was eager to have Ethan wait with him while we visited. Karen walked in ahead of me. Gary immediately perked up.

"Hello, Miss Prescott," he said politely. "Nice to see you again."

She put a hand on his arm. "Hello, Gary. I was worried about you."

He grinned. "You were?"

She nodded. "I'm so glad you're improving."

Gary struggled to sit up, but suddenly felt weak and fell back down. Karen patted his arm again.

"Look, Gary, when you feel better I'll come visit you at home again. You can make coffee for me, all right?"

He nodded and smiled. "Yes. I would very much enjoy that, Miss Prescott."

"Call me Karen."

He beamed. "Karen. That's a very pretty name."

"Thank you, Gary." She kissed his forehead. "Take care. I'll see you when you get better." We said our goodbyes and left.

There was a Greek restaurant I liked on Mount Pleasant Road. We ate quietly, tired from the long day. Our table faced the street. We watched people walk home in the mild evening, enjoying the warm air of early spring as they sauntered lazily past us. I felt the sunlight streaming through the window, feeling like a cat on a windowsill. The owner brought us coffee and dessert. I complimented him on the meal. He smiled and turned to Karen.

"And you, Mrs., how's your coffee?"

She gave a wry smile. "It's very good, thank you."

He left, pleased. I stared at Karen.

"Mrs., huh?"

She looked up sheepishly. "It was too complicated to explain."

I smiled, wondering if it might be an omen for the future. "Hey, sport," I said to Ethan. "Want to see something neat?"

Ethan smiled and nodded. Karen stiffened up. "Are you sure?" she asked, an edge to her voice.

"Surer than I've ever been in my life."

We rolled up the driveway to my house. I went ahead, fumbling for the keys. Ethan pulled Karen along as he chased me. I opened the front door, and he broke free, running through the living room to the smaller bedroom in the rear. He squealed with delight and ran back to us.

"Mom! Can this be my room?" He ran again to the bedroom. We followed. "Look! A closet and doors, and a yard and everything." He pressed his nose against the window, twisting his face to look left and right. "There's a garden, and a yard, and a forest and stuff." He recited as he looked out.

Karen looked up at me. "I guess he likes it, huh?"

I crouched down. "Ethan, do you think you would like to live here?"

"Yes," he said firmly.

"OK. But it wouldn't happen for quite a while, because we have to paint the walls and get carpets and stuff, OK?"

He hugged me, then he kissed my cheek. I was overwhelmed. Karen knelt down and smiled. She caressed my cheek.

"You know, I do love you," she said.

My eyes welled up. I was having trouble seeing. I

blinked hard. "Love you, too."

The tour of the backyard was just as much fun for Ethan. The ground had dried out in the last few days, and we plodded around happily, planning flower beds, choosing places for backyard tents and clothes lines. The garage was small; it would hold my Fiat and some tools, little more. Even so, it was usable and solid.

We reluctantly headed back to my place. Ethan watched TV till he got tired. At nine thirty, we picked up his sleeping body and tucked him into my bed. Frank called shortly after that.

"Hey, kid, how's it going?" he slurred.

"Enjoy Palumbo's dinner, Frank?"

"Yup. Good food, too. But man, that grappa really hits the brain hard, you know?"

"Learn anything good?" I heard rustling paper.

"Had to write this in the john before I forgot. Wait a sec." More rustling. "Maureen Zimmerman works for her old man part time. Nice girl, great boobs. Husband's a dick." I heard Helen scold him in the background. "Palumbo put an insurance policy on everybody. Maybe it's the 'evil eye' theory that having a policy on people meant he wouldn't collect on it. Bruno's father was in the insurance business and got them a deal."

"Was it Bruno that really decided on the policies, then?" It seemed logical.

"I thought so, but Palumbo insists it was his idea. Never collected, though."

"Interesting. Any other tidbits?"

"Yeah. His lasagna is definitely not better than yours. And I'm not just saying that for free food, you understand, especially not on Friday when I'll want lasagna again."

I smiled. "I'll keep that in mind. Friday is fine. Is Helen OK?"

He sighed. "Yeah, kid, we're both fine. Thanks. Listen, tell Ethan we send our love, OK?"

I smiled to myself. "Okey-dokey, Uncle Frank."

"Tomorrow morning, nine o'clock."

"Good night, Frank."

I sat on the sofa. The TV was off, the room dark. Karen sat beside me.

"What's wrong?" she asked.

I shook my head. "I'm missing something vital. Palumbo puts an insurance policy on everybody, but doesn't care about the payout. Why bother?"

She leaned back and thought for a moment. "Often, people have to have life insurance to get a loan or a line of credit. That way, if they died, we'd use the insurance to pay outstanding claims."

I thought about that. "So, when Palumbo's daughter started her business, would he have arranged a policy to get a loan?"

She nodded. "Also, at that point, it might be a logical step to just take out a policy on everybody."

I smiled. "You're not just a pretty face, huh?"

I woke up in the living room, feeling that I was falling. I tried to sit up. One leg slipped off the sofa, and I bobbed upright to avoid tumbling onto the floor. The clock on the stove said five fifteen. I rubbed my face, stretched, and made coffee.

Karen and Ethan were fast asleep in my bed. I dressed, strapped on my holster, tucked my badge into my pocket, and woke Karen up. We had breakfast. Karen sat on my knee eating toast. She was smiling a lot this morning.

"What's got you so chipper?" I asked, smiling back.

She kissed my nose. "You, that's all." She straightened her bathrobe.

I took a bite of her toast, and she exaggerated a frown.

"What about me?" I asked.

"You like Ethan, you're nice, kind, handsome . . ."

I tickled her side. "Don't stop, I like the compliments," I teased.

We became aware of movement in the room— Ethan staring at us. "Whatcha doing?" he asked, pajamas dragging under his heels.

"C'mere sport," I said. I sat him on my other knee.

"Want breakfast?"

He nodded eagerly. Karen beamed.

We dressed for the day and dropped Ethan at Mrs. Waleski's. The morning was pleasantly warm. It was sunny, and the few wet patches on lawns and sidewalks were drying before our eyes. Karen wore a short jacket, a black wool skirt that was not quite a mini, and a navy satin blouse. Her high heels made her legs seem a mile long.

I half-wished I could bring her in to my office today, but then everyone would know how she looked in a short skirt—not a good idea, I thought. I drove downtown.

We agreed on dinner and to spending the night at her place, then I walked her to the elevator, kissed her discreetly goodbye, and went back to the car, humming.

At the station house, Frank was telling his morning joke. "So the Pope says, 'But the bad news is, we lost the Wonder Bread account.'"

The men laughed. I sat at my desk. Frank sat on the edge of the desk and smirked.

"Another fun shower?"

I smiled back. "Not today. Any developments in the case?"

He slid down onto a plastic chair. "We checked the papers and TV stations. Nobody sent reporters to see Gary. Must have been the guys who stabbed him. But how did they know out where he was?"

"Fairly simple. There are what, five hospitals he would have been brought to? Ask the admissions desk at those five places, see if anyone was asking about him. I can call around and get the answer in an hour, Frank."

He thought for a second. "Good plan, do that. Afterwards, let's go visit DiNardo again."

I called the other likely hospitals—Northwestern, Branson, Toronto General, Scarborough. Nobody had been approached by two men asking if Gary had been admitted. On a hunch, I called the admissions desk at Sunnybrook.

The woman who answered remembered seeing two suspicious men. She said they asked for the recovery floor specifically, and when questioned, they said, "We're just here to get his story." She thought it was odd at the time, but she soon forgot about it.

I asked her for a description of the men. One was hanging back, so she didn't see him well. The other was very large. She mentioned that part of one thumb was missing.

We drove to DiNardo's warehouse; Frank wanted to barge straight in and ask questions, but I wanted to check out a hunch first. We drove around to the back of the building. Beside a loading dock, half a dozen cars were parked against a chain link fence. One was a dark blue LTD.

"Frank, that's the car I saw leaving the hospital yesterday."

He wrote the license number down. "You sure?"

"Absolutely."

"What made you think of checking the lot?"

"We talk to DiNardo, and someone visits the hospital. Too much of a coincidence."

We parked out front and entered the office. The ashtray had been emptied, and an arrangement of fresh flowers was on the table. The same blonde was sitting at the desk. She looked up.

"Yes?" she said, slight irritation in her voice.

Frank smiled. "Remember us?"

She nodded. "Mr. DiNardo is not in today. I can get him to call you."

I shook my head. "Do you know who owns the dark blue LTD in the back?"

She frowned. "That belongs to Leo, our warehouse manager."

"Leo who?"

"Leo Bernardin."

"Is he available? This will only take a minute of his time." I smiled genially.

She frowned and picked up the phone. "Leo?" She started. "Can you come up front? Two police officers here need to talk to you." She listened, then looked up with a fake smile.

"He'll be out shortly. Please take a seat."

Frank glared at me. I understood the look. I jumped into the Fury and raced around back, just as the driver's door was closing on the LTD. I stopped fast, blocking it from leaving.

The driver got out. It was the large man that we'd seen before with DiNardo. I walked toward him, smiling. He wore a light gray suit, which didn't make him look any smaller. He was a good two inches taller than me, and glaring down angrily.

"Leo?" I asked. "Can you come in for a moment? We need to talk to you."

"You're in my way," he said, his voice a tuba in a tunnel.

"This won't take long," I insisted. "We just need to ask you a couple of questions."

He poked his finger against my chest and pushed for emphasis. "You-are-in-my-way," he snarled.

"And I said we need to ask you some questions. This won't take long."

He turned bright red, gripped my arm, and hauled back to punch me. I grabbed his wrist, stepped back, and flipped him over my hip. He sailed high over me, astonished, and landed in the gravel. I still had his wrist in my hands; I twisted his arm, and he lay on his shoulder, his back arched. I stepped on his throat and pressed down, gently.

"Please come inside," I said with a smile.

He nodded, gritting his teeth. He stood and brushed himself off, watching me warily. "You're real quick," he grunted.

"Thanks. Listen, there's no reason to run. Honest, we just need to talk to you."

He nodded. "Fair enough. I was just worried, you know."

"About what?"

"That you were trying to pin something on me."

I brushed the dust off his jacket. He seemed genuinely surprised at the courtesy. "Thanks, man," he said warmly.

"What happened?" Frank asked, looking at us.

"He slipped in the gravel." I shrugged.

The big man looked at me, astonished that I covered for him. "Yeah," he said. The word filled the room with sound.

Frank turned to the blonde. "Do you have a place where we could talk privately?"

She opened an empty office. Frank got out his Moleskine book, and we handed Leo our cards.

"You went to the hospital where our witness is recovering," I stated. "Why?"

Leo shrugged. "I wanted to find out who did it to him."

"Why?"

"Why do you think? The guy who stabbed him hurt Palumbo's boy."

"He can't identify him," I explained. "He can't recognize people. Part of his handicap."

"Good. Saves me a trip."

"How did you lose the thumb?" I asked.

"Cooking class, chopping celery."

I glared at him. He grinned. "Band saw, in a furniture shop."

I winced. "Ouch. Hurt much?"

"Like a bitch."

"How did you know which hospital to go to?"

"Best trauma ward, figured he'd go there."

Frank stepped in. "Who was at the hospital with you?"

"Chooch."

"Chooch?" Frank repeated.

"Vincent Ciucciaro. Everyone calls him Chooch."

"Is he here?"

"No."

"Where does he work?"

"He's self-employed."

"Doing what?"

"Basket weaving," Leo growled.

"Bullshit," Frank snapped.

Leo shrugged. "Prove me wrong."

"Why did you take off, back at the hospital?" Frank stared at him.

"Chooch hates cops."

Frank stopped writing. "Why do you want the guy who hurt the Palumbo kid?"

"You expect me to answer a stupid question like that?"

"Are you saying he's a wanted man?"

"Let's just say he's on the hit parade."

"Can't let you do that." Frank shook his head. "This guy is ours."

Leo read my card, recognizing my name. "You're that cop—the restaurant robbery."

"Yeah?" I frowned.

"Nice work."

"Thanks. What would you get from whacking the Palumbo boy's assailant?"

He smiled. "Let's say Palumbo and DiNardo get friendly again. Think of the goodwill from finding the person who hurt his family. Brownie points for me. Good news all around."

Frank put his pen down. "All that from killing this guy?"

"I said *finding*."

"So you did," Frank replied.

I nodded. "So what you're saying is that we're both on the same side here."

"For now, yeah."

I shrugged. "Don't do anything dumb without telling us first, OK?"

He raised an eyebrow. "Should I call you for permission or what?"

"I'm just trying to keep you out of jail."

"Appreciate that. OK. No action unless I am sure of the—" he searched for the word, "—ramifications, and then I'll let you know."

The blonde looked up as we returned to the reception area. "Get what you needed?" she asked sharply.

Frank nodded. "Can I ask, what's your relationship with Mr. DiNardo?"

She glowered at him. "None of your effing business!"

He smirked. "I mean, are you a relative of his?"

She blushed slightly. "Oh. Yes. Yes, he's my cousin."

"It's a family business, then?"

She was still seething. "Yes. Anything else?"

"When do you expect him back in the office?"

"Next Tuesday. He's in Las Vegas."

"Gambling?"

"Trade show." She picked up her phone.

Frank handed her a business card. "If you hear anything, please let us know."

We left the building. Frank chuckled to himself. "Cousin, huh?" he snickered. "Yeah, he has a tall blonde cousin called Judith. I bet."

"Pretty eyes," I commented.

"I didn't look that high up," Frank drawled.

The rest of the week flew past. Friday night, Frank and Helen came over for dinner. Frank and Ethan played with Hot Wheels on my living room floor, racing them into cardboard tube tunnels, making *vroom* sounds and squealing tire noises.

Everyone else ate lasagna; I had fish. Once a Catholic, always a Catholic. Helen and Karen talked in low whispers and giggled in our direction, then hugged goodbye like old friends at the end of the evening.

On Sunday, I went to church alone. None of the Palumbo family was there, and I was relieved to not think about work for an hour. Afterwards, we walked Ethan through High Park and fed seagulls at Lake Ontario. The waves, pounding in to shore on the brisk wind, reminded me of the beach scene with Burt Lancaster and Deborah Kerr in *From Here to Eternity*. We had a quiet dinner and watched TV till bedtime.

Monday morning, I sleepwalked through the detectives' meeting. I called a list of tradesmen and arranged for the house to be ready by mid-April. Frank sat on my desk.

"Thinking about Gary," he said.

"Uh huh?"

"How many people would you tell if you were hurting Palumbo's kids?"

I shrugged.

"You are whacking a wise guy's family," he reiterated. "How many people do you tell?"

"As few as possible?" I offered.

"Right, you'd use the same gang for both jobs. Our 'Walter Carpenter' was in Italy, as well as at Gary's. He stole the Impala twice; he crossed the border to get a Connecticut driver's license and his U.S. passport. He's the key to this mess."

I agreed. "Yes, if it's all the same guy. Let's ask Gary more questions."

The uniform at Sunnybrook was flirting with a nurse outside Gary's room, caressing her arm as she smiled bashfully. We flashed our warrant cards; he nodded and kept talking. Gary was sitting up, devouring a rice pudding.

"Hey, Gary," I said. "The food's improved, has it?"

He nodded. "I love rice pudding. I never had it before. I want it all the time now." He scraped the sides of the plastic bowl and licked his spoon.

Frank squatted and pulled out the Connecticut license photograph. "Gary, did this man come to your house?"

Gary looked at the picture. "He said his name was Walter Carpenter."

"Are you sure?"

"Yes, he said, 'I'm Officer Walter Carpenter, we have some questions for you.'"

Frank sighed. "The one who said he was Ian—was he the one who hurt the boy on the railroad tracks?"

"Maybe, could be."

"Would you recognize him again?"

"I don't know."

Frank sighed, frustrated. We left.

Back at the station, Van Hoeke motioned us to his

office and closed the door. He picked up his phone and dialed a number. "Can you come here for a sec? Thanks."

Van Hoeke picked up our activity report. I noticed an underlined paragraph, mentioning that Palumbo knew about the gun. A moment later, Parker came in.

"Captain?" he asked, clearly puzzled.

Van Hoeke smiled sweetly. "We were discussing loss. You recently lost someone close, didn't you?"

Parker nodded. "Yeah, my sister-in-law."

Van Hoeke leaned forward. "What was her name?"

"Regina."

The smile faded. "Regina what?"

"Regina Fitzpatrick."

Van Hoeke leaned back. "What was her *married* name?"

Parker got nervous. "Captain, I just, you know."

Van Hoeke glared at him. "Regina Palumbo?"

Frank gasped. "You! You told him! You little shit!"

Parker shook his head, scared. "No, no. All I did was talk to my mother-in-law. Guys, she's lost a daughter and a grandson. She's an old lady, she's mourning for the second time in three years. I only told her we'd get to the bottom of it. That's all. Honest."

Van Hoeke held his hand up, and Parker stopped talking. "You told her about the Italian police report, the gun we found, and our witness in hospital. That's wrong, Terry."

Parker shrank back; Frank looked ready to punch him.

Van Hoeke said slowly, "You've got some vacation time, Terry. Take a couple of weeks. Paint the basement. Visit your folks in Halifax." He scowled. "Clear your head."

Parker sat up, indignant. "Is this an official reprimand?"

Van Hoeke's eyes opened wide. "A reprimand for what? It's a vacation."

Frank still looked like he might kill. Parker looked at him and shrank. "I'll leave next week."

Van Hoeke sneered. "Use the rest of this week to pack. Don't come back in."

Parker opened his mouth, silently closed it, and left. Frank turned to the Captain.

"How did you know?"

Van Hoeke waved at the door. "Discounting you two, I only had to look through fourteen records to find a link. I wasn't always just a desk jockey, you know." He turned to me. "The show's over. Go back to work."

Frank sat in a window seat at the diner, watching the traffic as we waited for our food. I tried to cheer him up. "Leafs are playing the Wings tomorrow. You going?"

He grunted. "They'll lose. Four-game slump already, they'll lose."

I shrugged. "Maybe. Still a good game, though." I sighed. "What does Chooch look like?"

He sat up. "What?"

"What does he look like? We never asked Leo."

He leaned back. "No, we didn't. Pay phone." He dug through his pockets, bringing out a handful of change, then headed for the phone in the corner.

He dialed, reading the number as he did. He talked animatedly, nodded, and wrote. A man walked up, motioning for Frank to hurry. Frank whispered, "Go away." The man tapped his watch. Frank pulled out his badge. The man slinked off. Sixty seconds later, Frank rushed back and sat down hard.

"Big blonde gal—Judith—says Leo didn't come in or call this morning. Extremely odd; he's always very punctual. She's worried."

"Do we know where he lives?"

Frank waved his book. "Got it here. I also asked her about Chooch. She described a big guy with curly hair, like a clown wig."

"Holy shit."

"Rain check on lunch," Frank said. "Let's go." We left a ten-dollar bill and our apologies and ran out the door.

Judith said that Leo lived on Roseneath Gardens, in the heart of Little Italy, close to the stores and restaurants a short walk away on St. Clair Avenue. The house was a brick story-and-a-half. It was neat, the trim painted, the windows clean, the side driveway swept—the house of someone who didn't want to stand out.

The side kitchen door, facing the driveway, had pale curtains for privacy. There was even an empty flower box under the kitchen window, waiting for spring. The navy blue LTD sat at the bottom of the driveway. We approached it slowly and peered into the car. No slumped body, no blood stains, no messy papers or anything.

I relaxed; it seemed we were needlessly worried. Frank marched up the stairs and knocked on the front door. It creaked open a few inches and stopped. He gestured at the side door. I ran past the LTD and squatted under the flower box, hidden from anyone who might be looking out.

"Ian!" Frank bellowed out, regret clear in his voice.

I sighed. I knew why he yelled. I sauntered up the front porch and joined him.

Leo was on his back, one leg comically over a coffee table, staring at the ceiling. Three bullet holes in his white cotton shirt were framed in dried blood. His mouth was open, as if he wanted to tell us what happened.

I touched his wrist; it was stone cold. Frank picked up the phone with a handkerchief and called for the meat wagon. One coffee cup sat on the kitchen counter, one glass in the dish tray, six eggs in the fridge, a small box of Cheerios on a shelf. It shouted that he lived alone.

One bedroom had a plain double bed and dresser, with a crucifix over the headboard. The other one was set up as an office: papers neatly stacked on a desk, an Olivetti typewriter and pens in a cup completing the arrangement.

The living room had a small loveseat and chair facing the TV, with a telephone table beside the chair. Coffee rings, a TV guide, and bread crumbs on the telephone table confirmed the story of someone who ate alone, watching TV.

We searched the rest of the house, guns drawn in case we had unwanted company. There were no signs of forced entry, no scuff marks on the floor from a fight—

nothing. It seemed he'd just opened the door, backed up, and been shot.

Two cruisers showed up, and we canvassed the street as we waited for the meat wagon. Frank paced the sidewalk. A small crowd had formed, ogling the open front door as if something interesting might happen, while two uniforms kept them behind sawhorses. Frank asked if anyone had seen anything. All heads shook no.

The coroner showed up; he and Frank spoke in hushed voices. Frank came out a minute later.

"Well, he's officially dead."

"Do tell," I grunted.

"Yeah, but now it's official."

I looked up at the house. "Funny that this happened when DiNardo was out of town."

"You think he arranged this?"

"I doubt it. Maybe he had to be out of the way before someone dared do this."

Frank shrugged. "Either-or. Let's talk to Blondie Big Rockets."

"Any excuse, huh?"

We broke the news to Judith. She cried into a Kleenex, wiping her eyes and sniffling. Frank spoke calmly, trying to comfort her, all the while looking down her blouse. She was far too upset to notice. Frank had only told her that Leo died suddenly. She looked up, red-eyed and coughing.

"What happened? How did he die?" she moaned.

Frank spoke gently. "I'm afraid we suspect foul play. I can't tell you any more than that."

She sniffled. "He was a nice guy. Everybody liked him. Who would do such a thing?"

Frank brought out his Moleskine and pen. "Anyone you can think had a grudge against him—arguments, anything?"

She shook her head.

"Any staff fired recently, any jealous husbands or boyfriends?"

"He wasn't like that. He was a very nice man, despite how he seemed to you."

Frank nodded. "Did you and he have something going on?"

She glared at him. "Oh, please. Is that all you can think of?"

Frank took a deep breath. "Look, we need to ask the questions. If you think of anything, call me." We left; she was still crying.

Staff wandered up from the warehouse, curious. She told them what she knew; some gasped and covered their mouths; others shook their heads in disbelief.

"Funny," I said. "I never thought of him as a working stiff. Pardon the pun."

Frank finished writing.

"Something interesting?" I asked.

"Yes," he said. "Judith has freckles in her cleavage."

We headed back to the station. Death means paperwork.

"Frank," I asked, "do we know for sure this death is related to the Palumbo case?"

He looked up. "Go on."

"Maybe it's a coincidence. Maybe he was involved in stuff we don't know about. Was he killed because of the Palumbo kids, or something else?"

Frank shook his head. "It has to point back to Palumbo. Maybe he figured out who killed the older kid."

"You don't think he was our gun guy?"

"Not the type—not a nickel nine mil guy. Maybe a forty-five, or a revolver, but not a nickel nine."

"Nickel nine," I huffed. "Sounds like a candy bar." We joked to diffuse the emotions we felt at seeing death again. It only worked if neither of us said we were doing it.

Frank leaned back. "Do we know what the Walter Carpenter in the passport looks like?"

I shook my head. "We can get a photo from U.S. Immigration. It could take time, though."

"Let's do that."

It was another real spring day; the smell of growing things was in the air, birds were in the trees, and the afternoon sun was warm enough that I turned off the heat in the Fury and opened the window.

Comparing notes, we had both collected the same statements from everybody in the street. Nice guy, no trouble, gave away tomatoes, helped shovel snow. No noises, no parties, no cars blocking driveways, nothing. He just blended in with the neighborhood. I dropped Frank home and drove downtown to pick up Karen.

She walked up, smiling, then slowed as she saw my face. "What's wrong?" she asked.

"Bad afternoon," I told her. "A witness killed in his house."

"How awful. Anyone you knew?"

"I met him last week. He seemed OK."

She grabbed my jacket and kissed me passionately.

"What was that for?" I asked weakly.

"For being you."

I smiled, if a little feebly. "I want to show you something this evening."

Her eyes widened. "Another house?"

"No, just a toy."

I drove Karen home and asked her to be downstairs with Ethan in fifteen minutes. I parked the Fury and uncovered my summer car. The Fiat's motor roared to life, filling the garage with noise. I tossed the canvas cover in the corner and drove back to Karen's. Ethan came down the front stairs holding her hand. As I pulled up he squealed like a dolphin.

"It's a racing car!" he shouted. Karen smiled, cautiously stroking a beige fender.

I lifted Ethan into the back seat. It was too small for most adults, but just right for a four-year-old. He rested his arm on the folded top. Karen sat beside me, inspecting the red vinyl seats and the Italian gauges. She looked back often to make sure Ethan was sitting securely.

"Is this thing safe?" she asked.

"Define safe. Life isn't safe," I said morosely. I fired up the engine, gunned it for effect and took off, squealing the tires down Rogers Road then left up Silverthorn. I revved high, snaked around bends in the road, shifted through the gears like a race driver, and waved at pedestrians.

Ethan made engine noises. We drove till the chill in the evening air forced us to stop. I took us to some burger place for dinner, sat where we could watch the car through the window, then headed home and parked it reluctantly. For a brief time, I hadn't thought about Leo.

Ethan, in the driver's seat, pretended to drive, making engine noises with his lips. The *ting-ting* sounds as the motor cooled down added to the effect. We covered the car up again; Ethan caressed the canvas and the vehicle under it. I just wanted to forget the day.

Frank called a little before nine. "Kid, we got news. A late wire photo from the passport office. Guess who Walter Carpenter is?"

I grunted.

"Right. The big guy with the wig. And tell Ethan good night from Uncle Frank."

"Good night, Frank."

I walk into my house. The furniture is all set up. The stove hisses, gas escapes dangerously from the burners, but no flame is visible.

In the living room, the TV is on but the screen shows only static. I reach to turn it off, but a deep basso profundo voice grumbles, "Please don't, man, I'm watching."

In an armchair, which was not there a moment ago, sits Leo Bernardin, eating a bowl of Cheerios. The bullet holes in his chest bleed into his cereal. I move aside so he can watch the hissing TV.

"Thanks, man." His bloody teeth are glinting. He repeats it. "Thanks."

Four a.m. Karen was asleep beside me. Ethan was in my tent. I had to check that nobody was in the chair beside him. I lifted the tent flap. Ethan snoozed peacefully. There was nobody in the chair. I crawled back into bed and wrapped my arm around Karen.

She whispered, "Another bad dream?"

"Uh-huh."

"Are you OK?"

I squeezed her closer. "I am now."

She rolled over and wrapped her arms around my neck. "How's this?"

"Pretty damn good."

"*Shh*," she said. I fell back to sleep.

Six o'clock. I dressed and made coffee. Karen came through in my robe. "Hey, you."

I hooked a finger in the vee where the robe crossed her chest, and kissed her good morning.

"Good morning to you too, chatty," she said.

"Did I talk in my sleep?"

She shook her head. "You did make noises, though. You were grunting."

I shrugged. "Leo—the dead guy. I was thinking about him." I took a sip of coffee. The morning sunlight forced its way through clouds, warming the room and reflecting the wet sink onto the ceiling.

Karen grabbed the cup out of my hand and took a slurp. "Does that bother you?"

I nodded. "He was looking for the Palumbo boy's attacker. I think he died because he got too close, but nobody seems to know for sure."

The sun climbed slowly higher, the light through the window moving down toward the floor, and the color of the light changed from golden to yellow to white.

Ethan was fixated on my Fiat, and asked when we could ride in it again. Karen explained that it was only practical when the weather was good. Besides, it didn't have a siren or flashing lights. Ethan was insistent. I promised that if the weekend was mild, we'd go for a long drive in the country. That was good enough for him. He drew convertibles on scrap paper until we dropped him off at Mrs. Waleski's.

I thought about Leo as I drove downtown. There was no reason to kill him unless he knew something. Karen stared at me the whole time, but I only noticed at a red light.

"So, you remember I'm here, right?"

I shook my head. "I'm sorry, sweetheart. I was working."

She pulled me closer. "I know. You told me—that's what you do."

"I assume you'll keep this to yourself? It might get messy if anything got out."

She scratched my shoulder. "Sure, but after it's over can I tell my co-workers?"

"Much as you want."

"Including how excited you get when I wear your bathrobe?" she grinned.

"Now you're just trying to make me feel better."

"Is it working?"

"You bet."

She sighed. "You really put your heart into this job, don't you?"

"Yeah, I guess you're right," I agreed. "Someone has to speak for the dead. They deserve a voice."

We parked. She got out and held up spread fingers. Traffic almost drowned her out. "Five p.m.?" She walked away, swinging her hips provocatively.

Frank was at his desk, reading a sheet of paper. I bounced in, humming to myself. He looked up and raised an eyebrow. "Happy start to the morning?"

"Feeling good, that's all."

There was a stack of papers on my desk, in a folder marked *Leo Bernardin*. The coroner said that Leo had died quickly, the night before we found him. He hadn't fought back, and he had soiled himself at the moment of death—fairly common. The slugs in his chest were thirty-eight caliber, fired from about five feet away.

He had been standing when he was shot, and the angle of the bullets suggested a killer around five foot nine. Frank read the report over my shoulder. I handed him the page I was holding.

"What do you think?" I asked.

He shrugged. "The report is pretty cut-and-dry, but why would you let someone in to shoot you? Even someone as big as Leo?"

I had an idea. "One sec," I said. I walked into Van Hoeke's office. A small coffee table sat to one side of his desk. I borrowed it, then set it by my desk, at the distance Leo's coffee table was from his sofa.

Frank watched, amused. The other detectives gathered around, curious. Van Hoeke came out to see, too.

"OK," I said. "I'm six two, you're—"

"Watch it," Frank warned.

"—say five eight. Roughly the same as Leo and his killer."

"Fair enough."

I handed him a pencil. "You have a gun." I stood in front of the coffee table. "I let you in. You pull out your gun and shoot me."

Frank went *bang-bang-bang* and poked the eraser at me. I collapsed theatrically, one leg draped over the table, just like Leo. Frank shrugged. "Yeah, so what, Shakespeare?"

"OK, now, let's pretend I don't know or don't trust you." I took my place in front of the coffee table again, and raised my hands. "Wait, Bob, don't shoot. Think of the kids . . . I have your money . . . There's a spider behind you . . . I dated your sister . . ." The men chuckled. As I spoke, I backed slowly away.

Frank lowered the pencil. "Yeah, so?"

I pointed down. "I got the table between us—a natural reaction to a threat. Leo never did. It was someone he knew, someone he didn't fear."

Frank stared at the table. "Really. Shit."

Van Hoeke looked between us. "Any idea who that could be?"

"Walter Carpenter?" I suggested. "I don't know. Whoever shot him, I think he's the man Leo went with to see Gary. That's our only lead so far."

Van Hoeke nodded. "Check it out. You run with this one, Ian, as part of your Sergeant's test."

"Got it, Captain. Thanks."

CHAPTER TWELVE

"Pretty pleased with yourself, huh, kid?" Frank smirked as we drove. "Captain Hook figures you're Sergeant material."

"I worked hard for this, Frank," I said. "I want those stripes."

"I agree." Then he chuckled. "You'll need the pay hike to keep Karen and Ethan in the style you're accustoming them to."

I grinned—he didn't see it. I quickly put on a frown. "About that, Frank. I'm moving."

His head swiveled. "What? Where?" There was real panic in his voice.

"About three blocks from your place."

He settled back in the seat. "Nice. Find a bigger place?"

"I bought a house." I held my expression, but I was giggling inside.

He stared at me for a long time. "You're shitting me."

"Why?" I asked, playing dumb.

"You're pretty set on this girl, huh?"

I chuckled. "Sorry, Frank, I couldn't help it."

"What?"

"I own the house. I had a tenant till last month, but I decided to move in myself, since I have Karen and Ethan now."

"Nice," he said approvingly. "Can I see this place after we check on Gary?"

"I'd be proud to show it to you, Frank."

He looked down at his Moleskine book, thinking, then back up at me. "You said you were 'moving' just to pull my chain, right?"

I snickered.

"Asshole," he grumbled.

The constable on duty nodded and returned to his newspaper. Gary was watching TV.

"Hello, Detective. I'm glad to see you."

I patted his shoulder. "Hey, Gary. How are you doing?"

"I like this food. The nurses are nice, too." He pointed to the TV at the end of his bed. "I aligned the tuner. It wasn't picking up channel six."

Frank leaned forward. "Gary, do you remember me?"

"Detective Sergeant Frank Burghezian. I remember."

Frank pulled out a glossy picture. "Gary, do you remember this man?"

Gary stared at the photo. "He said his name was Walter Carpenter. He's a bad man, isn't he?"

"Yes, Gary. He's a bad man." Frank leaned forward. "Gary, the man who said he was Ian McBriar. Do you remember anything about him?"

Gary shrugged. "I don't think so. His car was loud. That's all."

I leaned forward. "You said you didn't see the car, Gary."

"No, I just heard it."

"Can you tell me what it sounded like?"

"It was a big V8, probably a 350 or a 396, dual exhaust, and it had a hole in one muffler."

Frank sighed and rubbed his face, dumbfounded. "Left or right muffler?"

Gary still didn't understand Frank's humor. "I couldn't tell."

"Anything else you remember?" Frank asked.

Gary shook his head.

I smiled. "You will probably be home soon, OK? Get some rest."

"Yes. Thank you, Ian."

"After you go home, I'll come by with Karen, to say hello." He beamed, and we headed for the elevator. "Do you think he can go back to a normal life?" I asked.

"Whatever he considers normal, yeah," Frank said.

Frank still wanted to see my house. He walked ahead, waiting patiently while I unlocked the door. He stood in the hallway, turning his head between the kitchen on one side and the living room on the other, hands on his hips.

"This is nice, kid, real nice. I hope you'll be happy here. What does Karen think?"

I told him about her kicking my ankles. He grinned. I didn't tell him about how I carried her downstairs.

Back at the station, I was greeted by a slip of pink paper, propped up in front of my stapler. I read it and passed it to Frank. "Seems DiNardo wants to talk to me."

"*I must speak with you today*," Frank read. "Sounds definite. Let's go."

Judith was at her desk as we came in. She was expecting us, but she looked about ready to faint. "Please go on through," she said meekly.

We knocked at DiNardo's office door and sat down. Frank pulled out his Moleskine, looked at me, and raised his eyebrows. I would lead. DiNardo sat, clutching his Zippo lighter, glaring at us.

"Mr. DiNardo," I started. "It appears that Leo Bernardin was the victim of foul play."

He gave me the look a crocodile gives a slow chicken. "Yeah. Tell me something I don't know."

"Did Leo have any enemies?"

"Leo was a good man. He never did *anything* to deserve this," he thundered. "No. No enemies I know of."

"Did he own a gun?" I asked.

"Didn't like them."

"Was he married?"

"His wife left years ago—moved back to Montreal. He lived alone."

"Sorry to hear that."

"He got over it. He was fine."

"Is there anyone we should notify? Friends, family?"

DiNardo looked down at his knuckles. "I will contact everyone that needs to be told."

"Do you know a Vincent Ciucciaro?"

"No. I know the name, but I never met him." He tilted his head slightly. "Is he involved in this?"

I shook my head. "We're just following up with any contacts Leo knew." I hoped he wouldn't see through the lie. I looked around the office. "It must have been hard, building up all this." I waved my hand at the displays filled with olive oil, cheeses, jars of vegetables and tomatoes.

He nodded. "Leo made this happen." He played with his lighter again. "He made this place run. Everybody liked working with him. He was good to the guys in the back, he made sure nobody goofed off, made sure they didn't steal. They respected him, and they worked hard for him." His eyes got moist.

"You asked to see me today," I said.

He leaned forward, gesturing with the flint side of the Zippo. "When you get the guy who did this, and I'm sure you will, I want to hear about it first. It will be very much worth your while."

I smiled involuntarily.

"What?" he asked.

"You're not the first person who's asked me that."

"Nick asked you the same thing." He paused. "And you told him no?"

"Believe me," I said, "I know how you feel."

"You lost someone close to you?" He pointed the Zippo again. "A parent. That's why you became a cop."

I shook my head. "You and Palumbo—I'd hate trying to lie to you."

He glanced at Frank. "Your Sergeant is letting you talk. I suspect neither of you can be persuaded."

"Why would you think otherwise?" Frank asked.

DiNardo gave a resigned smile. "You will let me know when this man is apprehended?" He stood up. "Thank you for coming. I appreciate the courtesy." He stuck a large arm out. We shook hands and walked back to the reception area.

Judith was still at her desk, morosely sipping tea from a glass mug. She looked up as we approached.

I smiled sympathetically. "I'm sorry again about Leo. He worked here a long time, I guess."

She nodded. "Good guy. He taught me a lot about this." She waved at the walls.

"How did you get this job?" I asked politely.

She looked me over, calculating. "I know what some people think. Tom treats me with respect. I'm family."

"You're his cousin, right?"

She sighed. She'd explained this before. "Tom's family is from Milan. My family is from Como, near Milan."

I wrinkled my forehead. "Judith?"

She shrugged. "Giuditta. Try getting Canadians to spell that. I just say Judith."

"Was Leo from Milan as well?"

"Yeah, he knew the family. He came to Canada as a woodworker, but he lost his thumb. So he started working for Tom, because he knew Tom's family. He was a decent guy, a great big teddy bear." She started to cry. I felt sorry for her, but I kept going.

"Do you know a Vincent Ciucciaro?" I asked.

"He sometimes called Leo. I've only seen him once, in Leo's car."

Frank pulled out the passport photo.

She nodded. "Yeah, that sort of looks like him."

"Any idea where we can find him?"

"Leo knows where." She sighed. "Only Leo knew where to find him."

"Mr. DiNardo wouldn't know?" Frank was double-checking, just in case.

She shook her head. "Once, he needed Chooch for

some work; Leo called him."

"What work?" I asked, curious.

"An employee's daughter ran off. Joined the Krishnas or something. Chooch found her." She leaned back, stretched, and rubbed her eyes. "I'm really busy; sorry, I have to arrange a funeral." She stood up, brushed her skirt, and headed to the back, all composed, strictly business. "Do you mind seeing yourselves out?" she called over her shoulder.

Frank watched her go, his head tilting as he watched her hips sway.

"What do you think?" I asked.

"I think her boobs *really* stick out when she leans back," he said, still following her.

"What about what she said?"

"She spoke?"

"You're a pig, Frank."

"What, you haven't ogled other women?"

I decided not to fight that fight. "Guilty."

We walked out to the car. A thought occurred to me. "Did we check if Vincent Ciucciaro has a driver's license?" I asked.

Frank slapped his forehead. "No, damn it, we didn't." He spoke quickly to the dispatcher, spelling "Ciucciaro" twice. He wrote down the information and hung the mike up, smiling. "Dundas East and Kingston Road."

"Other end of town."

The address we had for Chooch was in Scarborough, an east end copy of Leo's neighborhood. It too was on a quiet street, down the block from a church.

The house was an up-and-down duplex; Chooch lived on the upper floor. An outside staircase led to his floor; the lower floor was occupied by an old couple. They were sweeping the front steps and stopped to talk when we showed our badges.

They spoke little English, but when I said "Vincent Ciucciaro," they nodded at the stairs then waved down the road, indicating he had left. We asked when they'd seen him last. They spoke to each other quickly and agreed it was on Sunday—the day Leo had been killed. He lived alone, they said, nobody else home. We asked if Chooch had a car. They motioned to the garage door. Frank opened it and smiled. A shiny, dark green trunk reflected our faces.

"Look," he purred, "a Chevelle." He looked at a badge above the bumper. "SS 396." He knelt down. "Dual exhaust, hole in the left muffler. This is the car they drove to Gary's."

I opened the driver door. The interior was pristine, the glass and the dash were clean, and the carpets spotless, just like the Impala we found at the cemetery.

On a hunch, I walked back down the driveway, checking the pavement. Halfway along was a pool of liquid in a deep crack. I poked it with my pencil. The recent rain had diluted it, but I recognized the color.

"Frank," I called, "same antifreeze we saw in Wally's garage."

He nodded, mentally reconstructing events. "They parked the Impala here, drove it to Gary's, and chased the young kids." Frank looked up at the house. "Is he coming back, do you think?"

I shrugged. "He wouldn't just leave the Chevelle. He takes good care of it. He wouldn't just leave it. But he didn't hurt the younger kid. Gary described someone else who hurt the kid."

Frank looked up the stairs. "Let's check his place out." He sprinted up the steps and stopped at the top landing. I followed, trying not to stumble over him.

We looked through a small window in the door. The hallway was dim, with doors on either side that opened to darkened rooms. Frank turned to me with a serious expression.

"Do you smell gas? I smell gas. We should investigate."

I rolled my eyes at the old excuse for an illegal entry. He pulled a plastic Eaton's credit card from his wallet and slid it into the door jamb. The door swung open, creaking softly. He sniffed the air.

"Gee, no gas. I guess I was wrong." He grinned and

drew his revolver. He stepped into the hall and pointed his gun down, walking lightly. As he approached the first open door, he stopped short and peeked around the corner to be sure the room was empty. We checked everywhere. Nothing seemed out of place.

Frank got out his handkerchief to pull open drawers, lifting things with his pencil. He opened a shoe box and stood back.

"Kid, come here."

Inside the box I saw a revolver and a box of bullets. Frank poked his pencil into the barrel and lifted the gun up. He sniffed the barrel.

"Colt Detective Special, fired recently." He shook his head. "Thirty eight, same as killed Leo." He put the gun back.

If Chooch returned, we would arrest him with the gun in his possession. That would make conviction easier. We went through the apartment again, carefully.

Apparently, Chooch also lived alone. The food in the kitchen, like at Leo's, suggested a single person. In the living room, a big old TV/stereo console had a record on the turntable. I read the label.

"Handel's *Water Music*; he likes Chevys and classical music, huh?"

Frank shrugged. "You like Fiats and jazz."

We checked the bathroom and the bedroom. A double bed sat against one wall, a crucifix and a plaster Madonna over the doorway on the opposite wall. Just like at Leo's.

I thought we might be wrong about him living alone. There was a Styrofoam head on the dresser—Karen had one to hold hats. Maybe he had a wife. I looked closely at the dresser; a small number of curly brown fibers were scattered under the head. Frank joined me.

"He's bald," I said. "That's why he wears the clown wig."

"Nice work, kid. Let's arrange a welcoming committee."

We could get an unmarked Dart parked down the street, but not till five o'clock. I suggested lunch at a health-food place I knew. I ordered for us both. The restaurant faced a playground across the street, and children from a nearby school were playing on the swings. I imagined Ethan in a couple of years, going to school.

Frank squinted at the sky over Lake Ontario. Clouds sailed slowly in to shore, darkening as they approached.

"Looks like rain," he muttered.

The waitress brought us our food and nodded, recognizing me. Frank stared at his plate.

"What is this shit?" he moaned.

"It's vegetarian chili, Frank. You'll like it."

He winced. "It looks like grass cuttings. You eat this, huh?"

I started in on mine, enjoying the tofu and tomatoes. Frank took a spoonful, like a child tasting bad medicine, then he raised his eyebrows.

"This is good," he exclaimed. "Real good."

I talked him into trying organic apple pie. He liked it, too. Frank complimented the waitress and left a big tip. She was puzzled, but thanked him.

"Damn, I'm going to bring Helen," he said. "Don't think she's ever had hippie food."

We walked a while, strolling past the children. Frank stopped for a moment, watched them play, then moved on. He had his head down, thoughtful.

"You ever think about kids?" he asked.

"A brother or sister for Ethan? Yeah, I've thought a lot about it."

"Big step. You ready for it?"

"We'll talk about it when the time's right. We're still getting used to each other. We're not stable like you and Helen."

"Stable," he snickered. "She's a lot of things, but stable isn't one of them." He smirked, embarrassed by the admission. He exhaled. "She can be a huge pain in the ass. Honestly, I'd take a bullet for her and grin, but there are times I could happily join the Foreign Legion."

I smiled. "There's a term for that: normal."

"Thanks, kid," Frank chuckled. "I needed that." Frank went back to the restaurant and bought some apple pie to take home. He cradled it under his arm as we drove back to the station.

We told the Captain about Ciucciaro's apartment. He agreed we should arrest him with the gun in his possession. The ghost car would be there soon. Nothing to do now but wait. I dropped Frank off at home.

Just after four, I called Karen and offered to bring Ethan when I picked her up. She thought that was a great idea; she would leave a little early. Ethan was happy to come with me. We walked to the Fury, racing the coming rain, talking about his day and what he wanted to do when he grew up.

He loved the farm and said he wanted to be an animal doctor. I told him the name for that was a veterinarian; most people called them vets. He asked if Uncle Frank was an animal doctor, because he was a vet. I pointed out the different meanings of the word. He didn't understand.

I smiled through the elevator ride, trying not to let my panic show. Ethan clutched a Hot Wheels car, looking around at this exciting new place. Karen met us at the high counter, and I lifted Ethan over it to her side.

She'd never been able to bring him to work before. She paraded him proudly through the office. I could hear her introducing him to coworkers. Ten minutes later, they appeared beside me, ready to leave. She held Ethan in front of her on the elevator, one hand around his chest, her other hand pulling me close.

"Thanks for bringing him. It meant a lot to be able to show him off."

"Glad I could help. What would you two like for dinner?"

She bent down and kissed the top of Ethan's head. What do you want to eat, champ?"

He tilted his face up. "Sandwich and soup; Tommy says that's his favorite."

I smiled. "What do you think, Mom?"

Karen smiled at "Mom." "I agree. We can watch TV

till bedtime. OK by you, Dad?" She gazed softly up at me.

"Wonderful," I mumbled.

We ran through the light rain to the car, lifting Ethan, skipping his toes lightly over puddles as he laughed with glee. The rain became a downpour. I ran the last ten yards and opened the door, letting Ethan climb in on his own, and waited patiently as Karen slid in beside him before I walked around and unlocked my door. The deluge got heavier still. I drove gingerly as oncoming cars splashed my windshield, momentarily blinding me.

By the time we got to my place, the rain had lessened. The police radio was now just noise in the background that I listened to with one ear. One message caught me. The dispatcher repeated it.

"Fifty-two four-eight, this is dispatch."

I grabbed the mike as I pulled into my garage. "Four-eight, go dispatch."

The female voice sounded tired. "Four-eight, contact Sergeant Burghezian at home first possible."

"Four-eight, roger." We went upstairs. Karen took Ethan's wet coat and slipped her shoes off. I went to the phone. "Frank, you called?"

His voice sounded worried. "Big news, kid. Chooch came back."

"So we got him?"

He grunted. "Yeah. I mean, no. He came back early. He took the Chevelle and the gun. He's gone."

"Any chance DiNardo or Palumbo got him?"

"They'd leave the car and a body. They'd advertise."

"Sure. Want to ask either of them if they know where he is?"

"No, I doubt they know, and they sure won't tell us if they do."

I stared out the window. "Crap." I sat silent. I could hear Frank breathing. He spoke first.

"Why would he kill Leo?"

"Leo learned something that Chooch didn't want people to know?"

Frank sucked air noisily. "Where was Chooch from?" he asked.

"No idea. Why?"

Well," he started, "these people aren't in the Buy and Sell. You have to know someone who knows someone. Maybe he was from the same area as Leo."

"Let me call DiNardo," I offered.

"Fine. Let's get in early tomorrow; eight a.m. at my place."

I hoped that DiNardo worked long hours. Judith answered the phone. "Hi, Judith, it's Detective McBriar."

"Yes?" she said eagerly.

"Do you happen to know where Vincent Ciucciaro came from?"

She let out a sigh. "Near Como, same as Leo, I think Leo said once. Why?"

"I'm trying to find out why Leo was working with him in the first place."

There was a long pause. "Did Chooch do this to Leo?"

"We're just trying to fill in some details, that's all."

"Bullshit." Her voice went icy. "He did this, didn't he?"

"Judith . . ."

"Don't give me that crap. Where is Chooch now?"

"We don't know. Is Mr. DiNardo in?"

"He's out with Nick Palumbo." She hung up.

I called Palumbo's house, and the gravelly voice of the Truck came on. "Yes?"

"Hi, this is Detective Ian McBriar. Is Mr. Palumbo in?"

"Sorry, Detective, he's out. I can pass on a message when he gets back."

"Do you know if he's out with Thomas DiNardo?"

"Could be. I'm not sure."

I didn't believe that for a moment. I decided to risk the next question. "Do you know where I might find a Vincent Ciucciaro?"

"You're looking for Chooch?"

"Yes, do you know him?" I felt hopeful.

"What do you want him for?" The tone was definite.

"We believe he may have some information vital to

our investigation."

"Did he push Leo's button?"

That caught me off guard. "What?"

"Did Chooch kill Leo?" His voice went from low rumble to sustained thunder.

"Look, you know I can't discuss that. Do you know where Chooch is?"

There was a deep growl. "Call me when you find him." He hung up.

I stared at the kitchen window. Karen rubbed my arm. "Problems?" she asked.

"The usual stuff—murder and mayhem. I'll solve it in the morning."

"Wearing a cape and tights are we, Superman?"

"And I've got X-ray vision."

"Be careful."

"Yes, ma'am." I saluted.

We watched the Academy Awards show. I didn't care what was on TV. Karen was disappointed that *The Godfather* won best picture. I hadn't seen it. A movie about crime families didn't hold much appeal.

Ethan spent his time with a coloring book Mrs. Waleski had given him. By nine thirty, he was asleep on the carpet with a crayon in his hand. Karen carried him through to bed, tucked him in, closed the door, and sat beside me.

"Tired of me already?" she asked.

I grunted a *hmm?* in reply.

She smirked. "There was a time you'd take this opportunity to have your way with me."

"I'm worried. There's something I don't get. It's got me frustrated. Sorry, hon."

She put her feet in my lap. "Tell me."

"What?"

"Tell me what's hassling you."

I rubbed her toes. "Two guys are looking for a bad guy. One kills the other. Why would he do that?"

She nodded, listening. "Are they the men that attacked Gary?"

"We think maybe one of them did."

"Who else did?"

"No idea. That's got us puzzled, too."

"Maybe the dead guy was just unlucky to be working with his killer?"

"Go on."

She smiled. "Now you sound like Frank. You can't have a very big pool of people you call on to do this kind of work, right?"

"We said that, too. You don't look in the paper; you know who you know, period."

"Exactly," she agreed. "So maybe your dead guy's killer was working for someone else. He wouldn't say 'I can't help you, I was hired by the person you're looking for.' He'd just go along until the dead guy got too close."

I stared at her, intently. "How did you come by *your* superpowers?"

She beamed. "I have other talents, too."

Five in the morning. Ethan was asleep on the sofa, placed there late last night. Karen was under the sheets beside me. I had an arm over her waist, caressing her stomach. She backed up and snuggled in to me. She slowly rolled over and opened her eyes.

"What are you thinking?" she asked.

I pulled her closer. "Just how much I love you."

She threw an arm over my waist and thumped my side, softly.

"What was that for?" I asked, in mock irritation.

She giggled, went *shh*, and covered her mouth.

Seven thirty in the morning. Ethan ate breakfast, watching TV. I turned to Karen.

"Can you get yourself to work, hon? I need to run in early."

She nodded.

"Do you need subway fare? Do you want to cab it?" I felt for a wallet.

She shook her head. "I've taken the subway for years; I'm fine."

I fumbled for my car keys. Karen straightened my

collar.

"You know, I could buy you a real tie," she said, holding mine like a wet fish.

"Regulations."

"Ugly ties are regulation?"

I explained. "You're a bad guy. You want to punch me." I wrapped her hand around the tie. "And you pull on it to bring me close." I raised her other hand in a fist and pantomimed her swinging at me. I jerked back, and the tie came away in her hand. "Bingo," I said. I clipped the tie back on and kissed her. "Enjoy your day," I added. "Love you." I rubbed Ethan's head. "Be good, sport."

He chewed toast and nodded. Karen sipped her coffee, looking particularly wifely.

I barreled down Rogers Road, skidding off the slippery streetcar tracks, and raced up Keele Street to Frank's house. Frank was out on the sidewalk, pacing. Helen was on the porch in her robe, watching him. Frank got in before I could stop.

I hadn't driven Frank to work for three weeks. Three weeks. All at once, after meeting Karen, life had changed for me. At the station, he marched off immediately. I followed at a discreet distance to the detectives' room. Frank was finishing a joke.

"So he says, 'No, no, I meant the other way!'" The men laughed.

Captain Van Hoeke came over and yanked his head back toward his office. We followed him in and shut the door. "Where are we with the Bernardin case?" he asked.

"Ciucciaro came back," Frank said. "He took his car and the gun."

"We think it was the one that killed Bernardin," I added.

"Should you two put out a bulletin on him?" Van Hoeke was telling, not asking.

"Way ahead of you, boss," Frank said.

Frank called an alert on the Chevelle; Chooch might have switched plates, but it would still be a distinctive car. Neither of us believed he'd abandon the car, but we figured he might stash it. If he was in it, we'd spot him. We did some paperwork, killing time. I offered Frank a coffee and Danish; I went out and waited for the coffee truck.

A shiny stainless steel food box on wheels raced into the lot and screeched to a stop. A dozen people streamed out of the building, lining up patiently for food and drinks from the assorted trays. I brought back two large pastries.

Frank was on the phone, animated. He scribbled on a pad, said *uh-huh*, wrote some more, and stared at me. "Great, man, I owe you one." He put the phone down. "Kid, we got something." I handed him his Danish. "Thanks. The Impala—it got a parking ticket a year ago, when the older Palumbo kid died."

"Where?" I looked for a pencil.

"JFK," he mumbled through a mouthful of pastry.

"The president?"

"The airport. The NYPD sent a parking ticket to Wally Carpenter."

"What do you mean?"

"OK, sorry, running ahead." He breathed deeply. He waved a blue sheet of paper. "Every year, Canadians get thousands of parking tickets in the USA. Most ignore them. Still, the police mail them out. Wally Carpenter's car got tagged at—" he checked a note, "—Sutter Avenue and 134th Street in South Ozone Park—not Harlem, but not exactly Manhattan either—in March of last year.

"Now, Walter Carpenter was never in New York. He forgot all about the ticket until last week, then he mailed it to us. A buddy at the NYPD says there was a rash of burglaries in the area, and some locals were patrolling the neighborhood. Here comes a big white guy with clown hair, in an Impala with Ontario plates. He leaves the car there for days. The locals call the cops, but the car's gone before they can have it towed."

"Why park there?" I asked.

"Because," Frank said, leaning forward, "from there he can take a three dollar cab ride to JFK. Want to bet Chooch flew to Italy from JFK?"

I exhaled. "So, he kills the older boy and the Alfa owner. He brings the gun back with him. That ties him to everything. No wonder he disappeared."

"I also called our friend, Terry Parker. He's not exactly enjoying his vacation, *boo-hoo*. But his mother-in-law gave him a scoop: Palumbo knows about Chooch, and there's a big price on his head." Frank laughed.

"You're not concerned about him getting killed?"

"Hell, if they save us the cost of jailing his sorry ass, I won't kick."

I thought about that. I wanted to do this the right way, not just have him erased. "You know, he might have killed the boy in Italy, but he didn't attack the younger boy. According to Gary's description he wasn't the man on the tracks."

"Yeah?" Frank leaned back.

"Two guys attacked Gary. One was Chooch. Who was the other?"

"The other one hurt the younger boy?"

"Makes sense. Like we said, how many people do you involve in something like this?"

Frank made a quick note. "So, we need Chooch alive to get the other boy's attacker."

"It's a reason for Palumbo to not kill him yet," I offered, hopefully.

"If Palumbo gets him first, he'll just get the answers with a welding torch and vise-grips. Yeah, you're right, kid. We gotta nab him alive. Only way, I guess."

We went to the diner for lunch. Frank ate quickly then grabbed the pay phone, slouching and speaking warmly into the receiver. He smiled broadly, tipped one shoe up on its toe, and leaned back, pushing forward against it as he spoke. He hung up and came back.

"Helen OK?" I asked.

He smiled. "She's good. Sends you her love."

The rain had stopped, and the street was almost dry. Frank invited me back to his house for coffee. Helen served as we sat at the kitchen table.

"You know," Frank said, "I haven't had your chicken parmigiana in a while."

"How about Friday?"

"Wonderful. Six thirty?"

"I'll make a special dessert," I said. "How about cheesecake?"

Frank waited for Helen's response. "Cheesecake is fine," she said.

"Good," he said. "I love your cheesecake."

I got to Karen's office just after five. We rode down an empty elevator, necking like teenagers, and held hands walking to the car. The rain had started up again, pelting us with great globs of water. We ran to the Fury, dodging puddles. I got behind the wheel, ran my fingers through my hair, and shook my hands dry. The rain fell harder, fogging the windows.

Karen wrapped her arms around me. She kissed me, slowly and softly. I made a face like blowing out a candle. "Did you like that?" she asked playfully.

"Wow," I said. "Yeah, but if you do it again, I won't be able to steer."

The heavy rain had caused accidents all over; the police radio helped me to avoid them. I parked at Karen's and opened the passenger door. Karen helped Ethan in then jumped in after him. I stood patiently in the rain, closed her door, and got in the driver's side. Water ran off my hair and mustache, and my jacket was soggy.

I looked like a dog after a swim. Ethan giggled. I closed one eye and gave him a stern look, which made Karen giggle. I shook my hair like a wet spaniel, spraying them both. They laughed hysterically. We parked and sprinted across the lane to my apartment. The rain immediately stopped.

"Typical," I grumbled. Through the window, I could see the last quarter of the moon through the overcast, like a letter *D* in the sky. I checked the cupboard. Not much food here, I thought.

"What does everybody want for dinner?" I asked.

"You pick," Karen called, toweling her hair dry.

I stood in the kitchen for a minute. "Hey, guys," I called again, "tortellini and salad for dinner?"

"Sounds lovely," Karen yelled back.

In the gray evening light, the street lamps came on. It might be a starry evening. I looked forward to that; it would be romantic if it cleared up. I threw on a dry jacket.

"OK," I said, "I'll get some stuff and be right back."

I walked to the store and absentmindedly picked groceries for the next few days.

The only thought in my mind was if I should ask Karen to marry me. It seemed natural, logical, that she would say yes, but I was worried. She might say no. Reason said, "Of course she'll say yes," but a nagging doubt kept coming up. Could she do better than me? Was she as committed to me as I was to her?

I left the store and turned the corner onto my street. Maybe I shouldn't wait three weeks. I should ask her tonight, after Ethan fell asleep. If she said no, we could talk about it. Maybe she'd change her mind, or just carry on as we were, but still move into the house. I could ask her again, later. But would she still want to live there if she said no?

It started to rain again, and I quickened my step. A voice caught my attention. A man, his car window down, held out a map. "Excuse me, Officer?" said a rough, squeaky voice.

I walked toward him. The map came down. I saw four flashes of light, then I heard four shots. My body turned numb and soft.

The world went into slow motion. I crumpled, like a cowboy in a Western, onto the sidewalk, my groceries hovering in the air beside me. I wondered how he knew I was a policeman. His car—a green Chevelle—looked familiar, too. I slid into the gutter. The sound of a big V8 got loud, and he drove off, just missing me.

I'd often wondered what would go through my mind when I died. I remembered the scene in *Sunset Boulevard* with William Holden floating face down in a swimming pool. I was curious how they filmed that scene. I wanted to know how long he held his breath.

I was lying on my left arm, my nose in the gutter, trying to keep my mouth out of the water and breathe. My groceries were scattered over the sidewalk. That upset me. My ripe tomatoes had splatted all over the concrete.

The street was empty. I was relieved that I wouldn't be embarrassed by being found this way, but irritated that nobody would likely find me at all. It was getting harder to breathe.

My right eye was out of the water, and reflected in the slow-flowing stream I saw a man, walking toward me, with a gun in his hand. My revolver was pinned under me, useless. I rolled onto my back with all my might and reached for my gun.

The man came closer. In *Anatomy of a Murder*, a piece of music plays through the film, a Ray Nance trumpet solo that sounds like a screaming woman. I heard that music now. Why would I hear that?

I tilted my head up and saw some neighbors and Karen, her hands over her ears, knees bent. Her mouth was open; the Ray Nance was coming out of her mouth.

I thought, Karen, why are you screaming in trumpet? The trumpet faded, and I heard only her voice now, screaming.

The figure moved closer. I pushed my hand as far as I could and reached my revolver. I managed to tug it out of the holster. I tried to lift it, but it was too heavy.

The figure stepped over me and put his hand on my arm. I heard Frank's voice.

"Easy, kid. Easy." He took my gun away. I heard Frank's voice again, very loud, in slow motion. "Call an ambulance! Karen! Karen!" His voice was clear, but he was getting hazy. ". . . CALL . . . AMBULANCE!"

The world went quiet and dark.

CHAPTER THIRTEEN

I've never liked carnival rides. I rode the roller coaster in Yorkton once, but only because my brother dared me; I nearly threw up.

I feel like that now, twisting left and right down a hall. Fluorescent lights pass overhead, fuzzy and distant, turning as I turn.

There's a pain in my shoulder, and I hear speech, voices, but I can't see anyone.

". . . lost a lot of blood," says a woman.

"BP dropping," comes another.

A man's voice. "Get me four units of O-neg, stat."

Hurried footsteps.

I hear Frank. "You will not lose him. You hear? You will not lose him."

I still can't see anything. Then the first man, irritated. "We're short-staffed; there's only so much we can do."

Frank again. "If you say that again, I'll cripple you."

I feel very, very tired. I sleep.

I wake up, almost. I'm in Heaven, it seems, with blinding light all around me.

The blinding light is overhead now, and I see a chrome reflector circling it.

I hear music; soft, angelic music. Then I recognize it. It's Mantovani—"The Living Strings." Shopping center music. I hate that crap.

More voices. A man, confident. "We got all four slugs . . . bleeding profusely . . . need two more units."

A woman's voice. "Can't stop . . . clamp the artery?"

The man again. "Could remove the spleen, but I don't want . . . wait, got it . . . sutures are holding."

I bike home from school on a warm sunny day and walk in the front door. My mother turns to face me.

"What are you doing here, dear?" she asks with a smile.

I have no answer. She asks again.

"Why are you here, Ian? You shouldn't be here. It's not time." She squats down, puts her arms on my shoulders and shakes her head. "Son, you can't be here, not yet. It's not time. It's too soon." Her voice is firm, serious.

She pushes me out the door. I turn back to protest, but the house is empty.

A thumb peels back my eyelid, and a bright light shines in my eye. I wince, trying to hide from the beam, but I can't move my head.

A man's voice booms above me. "Getting a response." The light moves to the other eye. "No sign of swelling."

A woman's voice next. "The fiancée is outside."

Fiancée. I smile. The light goes out.

"Can you hear me, Mr. McBriar?"

I nod as much as I can. My face barely moves.

The woman again. "I think he's conscious, Doctor."

Then the man. "Let him rest. He needs to rest. Get some sleep, Detective."

I try to speak, but I can't make any sounds. I sleep.

I finally woke up. I had no idea how much time had passed. Sunlight peeked between a gap in the closed drapes, letting a triangle of light in the room. I opened my eyes. Frank was beside my bed, his head resting on the side rail.

Karen paced behind him, dressed for work: white blouse, navy skirt, and high heels. She was hugging herself for comfort as she walked. I tried to talk, but a throat tube muted me. I found I could lift my hand now. I touched Frank's arm. His head snapped up.

"Karen!" he barked. His eyes were wide open and deep red.

She reached the bed in two steps and leaned over the rail. She started to weep. I wanted to say, "I'm OK." I tried to say, "Don't cry," but I still couldn't make a noise. I crooked a finger, and she leaned toward me. I hooked the finger into her blouse and pulled on it. A button popped open. I managed a weak smile.

Frank smirked, then frowned. "You do that again," he growled, "I'll turn off your oxygen. Dumb Indian." He looked away and rubbed his eyes, then he turned back, stern. I gave him the finger. He laughed.

Karen slumped in the chair and buried her face in her hands. I stared at her bra. She looked down at the open blouse and smiled. "Dumbass," she said tenderly.

I tried to smile as well. I fell back to sleep.

The room was very dark, but I could make out a shadow in a chair. My throat tube was gone; a mask now covered my nose. I coughed, testing my vocal cords.

The shadow, a uniform, looked away from his newspaper and stood up. "Hey, Detective, how're you feeling?" he smiled. He squatted down and eyed me.

"Sore. Hurts to talk." I looked at him. "Why are you here?"

"We had a pool," he said solemnly. "I lost." He grinned.

I laughed a bit. "Nice," I joked. "Time?"

He looked at his wrist. "Eight twenty p.m. Listen, I have to call Sergeant Burghezian right away. If not, I'll be washing trucks next month." He grinned again and marched back out.

I heard him barking, "Phone! Now!"

My left arm burned from the neck to the elbow. I couldn't take a full breath, no matter how hard I tried. My eyes soon focused in the dim light; one side of the room was stacked high with flowers and cards. Crumpled up on one chair was a cardigan—Karen's. I imagined her, watching me, wondering whether I would get better.

The uniform came back in and squatted beside me.

"Can I get you anything?" he asked earnestly.

"Leafs make the playoffs?" I whispered.

He shook his head. "Next year, maybe."

I sighed. "I didn't think hell had frozen over."

He laughed, covering his face with a huge hand. "I know; I'm a Habs fan myself." He moved his chair closer and placed the hand on my shoulder. "Take a nap," he suggested. "You're getting company."

I woke up to loud voices in the hallway.

"Because this is police business, that's why. Do you want me to arrest your ass for hindering an investigation?"

I opened my eyes slowly. Frank squatted beside me. He turned to the uniform. "Thanks, John, take a break." Frank frowned at me. "You're supposed to be dead."

"Relieved, or disappointed?" I whispered.

"Do you know how tough it is to break in a new partner?" His expression didn't change.

"Tell me about it." I laughed and sucked air painfully.

He put a hand on my good arm. "Shush, you idiot."

I looked over his shoulder at two shapes in the door. Karen came through first and leaned over the bed.

"Hey, you." She stroked my hair softly.

"I forgot to duck," I whispered. She frowned, puzzled.

Frank grinned. "It's a quote—Jack Dempsey."

I nodded. "Good to see you."

"Good to see you, too." She sniffed.

"Ethan?" I asked.

"He's at Mrs. Waleski's."

I took her hand and squeezed with all the strength I had. It wasn't much. She looked down at me gripping her for dear life. I shook my head.

"Not going . . ." I inhaled, ". . . let you go. Ever."

Helen walked up beside her. "Hi, Helen," I said. "You OK?"

She smiled. "I'm fine. We were worried about you."

"How long?" I asked. I was tired, fading fast.

"Five days," Frank answered. "Like I said, kid, you should be dead."

Karen glared at him. "Why?" she asked sharply.

He looked down. "You were hit four times, point blank, with a thirty-eight. Now, admittedly, he was a lousy shot. But still, he got your lung, arm, and collarbone. You lost enough blood to float a battleship. The medics barely kept you alive till you got here."

"I owe them a case of scotch," I joked.

Karen shook her head slowly. "You never told me he was that badly hurt."

"No, I didn't," Frank admitted.

She touched his arm. "Thank you."

He nodded a "You're welcome."

"Mind if I sleep?" I asked. "Go home." I blinked at them.

Karen kissed me on the forehead and straightened up to go. "See you soon."

I pulled her hand toward me. "Important question to ask you," I whispered.

Her eyes widened. "Now? You want to ask me that now?"

"Not that. No, wouldn't. Not that." I shook my head. I sighed, fatigue washing over me. I struggled to talk. "I have to know, first time I bought you lunch, at work."

"I remember."

"You met me, you said, 'Hey you.'"

She nodded, puzzled.

"Why did you say, 'Hey you?'" I asked.

She put her fist in front of her mouth and smirked. "I'd forgotten your name," she confessed. She giggled, embarrassed.

I laughed, but it hurt like hell. She kissed me again softly, and I slept.

On Tuesday morning, I was propped up for an hour to watch TV. There was a drain in my chest to stop fluid buildup after surgery.

After lunch, Frank came in alone, pulled up a chair, and held out a torn newspaper.

I looked at the front page: "*HERO COP GUNNED DOWN! Third officer shot this year!*"

"Did they get my name right this time?"

He chuckled. "Yeah, finally. They interviewed me, but they couldn't print what I said." He put the paper down. "I got a question for you. When you were in the gutter, you were mumbling something. Do you remember what?"

"I was saying a Hail Mary, a prayer for the dying."

"Good thing you didn't finish it," he quipped.

"I need a big favor. I'll pay you back," I said.

"How do I know you won't skip out on me?" he deadpanned.

"You can hold my wallet."

He grinned. "Name it, kid."

On Thursday, the doctor took my mask off.

I had toast and slept till noon. I ate a plate of mushy beefy something and slept again.

At six thirty, Karen breezed up and kissed me hard on the lips. "Hey, you. How are you feeling?"

"I'd feel better if I didn't have a tube up my wiener."

"Guess how I got here?" she asked.

I shrugged.

"Someone parked a Beetle in front of my place and dropped the keys in my mailbox."

I raised my eyebrows. "Do tell?"

She undid her blouse and leaned forward. "Thank you."

I looked down and rolled my eyes. "God, that's torture, you know."

She sat back and buttoned up again. "Anyway, I can't say thank you enough."

"Does Ethan like it?"

She stared at me for a long time. "He thinks it's a big toy. He loves it." She kept staring.

"What?" I asked.

"You're recovering from being shot, and your first question is about Ethan."

"Yeah?"

"Are you trying to make me keep you, or what?"

"If I can," I answered honestly.

She put a finger on my lips. "I have to pick Ethan up. We'll be right back."

I woke up an hour later. Ethan was in the corner, drawing with crayons. Karen was reading a magazine, looking like Grace Kelly in *Rear Window*.

It felt like I was breathing through a thick blanket. I gasped to get enough air. Karen's eyes widened; she rushed out. I heard voices in the hallway, then footsteps.

I waited, as calmly as I could. The footsteps got very close. I heard voices. "BP dropping, pulse racing."

Another voice, "Get the mask on him, now."

I could breathe again. I opened my eyes to a doctor checking my pulse. "Feeling better?" he asked.

"Pneumothorax?" I whispered.

He shook his head. "Good guess, but no, just pneumonia. Let's get you well enough to go home, OK?"

I blinked "yes." Karen leaned over me.

"How are you?"

"Gotta sleep," I said softly.

"He'll be fine," the doctor reassured her. "He just needs rest."

"If anything happens to him," she waved her finger at his chest.

He turned to me. "She's a keeper."

I smiled behind the mask. "Go home. I'll be fine." I fell asleep.

Voices in the corridor woke me. The drapes were open; it was dark out. A familiar voice—tired, but recognizable—was outside the door.

My father walked into the room, his Fedora in his hand. He approached the bed gingerly.

"Hi, Pops," I whispered. The uniform escorting him

nodded and left.

"Hello, Ian." He looked at the equipment behind me. "You got yourself into some trouble, huh?"

I blinked "yes." "Stopped all four shots. Pretty good goalie, huh?" I asked.

"Your jokes are sicker than you are." He smiled.

I nodded. "Glad to see you. Sorry about the occasion."

"I'm just glad you're still with us," he said warmly.

"Dreamed of Mom," I said gently.

"Me too, son."

I shook my head. "No, dreamed of joining her. She said, 'Not your time.'"

His gray eyes smiled. "She'd know. She was usually right." He looked at his knuckles, knotted in a prayer grip.

"I miss her all the time," I said.

"Me too, son. Me too."

"Life OK, Pops?"

He nodded. "Been busy. Restaurant and hotel are doing fine."

"Heard from James?"

"They played Ottawa last month, met the Prime Minister. Said he's shorter in person."

"Good to hear," I chuckled. "I saw them here last year. They're a tight group."

"That's his passion. God gave him the gift, he's using it." He hung his head, thoughtful.

"How are you doing, Pops?" I asked.

"I'm all right. You know, it's been a long time." He looked down at his hands. "I was true to your mom, good times and bad. That was always so . . ." His voice trailed off.

"You met someone?"

He watched me, gauging my reaction. "Pam Krieger—you know her. Husband died years back. We're both too old for more kids, too young to be living alone."

I patted his hand. "That's good, Pops. Happy for you."

He smiled softly. "Thanks son. That means a lot. How about you—been dating since the doctor girl left?"

A figure moved behind him. I wheezed, laughing at the irony. He frowned, worried, then turned around to look. Karen smiled at him.

"Perhaps you should ask me that." She put a hand out. "Hi, I'm Karen Prescott."

He stood and looked her over. "Hello. John. John McBriar." He shook her hand then smiled broadly. "Let's get this straight—*you're* dating *him*?"

"That's right." She nodded, puzzled.

He looked her over again. "You know he's not a Rockefeller, right?"

She smirked. "It's not his money that I'm after."

His voice went soft. "He's incredibly lucky."

"Yes." Karen dropped her eyes. "He's alive."

My father stared at me. "Why? What? Frank only said you'd been shot. How bad was it?"

"He nearly died," she told him. "They still can't explain why he survived."

"What day is it?" I asked.

My father answered, "The fifth. Frank called me yesterday. I got here quick as I could."

I took the mask off, waved Karen close, and puckered up. Bashfully, she gave me a kiss.

"Hey, you," she whispered. "Frank and Helen are coming. Ethan is at Mrs. Waleski's."

"Ethan?" My father tilted his head.

"My son." She stiffened up. They faced each other for a minute, both silent.

My father smiled. "I'd love to meet him, if he's anything like you."

She beamed, lighting up the room. "I'm sure he'd love to meet you, too, John."

I ate most of my dinner. My father joked that meant I was either improving or very sick. He bought Karen a snack, chatting as they walked to the cafeteria. I slept.

When I woke up, my father and Karen were talking in the corner, their voices low.

"How are you feeling?" she asked, caressing my hair.

I raised a finger. "I see you're making time with him instead of me?"

"I dunno . . ." She smirked. "He's kind of cute."

"He's me, just older."

My father stood beside her. "I can see why you get along. You don't get many chances to be happy. I'd keep this one."

"What do you mean by that?" Karen asked, frowning.

"He always said Melissa and I weren't 'a match.'" I grinned. "I guess he feels we are."

"What can I say?" she joked, looking at my father, "your son has good taste."

Frank appeared, guarding Helen like a mother hen. He stretched a hand out. "We spoke on the phone, sir. Pleasure to finally meet you, Captain."

My father put his hand out. "Call me John. Pleasure meeting you too, Frank."

The four lined up at my bed rail. "If it gets any more crowded I'm selling tickets," I teased.

Helen picked up the clipboard by my bed. "Your fever is way down. Your lungs are almost clear. You should be home by Sunday."

I wrinkled my nose, calculating. "Nine days. I've been here for nine whole days?"

Frank shook his head. "You should be six feet under. Maybe you had help from the big man upstairs after all. Most people in your situation don't even make it to hospital."

I imagined getting out, moving in with Karen. Wait—move in. "Hey," I said, weakly, "I still need a bunch of work done on my house."

Frank coughed. "Uh, we figured you'd be sort of busy, so we hurried that along. It's amazing how cooperative trades are to a wounded cop."

Saturday, I was allowed to pee standing up. Karen walked me to the showers, stripped us down, and bathed us. I said that in my telling, this would end differently. She warned me that she would tell people I wasn't up for action. We were at a friendly Mexican standoff, she said coyly.

I held her for dear life. Even in the running water, I'm sure I saw her eyes tear up.

After a shave and clean pajamas, I felt truly alive for the first time in days. I ate all my lunch. Karen smuggled in some pie from the cafeteria.

I could take a full breath without pain, and I could raise my left arm to chest height without screaming in agony.

Ethan showed up with a Beetle Hot Wheels car. It was canary yellow, just like on the real car, he said. He raced it along the floor, to the end wall.

My father took Ethan and Karen to dinner on Friday night. They stayed up late, talking about me, Saskatchewan, and my mother. Ethan fell asleep in his lap. Karen passed muster in his books, apparently. She had a standing invitation to visit Esterhazy. There would be horses for Ethan to ride.

Dad flew home on Saturday night. Before he left, he showed me a photo of Pam Krieger, taken outside her house. I'd gone to school with her son, but I didn't remember him much. In the photo, she leaned against his truck, squinting in the bright sunlight. She looked a bit like my mother; the same hair, the same smile, the same open face that hid no secrets.

On Sunday, Karen brought my "street clothes." I dressed, ate sitting up, and waited patiently in a wheelchair to be pushed out the front door. The senior nurse gave me a hug, delighted at my recovery.

Karen wheeled me out to the Nova and climbed into the back with Frank, and I shuffled into the front seat beside Helen. The sunlight on this mild April morning felt warm and invigorating. I leaned against the glass like a cat in a windowsill, delighted at just being outside.

"We figured you're not up to many stairs, so we set up a room at our place," Frank said. "That way, Karen can come check on you whenever she wants."

"Thanks. I appreciate that." I turned to face him.

"When can I go back to work?"

"I bet that you'd ask that on the drive home," he chuckled. "I win." He got serious. "We're still looking for Chooch. That Chevelle hasn't turned up. He hasn't crossed the border, he hasn't sold it. We figure he's stashed it." He stared off, thoughtful. "Oh!" he remembered. "The bullets we pulled out of you match those we found in Leo."

"Good. Save them. I want cufflinks." I smiled.

Frank grinned. "Also, Vincent Ciucciaro has a rap sheet for car theft. We have his prints." He paused, debating whether to continue.

"And?" I prompted.

"And," Frank went on, "one curious forensics tech went back to the Beretta—the nickel nine we found in the Impala? The gun was wiped clean. The bullets were wiped clean. Chooch was very careful. But on one edge of the magazine clip we found a partial thumb print, so we compared it to Chooch's." He grinned. "We got him. Now we can tie him to Leo, the guy in Italy, and the older Palumbo boy. The guy in Italy was shot in the chest. Leo was too, and you became a dartboard."

I chuckled. "Dartboard. I like that. Good nickname."

Karen sighed. "Take care of him, Frank. He's not as invulnerable as he thinks."

"You bet, girl."

Helen glanced my way and smiled. "What are you thinking?" she asked.

"I'm lucky to have friends like you," I said sincerely. "Sometimes it takes getting shot to appreciate what you have, I suppose."

"Amen," Frank agreed.

Frank helped me up the steps to the living room. He made sure I was comfortable, then made Helen equally comfortable. Karen appeared with a suitcase full of my clothes in one hand, Ethan in the other.

He repeated that he wanted to be a doctor, but this time a people doctor, not an animal doctor. I said that was a great idea. I took a nap.

My eyes half-closed, I heard Helen and Karen

talking about us in the living room. Ethan watched cartoons and talked to Frank. I watched the mismatched pair crawl around on the floor, playing with Hot Wheels. I was grateful to Frank for putting me up, as I was that he found me when he did. That was something that had stuck in my mind. "Frank?"

"Yup." He didn't look up.

"When I got shot, how come you were there right away?"

"I wondered when you'd ask that," he said. He sat up, cross-legged. "A cruiser spotted Chooch, but he was on an elevated road, and they couldn't get to him. Dispatch called me. I called you. Karen said you went to the store. Helen drove me over, in case he was headed your way."

Helen drove? That made me think of something else. "I've never seen you drive, Frank."

He looked to the kitchen. Helen nodded approval.

"I don't drive."

I thought I'd misheard him. "Sorry?"

"It's not that I can't drive. I *don't* drive." He was matter-of-fact.

"Did they pull your license?" I teased.

He studied the floor for a moment, formulating an answer. "I'm epileptic, so I don't drive." He glared at me, a look that said, "Don't joke about this."

"I'm sorry; you never said," I stammered.

"Hey, it only affects my brain." He grinned.

Helen shot him an angry look then turned away. She and Karen giggled.

"Does Captain Hook know?"

He rolled his eyes. "He's a detective—of course he knows. Him, you . . . and nobody else."

The last three words came out slowly. I nodded. "I've never seen you have a seizure."

"Yes, you have," he corrected. "Sometimes if I'm distracted, or blank out for a moment, I'm having one. They're just not grand mal, like on TV, but they're still seizures."

I stared out the living room window. The sound of a large V8 got louder, and I cringed involuntarily. It took a minute to realize that it was only a truck. I settled down. Another thought came to mind.

"How did Chooch find me?"

"We figure Leo showed him our business cards. I'm not in the phone book, but you are."

"How did he know what I look like?"

"Probably the same way. Leo had no reason not to tell him."

I imagined Leo letting Chooch in, talking to him, telling him we saw the Palumbo accident as suspicious. I imagined Leo asking Chooch to help find the guy responsible. I thought of Chooch, standing in Leo's front hall, wondering if Leo would turn him in, or blackmail him, or kill him, or if Leo suspected Chooch of also killing Peter Palumbo.

"If you were Chooch, where would you go?" I asked Frank.

"I dunno. Find a hole to crawl in?"

I shook my head. "He's working for someone."

"Explain." Frank sat still.

"He isn't hitting Palumbo's kids as a hobby. This is a job he's doing."

"Yeah, so?" He was paying attention now.

"So you're working for someone and the heat's on. You call them and say, 'Hide me,' until you can sneak away."

Frank stood up. "Very good. I'll check on that tomorrow. Right now, eat and sleep. That's an order."

Chapter Fourteen

I woke up smelling beef stew, and ate what I could. My appetite was still off. Karen helped me through to the spare room. I slid into the double bed, at an angle so my feet didn't overhang. After the hospital linen, the fresh flannelette felt luxurious.

Frank and Ethan were downstairs, playing with the trains. I could hear Helen and Karen talking in the living room. I caught snippets of conversation.

Helen's voice. "—to marry you?" then "—great guy, Frank says he's just like a—" then laughter.

Karen's voice. "—never thought I'd—feels like—" and followed later by "Ethan adores him—settles that."

More laughter. I strained to hear more. I fell asleep.

I woke with a start. Where was my dresser? Had I been robbed? Where was I?

No. Frank's, I was at Frank's house. I rolled over, my shoulder less painful today. Karen? Of course, she was home. I sat up slowly. My arm felt like I'd been hit with a bat. I slipped on a robe, grabbed a vial of pain pills, and shuffled to the kitchen. Helen turned to me, her mouth open in surprise.

"Why are you out of bed?" she scolded.

"I can't let you cook alone," I protested.

"Sit." She shook her head. "That's an order."

I sat down. I felt dizzy, but I didn't want to tell her that. She looked me in the eye.

"Karen is serious about you, you know? But she worries about the future."

"I heard you talking. How worried?"

"She wants to know whether she should buy a black outfit. Get my drift?"

"Hey," I joked, "she got injured first."

"Very funny. I told her this was a fluke. I didn't lie, did I?" It was almost pleading.

I shook my head. "Most of us have never drawn our gun. It's called 'Toronto the Good' for a reason."

She moved bread around pointlessly and tidied cups on a tidy shelf. "Yeah," she mumbled. "It just scares the crap out of me, whenever I hear an ambulance."

"Tell me about it." I smiled. "It's even worse to ride in one. The suspension sucks."

She sighed. "We lost two boys earlier this year. Frank went to both funerals."

"Lothian and Maitland—I know. I didn't want to be the March pinup boy."

Frank came in, holding his jacket and clip-on tie. He glowered at me. "Morning. Still have your boyfriend over, huh?" He popped bread into the toaster. "How're you feeling, Ian?"

"Never better. We driving in together?"

He laughed. "In your dreams, kid. You're home until the medics say otherwise." He poured two coffees and slid one in front of me. I popped two pills into my mouth.

Helen stared at the vial. "Are you in pain?"

"This?" I shook the vial casually. "Nah, these are breath mints."

She shook her head. "You guys. I swear, I just don't get your macho shit."

Frank buttered his toast and sat across from me. "We should get confirmation of one thing today," he offered. "We sent the U.S. passport photo to the Italian police, see if Chooch was the witness."

"So can we link him to those two deaths—the older Palumbo boy and the Alfa driver?"

"Maybe, but we still don't know who he's working for."

*

Just before eight, a distinctive, cheery sound filled the front hall.

"My ride's here," Frank said with a grin. A moment later, I heard a soft knock. Frank opened the door; Ethan hopped in, giggling.

"Hi, Uncle Frank!" he squealed.

Frank held him up at eye level and pretended to struggle under the weight. "Whoa! You're getting too big! Stop growing, OK?"

Ethan ran up to me and gave me a hug. "Hi. How are you?" he asked.

"I'm fine, sport." Karen stood behind him, watching me. I smiled broadly. "Hi, sweetheart," I said. "I missed you."

She squatted beside me and planted a kiss, gently.

"So, I'll see you this evening, right?" I asked.

She nodded happily. "I'm driving Frank to work, then heading downtown."

"How's the car?" I kissed her nose.

"Ethan wants to drive it," she laughed. "You're OK, you know?"

Frank held the door open, and they walked out.

"Hey," I called to him. "You touch my girl, I kill you."

He pointed at Helen. "Ditto." He grinned. They left.

The sound of the motor faded as they drove up Keele Street. I smiled. Helen was watching me, studying me.

"What?" I asked.

"You're in love," she said simply.

"Does it show?"

"Like the nose on your face; same for her."

"Then maybe you could tell her that. She seems to think I'm staying with her out of pity."

"She's been hurt," Helen said. "Ethan's father leaving, raising him alone. She needs to know you're committed to her."

I sighed. "I've asked her to live with me. I spend every moment I can with her. I bought her a car. What more can I do?"

"Tell her you love her." Helen smiled.

I slept for most of the morning, while Helen marked student papers. After I woke up, I looked through her fridge and wrote a shopping list.

"Hey, Helen?" I called.

"Hi, you're up."

"Could I get you to pick this stuff up? I'll pay you back."

"Don't be silly." She scanned the list. "Do you really want all this?"

"Yep. It's for dinner."

I showered, dressed, watched TV, and waited for her to return from the store. She struggled up the stairs with two full grocery bags. I met her on the porch. I carefully put aside the items I wanted, took another nap, then made dinner.

At five thirty, a cruiser pulled up. Frank jumped out, taking the porch steps two at a time. He flung the door open, looked quickly around, and settled on Helen.

"Hello, sweetheart," he purred. "How are you?"

"I'm fine," she said happily.

He kissed her. "Where's the freeloader?"

I called from the kitchen. "Here, drinking your good scotch."

He laughed. "I know that's not true! How are you feeling, kid?"

"Good. Making dinner."

"What is it?" he asked, curious.

"You'll see when Karen gets here."

We talked briefly about work. One Italian policeman who had interviewed our fake Wally Carpenter was on vacation. The other had transferred to Naples, so they sent Chooch's photo down to him, but we wouldn't hear back till Wednesday. Two minutes later, the sound of a VW motor filled the front window.

Karen and Ethan knocked, and Helen let them in. Frank hugged Karen and lifted Ethan up, making the boy laugh.

"How were you today? Good?"

Ethan nodded. "We went to the store with Tommy's mom. We got broccoli. It was good."

Frank's eyes widened. "Wow! Far out! From now on, I buy broccoli. No more ice cream, only broccoli. C'mon, Ian made dinner. Let's see what he made."

Karen was still in the front hall. I kissed her tenderly.

"Hey, you." She smiled up at me.

"I love you more than I can say." The words just fell out.

Her eyes widened. "What brought that on?"

"I nearly died. It makes you appreciate things. I love you. Period."

She wrapped her arms around me and kissed me passionately. "That's good," she whispered, "because I love you too."

Frank and Ethan set the table. Karen brought through a salad. Helen brought in my main dish. Frank stared at the food as though it might jump up and bite him.

"Problem?" I asked.

He glared at me. "You made this?"

"Veal parmigiana, Frank. Try it."

"*You* made this." He took a bite. "So, you're moving in permanently, right?"

"Glad you like it, Frank."

Karen scratched my thigh playfully. "How are you feeling?" she asked quietly.

"Fine. Kinda horny," I whispered in her ear.

Frank devoured his veal as Helen and I discussed the finer points of preparing it. He snuck some off Helen's plate while she pretended not to notice.

Helen made coffee and brought in dessert. Ethan wrinkled his nose.

"What is this?" he asked.

Frank smiled like a cat cornering a mouse. "Cheesecake. Blueberry cheesecake."

The evening evaporated. Frank and Ethan watched *Gunsmoke* until Ethan fell asleep. Helen talked about her students. Karen wrapped an arm behind me and rubbed my back. The emotion I felt in that one casual gesture said more than a love poem could. I realized how much I missed being with her. These few days had seemed an eternity.

Looking at her, I saw a lovely twenty-five-year-old, mature, vibrant, playful, and sexy. I imagined how she would be in twenty years, and I still liked what my mind saw. I imagined us middle-aged, gray-haired, with grandchildren, in a cottage on a lake. Me reading the paper, Karen baking cookies. It was a future I could be happy with.

Karen noticed me looking. "What?"

"Ever think about growing old?" I asked.

"Sometimes. Why?"

"Ever think of who you'd want to grow old with?"

Helen gasped and ran out of the room. Karen leaned forward, serious. I took her hands.

"I can't think of another person that makes me as happy as you do. Would you consider growing old with me?"

She sat, silent. I didn't know if she was going to cry or slap me. She looked down at our hands and sighed.

Great, I thought, I'm an idiot. I've put my heart out, and she's going to impale it. At least I'm at Frank's; I can lick my wounds here till I get on with my life. Good thing she hasn't given notice. She can still stay at her place.

She looked up, her eyes wet. "That's the most romantic thing you've ever said to me. I would love to grow old with you. We'll talk later, OK?"

I wrapped my good arm around her and kissed her again.

"Hey, you," she said softly. "We have a house to get ready."

Helen magically reappeared, staring as though one of us was going to burst into flame. She grinned.

"So?"

"We'll let you know." I smiled.

Karen gave me another look I couldn't read.

"What is it?" I asked.

"Ethan doesn't have a dad, like Tommy does. He asked if you would be his."

"Thank you, yes. Sure, I can, yes," I stammered.

"What should he call you?" she asked. It was a logical question. I thought about my own father and smiled.

"He can call me Pops."

Tuesday morning, April 10, I felt was my first day of real improvement. Karen and Ethan ate breakfast with us. Helen drove Frank to work. I had an hour alone.

I tuned the radio to a Buffalo station. Joe Pass played "What Now My Love"—perfect. I walked to the local newsstand, bought a *Globe and Mail*, and walked back with nearly no pain. I did the crossword puzzle and stayed awake most of the day. I made chicken salad sandwiches for lunch, and served meat loaf for dinner.

Helen and Karen sat together, whispering and giggling. As we passed the food around, they talked about children, work, and life in general. Frank and Ethan, like a pair of army buddies, discussed cars and trains and foods they liked. I sat at the opposite end of the table, by myself.

"What are these things?" Frank pointed to his plate.

"Stir fried sugar peas in vinaigrette."

Ethan tasted one. "This is good."

"You like this food?" I smiled.

He nodded, the pillow under him wobbling slightly.

"Sure do, Pops," he said.

The room went quiet. Ethan didn't notice.

"Ethan, can you come here for a sec?" I said, trying to sound casual. He hopped off the pillow and walked up to me. I wrapped my good arm around him and kissed his cheek. "Thanks for the approval, son."

He hugged my neck and went back to his seat. I thought Helen and Karen were going to cry. Frank was stunned.

"What, you've never seen a kid eat vegetables

before?" I teased gently.

For dessert, I'd made banana cream pie. It looked spectacular. I assured Frank that, yes, there was a second one in the fridge.

After dinner, we talked till Ethan got very tired, and Karen said he should be home in bed. He fell asleep on the sofa. Fatigue overtook me, and I went to bed too.

I woke up early in the morning, feeling sore but stronger than the day before. I made pancakes for Helen. She got up as the first stack was ready, shuffling into the kitchen in her heavy robe and slippers. She peered up at me, bleary eyed.

"Hey, Helen. Pancakes?"

She nodded. "Love some."

Frank came through, his jacket over one arm. He sniffed the air. "What the hell? Pancakes?"

At seven thirty, Karen's Beetle squeaked to a halt outside. I heard footsteps up the stairs. She knocked and let herself in. She and Helen started talking quickly.

Karen kissed me hard. "Hey, you. Sleep well?"

My eyes widened. That kiss had excited me.

"Pancakes?" I wheezed.

She grinned. "Sure. Ethan, want pancakes?"

"Yay. Yes, please!"

"Let's see if he has room for pancakes," Frank challenged. He flipped the boy upside down in the air. Ethan giggled uncontrollably. "Yup. There's room there."

We ate silently for a while, then I turned to Frank. "Frank, what's the word on the Italian cop? Did he recognize Chooch?"

He gulped coffee and nodded. "Should hear today. I'll check when I get in."

"Have we heard anything more about Chooch? Any sightings?" Frank shot a look at Helen, then quickly went back to his food. "What?" I asked.

Frank took another swig of coffee and leaned back. "The OPP found his car, at Niagara Falls."

"What, in the river?"

"No, of course not. It was in a parking lot at the

Skylon Tower."

"What was he doing in Niagara Falls?"

"I dunno, getting married?"

It rained all afternoon, a warm, spring rain. I smelled flowers and mown lawns in it. Karen showed up with Ethan just before dinner; Frank arrived right after her. Frank pulled a handful of papers out of his pocket and handed them to me. "Bad news, kid. Chooch didn't kill the Palumbo boy."

I stared at the crumpled documents. "Who did, then?"

"Dunno, kid. We're stumped. But the cop who saw Chooch's photo in Italy says it definitely was not him. He describes Mister Average—average height, weight, age, et cetera."

"Great," I sighed. "But if Chooch didn't do it, why shoot me?"

"Dunno. We think he plugged Leo, and we know he attacked Gary."

"How is Gary?"

"He's home with his dog. Hospital stay did him good—he's making nice to the sister of the woman who watched the dog."

"Good." I smiled. "Then he'll leave Karen alone."

"Something else," Frank said, serious. "Chooch didn't empty his trash can. We found medicine, for Hashimoto's Disease."

"That's what makes him bald?"

"It has several symptoms—puffiness, rough voice, baldness. The treatment is—" he wrinkled his nose, thinking, "—levothyroxine sodium, by prescription only."

"So we can track him through his medication?"

"Could be. Meanwhile, let's work on getting you better."

I thought for a moment. "Niagara Falls. Maybe he went off to the States?"

"We thought about that. No way to tell. Once he's over the line he could drive down to Mexico, or sail to Bolivia, who knows."

*

Saturday, we all took a walk to my house. Karen held my arm, while Frank and Helen held Ethan between them. They lifted him up, flying over sidewalk cracks. It was a week to Easter, and I would have loved to have an egg hunt in our own home.

Our own home. It sounded so permanent when I said that. I imagined Karen and me getting old, mowing the lawn, planting flowers, raking leaves. Ethan was grown and married; he had a family. Like me, he had a brother, who also had a family, and we'd all gather for Thanksgiving dinners, Christmas carols, weddings, christenings; all the events that make up life. I saw it all. It warmed me to think of it.

The front yard now had flowers in the bed. The kitchen appliances were new. Inside, everything had been painted. My bed, dresser, and clothes were in the big bedroom. My stereo and TV were in the living room. It looked as though I'd lived there for some time, already. It was quite surreal. Ethan grabbed my hand.

"I wanna show you something," he gushed. He pulled me downstairs. The basement now had a furnished bedroom, complete with sheets and lamps.

"Let's show you the yard," Karen said.

We went out back. My Fiat sat in the garage, under a tarp. I smiled at the thoughtfulness. The backyard was in pretty good shape before, but now flowers ran along the property fence, and the vegetable garden was turned to bare soil for the spring. I was speechless.

"This is beautiful." I said, "You guys did amazing work."

Karen rubbed my back. "Glad you like it. After all, you're paying for it. What do you think?"

"Ask me in ten years," I answered.

We took a final quick look inside and strolled back to Frank's house. It was a mild afternoon; the first buds were sprouting on the maples, and squirrels, after the long winter, pleaded for handouts as we passed.

Ethan squealed with glee; Frank promised we'd come back with peanuts to feed them. Karen and I walked behind, strolling like any young couple on a spring day.

Back at Frank's, I slumped down onto the sofa, and we had a snack. Ethan helped scoop out ice cream. Helen sat in the easy chair and put her feet up on the coffee table, wiggling sore toes.

I leaned back. My house was beautiful. Karen loved it. Ethan loved it. I owed Frank and Helen more than I could ever repay for the kindness they'd shown me, and for doing up the house. I had to cook dinner.

I fell asleep.

I woke up, groggy. The others were talking in the kitchen. Ethan was asleep on the sofa. Karen heard me and came through.

"It's ten at night. How are you feeling?"

I shook my head. "Tired, very tired. I needed to sleep, I guess."

She helped me to bed and kissed me good night.

At six fifteen on Sunday morning, I showered, chose my best clothes, and put on some coffee. At a quarter after seven, Frank came into the kitchen, hugging an old robe. He shuffled slowly toward the sink.

"Late night?" I asked.

He grunted. "Those girls love to yak. Ethan slept on our bed till midnight." He eyed my cup.

"Fresh coffee?"

He grunted and nodded. He pulled down a blue mug that read *Top Cop*. He leaned against the sink, eyeing me. "Why are you up so early?"

I smiled. "Church. It's Palm Sunday. I called a cab. I'll be back by nine."

He shook his head. "Nope, nope, nope, nope. Let Helen drive you."

"She's asleep," I protested. "I'm taking a cab."

He sighed. "We'll be right here. Call us. You feel sick, tell the padre, and we'll get you, all right?"

The taxi driver stopped at the church steps, thanked me for the tip, and sped off. I sat in a back pew and had a chat with God, about life in general and Karen in particular.

The church was decorated with palm fronds, the smell of incense and candle wax filling the air. The church was crowded, as I expected it would be. Even so, I had the pew to myself. Five minutes before the service, the frail old man in a rumpled blue suit walked slowly down the nave toward the rear door. He froze when he saw me. He smiled slightly, nodded, and continued on to the back.

The air glowed as the back door let in gray sunlight onto the red patterned carpet, and dimmed again as the door closed. Thirty seconds later, Nick Palumbo walked in with his mother and the Truck. His mother and the Truck continued on to their pew. Palumbo peeled away and sat beside me. I held out my hand, and he clasped it with both of his.

"Ian. I am delighted you're here," he said with complete sincerity.

"Not as delighted as am I," I answered.

He smiled. "Is there anything—anything at all—that you need?"

"Thanks, I will keep that in mind."

His tone deepened. "You're looking for Vincent Ciucciaro."

"Yes." I was surprised by his bluntness.

"We may both be pursuing the same thing, then."

I smiled. "The truth?"

"Justice."

"Any idea where we can find him?" I asked.

"I wish I knew. That would solve a lot of issues for us both."

"We both have some questions only he can answer," I agreed carefully.

He nodded. "I hope they are all answered satisfactorily." He held his hand out. "Again, please accept my best wishes for your speedy recovery."

I shook it again, and he walked to his pew, genuflected quickly, and sat beside his mother. He leaned behind her and talked softly to the Truck, who turned to face me and said something. Both men looked forward; the service began.

After mass, I stood at the back of the church, looking for a pay phone. The Truck walked up to me.

"Detective, can I offer you a ride home?" His voiced rumbled.

"Sure. I'd appreciate that," I said.

"You're staying with Sergeant Burghezian, right?"

I hesitated, worried about revealing too much. I didn't trust him. "I was, but I'm back home now. Is that OK for you?" He nodded. "Thank you very much. Actually, you could drop me at Sergeant Burghezian's house, and save him picking me up for lunch." I hoped he would believe that.

He gave me a long look, green-brown eyes reading me. "Whatever, no problem," he said. He led me to a Buick wagon. It occurred to me that I didn't know his name.

"By the way, call me Ian," I said in, a friendly tone.

He nodded. Dead silence.

"What can I call you?"

A long silence. "Anthony."

"Anthony what?" I asked politely.

I was sure he made a face. "Just Anthony." He held the passenger door open and looked around, instinctively scanning the area. He let me sit, closed my door, then walked around and got behind the wheel. I gave him the address, and he grunted that he knew where Frank lived.

Of course he did, I told myself. He gave Frank the invitation for dinner. He drove smoothly, constantly looking around to see we weren't being followed.

"So, have you worked for Mr. Palumbo long?" I asked.

He shrugged. I tried to move the conversation along.

"Where did you work before that?"

"Here and there."

The big Buick turned noiselessly south onto Keele Street. I decided to go for broke. "Why did you get excited when I asked you about Chooch?"

He pulled immediately into a parking spot and faced me.

"You ever meet Chooch?" he growled.

"Briefly. He shot me."

He broke into a grin, discolored front teeth blending to yellow canines. "Funny. I like you," he said. "Look, if he's responsible, he pays the price."

"I'm the one he shot. Don't I get a say in what happens to him?"

"I wasn't talking about what happened to you."

I considered his answer. "Would it help to know that Chooch didn't kill Nick's son?"

He leaned back and studied me. "Yeah? Who did?"

"We don't know. Chooch and a mystery man attacked our witness; Chooch was in Italy when Peter died. Beyond that, we think he killed Leo Bernardin before he shot me."

Anthony stared at me for a long time. He nodded. "You're telling the truth. OK." He shifted into gear and pulled back into traffic. "Zanussi," he said.

"Excuse me?"

"My last name. Zanussi."

A small, subtle joke occurred to me. "Anthony Zanussi. From A to Z." I beamed.

He groaned. "Congratulations. You and my grade four class figured that one out." He smirked. "Listen, you were going to be a priest, right?"

"You're not going to give me your confession, are you?"

"No. I just need to know I can trust you."

"What do you mean?"

He looked around. We were almost at Frank's house. "If you find Chooch, will you tell me first?"

"I can't think of why I should," I said honestly.

"OK," he sighed. "If I find him, I'll call you—only you. You keep him safe. Agreed?" He pulled a smooth U-turn and stopped behind Helen's Nova.

"Why are you protecting him?" I asked.

"Can you keep a secret?" he asked, in a remarkably soft voice.

I nodded.

"He's my brother." He got out and opened my door.

I got out, turned, and looked at him. "Different last

Azzano

names," I said, stating the obvious.

"Same mother." He closed the passenger door and walked to his side of the car. "Good day, Detective."

I wanted Chooch alive. I thought of something that might help us both. "You know he has a condition, right?"

"What condition?"

"Hashimoto's Disease. That's why he lost his hair."

He squinted. "You shittin' me?"

"Look it up. He takes prescription medicine for it. We know."

He nodded, slowly. "More reason to find him fast, then."

Something else occurred to me. "Anthony?" He opened his door and looked at me. I pointed back and forth between us. "This stays right here, just you and me?" I asked.

He nodded. "Appreciate it. You tell your Sergeant though, and ask him to keep it quiet too."

There was sincerity there, one professional to another. He patted the Buick's roof. "Take care, Detective." He drove off.

Frank opened the door before I got to it, looked to see I was alone, then let me in. "You OK?"

I nodded. "Palumbo's man offered me a ride—too good a chance to pass up." I glanced down as Frank slowly released the hammer on a huge revolver. "Expectin' trouble, Marshall?" I quipped.

He adjusted an invisible Stetson. "No, pardner, but I'm ready if it done come callin'."

"Interesting development," I said. "Palumbo's man is Chooch's brother."

"That gorilla in the driveway?"

"Anthony Zanussi. He asked if you and I could keep that to ourselves."

Frank leaned against the door frame, thinking. "So he wants what, to get his brother out of this mess alive?"

"Got it in one. Only half-brother, actually. Different dads."

"And he asks the man his brother tried to kill."

"Yup."

"And you're thinking what?"

"You mean, do I want to kill Chooch? No. I want to find out who killed those people. Chooch didn't kill the Palumbo kid, so why kill Leo? And why shoot me?"

The chirp of a Beetle engine filled the doorway. Frank quickly put the revolver away. He opened the front door, and Ethan attacked him, climbing him like a Jungle Gym. Frank pretended to struggle under the weight of the boy, letting Ethan climb up his back, then tossing him over his shoulder and dangling him by one leg. Ethan squirmed like an eel. Karen smiled, enjoying their fun.

Frank made silly noises as Ethan climbed his hip.

"Put me down, Uncle Frank, I gotta pee," Ethan protested.

Frank groaned theatrically and deposited him gently on the floor. Ethan ran to the bathroom. Karen watched him go, still smiling.

"You two get along well," she said.

"We're both the same age," Frank joked.

"That's what Ian said." She wrapped an arm around my waist and pulled me tight. "Hey, you. How are you feeling?"

I grinned. "Fine. I went to mass. I'm hungry."

We had a late breakfast; I read the weekend paper. I fell asleep.

The evening is foggy. I can see stars above me, but up ahead the road disappears in mist. I am driving an Alfa on a winding country road, with trees to either side.

A figure stands in the road, blocking my way, and I get out of my car. The headlights illuminate him, like a stage light. I walk over to him, a large man with an orange clown wig. He looks over the edge of the road, at a car that has gone down a ravine.

"Too bad," he says. "He didn't need to end up that way."

I didn't remember going to bed. I woke up in the afternoon, sprawled on top of the sheets. A ticking sound woke me: sparrows in the backyard, chattering as they hunted for food. Spring was truly on its way.

I heard Karen in the kitchen, then footsteps heading my way. She poked her head in and smiled.

"Hey, you. You slept through lunch."

I walked through to the kitchen.

Frank frowned, serious. "You feeling OK, kid?"

"Feeling good, thanks. Did I miss lunch?"

He nodded. "Someone called, wants to talk to you. Chooch." He wasn't laughing.

"Serious?" I asked. "I dreamed about Chooch."

Frank's eyebrows rose up high. "He just phoned the dispatcher. Chooch wants to meet you—only you." Frank handed me a pink slip of paper. It said "*5 p.m. 75 Carlton St, doorway.*"

I shrugged. "Why me?"

Frank shrugged back. "I bet he wants a deal to save his sorry ass. This is dynamite, kid. What do you think?"

I looked up at the kitchen wall. The clock read a quarter after three. I double-checked with the clock on the stove. Same time.

"OK," I said. "How do we want to do it?"

Frank scratched his head, thinking. "It's out on the street, hard to post any officers without them being seen. He thought this out well. But first, are you sure you're OK with this?"

"What the hell," I sighed. Karen stared at me. "What?" I asked stupidly.

"You're an idiot."

"That's what they pay me for." I smiled.

She shook her head. "If you get yourself killed, I'll never forgive you." I tilted my head to one side and crossed my eyes. She smirked. "You know what I mean." She hit my good arm. "Asshole." She hugged me. My chest hurt, but I smiled. "Be careful, stupid," she whispered.

Helen drove me downtown, with Frank in the back seat. I wrote down some questions to ask, and answers to questions Chooch might ask. Helen drove slowly past the address, and Frank scanned doorways in the area.

At ten to five, Helen parked around the corner, by a phone booth. I wrote down the phone number and got out.

Frank climbed into the front seat and wished me luck.

I walked north then left onto Carlton. I felt excited, alive for the first time in days.

People streamed out of Maple Leaf Gardens, after some sports event. Chooch would stay away from the crowds, I figured—too easy to be caught.

The doorway at 75 Carlton was visible to the hotels and offices in the area. I imagined Chooch watching to be sure that I was alone before he met me.

A large man walked past; I cringed inside, but he kept walking. I calmed down. Maybe I gave Chooch too much credit, I thought. I checked my watch: four fifty-six. Would he be late? Would he even show up?

The pay phone rang behind me. I picked it up but said nothing. A man's voice spoke.

"Detective, you're alive," he said, as though greeting an old friend.

I crumpled up the paper with the questions and tossed it into the gutter. "Hey, Chooch, how's it going?" I started, an edge in my voice.

"OK. I miss my car. It's a bitch taking a bus from the Falls."

"Sorry to hear that. If you'd told me, I'd have arranged for a ride," I said sarcastically.

He laughed, his voice giving a slight *eek* as he inhaled.

"How's the Hashimoto's Disease—you holding up?" I asked.

A pause at his end. "You clued in on that, huh? Good. Very good."

I wanted to get under his skin, take control. I played the family card. "Your brother says hi."

Another pause. "Yeah, what brother?" he asked defiantly.

"Anthony. He wants me to keep you safe."

He sighed. "Yeah, OK. Hi back. So, what do we do now, Detective?"

My turn to pause: I wanted him to worry. "Look, three people are dead. You attacked me and a handicapped man, but we can still help you if you tell us who hired you to kill those people."

His voice rose up, angry and arrogant. "I didn't kill anyone, you son of a whore!"

I smiled. I'd gotten to him. "So, Leo committed suicide?"

"He attacked me; it was self-defense."

"No sign of a struggle," I pointed out.

"Yeah, well, believe what you want. I was defending myself," he said, suddenly casual.

"What about the Alfa owner in Italy? Was that self-defense?"

"That wasn't me. I just boosted the car, and—" he stopped himself. "And the person with me shot him. Period."

I felt good now. I was on a roll, and he was on the defensive. "You and 'this person' stabbed an autistic man. Why?"

Chooch sighed. "We just wanted to find out what he knew. His stupid dog went ape shit. Then the retard started yelling at us."

My turn to sigh. "Everyone else is always in the wrong, huh? It's just never your fault."

"They got in the way, that's not my problem," he roared.

I decided to play the soft cop for a while, to win him back. "Look, Vince, I don't blame you for shooting me. You must have been desperate, trying to get away. Can we cooperate here? Can we both get what we need?"

He grunted. "What do you got to offer?" His voice sounded calmer. It was working, I thought.

"How about a head start?" I said coyly.

I heard a pencil tapping a book. "I'm listening." He was receptive now. I didn't want to blow this chance.

"OK, how about this. We put your Chevelle on the street, gas it up, no tricks. You take it, say goodbye to the girlfriend, whatever, and then a couple weeks later turn yourself in. You plead guilty to aggravated assault, and you walk in a year."

"My car? In exchange for what?" He sounded interested.

"The person who hired you."

"You know, I ain't stupid. I tell you, I'm dead. Then I got nothing. No deal."

I sighed. Go for broke, I thought. "We can get him without you, you know. We know about the insurance scam, the fake passport, the fake driver's license. We know about you parking the Impala in New York and flying to Italy. We know about the gun—Peter's Beretta you brought back. It's now just a matter of connect the dots. You take my deal, you walk in a year. If not, your boss will think we got your help anyway. You decide."

He chuckled. "You know all that, huh? Then you know I can see you, right?"

I thought about the pen tapping on the book. "I know you're in the hotel across the street. I know that you're on about the fifth floor, and I know that you're almost out of your Hashimoto's medication. I also know you don't want to spend the next six months hiding until we find you. Because we will, Vince, we will."

He was silent. I was getting cold; the evening was chilly, and I was still weak. I didn't want to catch a cold, not in this debilitated condition. I sighed. "C'mon, Vince. You know what to do, and you know that your best chance is with us. I'm offering you a good deal here, OK?"

Even though it sounded like random thoughts, I chose my words carefully. No words like "jail" or "arrested." Nothing to scare him.

He grunted. "Tell you what. Be here in exactly one week—same time. It's tempting. Best I can say right now."

I smiled sincerely. I imagined him watching me, and I wanted him to feel I'd deliver. "Listen, stay safe, OK, Vince? We'll talk in a week." I thought about next Sunday. "Wait," I added. "That's Easter Sunday. I'm cooking turkey."

He chuckled. "I won't keep you long."

"Did you want to come over for dinner?" I asked. "Plenty for all."

He roared with laughter. "No, but thanks for the offer. Gas up my car, man."

I nodded, hoping he was watching. "Fine, one week

from now. It's a date."

I hung up and called the pay phone around the corner. Frank answered on the first ring.

"Frank, stay there. I'm walking back."

I walked briskly back to Helen's car. Frank was pretending to window shop at a closed shoe store, his revolver against his leg. He waited till I got close, then threw himself bodily into the back of the Nova. I slid into the passenger seat and said, "Drive."

Helen squealed the tires and fishtailed slightly as she took off. We headed south, turned right quickly onto Gerrard Street, then right again onto University. The wide sweeping boulevards of University Avenue calmed me down. The combination of open space and urban towers made me feel safe.

We all started talking at once. Frank nodded for me to go first.

"He called me on a pay phone. I think I got through to him," I said.

"Good," Frank said. We passed Queen's Park, with its walkways and green space crisscrossing a wide oval of parkland south of the government buildings.

I continued, "He says he didn't kill the guy in the Alfa, the 'person with him' did. He promised to consider my offer and call me back in a week."

"What offer?" Frank studied me.

"We put his car on the road, let him clear up old business, then he turns himself in and gives up his boss. He's thinking it over."

"Sounds dumb. Why would he go for that?"

"I didn't think he'd go for it. I just wanted to open the door. I think he'll come back with a counteroffer. He seemed keen on getting the car back, though."

Frank stared off, thinking. "We could offer to jail him out of province. That should buy him some security."

"Yeah, that works for me. Something else. I said his brother says hi, and he challenged me to prove that I knew his brother. He seemed impressed. I also did the Sherlock bit. I told him we knew about the gun, the car at JFK, the Alfa driver. He didn't deny it. Then I said that I knew he was watching me from the fifth floor of the Carlton Inn, across the street. He didn't deny that, either."

Helen glanced over at me, puzzled. "How on earth could you know that?"

"The hotel's balconies stick out a fair bit. He wouldn't see me if he was much higher than the fifth floor, and he wouldn't want to be too low—too easy to see him from the street. I heard him tapping a pencil or a pen on a book. I bet it was a Gideons bible, and I heard him making notes. He probably used a notepad from the hotel room."

"Very good, Sherlock." Helen rolled her eyes.

Frank smiled. "I suppose he's gone by now?"

"I doubt he checked in. I bet he just found an empty room and called me."

Helen looked up at the sky. The lights of the city reflected off the patchy clouds, giving them a pearly glow, and behind them the inky blue sky turned black as night approached. "Pretty evening," she said.

Frank turned to look at her. "You OK, hon?"

She smiled at him through the rearview mirror and said, "I'm fine."

Karen almost hit me with the screen door as I came up Frank's steps. She glowered at me. I felt loved nonetheless.

"Are you OK?" she barked. I nodded. She smacked my arm, hard. "You could have called to tell me, dumbass."

"I love you too." I kissed her nose.

She smiled sheepishly and wrapped her arms around me. She leaned against my chest and squeezed tight. "Don't get hurt again, OK? Don't. I couldn't take it."

"Where's Ethan?" I asked.

"Playing with the trains," she said.

"Anyone else feel like Chinese?" I offered. "My treat."

We sat around Frank's dining table swapping white cardboard boxes. We had coffee and leftover cheesecake, then watched *McMillan & Wife* on TV.

By ten o'clock, Ethan was exhausted, so Karen said

her farewells and I kissed her good night. She whispered something suggestive and smiled. I kissed her again.

Her Beetle disappeared down the road, the sound of the engine fading down the nearly deserted street as I waved goodbye. That left the three of us in the house.

"Frank," I started, "I want to go in with you tomorrow."

He looked me over, deciding something. "Fine," he snapped. "Get some sleep, kid. Good night."

I'd finished my second coffee by seven in the morning. I placed my badge and gun in the front closet. At seven fifteen, Frank came into the kitchen, tie in hand. Helen shuffled out behind him, squinting in the soft gray light.

Frank popped bread into the toaster and nodded at me. "Morning, kid," he sang.

I nodded back. Helen ignored the coffee, pulling a milk jug from the fridge. Frank leaned over her to grab a mug, then kissed her cheek. She playfully scratched his tummy and smiled.

I had decided on a turtleneck, with my corduroy jacket hung over one chair. Frank looked me over.

"*Hmph*," he grunted. "Going for the Steve McQueen look, are we?"

We ate and talked, Helen hunched on a chair with her bare feet tucked up, drinking milk and nibbling toast. She wrinkled her brow. "Why did you offer this fellow his car back?" she asked.

I shrugged. "He really likes the Chevelle. I think he's attached to it. That's why—as part of a deal."

"Did he seem interested in that?" She sipped her milk slowly.

"I think so. He sounded like he was." I shrugged.

She slid her feet down into her slippers and leaned forward. "Yes, but he must realize that by turning himself in, he'd lose the car anyway. Is there anything special about that particular car?"

I shook my head. "Quick car, comfy ride. Why?"

She shook her head. "That's not what I mean. Is

there anything specific about *that* car that means something to him?"

Frank's mouth opened. "We gotta get the forensics guys to go over that car again."

I nodded. "I don't know what we're looking for, but I think Helen's right, and it's in that car."

Helen smiled, self-satisfied. Frank stared at her and shook his head.

Karen and Ethan stomped up the front steps. Ethan was talking about Frank's train set. Karen knocked on the front door and let herself in. Ethan ran ahead, giggling.

"Hi, Uncle Frank!" he squealed. He threw himself onto Frank, climbing him like a tree. Their routine.

Frank gasped in mock panic and held Ethan up at arm's length, eyeing him like a bug. "Helen, we got kids," he grumbled.

Karen kissed me hello. "You doing OK?"

"Feeling groovy." I smiled.

We all chatted for a minute, then Karen smiled at Frank. "Want a lift?" she asked cheerily.

Frank grimaced and nodded at me.

"Actually," I said, "you can drop me at my Plymouth. I'm driving us to work today."

She stood very still. She looked me over, just noticing that I was dressed up. "Are you sure? Are you very, very sure?" she asked evenly. The room went quiet. Ethan stopped fidgeting and looked at us, puzzled by the strange adult behavior.

"Yes, sweetheart, I'm sure," I said firmly.

She pursed her lips and grabbed my arm. "Conference," she snapped. She dragged me through to the bathroom, closed the door, and turned on the tap. "What the hell do you think you're doing?" she hissed. "You're eleven days out of critical care, and you're going to *work*?" She spat the last word.

I smiled and tugged on her blouse buttons. "I want to get back to normal. That includes working for a living."

She slapped my hand away and poked a finger into my ribs. "You do *not* hurt yourself, do you hear me? You feel sick, or weak, or anything, you call me, and I'll come get you." She saw the look in my eyes and started to smile. "What, dumbass?" she asked affectionately.

I sat her on the vanity, turned the water off, and wrapped my arms around her. "Jeez, I miss this," I said.

She pulled me close and grabbed my face in her hands. "Be safe. Or else." We strolled back to the kitchen.

"Karen will give me a lift to the Fury," I announced. "I'll be right back to get you."

Ethan and I climbed into the Beetle. Karen drove me to my car. Ethan, in the back seat, steered with an imaginary wheel. I chuckled to myself.

"What is it?" Karen asked, curious.

"This is the first time I've been in your car."

She started to smile, then her eyes welled up. I felt guilty. Somehow I'd upset her.

"What did I say?" I asked.

"You said it was my car. I always thought of it as yours, not mine."

I smiled. "It's yours, tootsie, unless of course you decide to dump me." I looked off, smirking.

She shifted smoothly from second to third and accelerated onto Rogers Road. She grinned broadly. "No chance. You're stuck with me."

I grinned back and rubbed her knee. It was exciting to touch her again, even just her knee. We stopped outside my apartment and walked Ethan back to Mrs. Waleski's.

She was shocked at seeing me. I hadn't realized that I'd lost about twenty pounds and looked rather gaunt. I only knew my pants were loose, and my sweater seemed baggy. She kissed my cheek and said something that translated to "God was with you."

We walked back to my car, Karen clutching my arm tightly. "You better take care, you hear?" she said.

"Believe me, I wouldn't risk losing you." I smiled. I stared at the empty spot where the Fiat had been, feeling an irrational loss with it at my house. Karen opened the driver door to the Fury and let me in. I let it idle for a bit, then I stepped out and kissed her goodbye. She poked my chest.

"Be *careful*," she warned. She walked back to the Beetle and drove down Rogers Road, waving as she disappeared around the corner.

I sat behind the wheel for a minute. It seemed normal to be doing this, yet my life had changed so much. I was neither invulnerable nor as strong as I had been, and I now had two other people to worry about, not just me.

I turned onto Silverthorne without thinking, steering and navigating automatically. Out of habit, I turned the radio on, waited for a gap in the chatter, and called in. "Dispatch, fifty-two four eight."

A long pause, then a familiar female voice came back, incredulous. "Four eight?"

"Four eight, any messages?"

"Yes. *Why aren't you in bed?*" Laughter behind her.

"Is that an offer, Nadine?"

The voice came back, giggling. "Good to hear your voice too, Detective. No messages. Dispatch out."

Frank was on the sidewalk, shaking his head. He shrugged and got in.

"What?" I asked.

"Not right. I should've said no," he lamented.

"You can't keep a good man down, Frank." I drove to the station and parked. Frank stayed in his seat after I shut the engine off. "Problem?" I asked.

"I expect you to bail early today, you know," he informed me.

"OK, no heavy lifting," I promised. "Meet, greet, and beat retreat."

He studied me for a moment then got out.

We walked in together. The receptionist gasped and rushed up to give me a hug.

"Wow!" I said. "That makes it worth getting shot."

She blushed and sat down. We continued on to the back, and the detectives' room immediately fell silent. On the chalkboard was a chart with my name, a series of dates, and detectives' names listed beside the dates—the pool on when I would come back. Frank's name was missing—inside knowledge, of course.

Everybody turned to look at me. Someone started clapping. Then the avalanche of hooting and cheering started, and soon everyone in the building had crowded into the room, pressing me.

I flushed and nodded feebly, anxious at the close quarters. It took over a minute for the noise to die down. I felt tremendous relief when Captain Van Hoeke walked up, shook my hand, and hushed the group. He smiled.

"How're you feeling, Ian?"

"Pretty good, sir, considering." A small rumble of approval rose up.

"Any pains?"

"Just Frank." The crowd laughed.

"Well, it seems your sense of humor is healthy," he chuckled. He faced the room. "Back to work, everybody. We're not paying you to hear bad jokes. C'mon, back to work." He waved his arms as if shooing geese, and everyone slowly dispersed. Van Hoeke waved Frank and me to his office and closed the door. "Listen," the Captain said, "go home. Honestly, I'm surprised you're out of bed."

Frank snorted. "True—you should meet Karen."

Van Hoeke smirked. "Anyway," he continued, "you're too valuable to lose stupidly. Besides, we've put black armbands on twice this year. I don't want to do it again."

"Thanks, Captain. I'll go easy," I assured him.

The morning briefing was predictable. It was comforting to be doing familiar things again. Van Hoeke made a joke about "Officers who should be in bed," then moved on to business as usual. I was obsessed, thinking about Vince's car. Why did he perk up when I mentioned giving it back to him?

The forensics boys, half a dozen men in lab coats, dissected everything from radios to trucks. Vince's car sat in one corner of the floor, waiting to be hauled away. I endured the obligatory hand-shaking, questions, and good wishes, then I told the group about my conversation with Vince, and his unusual interest in the Chevelle. Did they have any idea what that might be, I asked? One man leaned forward. "What?" I looked at him.

He was a bookish man with curly hair and a pallid complexion. "Something I was thinking about last week," he started. He pushed back his glasses on his nose. The others bobbed their heads, listening. "He keeps this car in very good condition—everything is clean. Yet he has a rust hole in one muffler. The other muffler is fine, but that one has a hole in it."

We quickly threw the Chevelle on a hoist and clustered around the exhaust system. I pulled at the hole in the left muffler; there was a sticky remnant of silver exhaust tape around it, placed there to muffle engine noise. Something else caught my eye. I turned to one of the men. "Got a flashlight?"

He handed me a pocket penlight. I stood on a chair and squinted into the rust hole where the tape had been. A baffle, just inside the rust hole, had a piece of wire poking out of it.

With a pair of needle-nose pliers, I peeled back the rust, exposing the wire, and reached in, gently pulling the wire out. It held a small brass key. The men gave a collective *ahhh*.

Frank grinned like a schoolboy. "Nice work, Sergeant," he joked.

I handed the key to the curly-haired man. He looked at it and removed his glasses. He squinted at the key, took it to his desk, and pulled a thick catalog from a shelf. He flipped through the pages for maybe ten seconds, then nodded and faced us. "It's a locker key. Probably from a train station or a bus depot—I'd guess a bus depot."

Frank smiled broadly. "Can I buy you guys pizza?" he asked. "All you guys?"

We sat at our desks, speculating on Chooch's movements over the last few days. I leaned forward and pointed at Frank.

"You stash something in a locker, then hide the key in your car. Why?"

"So you can retrieve it later?" he suggested.

"Why not just mail yourself the key? He must have

known we'd tow the car."

"The key was insurance," Frank said. "He never meant us to find it, but he wanted it there just in case."

"Insurance against what?"

"You mean *who*."

It made sense that he must have hidden the thing, whatever it was, in Niagara Falls, then headed back to Toronto. We called an OPP contact, who agreed to take the key to Niagara Falls. The Niagara Falls police detachment would check if it opened a locker at the bus depot or train station, but it could take all day, they warned.

We went down the street to the diner. I was drained from the morning's exertion, but something stuck in my head. I wasn't sure why. "Why that hotel?" I asked.

Frank shrugged. "Which?"

"I'm pretty sure he was calling from The Carlton Inn. Why that hotel? If he went into an occupied room, he might get caught. So, why risk it?"

Frank leaned back. "He had inside help."

"He had inside help. Right." I smiled. I called it a day after lunch and went home to Frank's. Helen was in the living room marking student papers.

"Honey, I'm home," I called.

"How are you feeling?"

"Tired," I said.

"Of course you are, silly. Hungry?"

"No, thanks. Frank bought me soup. You were right about the car." I yawned deeply.

"Want to take a nap?"

"Yes, please."

I took off my shoes and jacket, and went into the back bedroom. The clock on the dresser said two thirty. I'd nap for an hour then help Helen with dinner. Help later— sleep now.

I woke up after six; Karen and Helen were putting dinner out. After dinner we had coffee in the living room. Ethan watched *Rowan & Martin's Laugh-In*, squealing hysterically, especially where someone got doused with water. I fell back to sleep right after dinner.

*

On Tuesday morning, I walked, alone, to my house. There was a cozy feeling to the place I hadn't felt before. Maybe I was imagining it, but it suddenly felt like home.

The phone would be connected in a week. The gas was turned on. The yard looked good, and most of our furniture was in place. It would take no time to complete the move.

I walked to the backyard and made sure the Fiat was secure. Out of the corner of my eye, I noticed a woman staring at me. A neighbor, over the low fence. She frowned at my unfamiliar face.

"Hello. Good morning," I said, waving.

She nodded, scraggly white hair and metal-rimmed glasses reflecting sunlight. She leaned on an inverted broom, like one half of the painting *American Gothic*.

"Hi," she answered. Her voice was like a long fart.

"Bet you're wondering who I am." I smiled.

"Who are you?" she replied, her expression suggesting she smelled something bad.

"Your new neighbor. It's my house—Gerald and Nancy were my tenants."

She sniffed slightly. "I liked Gerry. Nancy too. No kids. You got kids?"

I thought about how I wanted to answer that. "We're raising one child. He's four. His name's Ethan."

She sniffed again. "Sounds Jewish."

"Nope." I gritted my teeth. "Hindu Zoroastrians. Hope you don't mind animal sacrifices."

She wagged a finger at me, wide-eyed, "You can't do that in this neighborhood. We'll call the police."

I pulled out my warrant card. "Relax. I'm kidding. I'm a police officer."

She squinted at my name. "You're that cop, the one who got shot," she said, incredulous.

"And lived to tell about it, yeah. See you in a couple of weeks." I walked back to Frank's. The walk had taken its toll. I fell asleep.

A voice roused me. Helen. "He's waking up, Karen."

I swung upright and put my hands on my knees. I felt better, but still weak. I joined the women and tried, unsuccessfully, to help with dinner.

Frank came home, looking very pleased with himself. "Know who did time with Chooch?" He grinned. "Front desk guy at The Carlton Inn. They discovered he let Chooch stay there. Fired him next day, hasn't surfaced since."

"Really? I was right, then." I smiled.

We ate dinner; I did the crossword and fell immediately asleep again.

I wanted to drive Frank in on Thursday. The following day, Good Friday, everyone would be home. I had a plan.

Karen showed up at seven thirty; I told her I'd just drive Frank to work and come home. She agreed, grudgingly. Karen left; Frank and I drove off a minute later.

"Frank," I said, at a red light, "can you tell Helen I'll be out a while?"

"Going somewhere?" He didn't seem surprised.

"I want to see Gary. Besides, it's Maundy Thursday. I want to go to church."

"Fine, but I want you home early," he said with a scowl.

I snickered. "Yes, Dad."

He broke out in a wide smile. "Yeah, OK, right. Go, kid. Be careful."

Gary's house was different since my last visit. The aluminum screen door was clean, and the windows were now shiny. The wooden back stairs had been replaced by a neat series of blocks laid carefully against the house. I opened the screen door and knocked. The inner door opened.

A woman peered out, a young, smooth version of the one who'd taken care of Gary's dog. She wore faded jeans and a baggy sweater, and peered at me with a puzzled look.

"Yes?" she asked.

"Is Gary home?" It sounded strange to ask that.

"One moment, please." She looked over her

shoulder. "Gary, we have a visitor."

Gary appeared in a plaid shirt and pleated slacks. His hair was combed. "Detective McBriar," he gushed. "Please, please come in. Sit down." The woman stood off to one side, furtively looking back to the open bedroom door.

The mismatched dining set was gone, replaced by a newer table and chairs. The spice canisters on the counter were lined up by height—a woman's touch. Gary sat across from me, the woman beside him, holding his hand under the table.

I smiled. "I don't believe I've met your friend."

"This is Barb. My girlfriend." He giggled.

"Hi, Barb, I'm Ian." I reached out my arm.

She placed a bony hand in mine. "Hi, nice to meet you." She giggled as well.

Gary grinned at us. "Barb makes really good rice pudding. Would you like some rice pudding, Ian?"

I nodded. "I'd love some."

The woman put on a kettle and went to the fridge. Gary gazed after her. "Thanks, babe." They both giggled.

She made instant coffee, frowning as she scooped powder and poured boiling water. She carefully, slowly brought the coffee out, along with three bowls of pudding. Gary beamed as she sat back down, then he frowned and hung his head.

"You got hurt bad. It was my fault, wasn't it?"

I shook my head. "Gary, don't say that. Don't you ever say that. You were hurt by the same man I was. It's not your fault."

He shrugged, unconvinced.

"Tell you what," I said. "If you hadn't been stabbed, Dixie wouldn't have been taken away, and you would never have met Barb, isn't that right?"

"I guess."

"And I wouldn't have tasted this amazing pudding."

They both giggled. I assured Gary that he was out of danger. He seemed more relieved for Barb than for himself.

I left another of my business cards, just in case, and wished them well.

*

My last stop was at Immaculate Conception. The church was empty, except for two ladies cleaning pews. They'd prepared the church for Good Friday—removing all the decorations to respect the memory of the Crucifixion. The church was denuded, the flowers gone, the altar cloth stored until Easter. The church, even bare, was still a comforting place.

I sat in my usual pew, praying. Would Chooch also attend mass, I wondered? A door opened by the vestry, and the old man, this time in a cardigan, walked to the back. He stopped, stared at me, looked carefully around, and sat beside me.

"You OK?" he asked, in a thick accent.

"Better, thank you," I replied.

"Not good, shoot police. Bad business." He waved a hand in the air.

"Especially if it's me," I agreed.

He smiled sheepishly. "Mr. Nick say you a good cop. You gonna get Chooch for Mr. Nick?"

"I'm going to bring him to justice," I answered carefully.

"Same thing." He got up and left. I sat through Mass and went home.

Helen smiled at me as I came back in. "Everything OK?" she asked.

"Gary has a girlfriend; she's cute."

She leaned back, surprised. "Really? Learning from you, is he?"

"Thanks for that." I chuckled. "Something I've wanted to tell you both. Thank you for taking care of me, and for being great with Karen and Ethan."

She shook her head. "Don't be silly. And of course, stay here as long as you want."

"I really appreciate that. Now, mind if I cook dinner?"

"Have a blast, Ian." She grinned.

The grocer refused to take my money. He was just delighted that I was alive. After much arguing, I threatened to arrest him for bribing a policeman, and he relented, smiling. We loaded two paper grocery bags into the Fury, setting them carefully on the front seat.

Standing on the sidewalk holding a bag of groceries brought a brief shudder of déjà vu, memories of the last time I'd done that. I made dinner and took a nap.

At five thirty, a cruiser pulled up; Frank opened the front door and stopped dead.

"What's that smell?" he barked, sniffing the air.

"Ian made dinner." Helen kissed him.

"Good thing you're cuter than he is," Frank teased.

At a quarter after six, I heard small feet jumping up steps, and heels following them. Ethan opened the door and hugged me.

"Hi, Pops," he squealed.

I looked at Karen. She shrugged, mystified. She hadn't prompted him to say that.

"How are you, son?" I answered, squeezing him back with my good arm.

"Mrs. Waleski took us out," he gushed. "We saw lots of aminals."

"Really? What kind of aminals?"

"They had goats and cows and horses."

"Ah," I said, "you went to the dry cleaner's."

Ethan laughed at the joke. "No, at the zoo. Uncle Frank, can I play with your trains?"

"Course, sport, after dinner." Frank smiled. "Right now, let's eat." Frank waited for his food like a child waiting for Santa Claus.

Helen had grilled some vegetables. I'd made roast beef. Soon the house was silent, except for the clatter of cutlery on china.

Five minutes into the meal, Frank coughed. "Is there any of this stuff left?" he asked hopefully.

"There's lots. You'll be having leftovers till next week."

"Bless your heart, kid."

Nobody worked Good Friday, so we had a later night than usual. Helen pulled Frank aside and whispered, gesturing and nodding. He opened his mouth stupidly and smiled, then strolled over to me, casually.

"Hey, kid. Would you mind if we kept Ethan overnight? You can pick him up tomorrow. He'd need your room, of course, OK?"

"If it's fine with you guys," I said casually, "I'm sure I can stay with Karen."

"Fine, then." He nodded solemnly.

Karen and I fell over each other taking our clothes off. I deposited her on her bed and peeled her jeans away from her thighs. We embraced, skin to skin for the first time in weeks. I kissed her as passionately as I ever had. My shoulder hurt, and my arm was sore, but it didn't matter. We made love.

Afterwards, I brought us ginger ale. Karen sat up, rolling the glass back and forth between her hands. She frowned. "The man who shot you, how could talk to him so calmly?" Her eyes searched mine.

I shrugged. "He didn't do that to *you*, though. If he had, I'd have killed him." I slid back under the sheets. Karen embraced me.

"Keep safe," she said, rubbing her fingers over my lips. "I need you to be healthy, for a long, long time."

"Is that an answer?" I asked.

"Think of it as a notice of intent."

I woke up at five thirty, with Karen pressed into my ribs. I'd missed her so much it ached. I caressed her back and the curve of her spine. She lifted her head and looked up at me. She smiled.

"Hey, you."

"I missed you," I said. I kissed her forehead. "I can't tell you how much I missed you."

"Good. *Shh.*" She wrapped an arm over my waist. She fell back to sleep.

We showered and ate breakfast; just two people without a care in the world. Karen looked through to Ethan's bed and sighed.

"It's nice being without him. Is that wrong?"

"It's just natural. You've been both parents to Ethan for his whole life. That must be a tremendous strain

—no time to yourself, no time off." I waved at the half-empty room. "This is like being on vacation for you, I guess."

"Only with sexier room service."

Around nine I used the pay phone outside the drugstore and called Frank.

"Kid, amazing news," he enthused. "The OPP got lucky. The key opened a locker at the Greyhound depot. They're bringing the contents to the station now."

"I'll be over right away, Frank," I said eagerly.

Karen stayed with Helen. Frank and I drove to the office, excited. An OPP cop, a copper-haired youth by the name of Owen Murphy, stood at my desk, glowering at a metal box they'd brought from Niagara Falls. Frank swung the lid open.

Inside was the gun from Chooch's apartment, the box of bullets, and a thick envelope. Murphy reached into his shirt pocket and extracted a pencil. He poked it into the barrel of the revolver and lifted it out of the box. He turned the pencil around to examine the gun without touching it. "Four shots fired," he commented.

"Yeah, and I know where they went," I joked.

He laid the gun carefully back into the box and picked up the envelope. He pulled a pen from his shirt, used it to slit the flap open, and dumped the contents onto the desk. Five thick, banded wads of twenty dollar bills dropped out, accompanied by another three wads of fifties.

At the bottom of the box was a business card that read *Zimmerman of Toronto Fine Furniture—Maureen Zimmerman*. Frank handed it to me. "Think she's involved?" he asked.

I shook my head. "Why keep the business card, though?" I wondered aloud.

Frank flipped the card over. The back was blank—no note, message, phone number. "Could she be behind this?"

"Kill her own brother?" I said skeptically. "Maybe she's helping Chooch for Anthony's sake?"

Frank scratched his cheek. "Screw it. It will get clearer tomorrow."

Chapter Fifteen

I dropped Frank home around two thirty, went to mass, and got home by five. Frank was on the phone, making notes and talking quickly to the person on the other end.

Karen and Helen were making cookies as I came in; they smiled and went back to rolling dough. I felt both irritation and relief that I was no longer the center of attention.

I sat on the sofa and waited for Frank to finish his call. He nodded, went *uh huh*, and scribbled more notes. He hung up and looked my way. "OK, kid," he started. "On Sunday, you're talking to Chooch again, right?"

I nodded.

"This time, we'll have the phone tapped. If you talk to him for three minutes, we can trace him and nab him."

"I think he's smarter than we give him credit for."

"What do you mean?"

I leaned forward. "I think he's too smart to be caught like that. Last time, he sent a message for me to call him in under two hours. I doubt he'd use that phone if he knows we can trace him."

On Saturday, after breakfast, we all walked to my house. The movers would bring the last few things next week, then we'd be all done.

Ethan was thrilled by his room. He and Frank played at having tea, lounging on the sofa, their feet on the coffee table.

We toured every room, walked the backyard and admired the first buds of cherry blossoms on the trees beside the garage. Karen wrapped her arm around my waist.

"Happy?" she asked.

"Thrilled. I can't wait till May. How does Ethan feel about all this?"

"He can't wait either."

I placed my left arm on her shoulder and instantly felt like I'd been hit by lightning. "Damn." I dropped to my knees. "Damn, damn, damn."

Karen hugged me, panicked. "What's wrong? What is it, what happened?" she gasped.

Frank circled around me, his back to us, scanning the neighbors' houses and yards.

"It's not a sniper, Frank," I said. "It's shoulder pain."

He relaxed and faced me. "Is it bad, kid?"

"It doesn't tickle, Frank." I stood up, slowly.

Karen was still holding my waist. "What happened?" she repeated.

"Lifted my arm, felt a shock, hurt like hell," I said, gasping.

"You're going to hospital," she declared. We all wedged into the Beetle and drove to Northwestern.

The emergency room was crowded, but Frank whispered something to a nurse on duty, and they took me in right away. I sat on the edge of a cot, embarrassed at the fuss.

The doctor walked in, a Ben Casey type in a crisp white smock. "You've been overdoing it, Officer?" he scolded. He touched my shoulder. "Does this hurt?"

I shook my head. He touched something by the shoulder blade. The lightning hit me again. I bent forward, wincing.

The doctor went *hmm* and looked me in the eye. "Have you recently been sexually active?" he asked.

"Excuse me?" I said, indignant.

"I'll take that as a yes." He started writing something on a clipboard. "You'll have to take care. Sex now could damage your shoulder."

"Will I still be able to play the violin?" I joked.

He put his pen in a breast pocket and folded his hands in front of him. "You have brachial neuritis. It's not uncommon, but it can be painful."

"And?" I asked hopefully.

"Rest, physiotherapy, and you should be on stage with Jascha Heifetz in no time."

"Stéphane Grappelli, actually."

His eyes widened. "A jazz cat? Really." He looked at the ceiling, thinking. "McBriar, McBriar. Do you have a relative who plays trumpet?"

"My brother James; his band is The Scarlet Pimpernels."

He nodded. "I saw them in Montreal last year. They're very good."

I smiled. "I'll tell him you said so. He'll appreciate that."

He scribbled something and read the notes in the file. "You're lucky just to be alive." He gritted his teeth. "You've heard that before, I gather. Take my advice. Go easy. You're not Superman."

"Thanks, doc. And if you see James again, say hi for me."

"Stay cool, man." He grinned. "The nurse will give you some pain killers, and I'll write you a prescription for more. Go home and rest. No whoopee tonight."

"There goes the weekend," I said.

Helen and Karen made dinner. Frank and Ethan watched TV. I stared at the carpet.

"Penny for your thoughts?" Frank asked.

"Why leave the gun at the locker? It's pointless to stash it a hundred miles away."

He nodded. "I'm wondering why he had Maureen Zimmerman's business card. Did he take it, or did she give it to him?"

"We can ask her Monday. We'll drop by and—"

"We?" Frank snapped. "We, paleface? What do you mean, *we*? Forget it, kid. You're on crutch brigade until I say otherwise." He smiled icily. "Can you do *this?*" He clapped his hands over his head. I didn't move. He leaned close. "No? Then stay home."

I slept fretfully, alone, without Karen. I couldn't wait to get into the house.

Also, I felt something was wrong about the box from the bus depot. I felt we'd missed something vital. Forget it, I thought. Tomorrow was Easter Sunday. I had other things on my mind.

I got up at five thirty; nobody else was awake. I attended early mass. The Palumbos were absent—a mixed blessing. I was glad to be left alone, but I'd wanted to know if Chooch had contacted Anthony. I came home and put coffee on.

At eight in the morning, Karen drove up. Ethan, wearing paper rabbit ears, carried a paper grocery bag, cut up to look like a basket. We all watched him hunt for Easter eggs.

He hopped giddily, collecting chocolate goodies stashed around the house. A half hour later, he was tired and overwhelmed by the foil-wrapped loot in his basket, so we called off the chase and stopped for brunch.

I made pancakes, eggs, and bacon, covering the stove with pans and skillets, moving like a church organist playing a Bach oratorio.

We passed around food, coffee, and syrup to the sound of three conversations at once. Frank grunted approval, reaching for coffee while nodding and chewing. Ethan smiled, biting a bacon rasher dipped in ketchup.

"This is real good, Pops."

"Glad you like it, son. More milk?" I rubbed his hair. I took his glass through to the kitchen, vaguely aware I was being followed. I turned to see who needed what, and was attacked by a pair of lips.

Karen wrapped her arms around me and wrestled me to the wall. I didn't struggle. She kissed me, then she stood back. "That's for breakfast," she cooed.

"Really? Wow."

She wrapped one arm around me and kissed me

again. "That's for calling him son."

I smiled. "He deserves it. Actually he deserves better, but I'm all I got."

She propped one arm up against the wall and poked my ribs. "You're more than good enough. Believe me, you'll do."

"You're moving way up in my list of top three girls, you know."

"Good. Any way I can help?"

"Just bring more eggs, if you would."

"Right away, sweetheart."

I blushed. The "sweetheart" gave me a shiver that I hadn't expected.

Brunch went on till almost noon. I stuffed the turkey and put it in the fridge. We were all still full, so I suggested walking to my house to burn off the meal.

The walk felt good. My shoulder was not sore, and I could lift my arm without feeling too much discomfort, as long as I didn't overdo it.

Frank and Helen swung Ethan between them again as Karen and I walked behind. That now seemed natural, too. Ethan saw them as real relatives, a real aunt and uncle he'd only found a month ago.

We walked across the street from my house to the school playground. Something occurred to me—I didn't know Ethan's exact age. "Hon, when's Ethan's birthday?" I asked Karen.

"He'll be five in July, on the twenty-fourth." She smiled.

"So, he'll go to kindergarten here in September?"

Her face dropped.

"What is it?" I asked.

"He's growing up. I didn't think it would be so fast. He's growing up so fast."

I nodded gravely. "He can't have the car till grade three, though."

She hit my arm. "Idiot."

"Made you feel better."

"You always do."

Frank chased Ethan around the monkey bars and

showed him how to flip himself over the supports. Karen laughed at the two mismatched kids. They charged up and down the field, Frank huffing theatrically, chasing Ethan, never quite catching him. Ethan doubled over slightly.

"I gotta pee," he complained.

I smiled. "I know where you can go."

We crossed the street back to my house to let Ethan use the toilet. Helen and Karen discussed furniture, and Frank drank some water.

"Still like the place, kid?"

"Yep. It's perfect for a small family. It's also close to very good friends." I looked at him, very serious. He put his glass down.

"You're not gonna hug me, are you?"

"Maybe later."

As we got back to Frank's, the fatigue from the walk overpowered me. I put the turkey in the oven, instructing Helen how to baste it, and took a nap.

The smell of roasting turkey woke me. I sat upright and rotated my shoulder. I felt almost no pain. I clapped both hands above my head. Bad idea—it hurt like hell.

Frank was on the phone, scribbling notes on his Moleskine book as he listened. He closed the book. "Fine. We'll be there at ten to. Stay sharp." He looked my way. "Hey, kid. We got backup bodies for your call."

"Is that today? I forgot," I joked.

Frank smirked. "There's a tap on the phone. We got two plainclothes in the alley. We'll drive you down and stay out of sight, just like before."

"No." I shook my head. "Helen stays home. I'm driving."

Frank looked back and forth between her and me. He smiled. "OK. Thanks, kid." He was visibly relieved. Helen was anxious.

"What's the matter?" I asked her.

"Something's not right. I just feel it."

"Maybe it's just nerves? We'll be fine, you'll see."

Frank and I discussed how to keep Chooch talking, so we could trace the call. Frank had a walkie-talkie. He would hide in the Fury, talking to the plainclothes. When they had spotted Chooch, he'd tap the brake lights to signal me.

Just after four, Karen stared at me for a long time, then grabbed my face in her hands. "You," she whispered. She repeated it softly. "You."

"I know. I will." I kissed her nose. "C'mon, Frank, I want to be back in time for turkey."

"Damn straight." He sniffed the air. "Stuffing?"

"Mushroom chestnut stuffing."

He melted. "Hell, I'm staying home. You go alone."

We laughed and headed out. Helen wrung her hands. Karen just stared at us. We parked down the street from the phone booth, with Frank scrunched down so passersby would not see him.

The street was deserted. Toronto was out of the playoffs, and Maple Leaf Gardens was empty. The stores and restaurants had closed for Easter Sunday. Just before five, I walked to the phone booth. The phone rang immediately. I picked it up.

"Hello?"

"OK, cop, now I'm pissed off."

"Chooch? What's the matter? What's wrong?"

"There's a phone on the other side of the road. Run!" he yelled.

"But why are you upset—" The line went dead.

Helen was right. Chooch knew we would tap the phone, given a week. He was smart. We hadn't thought of tapping any other phones.

I ran across the street. Frank was staring through the Fury's back window wide-eyed, barking into the walkie-talkie. Just turn back, just walk away, I thought.

I kept going. The phone across the street was already ringing. I picked it up.

"Why are you mad at me, Vince?" I wheezed, winded.

"I just wanted to see you run, that's all." He laughed. He didn't want to get caught, I got that. I just hated being jerked around.

"What do you say, Vince? Consider my offer?" I was still panting.

"Let's talk," he growled.

"Sure. So, have you thought any more about my offer?"

"Still thinking it over," he taunted.

I was irritated by the dismissive tone. I decided to shake him up. "By the way, your car's real nice, but it was a little noisy, so we took it to a muffler shop. It'll be ready Tuesday, if you do want it back."

There was a long silence.

"Where did you take it?" There was panic his voice. I had him now. I sighed, pretending to think.

"Umm, some place on Jane Street."

"Why would you do that?" he bellowed.

"Like I said, it was noisy."

Another long silence; I glanced back. Frank had climbed into the driver's seat.

"So, you found the key, huh?" Chooch asked.

I smiled to myself. No, he didn't want us to find the key. I decided to play with him. "Yeah, well, what's the key for, that's the question?" I asked.

"Have fun figuring that out. Besides, I don't really need the key." He laughed.

"Even for a locker at the Greyhound bus depot in Niagara Falls?"

I heard him gasp. "You found my stuff?" he screamed.

Now I laughed. It was childish, but I enjoyed besting him. "What stuff was that?" I teased.

Silence again.

"Wait right there." He hung up.

I checked the time: five ten p.m. We would be home and eating dinner by six. When he called back, I'd dictate the rules for the next call.

A bus raced by. The roar of the bus's engine brought an involuntary shiver of fear. I leaned in, so I could hear the phone ringing over it, and waited.

Five minutes and no phone call yet. I was ready to leave. I looked back again and saw Frank, still on the walkie-talkie, still watching me. I waited.

I noticed a car driving past me, a big, two-door

Eldorado. It slowed in the deserted street, hung a quick U-turn, and stopped behind me. The passenger door opened and Chooch glared out at me, gripping the steering wheel.

"Get in!" he yelled.

I crouched beside the car. "Man, can't we talk for just a bit? Let's clear this up right here, OK?"

He gritted his teeth. "I said get in! *Now!*"

Walk away, I thought. Don't get in.

I got in, gingerly, but left the door open. Out of the corner of my eye I saw Frank scrambling to start the Fury. Chooch glanced in the rearview and saw it too.

He jammed the car into drive and accelerated. My door swung shut. "You got some balls, cop, taking my stuff!"

"So, are you driving me home?" I smiled, acting cool. "Thanks. Saves me bus fare."

"You stupid, cop?" he snarled. "You don't get it? I *worked* for that money."

I laughed. I was scared witless, but I had to stand up to him. "You already shot me. What else can you threaten me with?"

He bit his lip, furious. I didn't want to show I was terrified—I had him talking to me. He swung onto Yonge Street, cutting off two cars. They swerved, honking loudly.

He blasted through traffic, went a couple of blocks north, stomped on the brakes, and peeled right down a laneway. I couldn't see Frank behind us; I hoped he'd seen us turn. My door scraped along a brick wall, ripping off the outside mirror.

Chooch slammed to a stop and shifted into park. I braced my right elbow against the dashboard and clutched my waist theatrically with my right arm. Chooch poked my bad arm. It wasn't sore, but I winced as if it was.

"Hurts, cop?" he jeered. He poked me again, and I cringed convincingly.

"Pussy," he said. "Tell you what, you get me my money. It's mine. *Mine*, you hear? You get me my money. Then I talk."

I groaned and rubbed my shoulder. "There was no money in the box, Vince, just some newspaper."

"What? You serious?" His mouth hung opened.

"You had cash in there?" I acted surprised. "How much?"

"Twenty-five grand." He pursed his lips. "Where did it go?"

"I was there when they opened the box. There was no money, just newspaper."

He stared off, thinking. I couldn't lose this chance to get his accomplice's name.

I cringed slightly, still acting injured. "Who gave you the money?" I asked innocently.

He smiled and shook his head. He wouldn't fall for that. I tried a different approach. "Why was Maureen Zimmerman's business card in the box?"

"You tell me," he snapped. He studied me, deciding something. "OK," he said, "Easter present for you. Why did I use the name Carpenter?" He looked in the rearview mirror; the laneway was still empty.

I replied, "In German it's Zimmerman. Why did you get fake ID from Connecticut?"

He just smiled.

"Why was Maureen's card in the box?" I pressed.

He kept smiling. "Ever think I didn't load the box? All in good time, man. You want more clues, bring me my money. All twenty-five gees."

"Who has it?" I asked.

"Figure it out, man. You got all the pieces. Like I said, in good time." He took the key out of the ignition, jumped out, and slammed the door behind him.

He dragged over a garbage can, wedged it against his door handle and walked away. My door was against the wall. His door was wedged shut. I was trapped.

I felt the way I had on the elevator. I kicked with all my might but couldn't open the door. I sat there for about three minutes, breathing deeply and trying to stay calm.

The glow of headlights behind me lit the dashboard. I turned to see who it was. The Fury coasted to a stop behind me. Frank crept out, his gun pointed down.

He checked the back seat, holstered his revolver,

and dragged the garbage can away.

"You took your time," I joked.

"I stopped for donuts," he grunted. "Besides, the car's set for somebody eight inches taller." He rethought the statement. "Four inches taller."

We called dispatch to tow the Eldorado, took some notes, and headed home. I checked my watch: five forty. Helen and Karen would be worrying about us.

I stopped at a pay phone to call them. There was no point in going over the scary details, so I just said we were heading back. Frank agreed with that white lie.

I smiled and ate and joked with Ethan, but all I could think of was Chooch. We carved turkey, had gravy with stuffing and glazed carrots, but I tasted nothing.

After dinner, Frank called me down to the basement. He just stood there, facing me. "You took a big chance, kid," he said.

"Sorry?"

"You got into his car without backup, right?"

"You'd have done the same."

He nodded. "I've been there. I've put my head in the lion's mouth. Best I can say is to play it safe. He who turns and runs away, and all. We'll get him eventually."

"OK. I'll show more caution next time." I smiled. "Now, can we have dessert?"

"You better not get upstairs before me."

We were all home for Easter Monday. I asked Frank to take Ethan overnight again. It didn't take much persuading. Karen and I again fell all over each other getting naked.

Her apartment was bare now; the dresser and the beds were the only items in the room. The closet was empty, the carpet was gone, and even the drapes were replaced by tattered old sheets, kept for the sole purpose of covering the windows.

The apartment echoed; Karen turned on her radio so passersby would not hear us. The local CBC station was broadcasting big band music. We made love to "Sing, Sing, Sing" and "Moonlight Serenade."

*

I woke up at five in the morning, our four legs intertwined and my arm over Karen's waist, caressing her bottom. Her arm was over my shoulder, and her face was under my chin. I caressed her, softly, following the shape of her lower back. She tilted her head up slightly and kissed the underside of my chin.

"Morning," she whispered.

I pulled her closer. "Morning. Hungry?" I asked.

She nodded.

"Buy you breakfast?" I offered. I nibbled her ear.

"Big spender."

I went downstairs to the pay phone and called Frank. "Hey, how's Ethan?" I asked.

"Holy terror," he teased. "Are you decent enough to eat with us?"

"Sure. I wanted to treat everyone to breakfast out."

Frank cackled. "Hey, always accept free food. See you soon."

We drove the Fury to High Park, to a restaurant with a view of Grenadier Pond.

"Already spending like a Sergeant?" Frank asked.

"It's a special occasion, Frank. It's Easter."

We ate overlooking the gardens, then walked around the pond, tossing bread to the hungry ducks. The first spring flowers poked meekly through the soil. Here and there violets, finally convinced that winter was over, struggled out of the ground. Helen and Karen walked ahead, swinging Ethan between them. Frank and I hung back.

"So, you told him his money wasn't in the box," Frank said.

"Yes. He thinks his accomplice took the cash."

"We don't know where Chooch is. And we can't find that guy till Chooch finds him." Frank sighed.

"We have Maureen Zimmerman's card," I reminded him. "They're closed today though."

"Yeah. Are you up for some work tomorrow?"

"You bet, Frank."

Chapter Sixteen

I walk up the porch steps to Leo's house. He is in the living room, watching TV. I open the front door and walk in. He stands up and looks at me.

"Hi," he says. "Glad you're here."

He listens for a moment. I don't know what I've said.

"The cops found a car," he says. "A Chevy. Hey, you like Chevys, right?"

I fire three bullets into his chest. He looks at the holes in his shirt.

"Why?" he asks, puzzled. He falls backwards, staggering over the coffee table. "Why?" he asks again. He dies.

I woke up. There was a half-moon in the sky. Pale gray streetlight filled the bedroom. It was very early, and Leo was no longer haunting me. I went back to sleep.

Seven a.m. I dressed, made oatmeal and coffee, and put toast on.

Helen shuffled through in her robe and wrapped a friendly arm around me. "Morning, Ian." She sniffed the air. "Gosh, I'll miss having you here. By the way, you guys are more than welcome to stay with us, if needs be."

"Thanks. You're a good friend."

She reached up and kissed my cheek.

Frank came into the kitchen, tie in hand. "So, making a move on my old lady, huh?" he smirked.

"Second foxiest woman I know."

"Only second?" He scowled at me and kissed her.

Karen arrived and talked to Helen about September and Ethan's school. They agreed, to everyone's joy, that Ethan could walk to Helen's after kindergarten. It made sense. It was perfect. Ethan ate toast and played with a Hot Wheels car.

Karen kissed me goodbye and drove Ethan to Mrs. Waleski's. I sighed. I just wanted Maureen Zimmerman to help answer all our questions. My questions.

Zimmerman Fine Furniture didn't open till ten in the morning. We stopped by the station and wrapped up some loose paperwork. The Mohawk kids who had rolled over on the auto parts thieves were gone, but their information had helped us nab their bosses.

Forensics had matched Chooch's gun to the bullets taken out of me and Leo Bernardin. Chooch was as good as convicted. Just before ten, I called Zimmerman Fine Furniture. The saleswoman from before picked up the phone.

"Detective, they said you'd been hurt," she said, puzzled.

"Yes, but reports of my death were greatly exaggerated," I joked.

"How can I help you?" she asked, businesslike.

I tilted my chair back, trying to sound more at ease. "Is Maureen in the office today?"

"No, she isn't."

"Where can we find her, please?"

"We?" Her tone was pleasant but cautious.

I closed my eyes. Stupid, stupid, stupid, I thought. I should have said "I." I smiled, hoping the smile would carry through the phone. "I'm just trying to clear up some final bits. Do you know where I can find her?"

The woman hesitated. "She's on her way back from a family weekend. She should be in around five tonight."

I wrinkled my nose. Why would she come in so late in the day? "I'm sorry, where is she?"

More hesitation. "She and Mr. Zimmerman went to Connecticut."

My eyes widened. I banged my desk. Frank sat straight up.

"Connecticut? Why are they there?" I tried to sound casual, but not very convincingly.

There was a final moment of reluctance, then I sensed a wall falling. "Look, he's not a very nice man, but I need the job, OK? We have teenagers to feed."

I waved Frank over and leaned forward. "Listen," I urged her, "we've got a murder investigation going. Any information you give me will stay confidential."

She let out a long breath, making up her mind. "OK. But I told you nothing. *Nothing.*"

"Agreed. We got it from someone else. You have my word."

Frank sat, watching me. I heard the woman cup her hand around the receiver.

"I don't know what's going on," she whispered. "Something's up. They aren't yelling, or arguing, or anything, but a few weeks ago the bookkeeper was screaming at Bruno. He'd taken out a bank loan. She yelled, 'Why would you do that?' and 'Are you crazy?' He fired her on the spot. I don't get it. We're doing fine for sales, we're not short on cash."

Frank stared at me expectantly.

"Any idea how much the loan was for?" I asked. It was a long shot, I knew.

"Yeah," she confessed. "The bookkeeper is a friend of mine. She felt bad telling me, but said better I should find out in case they went broke owing me back pay." I heard footsteps on the phone. She paused, and the footsteps receded.

I wrote *Bruno—bank loan* and turned it so Frank could read. He mouthed, "How much?" I nodded and put my hand up.

The woman was clearly anxious about being overheard. "He got out twenty-five thousand dollars. Why would he do that? There's only three of us, plus him and his wife. Why would he do that?"

My eyes widened. Frank whispered, "What?" I wrote *$25G*.

Frank sat back, eyes wide, his mouth open. The woman coughed nervously.

"Look, I don't know what all this means. Keep this in confidence, that's all. Period."

"Sure. Thanks," I said sincerely. "Look, I know this is uncomfortable for you; I won't involve you beyond this. This could have come from anyone."

"Thanks, I appreciate that." She sounded relieved.

"I have a silly question," I added, cheerily. "Why are they in Connecticut?"

She lightened up. This subject was clearly more like gossip than betraying a secret. "Oh, Bruno's parents live in New Haven. His father retired there some time ago."

I kept writing. "Why does he live so far away?" I was just chatting, trying to put her at ease.

"He worked in insurance; he still owns a house in Hartford, Connecticut."

My mouth dropped open. Frank again hissed, "What?"

I closed my mouth and smiled. "Great," I replied cordially. "Anything else you can tell me?"

"No," she said. "Sorry, I have a customer. Goodbye." She hung up abruptly.

I put the phone down and smiled. "Bruno's father was in insurance. He mentioned that when you went to Palumbo's."

Frank nodded. "I remember."

"Did you know his father lived in Hartford, Connecticut?"

Frank sat back, making the connection. "Oh, shit. Bruno is Chooch's accomplice."

"Zimmerman will be in at five. We'll just wait around till then." I called Karen and offered to buy her lunch. She was delighted.

At eleven fifty-five I parked on Front Street, left my *Police Business* sign on the dash, and sprinted up the stairs to the lobby. The gray-haired security guard stood and stretched a hand out.

"Detective," he wheezed. "Glad to see you're doing

well."

I shook his hand. "Thanks. I'm heading up to twelve, OK?" He nodded and sat down.

The elevator door opened. I pushed the floor button and waited for the wave of panic. It didn't come. The door closed; I rode the car up to the twelfth floor, inhaled deeply, and stepped out into the dark hall. Again, I felt fine—no panic.

"Thank you, Chooch," I mumbled. "You made that go away, at least." After being hijacked and trapped in the Eldorado, this seemed trivial. The fear was gone.

I opened the door to Mortgages. Karen was on my side of the counter with several women, sorting through stacks of forms. They all stopped talking when they saw me.

"Hey, you," she said.

"Hello, gorgeous." I kissed her.

A collective *awww* came up from the group. Karen blushed a deep red.

"Shall we go?" I asked. The women giggled, and we headed out. We waited for the elevator. Karen watched me, ready to calm me down. I hummed softly, casually watching the floor numbers on the display.

"You aren't upset?" she asked, curious.

I spoke without thinking. "After Sunday, this is a piece of cake."

"What happened on Sunday?" she snapped, suddenly alert. Her eyes drilled into me.

"Oh, crap." I cringed, realizing what I'd said.

"What happened?" she repeated. "What did he do to you?"

"Fine." I sighed. "Tell you over lunch."

I took us to a good restaurant, specifically to put her at ease. She'd also be less inclined to make a fuss in a place like that. I told her that Chooch had lured me to a different phone. She turned pale.

I quickly said that Frank was always right there beside me, and I was never in danger. I then told her that, after the phone call, Frank and I saw Chooch drive past us, but we couldn't catch him. She picked at her salad and smiled cynically.

"Bullshit," she said. "I don't believe you."

"Sorry?"

"You are so full of crap, Ian." She put her fork down and cradled her face in her hands. "And you are a rotten liar. Now, tell me what *really* happened."

I sighed and told her the whole story. "Please don't tell Helen," I pleaded, finally.

She shook her head. "Do you keep things from Frank?" she asked.

"That's different."

"No, it's not. He's your friend, and she's my friend."

"Not being told stops her from worrying, but not knowing might get Frank shot."

She leaned back and thought for a minute. "Got me there." She pointed her fork at me. "But if this happens again . . ."

"OK, here's a quote for you," I said. "Love is not in our choice but in our fate.'"

She snorted. "Meaning?"

"I couldn't love you more." I leaned forward. "I couldn't stop loving you either."

"Smooth-talking bastard," she said. But she smiled.

After lunch I stopped by Gary's house. Barb was in one of Gary's shirts, weeding the yard. The dog followed her, wagging its tail. I leaned on the fence, and she waved at me.

"Hi," I said. "Lovely day. It's Barb, isn't it?"

"Hello, Detective McBriar." She giggled and pulled off a gardening glove. "Nice to see you again, Detective." She held her bony hand out.

"Call me Ian. Can I call you babe?" I joked.

She giggled again. "Only Gary calls me that."

Gary came out the side door with a glass of lemonade. He handed it to Barb and she kissed his cheek. He placed an arm around her waist.

"Looks like it's going well for you two," I said.

Barb beamed. "We've been going for walks. Gary can walk all the way to St. Clair Avenue now. We even went to a movie last week."

"What did you see?" I asked.

"We saw *Tom Sawyer*," he said happily. "It was fun. There was singing and dancing and stuff. Babe really likes those movies, don't you, sweetie?"

"Yep, I do." She giggled again. Gary looked at the glass in her hand.

"Would you like some lemonade, Detective?"

"Thanks, but it's just a quick visit. If you need anything, you have my card, right?"

He nodded. Barb hugged his arm.

"Take care. Goodbye, you two." I drove back to the station. Frank was at his desk, reading.

"Have a romantic lunch?"

I nodded. I decided to keep my conversation with Karen to myself. "Went to see Gary too. He's a happy guy; got the girlfriend living there, looks like."

"Am I the only one who doesn't have a new girlfriend?" Frank snorted.

I snickered. "Something you and Ethan have in common."

He laughed and gently threw a pencil at me. "Dick." He leaned forward, serious. "Guess what I've been doing while you gallivant around eating lunch?"

"Gallivant? That's a big word, Frank."

He ignored the jab and slid a sheet of paper at me. "Bruno Zimmerman's father was a claims agent for the Empire State Life Insurance Company, which operated in New York and Connecticut. They were bought up this year by some big outfit. Anyway, my buddy in the business did some checking.

"Back in forty-eight, the old man handled a claim for some kid who died of pneumonia in Waterbury, Connecticut. Seems Zimmerman Sr. is a stand-up guy. The company didn't want to pay, said the pneumonia was negligence on the part of the family—they couldn't afford a doctor. But he argued for them and got them the cash. Cost him years of promotions. It was well known that he often took files home. That would include, of course . . ."

"Birth certificates," I finished.

"Birth certificates. So numbnuts digs through Dad's old files, finds a birth certificate for someone around Chooch's birthdate, a two-year-old who died of pneumonia, and gets Chooch a passport. I'd be drawn to a name that's the English version of my name, wouldn't you? He gets a bogus Ontario driver's license. With it, plus the U.S. passport, he gets a Connecticut driver's license. He then uses them to get a real Ontario license. Smart."

"But how did he find the real Wally to steal a car from?"

Frank smirked. "From whom to steal a car. Watch your prepositions, kid." I rolled my eyes. He continued. "I called Walter Carpenter. A year or so ago, he got a call from a man who offered him cheap car insurance. Said the guy was keen on the fact that Walter only drove the car once or twice a month. Visited him and said he'd be in touch. But the guy never came back with a quote so he forgot about it. On a hunch, I called the other six W. Carpenters in the phone book. Four were home. Two remember being contacted about car insurance, but the guy never showed up."

"Did Walter give us a description of this insurance guy?" I asked.

"Yeah. Bruno Zimmerman to a tee."

"Big surprise." I felt pieces of the puzzle fitting together. "Does that give us enough to bring him in?" I asked.

"There's more," Frank said. "Anthony told you that Chooch was his brother."

"Half-brother," I corrected.

"Right. Chooch was born in Como, Italy. When he was three, his parents split. His father took him to Lugano, Switzerland—it's on his rap sheet. He certainly knew Zimmerman; Bruno's father and Chooch's father once worked together. It makes for one of those 'Isn't it a small world' moments. Maureen marries Bruno. Chooch visits brother Anthony, sees Bruno. They team up."

"Shit," I mumbled. "If Palumbo connects the dots, Chooch and Bruno are both dead."

Frank agreed. "Think about it. Bruno and Chooch

fly to Italy. Bruno 'accidentally' runs into Palumbo's older boy. The kid would feel safe in a car with his own brother-in-law. Bruno takes the kid's gun. They steal an Alfa and kill the owner. They can always pin his death on the kid if things go bad. Bruno gets Peter drunk, drives him from Figaro—"

"—Foligno," I corrected.

"Whatever. And they push him off the cliff. Chooch hides in the bushes, figuratively speaking, while Bruno calls the cops. Bruno has a fake U.S. passport, with his own photo, in the name of Walter Carpenter. He probably got it made by whoever made the fake driver's license.

"He figures they won't check a witness for a bogus passport, and he's right. The most they might do is write down his name and passport number, and both are the same as the real 'Walter Carpenter' passport held by Chooch. It's perfect.

"They make sure the kid's dead and fly back to New York. Chooch travels on his 'Walter Carpenter' passport, and Bruno and Chooch come back to Canada in the Impala. Bruno tells everyone he was in New Jersey buying furniture at the time of the death. Chooch isn't on anyone's radar. Peter Palumbo died as a result of a drunken accident, and nobody connects the dots to the Alfa owner," he finished. I thought about his theory.

"Neat. Crisp," I mumbled. "Makes sense."

"Yup," Frank said. "It holds water, doesn't it?"

Parker sat down with us. Frank smiled. The anger he'd felt toward him earlier was gone. "Well, Terry, what do you think?" Frank asked.

Parker shook his head. "I wouldn't want to be the one to break this news to Palumbo. Imagine how furious he'd be at his daughter, for marrying this schmuck. I also imagine Bruno will evaporate."

"You staying out of this mess, then?" Frank asked.

"Call me when the dust settles," Parker replied emphatically. "I don't want another vacation. However, I think I can shed some light on one of your dead guys— Leo? Leo met Bruno when Chooch visited Anthony, yes? And Leo is looking for the younger kid's attacker, not knowing that it was Bruno?"

I sighed. "Nick. Gosh, he got lost in the crowd. Yeah, Chooch prefers GM—Impala, Eldorado, Chevelle. He stole the Impala twice, and Bruno used it to follow Nick Jr."

"Poor Nicky," Parker said sadly. "Yeah, the guy stole a Chevy. So Leo, the Boy Scout, asks someone with a prior for car theft if he knows who might have done it. Chooch misunderstands the question and figures he's been caught. He shoots Leo."

I finally saw how everything fit together. "Dear Lord, that's it."

Frank frowned. "But why leave the cash in the locker?"

I smiled. "Easy. Bruno pays Chooch to shoot me and leave town. He figures that will confuse us and draw attention away from him. Unfortunately, I survived. Chooch hides the money, but he comes back to make a deal with us. Even if we put him away, he still keeps the twenty-five grand, and Palumbo will take care of Bruno."

Frank went *hmm*, thinking. "And the business card in the box?"

"I thought about that, too," I said. "If we found it first, he'd claim Maureen was in on it. Then he'd make a deal to finger her in exchange for a shorter sentence. If Bruno found him first, he'd say he had insurance, that he could finger Bruno for all the murders. It's a bluff—all Chooch had was a business card."

"Yep, neat all right. Terry, any questions?" Frank asked.

"You guys wrap this up." Parker stood up. "Let me know when you're done."

Frank leaned back and rubbed his face with his palms. "OK, at five o'clock we clean this mess, once and for all." He called Helen to say we'd be late. He promised to be careful.

I sat at my desk, thinking. There was a nagging loose end, somewhere. "Oh, shit," I groaned. "I told Chooch his money wasn't in the locker."

"And?" Frank asked, unconcerned.

"Chooch must think Bruno took his cash."

Frank's eyes widened. "Call the furniture store."

I dialed the number. The same woman answered the phone. "Hello, Detective," she sang pleasantly. "Did you need something else?"

"Look," I started, "have you had any calls today asking for Bruno?"

"Of course, several."

"Did one come from a man with a raspy, squeaky voice? He would have sounded gruff."

"Yes. He was very insistent. I said Bruno would be back at five." Now she was worried.

"Listen," I told her, "we'll be there at four thirty. I want you to clear the building and go home as soon as we show up."

There was a long silence. "Are you serious?"

"Yes, I am."

"What the hell is going on?"

"This man is dangerous. He's a murder suspect. Is that clear?" I demanded.

"Fine," she snapped. "If you're not here at four thirty, I'll be gone." She hung up.

I checked my watch. Three fifty; plenty of time to prepare. I had handcuffs in my jacket, and I stuck a spare pair in my pants pocket. Frank drew his service revolver, checked the cylinder, and holstered it. He smoothed his hair and sighed; a long, tired sigh.

"C'mon, kid, let's finish this shit. My wife needs me at home."

We drove in silence to Zimmerman's store, the evening sunlight behind us, casting a long shadow ahead of us as we drove.

"Frank," I asked, "where do you want to park?"

"Good point. There's a loading bay out back, right?"

The *Shoppers' Mecca* sign shimmered in the light wind. Frank looked to one side as I looked to the other, searching for Chooch in a car. We drove around back, to a spot marked *Zimmerman Fine Furniture—Private Parking*. It was now twenty-five after four. It reminded me of the climax of *High Noon*. I was Gary Cooper, I thought, waiting for the bad guys on the train.

We walked in through the back entrance, still looking around constantly. Frank searched the offices, and I checked the warehouse. The place was empty.

We picked our way through to the front door, from dim display to dim display, dodging near-invisible furniture to the front entrance, then we sat and waited for Bruno to arrive.

A few minutes later the warehouse door opened. A male voice said, "Where is everybody?" and a female voice answered, "Out, I guess."

The man grumbled about a long drive. The woman said it was *his* parents, after all. I stood up. Bruno and Maureen walked around a wall and saw us.

Maureen smiled a plastered-on smile. "Officers. How nice to see you again. Can we help you?"

Frank stepped forward. "We need to speak with you about recent developments," he said.

Bruno tucked a folio under his arm and shrugged. "Did you want me too, or just Maureen?"

"Actually," Frank said, "we have some questions specifically for you, Mr. Zimmerman."

"Shoot," Bruno said calmly.

Frank smiled. "Interesting choice of words. When were you last in Italy?"

"Not for some time. I used to go there more, but now we mostly buy from the States."

"So last March, you didn't go to Foligno?" Frank continued.

"Why would I? I don't have any suppliers near there."

Frank nodded. "It's a very small town. Interesting you'd know where it is, though. Why is that?"

Bruno's face dropped. He shrank back, his mouth open. Frank stared at him, hard.

"If we check flights out of JFK last March, will we find that you went to Florence? And if we ask the NYPD about an Impala left in South Ozone Park, an Impala with Ontario plates, driven by a big guy with a wig and his friend, what do you think they will tell us?" Frank was on a roll, now, the questions hitting hard.

Bruno licked his lips. "Listen," he stammered apologetically. "I never meant for this to happen."

Maureen glared at him, seething. She's just put it together, I thought. Bruno looked around at the furniture, hoping for inspiration.

"It was an accident, honest." He shook his head. "It was all a terrible accident, that's all."

Maureen stared, cold. She looked like her father now: hard and determined. "What did you do?" she said coldly.

Bruno's expression suddenly changed from panic to disgust. He pushed Maureen toward Frank, threw his folio at me, and pulled a gun out of his belt. He pointed it at the three of us.

"You think you're so smart," he scoffed. Maureen gasped at the weapon. "That insurance will buy me a whole new life. You won't take that away."

Maureen gritted her teeth. "My father will kill you. You won't live to see tomorrow."

Bruno pointed the gun at her face, glaring at her with hatred. She didn't flinch. Frank reached slowly for his revolver. Bruno swiveled back toward him.

"Don't! I'll shoot you all, if I have to," he barked.

The back door of the warehouse opened noisily. A soft aura of light glowed behind Bruno. I turned to see who was there, but the back door slammed shut, and the darkness returned. Soft footsteps echoed in the dark, getting closer. Bruno froze.

A high, raspy voice called out through the darkness. "Drop the gun," it commanded.

Bruno looked nervously behind him, not sure what to do next.

"Gun down. Now," the voice said, insistent.

Bruno licked his lips. "Chooch, is that you?" he asked softly.

"Where's my money?" The voice boomed. The footsteps came closer. Chooch appeared out of nowhere and put a pistol against Bruno's ear.

Bruno started to shake. He lowered his gun. "Vince,

I paid you your money," he whimpered. "You saw the money. You saw it."

Chooch stared at me, realizing he'd been tricked.

"You lied," he said reproachfully.

I smiled. "It worked. You're here."

Chooch stepped forward to come at me. Bruno poked his gun against Chooch's back. "My turn," he said smugly. "Give me the gun, Vincent."

Chooch sighed and reluctantly handed his gun back. Bruno now held a gun in each hand.

"Whole different ball game now, huh?" He laughed. He stepped back two paces. "I paid you, you stupid moron. But you come back and *threaten* me?" he snarled. He looked at us, deciding something, and smiled menacingly. "Looks like Vince shot you three, but then I shot him." He nodded, liking that scenario. Maureen just glared at him, her face filled with rage.

Chooch turned red and made a fist. Bruno aimed one gun at his stomach. "Don't do anything stupid, Vince. You can still walk out of here, if we work together."

"I ain't dumb," Chooch retorted. "You don't want to keep me alive."

Bruno smiled the smile he used to charm customers. "Vince, forget about the gun. You'll come out of it fine. Really. Trust me."

Chooch growled and spun around, swinging a wild fist. Bruno yelped and staggered back. One gun went off, the noise deafening. Chooch stumbled forward. He moaned softly, slumped onto his back, and died. Seeing him there, looking like Leo, I felt sorry for him. I shook my head and quietly said a prayer for Chooch's soul.

Bruno pointed the guns at us again. He gritted his teeth and hissed angrily. "Look what you made me do. Look! You and your meddling—you should have let us be. I'd have lived with the bitch—" he jerked his head at Maureen, "—I would have shared the money." He waved one gun at her. He sighed, as if preparing for tedious paperwork. "Now I have to figure out something else." He shook his head. "I won't give up that money. I worked for too long to give up that money."

I shook my head, speaking softly and calmly. "You still have a chance here, Bruno," I said. "That was an accident. It can still end OK if you give up now." I held my hand out. "Come on, Bruno. Do the smart thing."

Frank lowered his arms, casually moving a hand toward his holster. Bruno pointed one gun at Frank, still looking at me. "Don't try anything stupid, pig," he warned.

"Wouldn't dream of it." Frank smiled and raised his hands again.

Bruno huffed, angry. "This works. He shot you. I shot him. I keep the cash. Yeah, it works." Maureen stared at him, her face frozen in pure rage.

"Listen, Bruno," Frank soothed, "you can still get out of this all right. We'll help you."

Bruno shook his head. His expression went cold, unemotional. "Forget it. I just have to figure this out. I'm not going to jail."

In the darkness, I heard another noise; a clunk, like a car changing gears. A moment later I recognized the sound: someone cocking a pump-action shotgun. Out of the shadows stepped Anthony, pointing a very long barrel at Bruno. Bruno's face dropped.

Anthony came closer, scowling, gliding silently forward. He looked quickly down at Chooch, then back up at Bruno. His expression didn't change.

"Drop it," he growled.

Bruno looked around for a place to run. "Look, Tony, let's talk. I can explain."

Anthony aimed the shotgun directly at Bruno's eyes. "Drop it, or you die right now."

Bruno pursed his lips and slowly placed one gun on a coffee table.

"Both guns. Back up," Anthony ordered.

Bruno reluctantly put the second gun down. He took a hesitant step back, then stopped and opened his mouth to speak.

Anthony lunged forward and pressed the shotgun barrel into Bruno's mouth. Bruno backed up some more, stopping when his back hit a wall a few feet along.

"Detective, get the guns," Anthony instructed.

I quietly picked up both pistols. Anthony reached behind him, one hand holding the shotgun against Bruno's mouth. "Give," he said.

I looked behind me; Frank nodded, slowly. I handed the pistols to Anthony. I wasn't completely sure why I should. He pocketed them, his stare still fixed on Bruno, and stepped back slightly.

"Vince," Anthony rumbled. "Vince was my brother."

Bruno's face dropped. "Tony—I didn't know. Man, if you'd just told me—I didn't know."

Anthony shook his head, turning red with anger. He gritted his teeth. "Shut up. Too late for you—way too late. Shut up."

Bruno began shaking, terrified. He started to cry. Anthony tilted his head back at us, still staring ahead.

"Come back in five minutes. I was never here. Maureen neither."

Frank seemed to know what was happening next.

"Anthony, are you sure?" he asked, calmly.

Anthony nodded slowly, certainly. "Yeah, this is just how you guys want it, nice and neat."

Frank grabbed my arm and pulled me into the dark warehouse. "C'mon, kid. We're taking a walk."

I looked back; Bruno was against the wall, Anthony holding him there with the shotgun.

Maureen stared at Bruno. He looked at her, pleading, tears in his eyes. "Maureen, sweetheart, stop him, please. You can stop him—Maureen, please."

She glared at him, like she was looking at something dead on the road. "Goodbye, Bruno," she said simply, and walked away.

Anthony's eyes stayed on Bruno. Vince lay lifeless behind him. It was surreal. Bruno pleaded with Anthony, offered him money, called to us, crying. Anthony hit Bruno in the stomach with the butt of the shotgun. Bruno sobbed. Maureen walked past us, got into Anthony's Buick and just stared at the dashboard.

Frank pulled me along behind him and out the door.

"We can't just let this happen," I protested.

"It's already happened, kid," Frank spat. "We're just sweeping up after the parade."

"We shouldn't," I said passionately. "We can't let him, Frank. We have to stop this."

"Stop what?" Frank poked a finger at me. "Grow up, kid. Five minutes ago, we were facing a short ride in a pine box. Now we've solved four murders. It's a good day."

Ignoring all my complaints, Frank dragged me to the Fury. He pushed me behind the wheel, closed the door, then got in the right seat. We waited till the Buick wagon cruised past us and out to the street. "Park out front," Frank said.

I drove around to the front door and shut off the engine. I sat still, paralyzed. Frank picked up the microphone and called dispatch, barking, "Shots fired, shots fired."

Four minutes after that, a yellow cruiser raced up, and two uniforms joined us. Frank jumped out of the car. I just followed him and went through the motions. We all went in through the front door together, looking around in the gloom.

With his flashlight, one uniform spotted two bodies on the floor. The other headed back to his cruiser and called the meat wagon. Frank pretended to be surprised, pretended to inventory the scene, pretended to reconstruct a series of events. The uniform said it looked like a robbery gone bad.

Bruno was on his back, two bullets through his stomach, a gun in his hand. Chooch was on the floor near him, a bullet hole in his chest, his gun in his hand. The uniform was right; it looked like Bruno had died defending himself.

The forensics boys photographed and dusted and measured and did all the things they do. We stayed until the meat wagon took the bodies away.

It was eight at night; Frank called Helen and said we were heading home. He spoke for a minute, then smiled sadly, saying, "We're glad it's over too." He hung up. "Let's go home, kid," he whispered. "We have women waiting for us."

"Couldn't we have done anything differently?" I insisted.

"How?" he snapped. "Get Anthony to drop the shotgun? Then what? Months of trials, stacks of paperwork, sitting in court, and letting other crimes slide. This way was best."

I looked down at my hands. I was shaking like a leaf. "Anthony killed Bruno. Does he just get away with that?"

Frank stared at me. "Did you see him kill Bruno? Were you in the building when he did? No? Then it's just speculation, isn't it? What they say happened, happened. Let it go, kid, just let it go."

It was dark when we pulled up to Frank's house. My arm was sore, my back hurt, my head was splitting. My stomach was in knots. Karen squeezed me tight.

Helen kissed Frank softly and asked him how he was doing.

I had some soup, then I went to bed. I felt sick, cold, tired, sad, and miserable.

Frank told a fictional version of events, the version he would put into a report. I didn't care anymore. I fell asleep.

I am sitting in a bright room. Huge, cartoonish furniture surrounds me: overstuffed chairs in dazzling colors, impossible lamps, and zebra-striped sofas on a pure white marble floor. Classical music plays in the background. It reminds me of the white room in the closing scenes of 2001: A Space Odyssey.

I'm in a chair with crazy legs, a back floating in space, and a wild pulsating fabric seat. Bruno Zimmerman walks up to me, dressed in a gaudy green suit. He smiles happily.

"How's the chair?" he asks.

I nod.

"Are you comfortable?"

I shake my head.

He smiles. "It takes a while to get comfortable. But you will, Detective, you will."

*

I woke up. Six in the morning: I'd slept through the night. My shoulder was still sore, but otherwise I felt better. This made me angry and pleased at the same time. I showered, dressed, made coffee, and just sat, staring down at the liquid in my cup.

Helen shuffled through and poured herself some milk. "Hi, Ian," she said gently. "Are you all right?"

I shook my head. "There was no right way for it to end. It was bad, but there was no right way. That's all."

She leaned against the kitchen counter, staring down at the glass in her hand. "I teach the child of a surgeon. He has saved hundreds—thousands—of lives. He only remembers the ones he lost."

I smiled. "So you're saying what, enjoy the victories?"

She shook her head. "You're a human being, in the moral sense. It would be impossible for you to not feel compassion for someone, even someone who's pointing a gun at you."

I shook my head. That's not what Frank had told her. "No, that's not what happened."

She smiled kindly. "Don't you think I recognize a comforting lie? I know almost everything that happened to you two, but I also know that it's vital for Frank to say what he said, for all our sakes. It goes with the territory, Sergeant."

"Constable," I corrected.

She smirked. "Want to bet?" She sipped her milk.

We parked at the station house. Frank sat in the car for a moment. "Let me do this, OK?" he said.

I nodded, grateful.

After the obligatory congratulations, questions, and back-patting from the others, Van Hoeke called us into his office. Frank straightened up, prepared for a grilling. I walked in first, and froze. Nick Palumbo was sitting across from Van Hoeke.

"I believe you gentlemen know each other," the Captain said. We nodded. "Mr. Palumbo is here because we have already informed him of the tragedy that occurred yesterday, and we've assured him that our investigation will reach a swift conclusion."

Palumbo sat still, his expression undecipherable.

"Mr. Palumbo, my deepest condolences, sir," I said.

He stood and took my hand. "Thanks," he said. "I appreciate everything you've done." He stressed the "everything."

Frank extended a hand. Palumbo shook it silently. Van Hoeke continued. "As I say, we are very near resolution, Mr. Palumbo. You have my word."

Palumbo stood up to leave. He turned to me. "My daughter is resting, on doctor's advice. Understandably, she is distraught at losing her husband to a burglar. That said, we're having a memorial for Peter. May we count on seeing you at the service?"

"It would be an honor, sir. I will be there," I promised.

"Detective," he said. "If I could ask you for a few words of comfort?" His voice broke. He looked at me with pleading eyes. I thought for a moment.

"There are souls in this world which have the gift of finding joy everywhere and of leaving it behind them when they go," I said, softly.

"Jean Paul Richter," he said with a smile. "I like that. Thank you."

"If there's any way I can help, sir. Again, please accept my best wishes."

He shook my hand a second time. "We're having a small service for Bruno. Only family will attend," he said firmly.

"I understand. Will he be interred in Connecticut?"

Palumbo stifled a smile. "Actually, some time ago he expressed the desire to be cremated. We will be scattering his ashes in the place where Peter died. I think that's appropriate, don't you?"

Frank rubbed his nose to hide a smirk. Palumbo bowed his head slightly at us and left. Anthony appeared from nowhere and followed him out of the building.

Van Hoeke frowned. "Frank, you're on vacation. Go

spend some time with your wife." He stared at me. "Ian, you're still sick. Go home."

Frank leaned forward. "With all due respect, Martin, we still have to wrap up the case."

"No, you don't," the Captain snapped. Parker walked in silently and sat down. "Terry, I want you to write up this case. Do you think it was a botched robbery?"

"That's how it looks, Captain," Parker said solemnly. "Ciucciaro killed Leo and the Palumbo boy. He shot Bruno. Bruno shot him before dying."

Van Hoeke added, to me, "Your Sergeant's exam. We'll talk about it when you're back."

"Yes, sir. Thank you, sir," I stammered.

Van Hoeke waved at us. "Go, get. Scram, beat it."

We left the building. I felt liberated. I could use time away, I thought. Set up the house, get settled, have Frank and Helen over for a barbecue.

The morning was warm, and the parking lot, foggy with evaporating drizzle, looked like the final airport scene in *Casablanca*. I chuckled at the absurdity of the thought. Frank turned to me, curious.

"What's so funny, kid?"

"Louie," I quoted, "I think this is the beginning of a beautiful friendship."

Frank shook his head. "You hug me, kid, so help me God, I'll deck you."

ACKNOWLEDGEMENTS

Any endeavor needs both the support and encouragement of others to succeed. I would never have been able to complete this book were it not for the support of these people.

First and foremost, thanks to my wife Alison. She has always held me in higher regard than I hold myself, and for that I will always love her. She has always placed my needs and those of our children ahead of hers, and has kept a level head, even in chaotic times. She has laughed at my tired jokes and complimented my middling food, and she has made me feel far better-looking than I am.

Second, thanks to Michael and Jennifer, who have always made me proud to be their father. I hope I have instilled in them the determination and dedication to do not only what is fun, but also what is right. Having them as an audience made me consider every decision I made and everything they saw me do.

Third, the gang at The Running Room and (alphabetically) Anne, Carol, Danielle, Patricia, Shawn, and the rest of the group known affectionately as "Team Ish."

ABOUT THE AUTHOR

Mauro Azzano was born on a farm in the Veneto region of Italy and moved to Australia at age three. He didn't learn English until he started school, and he didn't move to Canada until he was twelve. Having that as a starting point in life, he says, always made him look at language a little differently.

He has worked as a skydiver pilot, photocopier technician, band saw repairman, and pizza driver. He currently works in the technology sector, troubleshooting computer networks.

He has traveled extensively, but he currently lives in British Columbia with his family. He spends his time writing, gardening and running marathons—"not competitively," as he puts it.

For more information on this author, please visit www.mauroazzano.webs.com.

CPSIA information can be obtained at www.ICGtesting.com
Printed in the USA
LVOW12s1753190913

353232LV00001B/93/P

9 780985 446468